ACT

OF

OBLIVION

Also by Robert Harris

ROBERT HARRIS

ACT
OF
OBLIVION

RANDOM HOUSE CANADA

Library and Archives Canada Cataloguing in Publication
Title: Act of oblivion / Robert Harris.
Names: Harris, Robert, 1957- author.
Identifiers: Canadiana (print) 20220224536 | Canadiana (ebook) 20220224552 |
ISBN 9780735282124 (softcover) | ISBN 9780735282131 (EPUB)
Classification: LCC PR6058.A69147 A38 2022 | DDC 823/.914—dc23

Typeset in 12.5/16.5 pt Dante MT Std by Jouve (UK), Milton Keynes

Cover design: Glenn O'Neill
Image credits: (figures) Colin Thomas; (mountains) KenCanning, (wolves)
bazilfoto, (horses) Conny Marshaus and DaydreamsGirl / all Getty Images
Image of death warrant of Charles I: Bridgeman Images
Map: Neil Gower

Printed in the United States of America

2 4 6 8 9 7 5 3 1

Penguin
Random House
RANDOM HOUSE CANADA

To Gill

CONTENTS

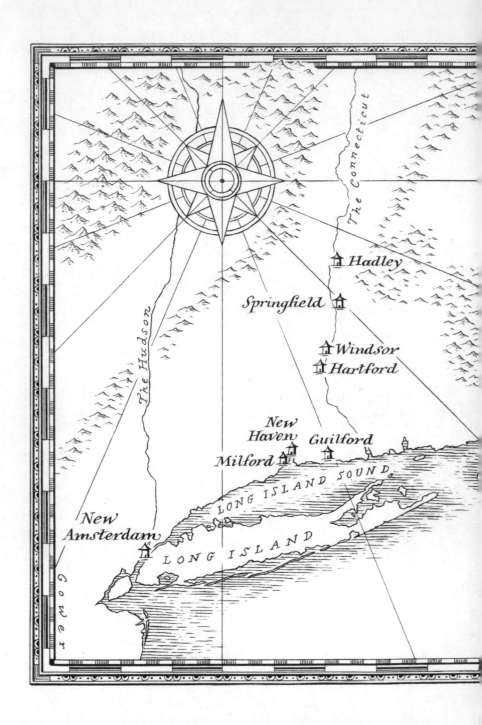

AUTHOR'S NOTE

This novel is an imaginative re-creation of a true story: the tracking down of the 'regicides', the killers of King Charles I, the greatest manhunt of the seventeenth century – in particular, the pursuit of Edward Whalley and William Goffe across New England. The events, dates and locations are accurate, and almost every character is real, apart from Richard Nayler. I suspect there must have been such a person – you cannot sustain a manhunt without a manhunter – but whoever he was, his identity is lost to history.

Otherwise, I have tried to stick to the known facts, and even discovered a few that were previously unknown, such as the date and place of Goffe's birth and the identity of Whalley's second wife. But it *is* a novel, and readers who want to investigate the story further will find a list of sources in the acknowledgements.

Robert Harris
20 June 2022

DRAMATIS PERSONAE

The regicides

Colonel Edward Whalley
Colonel William Goffe

In Massachusetts

Daniel Gookin a settler in Cambridge, Massachusetts
Mary Gookin Daniel Gookin's wife
Mary, Elizabeth, Daniel, Samuel, Nathaniel the Gookins' children
John Endecott governor of Massachusetts
Jonathan Mitchell Cambridge minister
John Norton minister of the Boston First Church
Captain Thomas Breedon Boston merchant, shipowner, Royalist
Thomas Kellond shipowner, Royalist
Captain Thomas Kirke Royalist
John Chapin Nayler's guide
John Stewart, William Mackwater, Niven Agnew, John Ross Scotsmen, members of Nayler's hunting party
John Dixwell regicide

In New Haven

Reverend John Davenport minister and co-founder of New Haven

Nicholas Street assistant minister and headteacher in New Haven

William Jones resident of New Haven

Hannah Jones William Jones's wife

William Leete governor of New Haven

Dennis Crampton resident of New Haven

Richard Sperry farmer

In Connecticut

John Winthrop governor of Connecticut

Simon Lobdell guide

Micah Tomkins general store owner in Milford

Captain Thomas Bull Puritan in Hartford

John Russell minister in Hadley

In London

Richard Nayler clerk to the Privy Council

Katherine Whalley Edward Whalley's wife

Frances Goffe William Goffe's wife, Edward Whalley's daughter

Frankie, Betty, Nan, Judith, Richard the Goffes' children

Reverend William Hooke Edward Whalley's brother-in-law

Jane Hooke William Hooke's wife, Edward Whalley's sister

Colonel Hacker former commander of the troops guarding King Charles I

Isabelle Hacker Colonel Hacker's wife

Sir Edward Hyde (later Earl of Clarendon) Lord Chancellor
Sir William Morice Secretary of State
Sir Arthur Annesley, Sir Anthony Ashley-Cooper Privy
  Councillors
Barbara Palmer (later Lady Castlemaine) Charles II's mistress
Samuel Nokes Nayler's secretary
Duke of York King Charles II's younger brother
Samuel Wilson merchant

In Europe

Sir George Downing His Majesty's ambassador at The Hague
Sir John Barkstead, John Dixwell, Colonel John Okey,
  Miles Corbet, Edmund Ludlow signatories of the King's
  death warrant
James Fitz Edmond Cotter, Miles Crowley, John Rierdan
  Irish Royalist officers
Sir John Lisle lawyer who managed King Charles I's trial

In the Civil War

Oliver Cromwell Edward Whalley's cousin
Henry Ireton Cromwell's son-in-law
General Fairfax Parliamentary commander
Cornet George Joyce soldier who arrested the King
John Bradshaw president of the court at Charles I's trial
John Cooke prosecuting attorney at Charles I's trial
Thomas Harrison signatory of the King's death warrant

PART ONE

HUNT
1660

CHAPTER ONE

I F YOU HAD set out in the summer of 1660 to travel the four miles from Boston to Cambridge, Massachusetts, the first house you would have come to after crossing the Charles River would have been the Gookins'. It stood beside the road on the southern edge of the small settlement, just past the creek, midway across the marshy land between the river and Harvard College – a confident, two-storey timbered property in its own fenced lot with an attic in its steep roof commanding a clear view of the Charles. That year, the colony was building its first bridge across the river. Thick wooden piles were being driven into the mud close to the ramp where the ferryboat ran. The sound of hammering and sawing and the shouts of the workmen drifted up to the house on the drowsy midsummer air.

On this particular day – Friday 27 July – the front door was flung wide open, and a childish sign reading *Welcome Home* had been nailed to the gatepost. A passing student had reported that a ship from London, the *Prudent Mary*, had dropped anchor that morning between Boston and Charlestown. Among her passengers was believed to be Mr Daniel Gookin, the master of the property, returning to America after an absence of two years.

The house, spotless enough to begin with, had been quickly swept and tidied, the children scrubbed and forced into their best Sabbath clothes. By early afternoon, all five were waiting with Mrs Gookin in the parlour: Mary, who was twenty and named after her mother; Elizabeth, eighteen; and their three younger brothers, Daniel, ten, Samuel, eight, and four-year-old Nathaniel, who had no memory of his father and was fidgeting in his chair.

Mrs Gookin knew it was the prospect of the meeting, rather than being cooped up indoors, that was making him so fretful. She took him onto her lap, stroked his hair and spoke of the man who would soon walk through the door – of his goodness and kindness and his important work for the government in London, where he had been summoned by the Lord Protector himself. 'He loves you, Nat, and God will make it so that you love him.'

'What's a Lord Protect Her?'

'Protector, child. He was the ruler of England and America.'

'Like a king?'

'Yes, like a king, only better, because he was chosen by Parliament. But the Protector is dead now. That's why your father is coming home.'

Nat's eyes widened. 'If the Protector is dead, then who will protect us?'

It was a question that had defeated the cleverest minds in England, and Mrs Gookin found herself stuck for an answer. She spoke over Nathaniel's head to her daughter. 'Mary, go to the attic, will you, and see if your father is coming.'

Mary ran upstairs, and returned a minute later to report that the ferryboat was still moored on the opposite bank and there was no sign of anyone on the road.

From then on, the children took it in turns every quarter-hour to climb up to the attic and be the lookout, each time descending with the same answer. An awful conviction began to grow in Mrs Gookin's mind that her husband would not be coming after all – that his ship had not arrived, or that it had anchored but he was not on board. Perhaps he had never embarked from London, or some calamity had befallen him during the crossing. The shrouded body, the brief prayers, the corpse weighted at the neck sliding head-first down the gangplank into the waves – she could see it all. It had happened twice during their original voyage from England nearly twenty years before.

'Go outside, boys, and wait for him there.'

Nat scrambled off her lap and all three darted for the door like cats released from a sack.

'But don't dirty your clothes . . .'

The girls remained in their places. Mary, who was most like her mother in her stolid good sense, and who had acted the man's role in the household over the past two years, said, 'I'm sure there's no need to worry yourself, Mama. God will have watched over him.'

At which Elizabeth – prettier and always grumbling about her chores – burst out, 'But it must be seven hours since his ship arrived, and it's only an hour to Boston.'

'Don't criticise your father,' said Mrs Gookin. 'If he is delayed, he'll have good reason.'

A few minutes later, Daniel called from outside, 'Someone's coming!'

They hurried out of the house, through the gate and onto the dried rutted mud of the road. Mrs Gookin squinted in the direction of the river. Her eyesight had worsened since her husband's departure. All she could make out was the dark shape of the ferry, like a water beetle, halfway across the bright ribbon of water. The boys were shouting, 'It's a cart! It's a cart! It's Papa in a cart!'

They dashed down the road to meet it, Nat's short legs pumping to keep up with his brothers.

'Is it really him?' asked Mrs Gookin, peering helplessly.

'It's him,' said Elizabeth. 'See – look – he's waving.'

'Oh, thank God.' Mrs Gookin fell to her knees. 'Thank God.'

'Yes, it's him,' repeated Mary, shielding her eyes from the sun, before adding, in a puzzled voice, 'but he has two men with him.'

In the immediate flurry of kisses and embraces, of tears and laughter, of children being tossed into the air and whirled around, the pair of strangers, who remained throughout politely seated in the back of the cart among the luggage, were at first ignored.

Daniel Gookin hoisted Nat up onto his shoulders, tucked Dan and Sam under either arm and ran with them around the yard, scattering the chickens, then turned his attention to the shrieking girls. Mary had forgotten how big her husband was, how handsome, how large a presence. She could not take her eyes off him.

Finally, Gookin set down the girls, placed his hand around her waist, whispered, 'There are men here you must meet; do not be alarmed,' and ushered her towards the cart. 'Gentlemen, I fear I have plain forgot my manners. Allow me to present my wife, the true Prudent Mary – in flesh and blood at last.'

A pair of weather-beaten, ragged-bearded heads turned to examine her. Hats were lifted to reveal long, matted hair. They wore buff leather overcoats, caked with salt, and high-sided scuffed brown boots. As they stood, somewhat stiffly, the thick leather creaked and Mary caught a whiff of sea and sweat and mildew, as if they had been fished up from the bed of the Atlantic.

'Mary,' continued Gookin, 'these are two good friends of mine, who shared the crossing with me – Colonel Edward Whalley, and his son-in-law, Colonel William Goffe.'

Whalley said, 'Indeed it is a pleasure to meet you, Mrs Gookin.'

She forced a smile and glanced at her husband – *two colonels?* – but already he had withdrawn his hand and was moving to help the pair down from the cart. She noticed how deferential he was in their presence, and how when they put their feet to the ground after so many weeks at sea, both men swayed slightly, and laughed, and steadied one another. The children gawped.

Colonel Goffe, the younger one, said, 'Let us give thanks for our deliverance.' Beneath his beard he had a fine, keen, pious face; his voice carried a musical lilt. He held up his hands, palms flat, and cast his eyes to the heavens. The Gookin family quickly wrenched their fascinated gaze from him and lowered their heads. 'We remember Psalm One Hundred and Seven. "O that men would praise the Lord for his goodness, and for his wonderful works to the children of men! They that go down to the sea in ships, that do business in great waters. These see the works of the Lord, and his wonders in the deep." Amen.'

'Amen.'

'And who do we have here?' asked Colonel Whalley. He moved along the line of children, collecting their names. At the end, he pointed to each in turn. 'Mary. Elizabeth. Daniel. Sam. Nathaniel. Very good. I am Ned, and this is Will.'

Nathaniel said, 'Did you know the Lord Protect Her, Ned?'

'I did, very well.'

'He's dead, you know.'

'Hush,' said Mrs Gookin.

'Yes, Nathaniel, that he is,' replied Ned sadly. 'More's the pity.'
There was a silence.

Mr Gookin clapped his hands. 'Boys, fetch the colonels' bags
for them.'

Until that moment, Mary Gookin had nursed a hope that her
husband had merely offered the men a ride. Now, as she watched
them unload their luggage from the cart and hand it to her sons,
she felt dismay. It was hardly the homecoming she had dreamed
of – to feed and shelter two senior officers of the English army.

'And where are we to put them, Daniel?' She spoke quietly, so
they could not hear, and took care not to look at him, the easier
to keep her temper.

'The boys can give up their beds and sleep downstairs.'

'How long are they to stay?'

'As long as it is necessary.'

'What is that? A day? A month? A year?'

'I cannot say.'

'Why here? Are there no rooms to be had in Boston? Are colonels too poor to pay for their own beds?'

'The governor believes Cambridge a safer lodging place than
Boston.'

Safer . . .

'You've consulted the governor about their accommodation?'

'We've been with him half the day. He gave us dinner.'

So that was why his journey from Boston had taken him so
long. She watched the boys struggling under the weight of the
large bags, the two colonels walking behind them towards the
house, talking to the girls. To her feelings of dismay and irritation
was suddenly added an altogether sharper emotion. Fear.

'And why,' she began hesitantly, 'why does the governor believe
Cambridge is safer than Boston?'

'Because Boston is full of rogues and royalists, whereas here they will be among the godly.'

'They're not visitors from England, then, so much as . . . fugitives?' He made no answer. 'From what is it they run?'

Gookin took a while to reply. By the time he spoke, the men had gone inside. He said quietly, 'They killed the King.'

CHAPTER TWO

I N ENGLAND, IT was almost nine in the evening, the sun just setting. Isabelle Hacker, her plain blue Quaker dress coated brown with dust after two days on the road, was riding into her home village of Stathern, Leicestershire.

Close behind her rode another figure. His constant proximity unnerved her. So did his silence. He had followed her all the way north from London. Even when they broke their journey for the night, he had barely directed a word at her. In his pocket she knew he carried a commission from the House of Lords issued three days earlier. He had shown it when he came to her door in London: *Hereupon it is Ordered, That Colonel Hacker do forthwith send his Wife into the Country, to fetch the said Warrant; and that the Gentleman Usher attending this House do send a Man along with her for that Purpose.*

He said, 'I am that man.'

Mrs Hacker had agreed at once to accompany him to the country. She was ready to do anything to help her husband, at that moment held in the Tower on suspicion of treason, for which the punishment was a death of an almost unimaginable and protracted horror: to be hanged until the point of unconsciousness, cut down, revived, castrated, disembowelled – the entrails dragged out and burned in front of the living victim – then beheaded and his body cut into four quarters for public display. Unimaginable, yet she could not stop tormenting herself by picturing it. Almost the worst part was that he would leave this world in a welter of agony and at the end she would not even have a body to lay to rest.

She had said goodbye to her children and within the hour they had been on the road. By surreptitious observation, she guessed the man to be roughly forty – a few years younger than herself – and that he had suffered some wound or defect at birth that caused him to walk with a barely perceptible limp. His torso was broad, his legs short, his voice when he chose to use it oddly soft. He had told her his name was Richard Nayler. She gathered he was some kind of clerk to the Privy Council. He rode well. More than that she could not say.

The day had been hot, the evening still warm. A few villagers strolled in the lane or idled at their cottage gates. When they heard the clip of horses' hooves, they swung around to stare then quickly looked away. Men who a month ago would have swept off their hats or touched their forelocks were now too afraid, or appalled, to acknowledge her existence. Isabelle Hacker, pious Quaker and lady of the manor though she might be, was also the wife of a revolutionary. She stared down at them with contempt.

Stathern Hall, the grandest house in the village, stood close to St Guthlac's church. The ninth chime of the hour was just dying away as she turned off the road and passed through the open gate. In the weeks she had been away rallying support for the colonel, she saw weeds had taken hold in the vegetable garden. The grass around the orchard was a meadow. In the gathering dusk, the big house loomed dark and seemingly abandoned.

Her horse picked its way along the drive towards the front. She dismounted, tied the reins to the iron railing beside the entrance, and without glancing back at Mr Nayler, took her key from her pocket and unlocked the heavy door. She wanted to be done with this man as fast as possible.

She crossed the flagstone floor and called upstairs into an echoing silence. Even the servants must have fled. The hall darkened slightly as Nayler loomed in the doorway behind her. As she went to her husband's study, she heard his footsteps quickening to catch her up. Clearly he wished to forestall any last-minute act of destruction. Inside the study, the air was stuffy. In the trees beyond the leaded windows, nightingales were singing. From a drawer she took a small box and extracted a key, then knelt in front of the safe. She had never read it, but she knew what it looked like. Give it to him, save Francis from the hangman-butcher, get him gone.

Nayler had not until that moment allowed himself to believe that the document still existed. Nobody had seen it for eleven years. Desperate men, in his experience, would say anything to buy themselves a little time – and Colonel Hacker's predicament was nothing if not desperate. But here was his dreary wife, her narrow back presented to him in this gloomy chamber, rummaging through the estate deeds and household accounts and whatnot, pulling out something – he could not quite see it – and slowly rising to her feet.

He had expected, if it did exist, a grand parchment in the style of an Act of Parliament: some scroll appropriate to the magnitude of the crime. But what she held out to him was a footling little thing, eight inches long or thereabouts, like a bill of sale for a horse or a cask of wine, rolled up and tied with a frayed black ribbon. It was promisingly heavy for its size, though. Parchment, not paper. He carried it over to the window and in the dim light untied the ribbon and unrolled it to its full width of seventeen inches. The death warrant of Charles Stuart, King of England, Scotland and Ireland, as handed to Colonel Francis Hacker, commander of the troops guarding the King, on the morning of His Majesty's execution, by Oliver Cromwell himself.

He laid it on the colonel's desk, where it immediately coiled up again, like a serpent protecting itself. He sat, removed his hat, placed it to one side, and wiped his hands on his coat.

'Some light, Mrs Hacker, if you'd be so kind.'

She went back into the hall, to the chest where the candles were kept. It took her a while, with shaking fingers, to strike a spark from the steel and flint. When she returned to the study carrying two candelabra, he was exactly where she had left him, motionless at the desk beside the window, his head silhouetted against the purple light. She set down the candles. He pulled them towards him without acknowledgement and unrolled the parchment.

The writing, he noted with interest, was full of erasures and insertions. Evidence of what? he wondered. Haste, perhaps. Confusion. Second thoughts? He began reading it aloud, to get it clear in his head, rather than for the benefit of Isabelle Hacker, who was watching him intently.

' "Whereas Charles Stuart King of England is and stands convicted attainted and condemned of High Treason and other high crimes, and sentence upon Saturday last was pronounced against him by this Court to be put to death by the severing of his head from his body, of which sentence execution yet remains to be done, these are therefore to will and require you to see the said sentence executed in the open street before Whitehall upon the morrow being the thirtieth day of this month of January between the hour of ten in the morning and five in the afternoon of the same day with full effect . . ." '

The awful, momentous words were thick in his throat. He had to cough and swallow before he could continue.

' ". . . and for so doing this shall be your sufficient warrant. And these are to require all officers and soldiers and the other good people of this nation of England to be assisting you in this service. Given under our hands and seals . . ." ' He stopped. 'And here are the names.' He scanned the fifty-odd signatures beneath the text, arranged in seven columns. Beside each man's name was a red wax seal. They spattered across the document like drops of blood.

'But my husband's name is not among them?'

His gaze travelled back over the signatories, lighting on a few here and there. Gregory Clements . . . Edmund Ludlow . . . Thomas Harrison . . . William Goffe . . .

'No. He did not sign.'

She let out her breath. 'You see – he told the truth. He was not one of the King's judges and nor did he put his hand to the death warrant.'

'No. But his name is here nonetheless. "To Colonel Francis Hacker, Colonel Huncks and Lieutenant Colonel Phayre." ' He turned the parchment round and pointed. 'The warrant is in fact addressed to your husband first and foremost – the reason, I assume, why it's in his possession.'

'But only as a soldier,' she protested. 'As an officer obeying orders, not issuing them.'

'That will be for the court to decide.' He quickly pulled the warrant away in case she tried to snatch it back. Hacker had super-vised the execution. His guilt was plain in black and white. She might just as well have handed him a noose to put around her husband's neck. She seemed suddenly to realise it, swaying in front of the desk, face as waxy as the candles. He was keen to be rid of her now. She had played her part. He wanted to study the warrant in peace. 'It's late, Mrs Hacker. You should retire.' He saw a couch in a corner of the room. 'I'll spend the night in here, with your permission, and leave at first light.'

She could not bring herself to accept this calamity. The abruptness of it, the cruelty. Two days on the road for this. 'But we have done what their lordships asked, Mr Nayler. That must count for something.'

'It's not my place to say. I suggest you withdraw for the night and pray for your husband.' His mouth twitched in a slight smile. 'Whatever happens next is God's will, after all.'

How many times had he heard that sanctimonious formula over the past eleven years? Let them see how they liked it now.

She continued to gaze at him, holding his eyes with hers. It was not enough for this man to hunt down, imprison and execute the King's enemies. He must mock their faith as well. But the Devil in his triumph was full of pride, and he did not flinch. He returned her stare until eventually she turned and walked unsteadily out of the study, up the stairs and into her bedroom, where she collapsed in a faint on the floor.

Despite his long day's travelling, Nayler felt neither hunger nor thirst. The warrant was sufficient meat and drink for him. He sat at the colonel's desk and read it again. *The severing of his head from his body . . . in the open street before Whitehall . . .* It still had the power to shock. He opened his jacket, unbuttoned his shirt, and bowed his head to remove the leather cord that had hung around his neck for the past eleven years. Attached to it was a small pouch. Inside the pouch was a tiny piece of bloodstained linen. He turned it over between his fingers.

He remembered everything about that midwinter day – slipping out of Essex House at first light, the bitter wind off the Thames, hurrying along the Strand, past the big mansions that backed onto the river, the feel of his old army knife and pistol hidden beneath his coat. It was all unreal to him. To cut off the head of an anointed king? Impossible. Barbarous. A sacrilege. The army would never go through with it. Either General Fairfax, the Parliamentary commander, would put a stop to it, or the thousands of Royalists lying low in the city would rise up to prevent it. He for one was ready if the word was given to sacrifice his life to rescue his sovereign.

Then he had turned at Charing Cross towards Whitehall and his hopes had collapsed. The crowd in King Street was certainly large enough – five or six hundred – to cause trouble. But the number of troops was greater, a thousand or more: lines of pikemen shoulder to shoulder, holding people back, then cavalry packing the middle of the wide thoroughfare to prevent any attempt to reach the scaffold. The makeshift timber platform, draped in black, adjoined the side of the Banqueting House. There was no ladder from the street. It was accessible only from an upper window. An organised mind, a military mind, had thought this all out very carefully.

He pushed his way through the mob. There was none of the holiday atmosphere that usually attended an execution. Even the most radical republicans, the Levellers, recognisable by the sea-green ribbons attached to their coats and hats, were keeping their mouths shut for once. He worked his way down the back of the silent crowd, along the wall separating Whitehall from the Tilt Yard. People were standing on it for a better view, or sitting perched, legs dangling. He saw a gap, demanded to be allowed up, and when no one moved, he grabbed the nearest man by his feet and threatened to pull him down unless he made room. He had the physique of a wrestler. They shifted along.

Standing on the parapet, he had a good view over the heads of the crowd and the soldiers. The scaffold was about thirty yards away. Most of the windows of the Banqueting House were boarded up, but one on the first floor gave access to the platform. From time to time an officer would step out and patrol around it, scan the scene, then retreat out of the cold, shutting the window behind him. There were five small objects in the centre of the platform, and it took Nayler a while to work out their purpose. One was a very low wooden chopping block, barely higher than a man's hand, with iron hoops on either side of it and two more set close together a little further back. Clearly the intention, if the King put up a struggle or tried to rouse the crowd, would be to tie him down by his hands and feet and cut off his head while he was lying prone. Thorough staff work again. Barbarous.

The day did not get warmer. No sun tempered the iron frost, just the occasional flurry of snow and a grey sky so heavy it seemed to press all the colour from the buildings. Time itself felt frozen. Nayler had to keep his hands in his pockets and shuffle from foot to foot to ward off the numbness. Eventually, half a mile to the south, the abbey bell tolled nine o'clock. The old wound in his thigh ached like a knife jabbed in the bone. His mind became as blank as the sky; there was only the pain in his leg and the cold and the dread. Another hour passed. He counted the chimes of ten o'clock, and then not long afterwards he heard a faint drumbeat coming from somewhere behind him, from St James's Park: a slow funereal pulse. After a few minutes, the beat ceased.

He looked to his right, to the Holbein Gate. Above its arch an enclosed passageway led across the street to the Banqueting House. Figures appeared behind the mullioned windows: soldiers first, followed by a shorter man with a familiar profile who turned briefly to look down at the crowd and the scaffold, then a pair of clergymen, and finally more soldiers. In the instant of recognition, all the air seemed to go from Nayler's body. A moment later, the procession vanished. But others had seen it too, and the word went round: 'He's here!'

Still nothing happened. Eleven o'clock struck. Noon. With each passing minute, Nayler's hopes revived. Rumours of the reasons for the delay swirled across the crowd: that the House of Commons was at that moment sitting in debate and cancelling the verdict, that the King had agreed to abdicate in favour of his son, that the Dutch had offered half a million pounds to purchase a reprieve. He tried not to imagine what must be going through His Majesty's mind as he sat in the Banqueting House. Evil enough to cut off a man's head; cruel beyond measure to drag out his agony.

One o'clock came and went, and then, just before two, there was activity. The window opened, and through it poured a file of soldiers with their officers, followed by the executioner and his assistant, clad in long black woollen coats and black leggings, their faces covered by black masks, with grotesque ill-fitting grey wigs and false beards. The shorter of them carried an axe, its long shaft resting on his broad shoulder. A bishop appeared behind him with a prayer book open.

The King stepped out of the window last – a slight figure, bare-headed, scarcely five feet three inches, although he carried himself, as he always did, even in these final minutes, as if he were a giant. He went straight to the low block, and it was clear he was remonstrating with the officers at this affront to his dignity, that he should have to lie on his stomach to be killed. They looked at one another, shook their heads. The King turned his back on them. Producing a small piece of paper from beneath his cloak, he stepped to the front of the scaffold. He surveyed the soldiers, the cavalry, and the crowd beyond. He seemed to realise his words wouldn't carry, so returned to the middle of the platform and read his speech to the officers. Nayler could not hear a word of it, although by the following day it was printed and available to buy on half the streets in London. *If I would have given way to an arbitrary way, for to have all laws changed according to the power of the sword, I needed not to have come here; and therefore I tell you (and I pray God it be not laid to your charge) that I am the Martyr of the people . . .*

The King unfastened his cloak and removed it, took off his jacket and handed it to the bishop, along with some glittering decoration. He stood in his white shirt in the freezing cold and gathered up his long hair into a cap. He did not tremble. He said something to the executioner and gestured again to the block in protest, then shrugged, got down to his knees and lay full-length, adjusting his neck on the block until it was comfortable. He stretched his arms out behind him. The executioner braced his legs apart and lifted the axe as far as he could swing it behind his shoulder. A few moments passed, then the King made a gesture with his hands, a graceful flick, as if he were about to launch himself into a dive, and the blade descended with such force that in the silence the sound of the blow could be heard all the way down Whitehall.

Blood jetted out of the severed torso. The nearest soldiers twisted aside to avoid the flow until it settled into a steady glug, like an upended barrel. The executioner, still holding the axe, picked up the head by the hair, strode to the front and showed the King's face to the crowd. He shouted something, but his words were lost in the great roar that rose from the spectators, a mingling of exultation, horror and dismay. Part of the crowd pushed forward through the distracted pikemen, who had turned to watch the spectacle, and darted between the cavalry. Nayler jumped down from the wall and loped across Whitehall after them.

Beneath the platform, the blood was seeping between the planks. It pattered in the kind of heavy droplets that herald the beginning of a storm. People were slipping and scrambling all around him. He held up his handkerchief and watched it spot crimson – once, twice, three times, the spots spreading across the linen fibres and merging to form a single patch – then he fought his way out into the winter afternoon, up Whitehall and back along the Strand to the chapel of Essex House, where his patron, the Marquess of Hertford, and his family were kneeling at the altar, waiting to hear the news.

The martyr's blood had dried over the years to a faded rusty colour. Perhaps one day it would disappear. But as long as it existed, Nayler had vowed to do all in his power to avenge the events of that January day. He kissed it, folded the linen carefully, returned it to his pouch and retied the cord around his neck so that the relic lay close to his heart.

It was dark in the study now, apart from the flickering pool of candlelight. Beyond the window, the birds had ceased to sing.

He counted the signatures on the death warrant, and made it fifty-nine. Some of the names were famous, some obscure, but all had become familiar to him over the past ten weeks as he had tracked their footprints through the dusty records of the King's trial. Yet it was one thing to know that such-and-such a man had sat in judgement on Charles Stuart in Westminster Hall on such-and-such a day; it was quite another to prove that he had actually dipped his hand in blood. What the warrant provided at last was incontrovertible proof of guilt. The slippery Colonel Ingoldsby, for example, had already confessed to signing, but had insisted he was held down by violence and that Cromwell, laughing at his squeamishness, had thrust the pen between his fingers and guided his hand by force. Yet here was Ingoldsby's signature in the fifth column, clear and true and unhurried, with his seal placed neat beside it.

He transferred his attention to the names at the head of the initial column. The first signature was that of John Bradshaw, the jobbing lawyer promoted to be president of the court, so fearful of assassination that throughout the hearings he had worn a suit of armour beneath his robes and a bulletproof hat of beaver fur lined with steel: luckily for him, he had been dead for nearly a year, so he would escape retribution. The second signature belonged to Thomas Grey – Lord Grey of Groby, 'the Leveller Lord' – a man too radical even for Cromwell, who had eventually had him thrown in jail: he too was dead. The third signatory was Cromwell himself, the true architect of the entire diabolical procedure – dead, of course, and burning in hell. But the fourth signature, directly beneath Cromwell's, belonged to a man who was still alive as far as Nayler was aware – a man whom he had cause to know well.

He must make a new list.

He took a sheet of paper from Hacker's desk, dipped his pen in the inkpot, and wrote, in his careful hand, *Col. Edw. Whalley.*

CHAPTER THREE

T HE THREE GOOKIN boys shared a room at the back of
the house. It looked out over the village of Cambridge,
and beyond it to the looming roofs and broad chimneys and thin spire of Harvard College, gilded like a lance by
the late-afternoon sun. When Mary hurried in, Colonel Whalley
and Colonel Goffe were standing at the window, studying the view
and being studied in their turn by Daniel, Sam and Nathaniel. At
the soldiers' feet were what looked like their old army bags. She
registered the scratched leather, stitched and patched. Scant luggage, she thought, for a voyage halfway across the world. They
must have left in a hurry.

'Boys, go downstairs and leave the gentlemen in peace.'

'But Mama—'

'Downstairs!'

They descended the steps in a chattering, tumbling continuous
thump.

Mary said, 'The boys have had this room since birth. Whatever
Mr Gookin might have promised – forgive me – I believe it would
be best for them to keep it.'

'They're fine lads,' said Colonel Whalley. 'They remind me of my own at that age.' He turned from the window, and for the first time she got a good look at his face close up. A strong nose, dark eyes, a grey beard streaked with black. 'We wouldn't ask them to give up their beds to us.'

'I don't wish to seem inhospitable . . .'

'Think nothing of it.' He glanced up. 'What's above? An attic?'

'Oh, that is merely a servant's room.'

'You have a servant? I've not seen one.'

'Not at present,' she conceded. 'But the attic is not at all comfortable.'

'After the ship, it will seem a palace.'

The two soldiers hoisted their bags onto their shoulders. Colonel Whalley was plainly a gentleman by birth: polite, accustomed to deference, not easy to deny. She hesitated, but lacking the inspiration for any fresh objection, she felt she had no choice but to lead them out onto the landing and up the narrow staircase.

The attic ran the length of the house. Its ceiling sloped according to the angle of the roof, and Whalley was tall – perhaps a head higher than his son-in-law – so it was only in the central section that he could stand upright, and even then he had to duck as he walked to the window, to avoid striking his head on the cross-beams. He unfastened the latch and leaned out, looked this way and that, then withdrew.

'This is perfect. We shall be most content up here, shall we not, Will?'

'Indeed. And at least, Mrs Gookin, we'll be somewhat out of your way. We do so much regret this unexpected imposition.'

She glanced doubtfully along the cramped, narrow space. There was a single wooden bed they would have to share, with a straw mattress, too short for Whalley – his feet would hang over the edge for sure. In the gloom at the far end were various items of furniture, no longer used. There was an old chair among it all somewhere, and a chest. She surrendered.

'Take what you need. I'll have the girls bring you linen and blankets.'

'Most kind.' Colonel Whalley was already back at the window. He took a small telescope from the inner recesses of his coat, extended it, adjusted the focus, and scanned the river. 'That bridge will make the journey from Boston much quicker. There must be thirty men working on it. When will the job be done?'

'They say another half-year.'

'So, January then.' The answer seemed to satisfy him. 'Perfect,' he repeated. He snapped the telescope shut.

Daniel Gookin was in their bedroom, lying on the bed with his arms flung wide, his eyes closed, sound asleep. He hadn't bothered to take off his boots. She leaned over and studied him for a moment. He was forty-eight, thinner than she remembered. The greying at his temples rendered him more distinguished. She felt a surge of love. The colonels were not the first men in need of help he had taken pity on, and would surely not be the last. They had even had local Indians sleeping under their roof before now. Daniel was dedicated to the cause of teaching them the Scriptures. Such faults as he possessed came only from a good heart. She knelt at the foot of the bed and began to unlace his boots. He felt the movement, opened his eyes and raised his head to look at her.

'Leave the boots and come and lie beside me.'

'Hold your impatience, Mr Gookin.' She finished the unlacing, grasped the heel and worked the boot off, then did the same to the other. The climacteric had come upon her while he was away. There would be no more children, for which she thanked God.

Fifteen pregnancies had been more than enough. She lifted her skirt and climbed onto the bed.

Ten minutes later, there was a thud above their heads, followed by another, and then the scrape of a heavy object being dragged across the floor.

He looked at the ceiling. 'You have lodged them in the attic?'

'It was their choice. Do you disapprove?' She climbed off the bed and searched around the floor for her underclothes.

'No, not if they are content with it.'

'If you like them so much, they may sleep in here with us if you prefer.'

He laughed and made a grab for her, but she twisted away and finished dressing.

Another thump came from the attic.

'How did you come to know them, Dan?'

He swung his feet to the floor and sat on the edge of the bed. 'You remember Reverend Hooke of New Haven, who returned to England some years ago?'

'Of course.'

'His wife is Colonel Whalley's sister. When Hooke discovered it was my intention to sail back to America with Captain Pierce, he asked me to arrange passage for his brother-in-law. And then Ned persuaded Will to join us. He was reluctant – he has a young family.'

'And why was it so urgent for them to leave?'

'To put the matter briefly, the King's son is returning to the throne by invitation of Parliament, the army has agreed – or most of it – and England is to be a republic no more.'

The information came in such a rush, was so overwhelming and unexpected, she had to sit on the bed beside him to absorb it. After a few moments she said, 'Why did the army agree to such a thing?'

'A new law, what they call an Act of Oblivion, has been laid before Parliament. The past is to be forgotten. There's to be an amnesty for all who took up arms against the late King – with one exception. All those regicides, as they call them, who had direct involvement in the trial and execution of Charles Stuart are required to surrender themselves for judgement.' He took her hand. 'There you have it, as plain as I can tell it. This was ten weeks ago. Ours is the first ship to reach Boston with the news. That's what I had to go and tell the governor as soon as we came ashore.'

'How many of these regicides came over with you?'

'These two only.'

'And the rest?'

'Some are already fled to Holland. Most are lying low in England. Others were planning to surrender in the hope of mercy. The ports were closing even as we left. It will be hard for them to get away now.' His fingers tightened on hers, as if he could somehow transfer his strength and belief by the force of his grip. 'They are good men, Mary. Ned was Cromwell's cousin. He commanded the cavalry in the campaign against the Scots. Will commanded Cromwell's regiment of foot. They're in need of sanctuary until things quieten down. There's nothing to fear. No one knows they're here, save you and me and the governor.'

'Colonel Whalley was Cromwell's *cousin*? Oh Daniel!' She pulled her hand away. 'Things will never quieten down. They'll come after them for sure. Nothing is more certain.'

Above their heads, another piece of furniture was being dragged into position. In her anxious imagination, it sounded as if they were already building a barricade.

Down on the river, the workmen had finished for the day. Both banks were deserted. Water glistened invitingly in the sunlight. Ned, back at his post at the window, felt a rush of contentment.

He liked the Gookin family. He liked this place. America would suit them very well.

Behind him, Will was laying out their armoury on the bed: four matchlock pistols, two bags of powder, a box of bullets, two knives, a pair of swords. He had barely spoken since they came into the house.

'Leave that, Will.' Ned searched through his bag, pulled out two clean shirts and threw one to him. They had not been out of one another's company for the past four months. His son-in-law's face had become like a pane of glass to him – he could see everything that passed through his mind. 'Let's go down to the river. It'll do us good to be rid of this salt.'

Will looked dubious. 'What if we're seen?'

'There's no one to observe us. And if they do, what of it? We're merely two men bathing.'

'Shouldn't we ask Gookin first?'

'He's our host, not our gaoler. The governor said it was safe for us to move freely here.' He took a step forward, gripped Will by the forearms and shook him gently. 'You'll see your wife and little ones again, I'm sure of it – my sweet Frances, and the grand-children. God will not allow the wicked to triumph for long. We must have patience, and faith.'

Will nodded. 'You're right. Forgive me.'

'Good.' Ned released him.

Together they put the weapons into the chest and covered it with a blanket, then Ned led the way downstairs. The two bed-room doors facing one another on the landing beneath the attic were both closed.

Mary, sitting on the bed, heard the boards creak as they passed. She glanced at her husband. 'What now, do you suppose?' she whispered. He shook his head, had no idea.

The two officers passed through the parlour, out into the front yard, through the gate, and set off down the slope to the river.

Gookin had taken them straight from the *Prudent Mary* to the home of the governor, John Endecott, an old man in a lace collar and black cap who seemed to Ned to have stepped out of the England of Queen Elizabeth. They had handed him their letters of introduction – Will's from John Rowe and Seth Wood, the preachers at Westminster Abbey, Ned's from Dr Thomas Goodwin of the Independent Church in Fetter Lane – and while the old man held them close to his eyes and studied them, Ned had sketched the circumstances of their departure: how for two days at Gravesend they had been obliged to hide below decks while on the quayside the common people had celebrated the imminent return of Charles II, son of the dead king. The sky above the town had glowed a diabolic red from their bonfires, the air had been filled with the noise of their carousing and the sizzle of their roasting meat. The revels had gone on disgracefully late into the Sabbath. On the Monday, when news was brought from Parliament that his name and Will's were on the list of those wanted for the death of Charles I, Captain Pierce had given the order to put to sea.

'But for our good friend Mr Gookin here,' concluded Ned, 'we were likely to have been taken.'

'So you both were judges of the King?'

'Yes, and signed his death warrant. And let me be plain with you, Mr Endecott, for I would not live here under false pretences. We would do the same tomorrow.'

'Would you indeed!' Endecott set down the letters and studied the two visitors through moist occluded eyes, pale grey as oysters. He gripped the edge of his desk. Amid a fusillade of cracking joints, he pulled himself to his feet. 'Then let me shake the hands that signed it, and bid you welcome to Massachusetts. You will find yourselves among good friends here.'

They scouted out a place a little way off the road, where part of the riverbank had been eroded by the current to form a nat-ural pool. Trees hung down almost to the surface. Someone had tied a rope to a branch to make a swing. A long green dragonfly, more exotic than anything they had seen in England, skimmed between the reeds. Wood pigeons cooed amid the foliage. Ned pulled off his boots and briefly dipped his feet into the cool flow, then stripped off his brine-stiffened clothes and waded naked into the river. The cold made him shout out loud. He ducked his shoulders beneath the surface until after a minute he became used to the temperature. On the bank, Will had taken off his own boots and leather coat but seemed to be hesitating. Ned waded back, cupped his hands full of water and splashed him. Will laughed, danced away and shouted in protest, then pulled his shirt over his head and quickly removed the rest of his clothes.

What a sight they made, thought Ned, with their dead white bodies and their battle scars, like phantoms amid all this lush greenery. He'd seen corpses that looked better. Their skin, front and back, was covered in nicks and welts. Will had a jagged line across his stomach from a royalist pike at Naseby, he himself an ugly fist-sized crater beneath his right shoulder, sustained when he was knocked off his horse at Dunbar. Will stood on the water's edge and lifted his arms above his head. At forty-two, he was still slender as a boy. To Ned's surprise he launched himself into a dive, full-length. He disappeared beneath the surface, then bobbed up moments later.

Was there any sensation more delicious than this – to wash stale salt off sweating skin in fresh water on a summer's day? Praise

God, praise God in all His glory, for bringing us in safety to this place! Ned flexed his toes in the soft mud. It was years since he had swum. He was always poor in the water, even as a boy. But he stretched out his arms and allowed himself to topple forwards, and presently rolled over onto his back. Katherine floated into his mind, and for once he did not try to shut out the memory, but allowed her to take shape. Where was she? How was she? It was four years since she had miscarried and almost died, and her health and spirit had never properly recovered. But what was the use of tormenting himself, as Will did every night, with impossible speculations? One of them must be strong. They had a duty to stay alive, not for themselves but for the cause. His text, which in the end was what had persuaded Will to join him, was Christ's injunction to his disciples: 'But when they persecute you in this city, flee ye into another; for verily I say unto you, Ye shall not have gone over the cities of Israel, till the Son of man be come.'

When he rolled over again onto his stomach, the riverbank was suddenly a long way off. As he struck towards the land, he could feel the pull of the current trying to carry him out towards Massachusetts Bay. Will was standing up to his waist in the river, arms akimbo, watching him. Ned trod water for a moment and waved to him, and in that instant saw a figure in the shadow of the trees behind him. It was hard to make the stranger out. He was dressed in black, with dark hair and a short dark beard, and he was standing perfectly still. No sooner had Ned registered him than he realised he was drifting again. The force felt strong enough to drag him all the way back to England if only he would let it. He had to put his head down and swim – swim hard, on the edge of panic, pulling with his arms and kicking with his legs – to save himself. When his feet at last touched the muddy riverbed and he was able to stand, the man had disappeared.

He staggered through the water and threw himself down on the grass, breathless, heart pounding. Will splashed his way out and stood over him, laughing, blocking the sun. 'I swear I never saw a man swim so fast in my life! You looked as if Leviathan was after you!'

Now here was a sound Ned hadn't heard in a long while: Will's laughter. He propped himself up on his elbows, coughed, and brought up a mouthful of river. He glanced at the trees, rustling in the slight breeze. Perhaps the figure had existed only in his mind. He decided to say nothing that might spoil his son-in-law's mood. 'That river's like the man it's named for. The surface may look friendly enough, but beneath it means to kill you.'

Will laughed again, put out his hand and pulled him to his feet. They dried themselves in the sun, donned their clean shirts, and made their way back up the empty road towards the house, the two English regicides, arm in arm.

Mrs Gookin was in her apron in the kitchen preparing supper when Ned ducked his head beneath the lintel and asked if she had such things as a pair of scissors and a broom – and if so, might he borrow them?

Naturally she had scissors, their blades as sharp as penknives, and of course a broom as well. She fetched them from the cupboard.

'And a mirror, by any chance?'

She handed it over and watched as he climbed the stairs. On the threshold where he had been standing, he had left a damp patch.

Elizabeth, laying the table, asked, 'How long will they be staying, Mama?'

'As long as they desire. Your father is quite firm on the matter.'

'But why have they come from England to Massachusetts? Are they on official business?'

'Enough questions. Go fetch some water.'

In the attic, Ned placed the chair next to the window, invited Will to sit, and began to cut his hair. They had been on the run since April – a month and a half in England, sleeping in strangers' houses and in barns and hedgerows, wanted by Parliament for trying to rouse the army to oppose the deal with the exiled Charles II, then ten weeks cooped up on that stinking ship. Will's dark locks came away in handfuls.

After a while he protested, 'Enough, Ned, surely? I shall be bald as an egg.'

'Not enough yet if you are to look respectable, which is how we must appear. If we look like escaped prisoners, we shall be treated as such. Front face, soldier. That beard must come off now.'

He squatted in front of Will and set about the tangle of hair that reached down almost to his son-in-law's chest. He wielded the scissors deftly. Long ago, in the twenties, before the war, he had been apprenticed to the Merchant Taylors' Company to learn the cloth trade from top to bottom, and the skill of cutting had not deserted his fingers. The face that emerged once most of the beard was gone was strong and delicate, full of spiritual force – a face straight out of *Foxe's Book of Martyrs*, thought Ned, which was exactly what the younger man would have become if he hadn't persuaded him to run.

'That will do well enough.' He showed him the result in the mirror, then handed him the scissors and took his place in the chair. 'Now you trim me.'

Will hesitated. His father-in-law had always been a man of distinguished appearance, what with his embroidered waistcoats and his fine shoes, and his splendid house in King Street next to Whitehall Palace. The Levellers were not the only ones who had accused him of vanity. The old man must miss it all, surely, yet not once had he complained. Under the strain of the past year, his hair had turned entirely grey.

He made a tentative cut.

'Hack away, Will,' commanded Ned cheerfully, but as he watched the clumps start falling to the floor, he noticed they were the colour of goose down, and when he picked up the mirror and studied himself, he realised with a shock that he had become grizzled, like one of the old Royalist soldiers begging in the City of London. He put the mirror aside.

Half an hour later, when they came down to the kitchen for supper, their appearance was transformed. They had discarded their stinking leather army jackets. They smelled clean from the river. Sitting in their shirtsleeves at the table with the Gookin family, the pair looked no different to any of the other Englishmen of Massachusetts, for which, thought Mary Gookin, God be thanked. Perhaps they would pass unnoticed after all.

Daniel bowed his head. 'Blessed by thy holy name, O Lord, for these thy good benefits wherewith thou has refreshed us at this time. Lord forgive us all our sins and frailties, save and defend thy whole church in these times of trouble, and grant us health, peace, and truth, in Christ our only Saviour. Amen.'

'Amen.'

Daniel looked up, smiled, and spread his hands. 'Eat.'

It was a simple enough supper – fresh-baked bread, cheese, pickled tongue – and their visitors set about it like men half starved, although they tried to show the residue of good manners, breaking their bread into small pieces and finishing each mouthful before wolfing down another. Daniel fetched a jug of beer. Ned accepted, but Will declined, and Daniel remarked to his wife, as if in explanation of his abstinence, 'Will's father was a minister of strict Puritan principles.'

'Is that so, Colonel Goffe?' she asked politely.

Will swallowed his bread before replying. 'Most strict. He refused to make the sign of the cross during baptism, or permit the exchange of rings in the marriage service, or wear a surplice. He signed a petition to the King objecting to such practices and lost his living in Sussex because of it. He was obliged to move to Wales.'

'Now that is a harsh punishment for any man,' said Ned.

Will smiled and shook his head. 'You must excuse him, Mrs Gookin. I've had to suffer these jokes for years. I was born in Wales, you see – as you may perhaps tell from my voice.'

Mary smiled. 'Then *you* are not Welsh, I take it, Colonel Whalley?'

'No, God be thanked, I am a Nottinghamshire man.' Ned drank his beer. 'But Wales breeds good preachers, I must grant them that, and Will here is blessed with the gift. Oliver thought him the finest speaker in the army.'

Oliver. The easy familiarity with which he dropped the name silenced the table, and Gookin couldn't resist explaining to the children, 'Ned was the Lord Protector's cousin.'

He regretted it at once. Mary gave him a sharp look, while the young ones lit up with interest.

'What was he like?'

'Did you see him often?'

'Tell us about the Protect Her, Ned . . .'

Ned laughed, held up his hand. 'Too many questions all at once.'

'But you knew His Highness well?'

'Aye, aye, well enough.'

He could have said that they had been born within a year of

one another, were friends from boyhood, went around together at university, rode and hawked and gambled together – this was before Oliver's conversion – shared a house in London for a time before they were both married; that Oliver had persuaded him to become a soldier, promoting him in time to be commissary general of the entire English cavalry, that they had fought together at Marston Moor and Naseby and a dozen other battles, that during Cromwell's rule he was in charge of the Protector's military security, that he was a witness at his deathbed, that but for Oliver he would have lived an obscure life as an unsuccessful cloth merchant and a failed farmer, he would never have signed the King's death warrant, and therefore would not have found himself here in his old age on the other side of the world sleeping in an attic.

Instead, he merely said, 'I shall speak of him some other time.'

Gookin said quickly, to change the subject, 'Perhaps you will favour us with a lecture in our meeting house here, Will? We should be glad of your instruction.'

'Is that wise?' asked Mary. 'For them to show themselves so openly?'

'A fair point,' agreed Will. He glanced at Ned for guidance. 'And I am out of the habit of public speaking.'

'We came to Cambridge to be with men and women of like mind,' said Ned. 'If they invite us to join them in studying the Scriptures, we should do so, else why are we here? After all, Mrs Gookin, although your attic is a splendid place, we cannot spend the rest of our lives locked up like prisoners in a single room.'

Mary opened her mouth to speak, but thought better of it.

After they had finished their meal, the officers wished their hosts goodnight and retired to their attic.

Ned stood smoking his pipe, looking down at the river, bluish grey in the fading light, the dark piers of the unfinished bridge piercing the surface like the spars of a shipwreck at low tide. He opened the window. A slight breath of air rippled the drifting layers of smoke. Often in the past, at just this time of an evening, he would walk from his house next door to Whitehall Palace to share a pipe with the Protector, who loved tobacco almost as much as he did music – sometimes, if he heard someone playing, or better still singing, he would roam his official residence until he found the source, and stand there listening with tears in his eyes.

If you want to know what he was like, there is something for you; something that you might not have expected.

Will sat nearby at the table, bent over the small pocket notebook in which he kept his journal. He wrote in shorthand, both for privacy and to save paper: he had managed to bring only a few volumes with him and had no idea when he would be able to acquire more.

27 July 1660. We came to anchor between Boston, and Charlestown; between 8. & 9. in the morning: All in good health through the good hand of God upon us: oh! That men would praise the Lord for his goodness, as psalm 107.21, &c.

He was too exhausted to write more. He blew on the ink to dry it, then knelt by the bed to pray for Frances and their five children. The eldest was only six, the youngest a baby born while he was on the run, whom he had never even seen. 'Dick, Betty, Frankie, Nan and Judith – protect and preserve them, Lord, from evil, and deliver them into thy holy grace.' Ned was right: it was foolish to dwell on them too often. He must have faith that they would meet again. Their separation could only be God's plan. But the sight of the Gookins' children had brought his own to the forefront of his mind. And yet he found that their images were becoming hazier with each passing day. The little ones must be walking now, and talking. They could not be as he remembered them. He saw them as if through fog.

A tapping sound recalled him to the present. Ned was knocking the bowl of his pipe against the windowsill. Will's mind had seized with tiredness. It was all he could do to drag himself up onto the bed. The strangeness of lying on a mattress rather than in a hammock – the solidity of it, the absence of the motion of the sea, the lack of shouts or footsteps on the deck above; the silence. He was barely conscious of the mattress creaking as Ned stretched out beside him, and in an instant, he was fast asleep.

CHAPTER FOUR

RICHARD NAYLER LET himself out of Stathern Hall on Saturday morning as soon as it was light. As a precaution, he carried his pistol tucked into his belt. Colonel Hacker might well have left weapons on the property. Who knew what his wife in her desperation might be capable of? He closed the door quietly behind him.

He untethered his horse and fetched her a bucket of water. While she grazed on the long grass in the orchard, he wrapped the death warrant in a piece of cloth, placed it carefully in one of the saddlebags and strapped it tight. Just before he mounted, he took a final glance back at the house. The windows were dark and blank, as lifeless as a mausoleum. By five, he was on his way.

He rode at a gallop, leaning forwards in the summer morning, up out of his saddle, elbows close to his knees, eyes fixed straight ahead, along the twisting deserted lanes, through villages only just starting to wake, and he didn't let up until he had put a couple of miles between himself and Stathern Hall. By nine, he was at the ruins of the old Roman fort that marked the crossing point of the Fosse Way and Watling Street. The ancient road stretched straight to the south.

As the day went on, he changed his exhausted horses twice, first at Burbage then at Towcester, and the only time he slowed his pace was early in the afternoon, when he recognised from the milestones that he must be passing close to the battlefield of Naseby. He trotted for a mile or two, peering left across the flat Northamptonshire countryside, trying to identify a landmark from that dreadful June morning fifteen years ago. Somewhere near here, Prince Rupert's cavalry had charged uphill towards the enemy through a tangle of furze bushes and rabbit warrens, only to find a thousand Ironsides roaring 'God is our strength!' thundering down upon them from their flank through the early-summer mist – commanded, he discovered afterwards, by Colonel Edward Whalley. He had managed to fire off a shot before the Roundhead cavalry smashed into their front line and his mount was cut from under him.

He had lain among the dead all day, trapped beneath his slain horse, bleeding, his ribs shattered, hip broken, unable to move, listening to his fellow wounded moaning and expiring. At nightfall, he fell unconscious. The next thing he remembered was the sound of gunshots and the agony of something sharp prodding his chest. When he opened his eyes, two Roundhead musketeers were standing over him with their weapons loaded, discussing whether to finish him off or not. 'Hold on,' said one. 'He's looking at us.' They had slung him into a cart, and he had survived, although often in the following months he wished that he had not. But here he was, against all odds, alive and on the winning side, and *he* would not make the mistake of showing mercy.

He spurred his horse and resumed his southern dash – a streak of dust, an avenging fury.

He passed that night at St Albans, twenty miles north of London, sharing a bed in the White Hart inn with two other travellers – a corn merchant from Lincoln and a captain of foot on his way to join his regiment in Yorkshire – and left on Sunday while both were still snoring. By the middle of the morning, he was riding down Ludgate Hill through the City of London, the bells of St Paul's ringing in his ears as if to welcome him home in triumph. He made directly for Worcester House on the Strand, but had barely gone ten paces past the entrance when he was stopped by one of the Lord Chancellor's guards.

'Richard Nayler,' he announced, 'to see Sir Edward Hyde.' He was grubby, unshaven, clutching his dirty saddlebag, sweating from the pain of old wounds and cramp. He tried to step around the guard, who moved at once to block him.

'Sir Edward is at worship with his family.'

'As soon as he is finished, then.'

The guard looked him up and down. 'You know it is a day of rest?'

'I know you are a dolt. Tell him I have the warrant – exactly that, you understand? He will grasp the meaning.'

He limped across the passage to a reception room and lowered himself into a chair. He was not offended by the guard's rudeness. He was used to passing unrecognised. Indeed, he preferred it. A man could be more effective anonymous. People talked and gave themselves away. Prior to his present position, he had been confidential secretary to the Marquess of Hertford; when the King was restored, it was the marquess who had secured him a place in the new administration as a reward for his long years of loyal service.

He could have had any post he wanted, within reason – at the Exchequer, the Navy, the Chancery Department – but he had requested the Privy Council, and in particular the committee established to apprehend the regicides. The work suited him. He had no wife or children to distract him. Leisure he had no time for. His reputation was already growing. He was one of those shadows who moves, anonymous, along the private passages and through the council chambers of every nation in every age – a word here, a warning there, a secret imparted, a person betrayed – a most useful shadow; a shadow who causes things to happen. He stretched out his leg and began massaging his aching muscle.

After a few minutes, one of the Lord Chancellor's secretaries appeared, a foppish, indolent-looking young fellow, doubtless some courtier's relative. 'Sir Edward is presently at dinner.' He held out his hand; lace at the wrist, fingers heavy with rings. 'However, he wishes to see the document you mentioned.'

Nayler hesitated before taking the warrant from his saddlebag, then watched with some envy as it was carried off upstairs. Knowing the foibles of great men, he had hoped to place it in Sir Edward's hands himself. But as time passed, he was gratified to observe the effect it seemed to be having. The great mansion suddenly roused itself from its Sabbath torpor, with shouted summonses and a glimpse of messengers rushing past the open door. After about a half-hour came the noise of a coach pulling into the courtyard, and the long-nosed, bloodhound figure of Sir William Morice, Secretary of State for the Northern Department, went shuffling down the passage. He was followed shortly afterwards by Sir Anthony Ashley-Cooper and Sir Arthur Annesley, both Privy Councillors, who as usual arrived together, and soon after that the foppish secretary reappeared in the doorway, his manner now more deferential.

'Sir Edward sends his compliments, Mr Nayler, and requests your attendance at a committee meeting of the Council.'

Nayler picked up his bag and followed the secretary's slim hips into the galleried hall, up the central staircase and through a succession of reception rooms looking out over the garden to the

Thames, until they reached the Lord Chancellor's private study, where the secretary stood aside and indicated that he should enter.

He was struck, as always, by how small it was, little more than a closet – wood-panelled, low-ceilinged, airless, gloomy, with one leaded window so tiny that even on this summer day there were candles burning. Yet it was from here that England was run. A heavy table covered with a Turkish rug occupied most of the floor. He took in the committee at a glance: Morice on one side, Ashley-Cooper and Annesley opposite him, and at the head of the table facing the door, the King's first minister, Sir Edward Hyde. Immensely fat, he sat away from the table and sideways to the others, his arthritic, gout-swollen legs propped up on a stool. He was reading the warrant. He did not look up.

'What kind of man preserves such a document, even when his enemies have returned to power and he knows it must hang him? Can you answer me that, Mr Nayler?'

'A fanatic, my lord.'

'Well then, I believe he has met his match in you.' Hyde lifted his gaze from the warrant and studied Nayler out of the corner of his eye. 'Leicestershire and back in four days – that is a feat. You did not think of sending someone else?'

'I considered it too important.'

Hyde nodded. 'It is. You are forgiven for disturbing our Sabbath.' He resumed his examination of the warrant and at the same time lifted a pudgy hand and pointed to a seat at the end of the table. 'Join us.'

Nayler removed his hat and took his place. 'Thank you, my lord, but in truth I am merely the messenger. The credit all lies with Sir Arthur and Sir Anthony for their skill in persuading Colonel Hacker to reveal the existence of the warrant.'

Persuaded – now that was a pretty euphemism. While Nayler

had sat taking notes in a corner during Hacker's interrogation, it was Annesley and Ashley-Cooper who had ordered the Tower's guards to beat the manacled colonel with clubs until he vomited up what he knew. Both were lawyers who had served under Cromwell before smoothly transferring their loyalties to the King. He glanced across at them. They nodded in acknowledgement. He knew they were anxious to demonstrate their zeal in tracking down their former comrades.

Hyde said, 'Hacker is even more of a dead man than he was before. And what of these other two officers who received the warrant – Phayre and Huncks?'

'Both in custody, my lord, and both insistent that they refused to obey the order. Huncks claims Cromwell abused him for his cowardice. Both put all the blame on Hacker.'

'We are now obliged to surrender the warrant to the House of Lords, I suppose?'

'Yes, my lord,' said Annesley. 'It must go first to the Lieutenant of the Tower, who will show it to Hacker and have him swear its authenticity, and then he is under instructions to provide it to the Lords.'

'And this must happen at once? Tomorrow?' Annesley and Ashley-Cooper both nodded. Hyde sighed. 'This will stir up Parliament again.' He trained his eye back on Nayler. 'How many of these signatories are still at liberty? That is the first question we shall be asked.'

'With your permission, my lord?' From his bag Nayler extracted the list he had made on Friday night in Hacker's study. 'I have been through the warrant. You will see that fifty-nine traitors signed it. By my reckoning, of these, twenty have since died. Twenty-five are in our custody, either surrendered or captured. One – Colonel Ingoldsby – has been granted a pardon by His

Majesty in return for his assistance in catching the others. Which leaves thirteen still at large.'

'And who are they?' asked Morice. Like Hyde, he had been with the King throughout his years in exile. But he was an old man, somewhat addled in the head and unlikely to last very long as secretary of state. Still, Nayler regarded him with more respect than he did Annesley and Ashley-Cooper, clever though they were. Let him serve out his time; he had earned it.

'Whalley,' he replied, running his finger down the names, 'Livesey, Okey, Goffe, Hewson, Blagrave, Ludlow, Barkstead, Dixwell, Walton, Say, Challoner and Corbet.'

'And how close are we to catching them?'

'Livesey we believe to be in the Low Countries with his wife and children. Okey and Barkstead have been sighted in Germany; so has Walton – very ill and old, by all accounts. Hewson is in Amsterdam. Blagrave, Challoner and Corbet are also rumoured to be in the Netherlands. Say is in Switzerland. The rest we do not know, as yet. We are keeping watch on their families.'

Hyde threw the warrant onto the table. 'There is no end to it. Only four men were to die for murdering the King – that was our agreement when we negotiated the Act of Oblivion. Then we found the records of the trial – or rather you did, Mr Nayler – and the four became eight, then the eight twelve, and now there are dozens of them. Every man in Parliament has some enemy he wishes to see excluded from pardon.'

Morice's pendulous jowls quivered. 'You are not suggesting we should leave these thirteen at liberty, my lord?'

'No, Sir William, indeed I am not. We must hunt them down. But in the meantime, we must move this business on more quickly, so that we can turn our minds to other matters.' Hyde lifted his wig and scratched his sweating scalp as he weighed the matter up.

Finally he settled it carefully back on his head. 'I propose we now concentrate our efforts on those we have in custody. The discovery of the warrant will help us close the case against them.' He turned to Nayler again. 'Those who surrendered in the hope of mercy – they are all still held without charge at Lambeth House rather than the Tower?'

Nayler nodded. 'To encourage others to follow their example.'

'Well, we may take it as certain that none of these fugitives will ever give themselves up willingly, otherwise they would have done so by now. Therefore, it is time to move to the next step.'

'Meaning what, my lord?'

'We should transfer the prisoners directly to the Tower and bring them to trial as quickly as possible.'

Ashley-Cooper said, 'So there's to be no pardon for any of them?'

'None.'

'And yet they gave themselves up in the expectation of mercy.'

'Then they were fools. I would have preferred it otherwise – God knows I warned the King what would happen – but the present mood in Parliament will not permit it. Do you disagree?'

Annesley said quickly, 'No, we all agree, my lord.'

'Mr Nayler?'

'They showed no mercy to the King; why should any be shown to them?'

'Well put. Then I shall recommend to the King and full Council that that is how we shall proceed.'

Nayler said, 'And the catching of the rest?'

'That can be your responsibility, Mr Nayler, since the work is plainly to your taste.' Hyde held out the warrant at arm's length and turned his head away, as if he found it distasteful merely to touch it. 'You had better deliver this to the Tower.' Nayler rose from his seat and went round the table to collect it. 'Keep us informed of your progress. Now I have a sensitive matter I wish to discuss with my colleagues.'

Nayler gathered he was dismissed. He picked up his bag and bowed to the committee. 'My lords.'

Outside the room, he lingered for a moment, ostensibly to put away the warrant but actually to listen.

He heard Morice's voice, approving: 'Now he's a zealous fellow.'

And then Hyde's high-pitched, wheezing rejoinder: 'A very zealous fellow. Two hundred miles in four days? What makes him run so hard, I wonder.'

He would have liked to have lingered to hear more, but Mr Secretary-Fop was waiting to escort him off the premises, obliging him to walk away from the open door, straining his ears in frustration as the voices behind him faded to a drone.

All along the south side of the Strand, for a distance of a mile, the great palaces and gardens of the nobility ran down to the Thames – first Somerset House in the east, then Worcester House, Arundel House and York House, right the way to Northumberland House on the edge of Whitehall. In the midst of these stately piles, dilapidated by civil war and the lean years of the Protectorate, stood Essex House, the Elizabethan mansion that served as the London residence of William Seymour, 1st Marquess of Hertford. It was not so much a house nowadays as a warren of lodgings spread across several buildings – forty-two bedrooms in all, mostly let to tenants to raise some income – and it was here, in this monument to Royalist decay, that Nayler had lived rent-free for the past fourteen years as part of the marquess's household.

He passed across the cobbled courtyard, through drifts of refuse rustling with rats, to a heavy oak door in the west wing, produced a bunch of keys, unlocked it, and climbed the staircase to the top floor. At the end of a dark passage, he unlocked a second door. None of the servants was allowed a key. The heat of four days' shut-up air struck his face like the opening of an oven. A column of flies circled in the centre of the room that served as his study. Others buzzed helplessly against the leaded windows. Every surface was covered with spreading heaps of yellowing papers – the case against the regicides, letters and minutes seized under warrant from neglected corners of lawyers' libraries and family archives, from hiding places in cellars and attics and rubbish heaps. Powdery with reddish dust and dirt and decay, they gave the room its peculiar aroma of mould and dryness. As he crossed to the window, treading carefully between the piles, his legs brushed against them. They rustled like dead leaves, and his footsteps on the carpet seemed to raise clouds of black spores. His nostrils clogged, and he sensed another of his nauseous headaches coming on, spreading from the back of his nose to behind his eyes.

He opened the window. The Thames flowed past sluggishly barely a hundred yards away. The tide was out, exposing black humps of oozing mud streaked with green weed. In the hot sunshine, it reeked of the sea and of decay. Figures were picking through it in the hope of finding something they could use or sell. Gulls wheeled and cried above their heads, occasionally swooping down, settling for an instant and lifting off again. At the bottom of the garden at the water's edge, an arch led to a private jetty. He craned his neck. The marquess's boat was gone. He guessed the old man must have been rowed upriver to see the King at Hampton Court.

In the hope of creating a draught, he went through to his small corner bedroom and opened another window. This was at the side of the house and looked down onto Milford Lane, which ran between Essex House and Arundel House – a notorious narrow street of alehouses, cheap shops, whorehouses and tenements that even the Cromwellians had not been able to bring to God. It was unusually quiet on this Sunday afternoon, whores and tapsters in his experience observing the Sabbath as keenly as anyone else. He had descended there a few times himself over the past couple of years, when his solitariness and the ache of desire had become too much to bear.

He continued to stare for a few more minutes, then turned and confronted the room. He kept it free of paper and bare of decoration, save for a miniature of his wife that hung above his dressing table. There was a candle beneath it that he liked to light at night so that he could fall asleep in her company. She gazed at him now from beneath her dark ringlets, somewhat in the manner of Sir Edward Hyde at the council table, her head in profile and half turned towards him, wearing a quizzical expression; intelligent, amused.

He had seen her last on Christmas Day 1657, when the household had gathered illegally in the private chapel to celebrate the Nativity. Just as the sermon ended and the priest was administering the Holy Sacrament at the altar rail – an ornament that was itself illegal – the doors banged open and a file of soldiers marched in and surrounded the congregation. They aimed their muskets but permitted the communicants to finish receiving their wine and wafers. There were no officers amongst them, Nayler noted as he escorted Sarah back to their pew, and he guessed those must be their orders. When they were seated, she took his hand and placed it on her belly. He felt the kick beneath his palm – he could feel it now, two and a half years later, a sharp thump, like a heartbeat. He realised afterwards it was her way of telling him not to do anything foolish, and he resolved as such.

But when after several hours of sitting as prisoners two officers – both colonels – did at last appear, and strutted up the aisle to the altar demanding to know the reason for this unlawful assembly, he felt a rage begin to rise within him.

'This is but a common Tuesday,' said the younger of the pair, 'an ordinary weekday like any other. To celebrate the superstition of the Nativity is forbidden by Act of Parliament. You are all liable for arrest.'

No one said a word, not even the marquess, sitting quietly at the front. In the silence, Nayler found himself muttering, 'It is not illegal to worship God.'

'What was that, sir?' demanded the officer.

'I said,' he repeated more loudly, 'it is not illegal to worship God.'

'It is illegal to use the Book of Common Prayer, which is but the Catholic Mass in English.'

He felt Sarah clutching at his arm, but he could not stop himself. 'And yet I thought you fought the war for liberty of conscience.'

'Liberty of conscience, sir, not treason. The Book of Common Prayer means you pray particularly for Charles Stuart – do you deny it?'

'We pray for all Christian kings, princes and governors.'

The older officer said, 'Then you pray for the King of Spain, who is an enemy and a papist.'

'We pray only to God to bless all rulers. There are no papists here.'

The colonels had had enough. 'Arrest him.'

He had no time to say goodbye to Sarah, or even properly to look at her. A pair of soldiers had already come up behind him, but he had been too full of anger to notice them. He heard her cry out, but before he could register what was happening, he felt himself hauled up and away, shoved and marched to the back of the chapel and out into the December cold, all the way through the empty streets – deserted because of Christmas Day, which was what had outraged the army – until they came to Newgate prison, where he was thrown into a cell and left to rot for the next six months, and when he came out he learned that the baby, a boy, had been born dead on the night of his arrest, the premature labour brought on by the shock, and that Sarah had died giving birth to him.

What makes him run so hard, I wonder.

Well, that would make a man run pretty hard, would you not say, your lordship? Especially when the two officers who had ordered his arrest were Colonel Whalley and Colonel Goffe, wanted for the murder of the King and still at liberty somewhere on God's fair earth – but not for long, sir; not if Mr Richard Nayler had anything to do with it.

CHAPTER FIVE

A S SOON AS it was light that Lord's Day morning, Will – barefoot, wearing shirt and breeches – slid out of bed so as not to wake his father-in-law and seated himself at the table. He took from his pocket a sheet of yellowing paper torn from the back of an old almanac, dipped his pen into the inkpot, and after some hesitation wrote across the top of the blank page – in the same carefully elaborate, curling script that he had used to sign the King's death warrant – *A Humble Petition to the Christian Congregation of Cambridge, Massachusetts, by William Goffe, Esq.*

He paused and looked up, searching the shadows of the slanting roof for inspiration. Plant him before an audience, however large, even with Cromwell himself in attendance, and the Lord would pour such a torrent of words into his head that he had only to open his mouth and they would gush forth like a fountain. Writing was a different matter. Perhaps if he had gone to Oxford like his two elder brothers, he would have been more confident. But by the time he was of age, his father had lost his living, and instead he had been apprenticed as a salter to 'Praying William' Vaughan, a Puritan grocer in London, and his education had come to an end.

Still, after a while his thoughts began to form, and eventually his nib started to scratch across the paper.

It took him the best part of an hour to finish. It was stilted and poorly punctuated but sincere, and it conveyed what he wished to say. He blew on the paper then sat back and waited until the sun was fully risen and he could hear sounds of movement downstairs before he went over to the bed and shook Ned gently by the shoulder.

'I have written something.'

'Let me see it then.' Ned took the petition, held it at arm's length and squinted at it through eyes still half asleep.

Having received much mercy from the Lord, at his leaving his native country, and in his passage through the great deeps; as also in this land; wherein he is a stranger; Now before the Lord in the congregation of his people, doth humbly desire that the praises due unto God, – may be rendered on his behalf. And that the Lord may be entreated yet to follow his poor unworthy servant with goodness and mercy; that he may walk as becomes the gospel, and forever cleave to the Lord; and love him, and serve him, in all conditions.

When he had finished reading, he nodded. 'That is well put.'

'And the grammar is good?'

'It will pass.'

'So, we are agreed? We shall reveal ourselves?'

Ned returned the petition. They had argued the matter back and forth for the whole of the previous day. He said, 'What would Oliver do in our place? He would not skulk up here in an attic, you may be sure. He would walk out with his head erect, and on the Lord's Day he would join in public worship.'

'Then I shall give it to our friend.'

Will pulled on his boots.

He found the Gookins downstairs in the parlour, preparing to leave for the meeting house. He gave the paper to Daniel, together with the testimonials of their ministers in London affirming that they had both experienced a revelation.

Gookin read the petition, frowning, chewing the inside of his lip. 'You understand I must be honest as to your true identities, and the reason why you have come to America?'

'We understand.'

'Mary, what is your opinion?'

Mary's opinion was that it was a little late in the day for him to start soliciting her views. But she was developing a fondness for Will – his quiet earnestness, his piety, the care he took in talking to the children. She did not wish to dishearten him. 'Whatever you feel best.'

In the distance, a bell began to toll. Gookin stuffed the papers into his pocket. 'I'll send word as soon as the members have voted.'

They left in an orderly procession, with Daniel at the head and little Nathaniel bringing up the rear. Will retreated to the attic. 'They have gone.'

Ned – stripped to the waist, bent over the basin, washing – grunted.

Will resumed his seat, closed his eyes, inserted his finger into the Bible and opened it at random. Somehow God always guided him to an appropriate passage, and so it was this morning. *Hear the right, O Lord, attend unto my cry, give ear unto my prayer, that goeth not out of feigned lips.*

Ned put on his shirt. He went over to the window and scanned the river through his spyglass. The ferry was approaching, carrying a horse-drawn cart laden with passengers and half a dozen men and women on foot. All middle-aged. No children. They looked to be in a hurry. As soon as they reached the Cambridge side and the ramp was lowered, they made haste up the road across the marshland, over the creek, past the house and out of sight. Not long afterwards, the bell ceased tolling and there was silence.

He closed the telescope and went and stretched out on the bed. In eighteen years as an officer, he had learned the importance of conveying confidence even when he didn't feel it. He was fairly sure they were right to reveal themselves, if only because so many people knew their true identities already – Captain Pierce, some of their fellow passengers on the *Prudent Mary*, Governor Endecott, the Gookin family . . . They could hardly expect talkative children to maintain such a secret. On the other hand, he was not convinced the Cambridge community would welcome them. And if the decision went against them – what then? They would have exposed themselves for nothing, and would have to move on quickly. But where? For such a vast land, it seemed to him at that moment mightily short of hiding places, at least for a man of sixty and another of forty-two with few practical skills and little money.

He was no further forward in devising an alternative plan a half-hour later, when he heard the front door open and footsteps come running up the stairs. He reached under his pillow and curled his finger around the trigger of his pistol, but when the door opened, it was only young Sam Gookin, bursting with self-importance.

'Father says you are to come at once!'

They picked up their Bibles and followed him downstairs, out onto the road and up the slope towards the village. They stared about them with curiosity. Half a dozen timber houses, identical to the Gookins', were set back from the road, spread far apart in their own fenced lots, all gleaming fresh in the morning sun. Ahead, the high roofs and chimneys of the college loomed above the settlement. No people were about, and the effect of such space and newness and emptiness was peculiarly disconcerting, like walking through a dream. Ned felt suddenly hollowed by homesickness. Dear God, he thought, I shall never get used to this.

Sam scampered on ahead.

The meeting house was a modest building, forty feet by forty, of two windowed storeys, clad in wooden shingles that had weathered to a silvery fish-scale grey, with a square pointed roof capped by a little hive-shaped belfry. A profusion of horses, carts and traps were drawn up outside it; but from inside came no sound. The only noise was birdsong. Sam opened the door and they passed into a chilly, well-lit space with a gallery. The ground floor and the upper section were packed with silent figures – men on one side, women on the other, children at the back – who all turned to stare as the two colonels entered, and at that moment, Ned was as certain as he had been of anything in his life that the vote had gone against them. But then Daniel Gookin stood and began to clap, and a moment later the others joined in, and suddenly the wooden building was filled with applause as the minister came down from the pulpit and advanced along the aisle towards them, smiling, his arms stretched wide in welcome.

The minister preached a sermon that began with a quotation from Deuteronomy about the need to be ready to die at any moment. 'Sinners should consider of death, that the thing is certain, and only the time uncertain, and that they run an infinite hazard if they neglect making sure of an interest in Christ one day longer.' He spoke in a strong, deep voice with a Yorkshire accent, his palms and eyes cast up to Heaven as he exhorted his listeners to seek God's grace in the act of hospitality.

As honoured visitors, Ned and Will were seated at the front. Will listened with his eyes closed throughout, nodding and murmuring

in agreement, but Ned, after the first half-hour, found his attention wandering. Moving his head only slightly, he glanced surreptitiously from side to side along the pew, first at the rapt faces
and then up to the crowded gallery above the preacher. Finally
he returned his gaze to the minister. He was in his thirties, thick-
set, dark-haired, with a short black beard and eyebrows that met
to form a continuous line across his forehead. Ned had a sudden
instinct that he had seen him before, and then it occurred to him
that this was the man who had watched them bathing.

He tried to put the matter out of his mind and to open his heart
to the Lord. When, after an hour, the sermon ended, he joined
loudly in the unaccompanied singing of the psalms ('I waited
patiently for the Lord') and the recitation of the Lord's Prayer.
He listened carefully to the discussion of a passage from the Book
of Isaiah ('Be strong, fear not: behold, your God will come with
vengeance . . .'). And after the meeting was over, when they were
standing outside in the sunshine, he made a mighty effort to
remember the names of all the members of the congregation
whom Daniel Gookin brought over to introduce to them, beginning with the Reverend Charles Chauncey, president of Harvard
College, a large and stately galleon of a man, some sixty-odd years
old, clad in black clerical robes and attended by a small fleet of
eager undergraduates, bobbing their heads respectfully.

'I am persuaded that the Lord has brought you to this country
both for your good and for ours.' He had a broad pink face, framed
on top by an orangey periwig and beneath by a white collar with
preaching bands. He intoned his words like a judge pronouncing
sentence. 'You must visit the college and dine.'

Ned said, 'We would be honoured, would we not, Will?'

'Indeed, Mr Chauncey: a pleasure – if it is not an imposition?'

'An imposition? You are as angels dropped from Heaven!'

After the president and his students had moved away, Gookin introduced the senior church elder, Mr Frost, who wheezed a welcome, and then came a blur of farmers, their faces picked thin by hard work and burnt by the sun, offering callused hands to shake – Thomas Danforth, Golden Moore, Nathaniel Sparrowhawk, Abraham Errington – who reminded Ned of the first recruits of Cromwell's regiment of horse.

Over their shoulders he kept an eye on the minister, who was positioned beside the entrance to the meeting house, greeting his congregation as they gathered outside. Eventually he seemed to sense he was under scrutiny. He glanced across at Ned, and a minute later he had excused himself and was walking across the grass to where the colonels stood.

'Now,' said Gookin, drawing him into the group, 'if your aching heads are not too a-buzz with names, permit me to introduce the Reverend Jonathan Mitchell. Jonathan, this is Edward Whalley and William Goffe.'

Mitchell bowed to each in turn.

Will said, 'We are not likely to forget *your* name, Mr Mitchell, after such a sermon.'

'Ah well,' the minister said modestly, 'you know how it goes, Mr Goffe, when the spirit takes you. The credit belongs entirely to God. I gather from Daniel that you are a fair preacher yourself.'

'On occasion.'

He turned to Ned. 'And how long do you propose to stay in Cambridge, Colonel Whalley?'

'That depends on how things go in England. I cannot believe the Lord will suffer his enemies to triumph for long. As soon as the government falls, we shall return home.'

'And in the meantime, we are to be your shelter from the storm, is that it?'

There was a slight edge to the remark that Ned did not like, although he could not say precisely what it was, and neither Will nor Daniel seemed to have noticed it. He said, 'We are thankful for a safe haven, certainly. Tell me,' he added casually, 'did I not see you down at the river the other day?'

Mitchell's thick brow creased as if he was trying to remember. 'No, I think not. I was in Boston until last night.' He looked beyond them. 'Now there is Mrs Simes, waiting patiently for a word – she was lately widowed. Let us talk more later.' And after bestowing another pair of bows, he was gone.

As they were walking down the hill towards the Gookins' house, Will said, 'You did not tell me you saw anyone by the river.'

'Only because I wasn't sure. It's no matter.'

Of one thing he was certain, however: the minister was lying. Which meant that if he had indeed been in Boston, there was a chance he had been making enquiries about them. And if he was not willing to admit to such enquiries, he was not the friend he pretended.

In the week that followed, the officers did indeed find themselves treated, as Chauncey had described them, like angels dropped from Heaven. They sat in the Gookins' parlour and received a succession of neighbours anxious to meet the two most senior Englishmen ever to set foot in America. In particular, the news that Ned was a blood relation of Cromwell had spread far and fast, and he found himself being asked repeatedly to confirm the rumour.

'Yes, I had that honour. My mother, Frances Cromwell, was the sister of His Highness's father.'

'And what was he like?' That question, again and again.

'He was remarkable,' was the most that Ned would say.

True to the spirit of hospitality, they were invited back to their visitors' houses to break bread and study the Scriptures, and having nothing else to do, they accepted, and so became quite familiar figures, their Bibles in their hands, walking around the grassy lanes, always together – up Wood Street to the meeting house off Cow Yard Lane, down Crooked Street and along Creek Lane. As they strolled, Ned committed the grid of streets to memory and took careful note of the lines of communication: the main road from Boston to the south that ran up between Ox Marsh and Ship Marsh, all the way through the town, past the college and out to the common land in the north where the cattle grazed; the track to Watertown to the west; and to the east, the path along the river to the oyster bank and the clay pit. Four roads gave access to the town, and more importantly exits out of it. It was not that he felt insecure in Cambridge, surrounded by so many kindred souls, but still, it was as well to know these things.

On their second Sabbath, the gathering at the meeting house was more crowded than the first, people having apparently come from miles around to gaze upon the colonels. Such fame made them both uneasy. Reverend Mitchell preached another fine sermon and carefully avoided them afterwards, or so it seemed to Ned.

It was on the morning of Thursday 9 August, thirteen days after their arrival in America, that matters took a decisive turn.

They were at Golden Moore's house, where the boys had taken them to see a litter of spaniel puppies that had just been whelped, when Mary Gookin appeared in the doorway of Old Moore's barn, flustered, wiping her hands on her apron, and announced that John Norton had come to see them.

Ned said, 'And who is John Norton?'

'Minister of the Boston First Church,' replied Golden Moore, who had retired from farming and was bent almost double with infirmity. 'A man of the utmost learning.'

'He has come all the way from Boston?' asked Will.

'Aye, he must have done.'

'If he is so distinguished,' said Ned, 'and has come so far, then we had best go and speak with him.'

The boys clamoured to stay and play with the puppies, to take one home. But Mary was firm and made them give them back, and they set off down the hill, Sam holding one of Will's hands and Nat the other, to find the Reverend Norton standing at the gate watching the building work on the river. He was a slender, dignified figure, perhaps fifty years of age, with long, thin hair parted in the middle and hanging in lank curtains on either side of a mournful face. He had brought with him a letter from the elders of his church inviting the colonels to attend a lecture to be given by him the following afternoon, with a gathering afterwards at his house. Ned read the letter and handed it to Will.

'Our members are most keen to meet you,' said Norton. 'I wished to impress that upon you in person.'

Will, studying the letter, shook his head. 'Governor Endecott advised us to remain in Cambridge.'

Ned said, 'But if our presence here is already known in Boston, what difference does it make? Those who wish us harm can find us easily enough.'

'We are a strict church,' Norton reassured Will, 'most careful as to whom we admit. You will be entirely among sympathisers.'

'I still say we should consult the governor first.'

Norton smiled. 'The governor will be there.'

Will had no reply to that.

Gookin said he couldn't accompany them as he was expecting a visitor. He drew them a map. 'It is a handsome church and cannot be missed. Merely direct yourselves towards the harbourfront.'

They set off shortly after noon the next day, wearing swords. As extra protection, they carried pistols concealed beneath their leather coats.

The ferry was a rickety wooden platform, large enough to carry a couple of wagons, attached to a cable slung across the river. They were obliged to wait a few minutes to see if any other passengers turned up. The ferryman kept staring at them. Finally, when no one else came, he drew up the ramp, spat on his hands, took the rope and started to haul them across.

It was cooler than of late – low clouds and a blustery Atlantic wind that whipped waves across the surface of the Charles and gave early threat that summer would soon be over. Ned looked back at the scattering of grey timber houses receding behind them and tried to imagine a winter stuck in such a place. Cambridge was already beginning to bore him. He was sure they were right to scout out the situation in Boston. They had barely fifty pounds between them. At some point they would need to make some money. A town was a better prospect.

'Perhaps we can go back to our old trades, Will?' He nudged his son-in-law with his elbow to cheer him up. 'You a salter and I a draper – what do you say? We could open a shop. Or you could become a minister – it always was your calling.'

Will looked up from the water long enough to give a brief smile, and then went back to his brooding. Frances, Dick, Betty, Frankie, Nan and Judith. What time was is it in England? What might they be doing?

It took little more than a minute to make the crossing. On the opposite bank, the road ran alongside the river. At first they had it to themselves – the fast-flowing water to their left, to their right, open country of gentle pasture with small patches of woodland, very like England, and in the distance, the start of a larger forest that draped itself like a dark blanket over the low hills. But presently they passed a horse and cart heading towards Cambridge, and signs of settlement appeared: isolated farmsteads, a windmill with a house and outbuildings, cattle in a fenced enclosure with a stall. After they had walked for perhaps half an hour, the river rounded a bend and widened to an estuary, and there ahead was Boston – a fort on the headland and the sea beyond it, dull as pewter, with half a dozen tall-masted ships moored in the channel. They hastened their pace towards it.

It was a marvellous thing, after so many months, to stroll freely again through a proper town, to clump along the wooden side-walks, to observe a busy market, to jostle through a crowd of sailors, smell freshly landed fish, admire fine buildings of brick and tile. Among so many hundreds, all intent on their own business, the colonels passed unnoticed, until Daniel Gookin's map brought them to an impressive three-storey building on a street corner near the waterfront, with a paved area in front of the door on which waited a welcoming party of Reverend Norton, Governor Endecott and half a dozen other men of the Boston First Church.

Norton had chosen as the subject of his lecture St Paul's Epistle to the Hebrews: to be precise, why did Christ assume human rather than angelic form? 'For verily he took not on him the nature of angels; but he took on him the seed of Abraham.'

Listening, Ned's heart was fuller than it had been for months – for years, in fact. Was this church not exactly what they had fought the Civil War to achieve? For the right to sit in a meeting house in the middle of the week, with a plain table instead of an altar; with clear glass in the windows instead of idolatrous coloured images of angels; with no fancy lace surplices or organ music to distract them from the truth; no high-and-mighty bishops in their palaces; no sinful king blasphemously posing as head of Christ's church – just the freedom to experience directly the word of the Lord?

'Amen!' he cried when the lecture was finished. 'Amen! Amen!'

Will glanced at him. He had never known his father-in-law to express such religious fervour.

Ned was still enraptured after the discussion ended and they were filing out onto the street. 'That was the case for the true faith proven, Will – and proven well!' He gripped his son-in-law's elbow. 'The Lord put a man of flesh and blood on earth for us to follow – a humble man, "the seed of Abraham" – and raised him above the angels so that he could teach us not to fear death.' They had emerged into the dull afternoon and were standing on the forecourt. 'The rest is all casuistry and popery—'

'Whalley!' shouted an astonished voice. 'Edward Whalley!'

Ned stopped speaking and looked around. A group of rough-looking fellows, apparently slouching into town from the direction of the harbour, had halted opposite the church, and one of them was pointing at him.

'It's old Ned Whalley!' the man repeated. His accent was guttural, slurred with drink – "Shauld Ned Woll-eye!' – but his words were clear enough. 'I know yon bastard!' he yelled to everyone within earshot. His arm was outstretched like an Old Testament prophet's. 'He took me prisoner at Dunbar!'

Norton, Endecott and the others all turned to see who was shouting. Someone said, 'He sounds as though he's off the Scottish ship that dropped anchor this morning.'

'Ah yes,' said Ned, recovering his composure. He tried to make light of it. 'A Scotchman – it had to be!'

Suddenly the rowdy group started heading across the street

towards them. Twenty or so members of the Boston First Church quickly formed a protective phalanx around the two colonels. 'My house is just next door,' said Norton. 'We should make haste.'

The Puritans moved off up the sidewalk. The Scotsman and his companions swerved to follow them and kept pace alongside. Quite a crowd was watching the spectacle now.

'Whalley, Whalley!' chanted his tormentor. 'And I'll warrant the other wee cunny's Goffe, his son-in-law. Both wanted for the murder of the King!'

Ned moved to draw his sword, but Will grabbed his arm to stop him. 'Not here, not yet.'

They reached Norton's house. Old Endecott – puffing, red in the face – swung round to face the Scotsman. 'I am the governor of this colony, and these friends are our honoured guests. Hold your tongue, or I shall have you arrested for disturbing the peace!' With that, he turned his back on him and gestured to the colonels to go inside the house.

The Scotsman, defeated, stood with his hands on his hips, his comrades crowded behind him. 'If it were not for those you walk with,' he shouted after them, 'we'd have you by the hair of your heads!'

Will called back over his shoulder, 'All the hairs of our heads are numbered by the Lord! We are not afraid of you!'

The door slammed shut behind them, and was barred and bolted.

Inside, the Puritans stood in hushed groups of two or three, occasionally glancing at the officers. Ned was breathing hard. His blood was up. He wished Will had let him draw his sword. He would have given that Scotch dog a cut or two, just to remind him to heed his manners in future.

Endecott said, 'It was ill luck he happened to pass by just then and see you, Colonel Whalley. You did not recognise him, I suppose?'

'We took five thousand prisoners at Dunbar, Mr Endecott – so no, sir, I did not recognise him.'

The mention of Dunbar made the wound beneath his shoulder start to throb. Now *that* had been a fight: outnumbered, their backs to the sea, and yet still, by the grace of God, they had surprised the Scots in the dark before dawn and chased them all the way back to Edinburgh. Most of the prisoners had been marched into England and imprisoned in Durham Cathedral. Sixteen hundred had died of hunger and disease – a bad business, nothing to do with him. The rest had been shipped off and sold as slave labour to the colonies. Three thousand pounds per shipload, if he remembered correctly: much-needed revenue.

He realised he had spoken too sharply. He added, in a more polite tone, 'Now I come to think of it, I do recall some Scotch were sent to Massachusetts.'

'They worked at the iron mines near here, and in the sawmills; various places. The last of them was only freed this year.' Endecott looked thoughtful. 'I had not realised you were at Dunbar. We have many Scotchmen in the colony, veterans of the King's army. Boston may be more hazardous for you than I anticipated.' He called over towards the window, where Norton was keeping watch on the street. 'Have the rogues gone, Mr Norton?'

'Yes, Governor. They have drifted away. Doubtless to cause trouble elsewhere.'

'Captain Michelson!' Endecott beckoned to a heavyset man. 'Would you be good enough to fetch some militiamen to escort our honoured guests back to Cambridge?' He turned to Ned. 'Captain Michelson is our marshal general.'

Ned said, 'You are kind to make the offer, Governor, but we are well used to looking after ourselves.'

'I don't doubt it. But it will signal that you are under our protection and may deter such rudeness in the future.'

As soon as Michelson had gone, the mood among the assembly eased a little. Norton's house was spacious: plain whitewashed walls, wide floorboards and a high ceiling. Plates of food and jugs of water had been laid out on a long table for his guests. Gradually the parlour became noisy with conversation. For the next hour, Norton conducted the colonels around the room. The members of the Boston church were of a different sort to Cambridge: fewer farmers, more merchants, lawyers, a doctor. Several ministers had attended the lecture, among them Jonathan Mitchell, who greeted them affably and commiserated on the unpleasant scene in the street. 'Drunken riff-raff', he called them, and that seemed to be the general view.

Ned took some bread and a piece of cheese. He would have liked a tumbler of beer, but it did not seem to be on offer.

'And this is Mr John Crowne,' said Norton, ushering forward a young man, 'an undergraduate of Harvard College who lodges with me.'

He was the last to be introduced, and it was clear at once that he was reluctant to make their acquaintance. He did not offer his hand. Instead he blurted out, 'And is it true, what the Scotsman said? That you are both wanted for the murder of the King?'

'No such warrant had been issued when we left England,' said Will. 'In any case, it wasn't murder.'

'And since then?'

'Now, John,' warned Norton, 'these men are guests in my house.'

'True, and of course you must entertain whom you please. But I wouldn't have been present had I known of the accusation.'

A silence had once again fallen on the room as people turned to witness the exchange.

Ned said pleasantly, 'How old are you, Mr Crowne?'

'Nineteen.'

'Nineteen! I thought as much – a babe in arms when the King was tried. You know nothing of the circumstances.'

'I know the fifth commandment: "Thou shalt not kill." '

'And we know Exodus,' said Will. ' "Eye for eye, tooth for tooth, hand for hand, foot for foot . . ." Charles Stuart was no innocent. He killed thousands.'

'But still he was your king – *our* king.'

'Crowne by name,' said Ned, with a grin, turning to the others in the room, 'and Crowne by nature, I see!'

There was laughter. Crowne flushed. 'Forgive me, Reverend Norton.' He bowed to his host. 'I cannot remain under this roof any longer.'

'John!'

'Let him speak as he wishes,' said Ned. 'He has a right to his opinion.'

A loud knock came at the door.

Endecott said, 'That will be Michelson. Let him in, Mr Norton.'

But when Norton unlocked the door, it was a very different figure who was standing on the threshold – tall, well dressed, erect and confident. Behind him was the Scotsman from earlier in the afternoon, along with his companions. Norton tried to shut the door, but the stranger stuck out his boot to keep it open. Ned drew his sword, and this time Will did the same.

'Mr Norton,' said the stranger politely. 'Good day to you.' He touched his hat. 'I am Captain Thomas Breedon.'

'I know who you are,' replied Norton. 'This is a private meeting.'

Breedon craned his neck to peer around him. 'And there is Mr

Endecott – good day to you, Governor – and there, if I am not mistaken, are Colonel Edward Whalley and Colonel William Goffe.'

'Move aside, Mr Norton,' commanded Endecott. He stepped in front of him. 'State your business, Captain Breedon.'

'*My* business, Governor? *Your* business, surely? Those men are wanted for the murder of the King.'

'So you say. I have received no warrant to that effect.'

'Then allow me to read you the latest London newsletter.' Breedon reached inside his coat and pulled out a printed sheet. 'It came upon the Scottish ship this very day and reports the following vote of Parliament: "Resolved, upon the Question, by the Commons assembled in Parliament on the 17th day of May 1660, that all the Persons who sat in Judgment upon the late King's Majesty, when Sentence of Death was pronounced against him, and the Estates both real and personal, of all and every of the said Persons, whether in their own Hands, or in the Hands of any other, who are fled, be forthwith seized and secured: And the respective Sheriffs, and other Officers, whom this may concern, are to take effectual Order accordingly." And here is the list of names of those who are to be seized, along with all their property. Do you see, sir?' He put his finger on the paper and thrust it in the governor's face. 'Those of Whalley and Goffe are quite plainly printed.'

'Be that as it may,' said Endecott, with a defiant upward tilt of his chin, 'that is a newsletter, not a warrant.'

'Then I insist that at least they should be arrested and held in custody until the warrant arrives.'

'You *insist*, sir?' The governor's voice was edged high with indignation. 'You may insist all you wish, Captain Breedon, but you have no standing in this matter. I have the authority in this colony.'

'You are still a servant of the Crown . . .'

As the argument continued, Ned whispered to Norton, 'Tell me, who is this Captain Breedon?'

'A merchant of some means. A shipowner. A Royalist. An enemy of the Puritan faith.'

He looked around. 'Is there a back way out of your property?'

'Of course.'

'What do you say, Will? Should we withdraw?'

Will took note of their position: the governor on the doorstep; the church members clustered at his back to give him support; Breedon at the head of his rabble, but so intent upon his heated dispute with Endecott he seemed temporarily to have forgotten the presence of his quarry.

'I think it would be prudent.'

The officers put away their swords and followed Norton through the kitchen, past a maidservant standing pressed to the table with her mouth agape, and out into a yard. The minister opened a gate in the wall, stepped into the street, looked up and down, and returned a moment later. 'The way is clear. If you go left and then right, you will reach the Cambridge road.'

Ned said, 'We are sorry to have brought our troubles to your house, Mr Norton.'

'It is no matter. The fault is ours. We should not have issued the invitation.'

'We shall gladly come again if you ask us.'

'Indeed. Indeed we shall.' But the hesitancy in his voice, in contrast to the urgency with which he ushered them out into the street, suggested to Will that they might well have seen the last of the Reverend Norton and the Boston First Church.

They moved quickly – not running, as that would have attracted suspicion, but walking with long and rapid strides – until very soon they were out of the town and back on the road beside the Charles. Only then did they risk glancing over their shoulders. No one seemed to be following.

It started to rain – big, heavy late-summer drops, surprisingly cold, that raked the river and the leaves of the trees beside the track like musket shot. They hunched their sodden shoulders and trudged on without speaking, each contemplating what had just occurred. It was no more than either had expected. Yet to see it published in the language of Parliament and flourished in public made their predicament seem much more real. And their property confiscated as well! That they had not foreseen. *The Estates both real and personal . . . whether in their own Hands, or in the Hands of any other . . .* What did it mean? The seizure not only of the houses that sheltered their wives and children, but of the very chairs they sat upon, and the knives and spoons they used to eat with? The property and lands whose rents provided their only income? It was utter ruination.

Ned could sense his son-in-law's resentment. Will's instinct had been right: they should never have ventured into Boston without making sure it was safe.

'Well,' he said eventually, to break the tension between them, 'at least we now know the true situation.'

Will gave him a bitter sideways look. His face was white, clenched, dripping rainwater. 'And in what way does that help us?'

'It shows us we must be more careful in the future.'

'You say that *now*?'

The younger man had never spoken to him in such a tone before. They both lapsed back into silence.

It took them an hour to reach the crossing point. It was late afternoon by then, gloomy in the rain. The ferry was on the Cambridge side and the ferryman plainly had decided to finish for the day. His hood was up, his back turned. He pretended not to hear them at first. They had to cup their hands to their mouths and holler and wave their arms to persuade him to come and fetch them.

Ned stood alone with his feet planted apart as they were hauled across the river. He wiped his sleeve across his eyes.

Behind him, he heard Will approach. 'Forgive my rough words earlier. As to my personal situation, you know I care nothing for either life or property. Yet I could not help but think of Frances and the little ones. It must be hard for them now. Harder than for us.'

'I know. I'm sorry.'

'We'd be wise to confine ourselves to Cambridge from now on, I think.' Will laid his hand upon Ned's shoulder. Together they contemplated the approaching settlement. It looked dark and dismal in the murk. 'We must have faith. "Be without covetousness and be content with such things as ye have. For he hath said, I will never leave thee, nor forsake."'

The ferry ran aground into the shallows of the riverbank causing both men to stumble slightly.

'Amen to that,' said Ned.

CHAPTER SIX

A LITTLE OVER TWO weeks later, on the final Saturday in August – as sweet an end-of-summer's day as one might ever hope to find in England – Mr Richard Nayler stood in the courtyard of Lambeth House, just across the Thames from Parliament, a pencil in one hand, a warrant from the House of Commons in the other ordering the transfer into his custody of all those prisoners presently held in Lambeth.

He knew each one by sight. Nevertheless, as the prisoners were brought up from the cellars, shackled at the wrists and ankles, he politely asked their names and marked them off on his list. Of the seventeen who passed before him, fourteen had signed the King's death warrant; the others had been judges at his trial. They had surrendered themselves to Parliament in the expectation of royal mercy, and as they emerged, one after another, maggot white after months underground, their eyes screwed up against the sudden sunshine, several among them, still not accustomed to their loss of status, demanded to know what was to happen to them now.

'A short trip downriver,' responded Nayler pleasantly, and gestured across the courtyard to the pier where the barge was waiting.

After the men had been loaded and he had signed the Serjeant-at-Arms' receipt confirming their delivery, he settled himself into the stern of the barge and pulled the brim of his hat down over his eyes. Once the boat had pushed off from the pier, he allowed his hand to brush the surface of the water. A second boat followed, filled with soldiers. As Hyde had predicted, the production of the death warrant had sparked a new frenzy for vengeance in Parliament. There seemed to be no limit to it. But it would all be ended well enough once they caught the thirteen who were on the run. He knew the rough whereabouts of most of them on the Continent. It was only Whalley and Goffe who eluded him entirely. The thought of that pair still enjoying freedom rankled almost enough to spoil his good mood.

The barge went under the centre of London Bridge and then swung left towards the Tower. As it passed beneath Traitor's Gate, a moan arose from some of the prisoners. By the time they had moored, the Lieutenant of the Tower, Sir John Robinson, was on the quayside with a dozen guards. Nayler did not care for him – a stupid, boastful merchant from the city. He climbed out of the boat, and Robinson signed immediately for the receipt of the prisoners, resting the paper on his thigh and marking it with a careless hand.

Nayler said, 'You do not wish to count them, Sir John?' Such sloppiness offended him.

'Your word is good enough for me, Mr Nayler.'

Robinson returned the receipt. The prisoners were hauled roughly out of the barge and shoved along the quayside. Colonel Scroope stumbled past with blood pouring from his head. Robinson said, 'Our new garrison are an Irish Catholic regiment. They remember Cromwell's massacres at Drogheda and Wexford. It will be a hard home for a regicide, I fear.'

Nayler waited until the last of the traitors had stumbled up the steps and been herded into the darkness of the interior, then boarded the empty barge for the voyage back to Whitehall. And for the first time in many years, as the oars dipped and he was pulled away from that grim grey-stone fortress, with its narrow slit windows and the gulls crying over the green-slimed rocks, he experienced an emotion he had almost forgotten: a twinge of human sympathy.

Over the next three days, Nayler was in perpetual motion, sleeping little, scurrying with his scuffed brown leather case of interrogation reports and compromising documents between his apartment in Essex House, his office off the Privy Council corridor in Whitehall Palace, the chambers of the Crown lawyers near Fleet Street, and the committee rooms of Parliament in Westminster. On Tuesday 28 August, the Act of Oblivion was approved by Parliament, and the following day, as a reward for his efforts, Nayler was invited to accompany Sir Edward Hyde in his carriage from Worcester House to the House of Lords to witness His Majesty sign it into law.

The Lord Chancellor, in his heavy velvet robes of black and gold, sat opposite Nayler, his fleshy face pouring sweat, his page boy beside him, his damp hands resting on the head of his walking stick. As they passed the Banqueting House, he glanced up at the window from which the martyred King had stepped on the day of his execution. 'The streets will run with blood for a week or two,' he muttered, 'and then let's hope we can make an end of it.' He didn't speak again until they were at Westminster, pulling up outside the peers' entrance. 'Well then,' he sighed, 'let's get this business over with.'

Nayler stood at the bar of the Lords' chamber and viewed the pageantry with detachment. The vividness of the colours, the roar of conversation of the peers and MPs assembled, the piercing note of the heralds' trumpets, the abrupt silence, the opening of the door beside the throne at the far end of the chamber that signalled the assembly should rise, even the appearance of the King himself, crowned and magnificently robed in red velvet trimmed with ermine – none of it moved him. It should have been a moment of triumph, but ever since the loss of Sarah, he had lost the capacity to feel content.

Hyde struggled up from his seat on the Woolsack and invited the King to speak.

Charles II was a big man, a foot or so taller than his father, and every inch the image of a king – virile, handsome, dark-haired, dark-eyed: 'the Black Boy', they'd called him when he was younger. In a voice of regal authority he read out the speech that Hyde had written for him and Nayler had checked.

'I have been here sometimes before with you, but never with more willingness than I am at this time. And there can be few men in the Kingdom who have longed more impatiently to have this Bill passed than I . . .'

Nayler looked across the chamber, picking out a few faces he knew – his patron, the Marquess of Hertford, now elevated to the dukedom of Somerset, looking old and frail; the Duke of York, the King's younger brother, sitting beside the throne with a bored expression; Sir Orlando Bridgeman, the Chief Justice, who would both help the prosecuting lawyers draft the charges against the regicides and then preside over their trial – so much for a fair hearing.

'. . . the same discretion and conscience which disposed me to that clemency which is most agreeable to my nature, will oblige me to rigour and severity. And I must conjure you all, my lords and gentlemen, to concur with me in this just and necessary severity . . .'

At the repetition of 'severity', a deep-throated masculine murmur of approval rose to the coffered roof.

It was soon over. The King finished his address with a plaintive appeal for money that he must have inserted himself at the last minute ('I have not been able to give my brothers one shilling since I came to England'), the Oblivion bill was presented to him by the clerks, he bent over the table, signed it, acknowledged the applause, then exited by the door through which he had entered, bowing to a few he recognised. Hyde tottered after him on his swollen legs. He beckoned Nayler to follow him into the crowded chamber behind the throne.

Half a dozen women – bejewelled, their hair piled fashionably high, their dresses cut fashionably low – were standing together, watching the King. One attendant at his back removed His Majesty's ermine robes; another, in front, on tiptoe, lifted off his crown. How ordinary he looked suddenly, Nayler thought. You would pass him in the street and think him just some Italian merchant on his way to meet his tailor.

The King was in profile, smiling and winking at the ladies. Hyde said, 'Your Majesty, may I present Mr Richard Nayler, who has been most diligent in the matter of bringing to justice the murderers of your late father?'

Reluctantly the King turned away from the women and held out his hand. Nayler bowed and kissed it. 'Your Majesty.' He had been presented twice before, but it was plain his sovereign had no memory of him.

'We are most grateful for your efforts . . .' The King looked at Hyde.

'Nayler,' said Hyde.

'Mr Nayler.' He smiled and nodded and turned back to Hyde. 'That went well enough, I think, Sir Edward.'

'Your presence was commanding, Your Majesty.'

The tallest of the women stepped in front of the Lord Chancellor. She took the King's arm. 'Enough politics for one day, Sir Edward, surely? I think His Majesty needs an hour or two of rest.'

The King laughed, showing large white teeth, and allowed himself to be led away.

Hyde tapped his stick against the floor. 'Rest – is that what she calls it?'

'She is a great beauty,' Nayler said carefully. 'Who is she?'

'She,' said Hyde with distaste, 'is Mrs Palmer. Don't tell me that you, with all your spies, have never heard of her? The King has just installed her in a house next to his palace.'

Nayler was on alert at once.

'And which house would that be, Sir Edward?'

'The closest one, of course – Whalley's old place.'

As soon as he could escape, which took about an hour, Nayler hurried out of the precincts of Westminster, past the taverns and the narrow little yards, up King Street towards Whitehall Palace.

A stream ran down the middle of the road. The houses nearest to the palace were all built in the Flemish style: three or four storeys, terraced and gabled, with diamond-paned bay windows jutting out over the street, their timbers gilded and brightly painted to match their occupants' coats of arms, which were fixed above the doors.

He knew exactly which had been Whalley's: he had had it watched since the end of May. On his instructions, Katherine

Whalley, together with her stepdaughter, Frances Goffe, and Goffe's brood of children, had been allowed to remain long after they should have been evicted. Unfortunately, the women had been careful; no clue as to the whereabouts of their menfolk had been discovered. Still, he preferred to have them where he could keep an eye on them, and he had believed he had an understanding with the Commissioner of Works. But now they had been moved out in favour of the King's mistress, and the Whalley family crest of three spouting whales' heads had been torn down, leaving marks in the brickwork.

He had lost them.

He crossed the street and pulled on the bell handle. The door was opened by an elderly porter.

'Yes?'

'Good day to you.' Nayler touched his hat. 'I'm looking for Mrs Whalley.'

'She has left.'

From the interior came the sound of music and women's laughter. There was a crash as something glass fell to the floor and shattered. The porter looked over his shoulder.

'Can you tell me where she has gone? I'm a friend of the family – a very good friend,' he added.

A man appeared in the passage behind the porter. His shirt was unbuttoned to the waist. He was holding the neck of a broken bottle. 'His Majesty needs more wine.' Nayler recognised the Duke of York.

The porter bowed. 'Yes, Your Highness.' He gave Nayler a brief glance of apology and closed the door.

Nayler stepped back into the street. Nothing shocked him; little surprised him. If this was the person God had anointed to be king, who was he to dispute it? But he cursed the man Charles Stuart for his rampant prick. He waited a few minutes and rang the bell again.

This time the old porter was ready for him. After another glance over his shoulder, he said, 'You are truly a friend of the family?'

'Of course.'

'Then you are a friend of mine. I was in their service for seven years. Honest, God-fearing people. They have lost everything. Not even a candlestick remains to them.'

'A cruel business,' said Nayler, clasping his hands as if in prayer, 'to punish the wives and children for the sins of the husbands and fathers. Where have they gone?'

The porter lowered his voice. 'To lodge with Mrs Whalley's brother-in-law, the Reverend Hooke, at the Savoy Hospital.'

'He has found them rooms?'

'They are in his gift. He is the master there.'

'*Porter!* Where in the devil's name are you?' It was the Duke of York again. The old man gave Nayler a sorrowful look and closed the door once more.

He set off at once, conscious of wearing his best court shoes with the silver buckles and his white silk stockings, which meant he had to keep his eyes on the ground and avoid the stinking piles of shit and pools of piss – equine and human – strewn across his path.

The Savoy Hospital was along the Strand from Essex House, a charitable refuge for the poor and sick that had served as a military hospital for the Roundheads in the Civil War. Nayler had never had cause to set foot in it before, thank God. He passed down a sunless alley, through a gate and into a crowded cemetery filled with crumbling grey slate stones from Tudor times, slanting all ways like rotten teeth. To his right, a chapel; ahead and to his left, a pair of red-brick fortresses, stained black by coal smoke, with tiny windows. The destitute of London, mere bundles of rags, crouched in the shadows of the walls. Wounded veterans, missing limbs and hobbling on crutches, swung themselves between the graves. A fearful, horrid place, it seemed to him, more a prison than a hospital. It reminded him of his long period of sickness after Naseby, and the gaol where he was kept after his wife had died.

He wandered around, through courtyards and a garden high with weeds, keeping an eye out for his quarry, until he encountered a woman with a bunch of keys attached to her belt who pointed him in the direction of the master's lodgings – an altogether more congenial building, ivy-covered, like a master's lodge in an Oxford college. He could imagine the Whalleys and the Goffes seeking sanctuary here. He hesitated, wondering if it was wise to show himself, and decided he had no choice. He would tell this Reverend Hooke he had a message for Katherine Whalley, and if she was at home devise some story on the spot. But when he rang the bell and a priest appeared, he saw at once that the regime had changed, for this man wore a surplice and was no Puritan.

'I am looking for Mr Hooke.'

'Hooke has gone,' said the priest, with great satisfaction. 'He was appointed by Cromwell, but now he has been purged.'

It cost Nayler some effort not to groan aloud. 'Gone? Gone where?'

The priest shrugged. 'I know only that he and his family departed a week ago.'

'How numerous was this family?'

'With children, I should say seven or eight.'

'Did they not leave some new address where they could be found?'

'They had only a day to pack and leave. I doubt they knew

themselves where they were going. There is nothing left in England for the likes of William Hooke, particularly at his age. He has no hope of finding a living.'

'Is he old?'

'Sixty, I believe.'

Nayler sighed and took a step backwards, 'If by chance you should hear any report of him, perhaps I might trouble you to send me word at the offices of the Privy Council? Richard Nayler is my name.'

The priest nodded, impressed. 'I shall indeed, Mr Nayler.' He was more eager to be helpful now he knew he was dealing with a man of power. 'You might do well to enquire among the Puritan meeting houses around Spitalfields. They look after one another like Jews.' Then, as an afterthought, 'I suppose it is always possible that Hooke will return to America.'

Nayler, who was just turning away, stopped and swung back to the priest. 'America?'

'Most certainly. He lived there nearly twenty years, ministering to some sect of zealots.'

The following afternoon, in his office – a small room directly across the corridor from the Privy Council chamber, overlooking the gardens of Whitehall Palace – Nayler convened a meeting of those most closely associated with the hunt for the regicides. Pinned to a board propped up on an easel was a chart of all the wanted traitors: their names and last known locations.

The usual four men attended: his secretary, Mr Samuel Nokes, a diligent young lawyer trained at Lincoln's Inn; Dr John Wallis, the Savilian Professor of Geometry at Oxford University, the greatest cryptanalyst in England and a supporter of Parliament in the Civil War, who had broken the cipher of the King's correspondence captured at Naseby, and who now, after some persuasion, was making his skills available to the new regime; Colonel Henry Bishop, the Postmaster General, who ensured the committee had prompt access to every letter that passed through the London sorting office; and Mr William Prynne, the MP for Bath, the most fanatical of the anti-regicides in Parliament, who always wore a black leather cowl to conceal the fact that his ears had been cut off in the pillory twenty years before.

Once Dr Wallis had reported on the latest coded messages intercepted between the fugitives in Holland and their sympathisers in England, Nayler raised the matter of Whalley and Goffe. He recounted how he had gone to the King Street house and learned that the families had left – tactfully he omitted to mention what else he had witnessed – then described his visit to Savoy Hospital and his discovery that they had moved on from there as well. As he spoke, he became aware of young Nokes regarding him with curiosity, and it occurred to him that it must seem odd that he should have undertaken such humdrum work himself. He quickly drew his report to a conclusion. 'So, to put the matter briefly, gentlemen, it is my belief that if we are to track down these particular traitors, we need to find their families. Goffe has young children. It is most likely that sooner or later he will seek to contact them. Affection is their weak point.'

Colonel Bishop said, 'Do we believe them still to be together? If so, that is another weakness. Two men travelling as a pair are more conspicuous than one alone.'

'My feeling is they are together,' said Nayler. He thought of them that Christmas Day, standing at the altar in Essex House, berating the congregation. 'They often were when Cromwell was alive.'

'I must confess I find the completeness of their disappearance a surprise,' said Wallis. He spoke as usual with a certain scholarly detachment: for him, the manhunt was merely a series of mathematical problems to be solved. 'None of the encoded messages between the other fugitives and their supporters has so much as mentioned them. They are a void – as if they have vanished from the earth.'

'I have begun to wonder,' said Nayler, 'if they might not have gone to America.' He had spent half the night turning the matter over in his mind. 'Colonel Whalley's sister is married to a Puritan minister named Hooke, who lived among some community of religious extremists over there for many years. If that is the case, it would explain why they seem to be so entirely removed from the rest.'

'Then they must have sailed before the end of May,' said Nokes, 'because we have checked every passenger leaving England since then. Unless they took ship from Holland.'

'Surely we would have heard of that? Have one of our men go to the Customs House, Mr Nokes, and consult the passenger manifests for vessels sailing to America in April and May. They may have travelled under assumed names.'

Nokes made a note. 'Yes, sir.'

'And do we have an informer among the Puritan community in Spitalfields?'

'We have several, Mr Nayler.'

'Then they should be directed to enquire – discreetly – after the whereabouts of Reverend Hooke. Hooke will lead us to the families, I am sure.'

'Bait the Hooke and we shall catch our fish,' said Prynne. His thin mouth twisted in amusement. His hollow cheeks were scarred with the letters 'SL', for 'seditious libeller', branded there on the orders of the Chief Justice at the same time as his ears had been severed. The letters had broken up over the years, leaving two dark brown jagged ridges, like cankers, and although the punishment had been inflicted under the government of Charles I, by some weird process of his remorseless logic, Prynne had ended up on the Royalist side. 'I know these men Whalley and Goffe,' he continued. 'They stood beside Colonel Pride and his soldiers and stopped me from entering Parliament because they knew I was one of those Members who would not vote for the trial of the King. I was held in a vile dungeon for weeks, and not released until after His Majesty had been murdered. I would dearly like to see them hanged and gutted alive.'

Nayler nodded in agreement but otherwise made no answer; indeed, he looked away, preferring not to glimpse his own reflection in those fanatical eyes.

Two days later, shortly after sunrise on Saturday, Nayler was in his office, composing a memorandum to Sir Orlando Bridgeman, when the door was thrown open and Nokes burst in.

'Hooke has been found. He has been lent a country house by a wealthy Puritan merchant in the city named Gold.'

Nayler threw down his pen, sat back in his chair and laughed in delight, then checked himself. 'Can it be true, though? A rich man named Gold? Are you sure this is not a joke?'

'No, sir,' said Nokes earnestly. 'The source is reliable. I had a watch placed on the house last night and this morning received a report that Hooke and his wife are indeed in residence, and others with them, women and children.'

'Whereabouts?'

'Just across the river, in Clapham village.'

'Were any other men observed?'

'None reported.'

'But it must have been dark?'

'True, sir.'

Nayler fell silent, tapping his forefinger on the table. He was thinking that it was possible – not at all likely, but still just conceivable – that Whalley and Goffe might be hiding with their families. 'Speak to the Serjeant-at-Arms,' he said. 'Explain the circumstances. Tell him we need a dozen armed men to surprise this house in Clapham, today.'

CHAPTER SEVEN

THERE WAS NOTHING to be said for the wretched state into which Frances Goffe now found herself plunged at the age of twenty-six, save perhaps that it allowed her no time to brood on the calamity that had engulfed her. In the space of a few months, she had lost her husband and her father, her position in society, her home, possessions, money, servants and all peace of mind, save for her strong and simple faith that God must have willed this for a purpose and that it was her duty to endure it. Had it not been for her devotion, she was sure she would have lost her reason.

She had five children under the age of eight – the middle girls, Betty and Nan, both sickly, were a particular worry – but they were less of a burden to her than her mother, who lay on the bed beside her, eyes open, unmoving, as Frances attempted to spoon some soup into her mouth while at the same time feeding her baby, Richard, who was sucking at her breast. It was just beginning to get light. Upstairs, she could hear Aunt Jane telling Frankie, the eldest, to help her sister Judith get dressed. Uncle William was in the kitchen, studying the Bible: of all of them, he seemed the least perturbed by the meanness of their surroundings.

The house was small, a cottage at the end of a lane half a mile out of the village, with two rooms upstairs. The Hookes had one, the four girls shared the other, while Frances slept downstairs in the parlour on a mattress rolled out each evening onto the damp floor between her mother's bed and Dickie's cot. Apart from the beds, and a table and half a dozen wooden chairs in the kitchen, there was no furniture: Mr Gold intended to pull the house down and build a new one on the site. But then they had no need of cupboards, chests and wardrobes, for they had nothing to put in them. They possessed the clothes they stood up in, a few spare shirts and nightgowns, the girls' dolls, and three family Bibles. The Hookes were better off – their possessions had not been seized – but their belongings were in a warehouse in the city. Uncle William, who had no head for money and who had given most of his savings to Will and Ned on their embarkation, had ten pounds that Mr Gold had loaned him. Aunt Jane took a few shillings and ventured out each day to the village to buy the household food, which she and Frances prepared between them. There was no servant. It was a long way from what Frances had been used to – the apartment in Somerset House, the place in King Street, the deference due to a family in the Protector's inner circle.

'Take heart, child,' said Uncle William whenever he found her crying. 'The Lord had less, and we still have one another.'

True. But she did not have her husband.

The baby had stopped suckling and had fallen asleep. She laid him in his cot and resumed her efforts to feed her mother. Katherine Whalley was not that old, barely more than forty – she was her stepmother, in fact: Frances's natural mother had died when she was a baby – but her hair had turned grey and her flesh was no more than a shroud over her bones. She had been ill for years, ever since her last miscarriage; now she seemed to have lost all comprehension, and twisted her head away like a sulky child. The soup trickled off her closed mouth and onto the pillow. Frances dabbed at it with a cloth, then lay down on her mattress and put her hand over her eyes.

Will . . . Will . . . Will . . .

He had set off to America nearly four months ago. She didn't know if he had arrived. It was too soon for word to have reached her. He hadn't wanted to go, but she had pleaded with him, for her sake and the children's, not to surrender to their enemies. The fact that he was with her father gave her some comfort: the old man was practical and cunning where Will was mystical and fatalistic – God forgive her for thinking so, but it was a fact. She had loved him since she was sixteen, had married him at eighteen, knew him better than anyone else in the world.

She sat up and felt around the edge of the mattress for the small cut she had made in the material. She inserted her fingers into the straw and pulled out the only three things she had left of him: a lock of his hair, a miniature portrait, and the last note he had sent her, on the day he took ship. Uncle William had brought it back from Gravesend after he had seen them off:

Dearest Heart, God will protect us, for He makes all things right on Earth. Pray for me, as I pray always for you; the greatest gift He has bestowed upon me. I will come back to you again as soon as I am able.

It was written in Will's elaborate hand on a small piece of paper torn roughly from a notebook. The ink was smudged. It was unsigned and undated. She read it through again. She smelled his lock of dark hair. She studied his dear face – wide eyes, thin nose, a small and delicate mouth – and kissed it.

She heard her aunt calling her name. She replaced her treasures deep inside the mattress and went upstairs to see what she could do to help.

Several hours later, towards the end of the morning, soon after Aunt Jane had returned from the village with bread and cheese and Frances had drawn water from the well to wash the children's nightclothes, Uncle William hurried in with apples from the orchard to report that soldiers on horseback were approaching down the lane. Frances saw the fear in his face.

'You think they're coming for us?'

'Ours is the only house. Where else might they be headed?'

She scooped Nan up from the kitchen floor and handed her to Frankie, told her to take her little sister and Judith up to their room, where Betty was still in bed. 'Stay there till I tell you to come down.'

From the garden came the sound of horses and men's voices. A pair of soldiers hurried past the kitchen window. The house was being surrounded. An instant later there was a hammering at the door. Uncle William opened it a little and was roughly pushed aside by men armed with pistols and drawn swords, who poured into the house. Some ran into the parlour. Others clumped upstairs. Two soldiers trained muskets on Frances and the Hookes and shouted at them not to move.

A moment later, a short, broad-shouldered man strolled into the kitchen. 'Reverend William Hooke, I assume?' He touched his hat politely and turned to Aunt Jane. 'And you are Mrs Katherine Whalley?'

'No, sir. My name is Jane Hooke.'

'Forgive me.' He looked at Frances. 'Therefore, you must be Mrs Goffe.' He studied her for a moment. His eyes were very dark. Something flickered in them, a kind of knowingness or intimacy that made her flesh shrink. 'Where is Mrs Katherine Whalley?'

Frances said, 'She is in bed, sir, ill.'

'Show me, please.'

Uncle William was beginning to recover from his shock. 'Wait,' he said. 'By what authority do you invade our house?'

'There is a warrant issued for the arrest of Colonel Whalley and Colonel Goffe – as you well know.'

One of the soldiers shouted downstairs, 'There's no one up here, Mr Nayler, save some young girls!'

Frances saw Nayler's mouth briefly set in disappointment. 'Well, that is no surprise.' He turned to her. 'You'll doubtless tell me you've no notion where they are.'

'I haven't seen my husband or my father for many months.'

'Is that so?' He called upstairs, 'Search the place thoroughly. Turn it upside down if needs be.' And then to Frances again, 'Take me to Mrs Whalley.'

She led him into the parlour. Her mother had drawn her blanket up to her chin and was staring at the ceiling. Nayler bent to examine her. He passed his hand above her eyes. There was no reaction. 'How long has she been this way?'

'Since she was put out of her house into the street with nothing to her name.'

'You've no brothers or sisters to help you?'

'One brother and two half-brothers, but they are not in England.'

'Where are they?'

'I do not know.' It was true. John and Henry were said to be in France, Edward in Ireland. The family was entirely broken.

The baby began to cry. Frances moved towards him, but Nayler was there before her. He lifted Dickie out of his cot and held him at arm's length, turning him from side to side, appraising him like a piglet at market. 'Now he is a fine little fellow. It must be a splendid thing to have a healthy baby boy.'

There were thuds upstairs, a splintering of wood. One of the girls was screaming. Frances held out her hands. 'Give him to me, please.'

Nayler cradled the baby against his chest and inhaled the scent of his downy hair. He began to rock him, stroking his back. The crying stopped. 'There, you see? I have a gift with infants. Tell me where your husband is, Mrs Goffe,' he said softly. 'Life will be better for your baby and for all of you.'

'I cannot tell you what I do not know.'

'Then I will tell you what I think.' He nodded towards Uncle William, who was watching from the doorway. 'I think Goffe and your father have gone to Mr Hooke's friends in America. That is my suspicion.' He called past him to the kitchen. 'Captain Weaver! Come and search in here, if you please.' Uncle William was shouldered out of the way. Weaver came in with two more soldiers. 'Start with the bed. Take your sword to the mattress.'

The captain glanced doubtfully at Katherine Whalley. 'What shall we do with her?'

'If she won't move, tip her out.'

Frances could hear seven-year-old Frankie upstairs calling, 'Mama! Mama!'

Aunt Jane said, 'This is not human, Mr Nayler!'

'What is not human is to kill your King in cold blood. Get on with it, Captain.'

In that instant, when time seemed to her suspended, Frances saw three things at once and with perfect clarity. They knew about America. They would find Will's note. The man was still holding her baby.

'Wait,' she said.

She untied the string around her mattress and rolled it out. She knelt and put her hand into the cut and extracted the note, the picture and the lock of hair. She offered them to Nayler. He looked at her, briefly mystified. Her hand was shaking. Finally he gave her the baby in exchange. She took her son and held him tight, and watched Nayler as he read the note.

'This is from your husband?'

She nodded.

'Frances!' warned Uncle William.

'When did you receive it?'

'A week ago.' The lie came easily.

'Who brought it?'

'I did not see. It was delivered in the night. It was here in the morning when I awoke.'

'And the likeness is his?'

'Yes.'

He read the message through again, noting the ornateness of the script. He studied the miniature portrait closely. He grasped the lock of hair between thumb and forefinger and held it to the light. To see such precious keepsakes in his hands made her feel faint. She tried to control her trembling.

'Good,' he said at last. 'The note and the picture I shall take. The hair you may keep.'

As soon as the door closed behind him, even before the soldiers had remounted their horses, Frances ran upstairs to the girls. Frankie was sitting with her legs stretched out, propped against the wall, holding Nan in her lap, trying not to cry. Judith had climbed into bed with Betty and pulled the blanket over their heads. Their few childish clothes and possessions had been tipped out onto the floor. Some of the boards had been prised up. One mattress had been slashed twice, crossways, and turned on its side. Straw had been trampled everywhere. The room smelled like a stable.

She went from one to another, hugging them, whispering the same reassurances to each: 'Don't be afraid . . . The men have gone . . . We are safe now . . .'

Frankie said, 'Why were the soldiers looking for Papa and Grandfather?'

'I will tell you one day. But always remember they have done nothing wrong.'

'When can we go home?'

'Wherever we are together is our home. Put all the things away, there's a good girl. I'll fetch needle and thread and we'll gather the straw, and the bed will soon be right again.'

Downstairs, Aunt Jane was in the parlour comforting Katherine. Her low, soothing voice carried through the doorway. Uncle William was seated at the kitchen table. His Bible was open, but he was staring straight ahead. She had only known him since he returned from America four years ago, to serve as one of Cromwell's personal chaplains, a position her father had obtained for him. His expression was stern. As soon as she entered, he stood. She was braced for a rebuke – in truth, she had always been a little frightened of him – but instead he held out his arms. 'Come here, child.'

'You're not angry with me?'

'Angry? Not at all. You thought quicker than I did.'

She fell against him in relief, rested her cheek against his shoulder. He felt as solid and immovable as stone. 'Even though I broke a commandment and told a lie?'

'The Bible says thou shalt not bear false witness against thy neighbour. That man was no neighbour. He was the Devil. You threw salt in his eyes, which is not to be accounted a sin. Although I fear he will be back when he discovers he was tricked.'

At eight o'clock the following Monday morning, Nayler presented himself at Worcester House and asked to see the Lord Chancellor. He waited in the reception room to be summoned, and then followed Mr Secretary-Fop upstairs. The young nobleman was subdued for once, and there seemed to Nayler to be a strange atmosphere in the place – whispered conversations at the ends of passages, doors left ajar that were quietly closed as he went past. As they entered the gallery that led to Sir Edward's study, Anne Hyde, the Chancellor's daughter, appeared hurrying from the opposite end, accompanied by a maid. Nayler had not seen her for several months. He stopped and took off his hat and bowed. Her appearance shocked him. Her pretty face was fat and flushed, her figure gone to ruin – she looked unfortunately like her father – and as she fled past without acknowledging him, he had a fancy she had been crying.

Sir Edward was seated in his usual place at the end of the table. He had taken off his wig and was leaning forward with his head in his hands. He spoke at the carpet. 'What is it, Mr Nayler?'

'It can be kept for a better occasion, my lord, if this is an inconvenient moment.'

'No.' Hyde raised his head wearily. 'Proceed.'

'It concerns Colonel Whalley and Colonel Goffe.' Hyde groaned. Nayler continued regardless. 'I have evidence they may be in England.'

At that, the Lord Chancellor looked up. 'What manner of evidence?'

'I have hunted down their families and found them living in Clapham. This is a message Frances Goffe says she received a week ago from her husband, delivered by an unseen hand.' He laid it on the table. 'The writing is most distinctive, similar to his signature on the death warrant.'

Hyde scanned it quickly. 'And you believe her?'

'I do. She's a frightened, artless creature, schooled by her religion not to lie. Moreover, her story fits the facts. No mention has been made of Whalley and Goffe in any of the correspondence of the regicides exiled in Europe. I suspect they fled to Holland in May or April but have now secretly returned.'

'Why would they do something so foolish?'

'Goffe is amongst the youngest of the regicides – only thirty at the time the King was murdered. He has infant children, one a baby. I suspect his children draw him home.'

'Ah yes,' said Hyde, gloomily, 'children. A destiny no one can escape.' He was silent for a moment. 'If they are in England, how do you propose to catch them?'

'By advertising their names in every town and village in the kingdom. By warning that anyone who harbours them will be regarded equally as a traitor. And above all by placing a reward on their heads. A hundred pounds apiece should do it. There's a chance we may yet find them in time to put them on trial with the others in October.'

Hyde shook his head. 'By God, Mr Nayler, I should not like to have you as my enemy!'

Nayler bowed obsequiously. 'That I shall never be, my lord.'

Hyde stared at him. 'Strangely, I am inclined to believe you.' He seemed to be weighing something up. 'Did you know my daughter, Anne, is to be married today, in this house?'

'No, Sir Edward, I did not.'

'It cannot be a public ceremony, for obvious reasons.' Hyde was watching for his reaction. 'She is with child – six or seven months gone, so I'm told. She is marrying the father. He claims to love her. He is the Duke of York.'

Nayler gaped. He could not help it. He had an unbidden image of the King's brother, half naked, in Whalley's old house.

Hyde said, 'I note you do not congratulate me,' and when Nayler started to protest, he cut him off: 'No, no, don't lie. I admire your instinct. Fools will think I am making a brilliant connection. But you and I both recognise a disaster. His Royal Highness is bedding half the court – the whole world knows it, apart from her. He'll make her very unhappy. And it will bring about my ruin. Oh, not at first – the King has been very gracious in the matter – but until he has an heir, my enemies will whisper that I am scheming to put my grandchild on the throne, and in time the King will turn on me. He denies it now, but I know him too well.' He sighed. 'Well, there it is. Go and do your business, Mr Nayler. There will soon be heads on spikes all over London. But bear in mind that one day one of them may be mine.'

For the first few days after the raid on the house, Frances's heart would jump every time someone passed along the lane. But the sinister Mr Nayler, whoever he was, did not return, and gradually the house settled into its former quiet rhythm. Uncle William ventured out occasionally across the river, to meet clandestinely with the Puritan preachers in the city and discover the latest news; no word was expected from America until the end of October. Frances and Aunt Jane stayed in Clapham with the children and Katherine Whalley. They saw no one, except on the Sabbath, when they attended the meeting house in the village, which seemed safe enough. The Puritan community south of the river was small and fearful; no one asked them any questions.

In the evenings, after the girls had gone to sleep and the baby had been fed, Jane would sit sewing by the hearth and tell stories of her life in America. She and William had spent eleven years in New Haven, newest of all the colonies, a religious community more than a hundred miles along the coast from Boston, co-founded by the Reverend John Davenport, 'a most mighty preacher and inspirer of men', and Mr Theophilus Eaton, a Puritan merchant of immense wealth. As she described the little wooden settlements enclosed by palisades, the endless expanses of encroaching forest filled with wolves and wildcats, the local native Indians with their burial grounds and heathen customs, the long winters and the hard work of planting and harvesting, Will seemed to Frances to be both closer to her (in that she could imagine him) and yet to recede from her. She wondered why her aunt and uncle had left.

One night, Jane told the tale of the *Great Ship*, a vessel of a hundred tons that the town had built and that had sailed from New Haven not long after she and Uncle William had arrived – how the colony had filled her hold with goods to trade in England, and had had to break the ice to get her out of the harbour, and how a few months later a vision of the ship appeared faintly in the starlit winter sky, and that was how they learned she had sunk, taking seventy of the town's citizens down with her. 'It was a tragedy from which it was hard to recover. Why does God punish the faithful so? How had we sinned?' She must have noticed Frances's horrified expression, for she suddenly broke off and said, 'How foolish of me to tell such a tale. Dear Will is safe, I am sure.'

A month or so after the soldiers' visit – it was hard sometimes to keep track of the days, when there was so little to differentiate them – Frances walked along the lane to Clapham to buy food for dinner. It was autumn, the leaves were falling in rustling red and golden showers, and she dawdled, gathering horse chestnuts into her apron for the girls to play with; they were gleaming, waxy, as if Nature had polished them. When she reached the lychgate of Trinity church, she saw that a notice had been pinned up on the board beside it. There was a crown at its head – a royal proclamation no less. She stepped closer and began to read.

Forasmuch as the execrable traitors Colonel Edward Whalley and Colonel William Goffe, having absented and withdrawn themselves beyond the Seas, are now, as We certainly understand, lately returned into Our Kingdom of England, and do privately lurk and obscure themselves in places unknown, We do hereby Require and Command Our Judges, Justices of the Peace, Mayors, Sheriffs, Bailiffs, Constables and all Our Subjects whatsoever, to be diligent in Inquiring, Searching for, Seizing and Apprehending them . . .

And We do hereby further Declare and Publish, That if any Person or Persons after this Our Proclamation published, shall Directly or Indirectly Conceal, Harbour, Keep, Retain, or Maintain the said Edward Whalley and William Goffe, or either of them, or shall Contrive or Connive at any means whereby they or either of them shall or may Escape from being Taken or Arrested We will proceed against them with all severity . . .

And lastly We do hereby Declare, That whosoever shall discover the said Edward Whalley or William Goffe, and shall cause them, or either of them, to be Apprehended, and brought in alive or dead, shall have a Reward of One hundred pounds in money for each of them.

Given at Our Court at Whitehall the Two and twentieth day of September. Charles R.

It was such a shock to see their names in print that for a while she could not move, but stood staring at the same few words: *Edward Whalley and William Goffe* . . . *alive or dead* . . . *One hundred pounds* . . . Her eyes travelled back to the top of the poster: *We certainly understand, lately returned into Our Kingdom of England* . . .

We certainly understand . . . This must be her doing. The King of England had sat in his palace and issued a proclamation because of *her*.

She felt weak at the implications and glanced around to see if anyone was watching her. The church appeared to be empty. On the common, a man with a boy and a dog was herding sheep into a pen. She let the horse chestnuts drop from her apron, tore down the proclamation, folded it and tucked it away, then turned and walked quickly back to the cottage to warn her aunt and uncle.

CHAPTER EIGHT

I N MASSACHUSETTS, IT was harvest time, the crops ripe, the wooded hills a distant, drawn-out fiery sunset of russet and pink, orange and gold, vaster and more vivid than anything they had ever seen in England.

'We are able-bodied,' said Ned to Daniel Gookin one day. 'Employ us in honest labour. Let us earn our keep.'

From then on, each weekday morning at first light, Ned and Will left the house to labour on the farm – bringing in the wheat and maize, and when that was done, digging ditches, mending fences, herding the sheep and cattle, stacking hay, felling trees, cutting logs in readiness for the winter. Their hands roughened with the use of scythe and axe, hoe and shovel. Their muscles hardened. If they were to survive, Ned thought, they would need to be fit. It was useful training.

And this labouring from dawn till dusk had another benefit: it dulled the pain of homesickness. At night, when they went up to bed exhausted, they fell into sleep so deep that even dreams of England did not disturb them. They received no word from home. On the Sabbath, they attended the meeting house. Three times they dined with President Chauncey at Harvard College. They visited their neighbours: men such as the Elder Beale, who suffered so much from the kidney stone he confessed that when he tried to pass water it tested his faith in God; and the Elder Frost, who received them with such love and kindness in his squalid house that Will declared as they were walking home, 'I would rather abide with this saint in his poor cottage than with any prince in the world.'

They confined themselves to Cambridge and kept clear of Boston. In any case, there were no more invitations. Whenever strangers visited the Gookins, the officers withdrew discreetly to their attic.

Gradually, it seemed possible that the outside world had forgotten them. Ned even began to wonder if they might yet live out their days as simple New England farmers. Perhaps they could send for their families? Frances and his grandchildren would take to the life, although it was hard for him to picture Katherine in America.

He kept an occasional eye on the bridge through his telescope. The days shortened. The air turned chilly.

CHAPTER NINE

For Nayler, the hour of retribution was approaching. Sometimes, when he left a meeting of the Crown lawyers preparing the prosecution in Serjeants' Inn to walk back to the Strand, he fancied that he could feel it almost physically, like a tumour swelling in the autumn air – a heavy grey stillness settling over the city. The second week of October was when it was fixed to begin. A festival of blood.

Just before sunset on Tuesday the ninth, he took a boat to the Tower and in the company of the Lieutenant, Sir John Robinson, and the Attorney General, Sir Geoffrey Palmer, spent the evening going from cell to cell, informing each of the twenty-nine prisoners held in solitary confinement that their trial would begin the following day. All, without exception, asked to know what charges they would face so that they might have the night at least to prepare their defence; all were told that they would discover the details the next morning in court. The lawyer John Cooke, who had been the prosecuting attorney at Charles I's trial, was especially outraged.

'It is a denial of all justice not to tell us of the indictment against us!'

'Is that so?' responded Nayler pleasantly. 'And yet that is exactly the way you treated the King, who only learned what crimes he was accused of when he was forced before your illegal court.' He banged on the door. 'Guard!'

The three officials stepped out of the cell. The guard slammed the door and locked it. Cooke started hammering, demanding they come back. His complaints pursued them all the way down the narrow passage. Palmer patted Nayler on the back. 'Well said, Mr Nayler, well said.'

A most useful shadow . . .

He refused the offer of supper and went straight to bed in Robinson's official residence, where he lay awake until after midnight, listening to the other two drinking toast after toast to the health of the King in the Lieutenant's fine French brandy, their voices increasingly slurred.

The following morning, he was woken at five by a clap of thunder. By six, he was in the courtyard, sheltering in a doorway, watching the prisoners as they were brought out into the darkness. The sky was a tumult of black cloud, edged silver by the sheets of lightning that lit the threads of rain. Drops hissed on the flaming torches. The regicides in their leg irons and handcuffs shuffled through the puddles. It was hard to believe that these broken old men were the revolutionaries who had made England a republic for eleven years. They were crammed into a line of carriages with blacked-out windows. A minute later, Palmer and Robinson emerged bleary-eyed; Nayler joined them in a separate coach, and the cortège set off under a heavy escort of cavalry and infantry.

Afterwards, he was to remember the next nine days as an

exhausting, sleepless blur from which certain distinct moments lodged themselves in his mind.

The immense crowd, almost invisible, shuffling and murmuring in the wet darkness like some great animal, waiting for the trial to begin.

The medieval court arranged like a theatre, with the judges and officials seated beneath a portico and the spectators standing under the open sky.

The jeers and jostling that greeted the regicides as they were led in batches of three or four from their holding cells in Newgate prison into the well of the Old Bailey.

The vast assemblage of notables who crowded the benches to watch the spectacle: the Lord Chancellor, the Lord Treasurer, the Treasurer of the Royal Household, the Lord Mayor, the Speaker of the House of Commons, the two secretaries of state; and the men who had served Cromwell – Annesley, Ashley-Cooper, General Monck, now elevated to Duke of Albemarle – Roundheads who but for the grace of God and some nimble footwork might have been on trial themselves.

The reading of the indictment by the clerk of the court to each of the accused, standing drenched before the bench: 'That he, together with others, not having the fear of God before his eyes, and being instigated by the Devil, did maliciously, treasonably and feloniously, contrary to his due allegiance and bounden duty, sit upon and condemn our late sovereign lord, Charles the First of ever-blessed memory, and also did upon the thirtieth of January, sign and seal a warrant for the execution of His late Sacred and Serene Majesty . . .'

The pathetic attempts of the accused to avoid pleading guilty or not guilty but instead to dispute the legality of the charge, and the way the Lord Chief Justice and the clerk of the court simply posed the question again and again, shouting over their protests until they were bludgeoned into answering.

The hush that fell when the death warrant was produced and read out to the court, and then shown to each prisoner. The way they were forced to confirm – some defiantly, some reluctantly – that they recognised their signatures and seals. The way that what little fight they had left in them seemed to vanish at that moment, shoulders slumping, heads bowed, men already dead.

The Lord Chief Justice placing a small square of black cloth upon his head and pronouncing the terrible sentence, again and again: 'The judgment of this court is that you be led back to the place from whence you came, and from thence to be drawn upon a hurdle to the place of execution, and there you shall be hanged by the neck, and being alive shall be cut down, and your privy members to be cut off, your entrails to be taken out of your body, and you living, the same to be burnt before your eyes, and your head to be cut off, your body to be divided into four quarters, and your head and quarters to be disposed of at the pleasure of the King's Majesty; and the Lord have mercy upon your soul.'

And the killings – above all, the killings – which went on for a week. The instruments of death set out at Charing Cross so that the ten regicides excluded from the mercy of life imprisonment could gaze their final hour upon the Banqueting House where they put the King to death – the scaffold with the ladders and the dangling nooses, the braziers with the roaring coals and the irons heating and the kettles boiling, the chopping block, the hurdles on which the prisoners were strapped and dragged from the Tower through the crowded cobbled streets so that they arrived with their backs rubbed raw and their faces covered in spittle, the mounting of the ladders, their final speeches, the hangman pushing them off, the brief dangling from the rope until consciousness was lost, the cutting-down, the bucket of water thrown in the face, the cutting-away of clothes, the sharp knife flourished to the crowd, the severing of the cock and balls, the screams, the blood, the ecstatic groans and cheers of the mob, the slash of the blade through the stomach lining, the dragging-out of the entrails with red-hot tongs and corkscrews – yard upon yard of glistening pink tubing, like strings of sausages dangling in a butcher's shop – cut up and thrown onto the coals, the stench of the frying innards, the pulsing heart plucked out and shown to the mob, the dragging of the lifeless empty carcass to the block, the sawing-off of the head, the thudding of the axe as the trunk was chopped into quarters, the King watching with his ladies from a window of the Holbein Gate with a handkerchief pressed to his nose, the stench carried on the wind so nauseating that the wealthy citizens living close to Charing Cross protested and the final killings were done at the traditional execution ground of Tyburn instead, the late-night visit to Nayler's apartment from Isabelle Hacker, the plea for mercy, the word with Hyde the following morning ('It is thanks to him we had the warrant, which made the trial run smoothly . . .'), and so the colonel by the King's gracious clemency, the last to die, was killed by hanging only and his remains returned to his family for burial.

The heads of the other nine regicides were placed on spikes around Westminster Hall, on London Bridge and in other public places. Their quarters were nailed over the city gates. For a week or two they drew curious spectators, but gradually people ceased to notice them – mere hunks of meat, pecked to white bone by crows. The Act of Oblivion had been accomplished, and the King's government turned with relief to other matters.

Except for Nayler.

*

At the end of November, he convened another meeting of his intelligence committee – Nokes, Wallis, Bishop, Prynne – to review the progress of the manhunt. He had been so busy with the trial and the aftermath, it was more than a month since they had met. He took satisfaction in revising his chart of wanted men, running a line through the names of all those who had been dealt with.

But of the rest, the news was entirely frustrating. Henry de Vic, the English ambassador in Brussels, had sent a cipher dispatch reporting that he had almost succeeded in laying his hands on John Lisle, one of the managers of the King's trial, but that Lisle had taken fright and was now believed to be in Hamburg. Even more irritatingly, Edmund Ludlow, a general in the Parliamentary army, who had signed the death warrant and who had almost handed himself in during the summer but then changed his mind, had somehow slipped across the Channel to Dieppe, and had now been sighted in Geneva, where he was protected by the Calvinist Swiss.

'How could such a thing have been allowed to happen?' demanded Nayler.

'The straits are narrow,' replied Nokes, who had taken charge of the inquiry while Nayler was in court. 'The weather was unseasonably calm in September. Most likely he crossed in a small vessel from a beach, avoiding the southern ports.'

'Perhaps Whalley and Goffe have done the same,' said Bishop. 'The King's proclamation and reward have most certainly yielded us nothing, except a few unfortunate fathers and sons falsely denounced by their neighbours.'

'It is disappointing, I agree,' said Nayler, 'and surprising.'

'I think perhaps,' said Nokes cautiously, 'they may never have come back to England in the first place.'

As the weeks had passed without result, Nayler had been forced to consider that possibility himself. He had thought often of Frances Goffe; often enough to feel slightly guilty. Some quality about her – a calmness, a certain stillness – reminded him of his late wife. He even entertained a fantasy that . . . But no, that was impossible. He was certainly reluctant to accept she might have tricked him. 'And why do you say that Mr Nokes?' There was a truculent edge to his voice.

'You may recall, sir, that you asked me to check the passenger manifests of ships leaving England for America in April and May.'

'I do recall. And was it done?'

'We stopped when the reward was offered, but have since gone back to it.' Nokes produced a sheet of paper and laid it on the table. 'This is the manifest of a vessel named the *Prudent Mary*. She sailed from Gravesend on the fourteenth of May. Her master, a Captain Pierce, is a well-known Puritan. So are some of her passengers – Daniel Gookin is probably the same man of that name who served as collector of customs under Cromwell; William Jones may be the son of Colonel John Jones, the regicide lately executed.'

'And what? Do you believe Whalley and Goffe were also on board?'

'They are not listed. But two names caught my eye – a Mr Richardson and a Mr Stephenson, written down one after the other, suggesting they were travelling together.'

'Those are common enough names, surely?'

'Indeed. But then I remembered that Whalley's father was named Richard, and Goffe's was called Stephen.'

After he had congratulated Nokes on his diligence with the best grace he could muster – which was in truth not much, for he hated to think he might have been made to look a fool – Nayler ended the meeting, took a horse from the stables in the Mews, crossed the Thames by ferry and rode at a gallop to Clapham. He dismounted a little way up the lane, drew his pistol and approached the cottage on foot.

If any Person or Persons . . . shall Directly or Indirectly Conceal, Harbour, Keep, Retain, or Maintain the said Edward Whalley and William Goffe . . . We will proceed against them with all severity . . .

That was the law, and he would enforce it. He would put her in jail. He would take away her baby. He would sweat the truth out of her. And out of the old man. And the old woman.

He opened the gate quietly and walked towards the house on the grass rather than the path so as not to make a noise. The door was locked. He cupped his hands to the glass and peered through the window into the parlour. Nothing. He worked his way around the side of the house, but it was the same when he looked in at the kitchen: bare boards, possessions gone, the place deserted.

The two open carts lumbered through Southwark towards London Bridge. William and Jane Hooke were sitting in the back of the first on either side of Katherine Whalley, who was lying on a mattress surrounded by their possessions. Frances Goffe was in the second, seated up on the bench next to the driver, cradling Richard in her lap. Behind her, Frankie was holding Nan. Judith and Betty were lying on their stomachs, hand in hand, looking over the tail of the cart, laughing and making faces at the people in the street. Frances had to keep turning round and telling them to be careful not to fall out.

She was exhausted by the strain of the past few weeks, from the effort of packing up the house and preparing to move to a new hiding place in the city – so much so that despite the cold and fear, she kept nearly dozing off, only to be saved by a jerk as the cart hit a rut and bounced her on the hard wooden seat. She was still in this drifting, semi-conscious state as they approached the gate leading to London Bridge. The cart bumped again, and she opened her eyes to a nightmare of waxy faces arrayed like kites in the wintry sky. They gazed down at her, slack-mouthed, ragged-necked, eyeless, set on long pikes above the portcullis. She recognised two of them, even at a distance: the republican preacher Hugh Peters, and Will's old Welsh friend Colonel John Jones.

She gasped, and instinctively laid her hand on the baby's face to shield him from the sight. But he slept on soundly, rocked by the motion of the cart as it went under the gate and onto the bridge and was swallowed up in the unheeding London traffic.

CHAPTER TEN

THE FIRST SNOWFALL of the winter came to Massachusetts in the middle of December. Unable to work in the fields, the two colonels stayed in their room.

Ned watched though his spyglass as the large flakes slowly obliterated the familiar landmarks of road and marshland, rubbing out the detail until only a few dark lines remained. That was when he noticed that the workmen on the bridge were laying planks between the piers, gradually building a causeway towards the middle of the river, and when he put on his hat and boots and went down to check, they proudly confirmed that the bridge would indeed be ready for use, if not properly finished, by the end of the month.

He stood for a while, heedless of the snow, frowning at the opposite bank. Not only would the bridge cut the journey time from Boston; because the ferry had never run at night, for the first time it would make Cambridge accessible after dark. Finally he turned on his heel and walked directly up the hill to the home of Golden Moore.

'Is there a puppy left from that litter of yours, Mr Moore?'

'Aye, Colonel, there's one, a pretty little bitch – though I'll be sorry to part with her.'

'I'd be very much obliged if you would.'

Ned carried the squirming spaniel hidden under his coat down to the house and presented her over supper as a surprise to the children. Mary Gookin didn't want a dog, had made that clear a hundred times, but there was nothing she could do about it once the children saw the puppy. And she *was* excessively pretty – even Mary had to concede that – entirely black apart from her white throat. The girls named her Bonny. She slept by the fire in the kitchen and barked every time someone came near the house.

And then, not long after that, at the end of December, a packet of mail arrived on a ship from Bristol. Daniel took it into the parlour to read at his desk. He said nothing about it for the rest of the day, but his mood was noticeably grim, and twice he disappeared with Mary to their bedroom. That night, just as Ned and Will were finishing their evening prayers before getting into bed, there was a knock at the attic door and the Gookins came in together. Without saying a word, Daniel held out a printed document.

Ned and Will sat on the bed to read it. It was a proclamation, signed by the King, offering a reward of one hundred pounds a head, dead or alive, for 'the execrable traitors Colonel Edward Whalley and Colonel William Goffe', and promising dire punishment to anyone caught harbouring them. The date showed that it had taken three months to travel from Whitehall Palace to Boston, Massachusetts.

'At least they think we are in England,' said Ned, whose nature was always to be hopeful. He looked up. 'They are on the wrong trail. That is good. And why does everyone always call me Colonel when I was Oliver's commissary general of horse? My head alone should be worth two hundred pounds.'

Daniel did not smile. 'Unfortunately, they will realise their error soon enough – everyone in Cambridge and plenty in Boston can testify that you are here – and Governor Endecott will find a royal warrant hard to ignore.'

Will lowered his head and clasped his hands behind his neck. 'We must leave your house.'

Daniel shook his head. 'No.'

'But our presence endangers you all. We must leave at once.'

'And where will you go in the middle of winter? This proclamation must be known already in Boston. Within a week, it will be displayed all over the colony. There's no place for you to run.' He exchanged a glance with Mary and took her hand. 'We have talked the matter through and are both agreed. We shall not abandon you.'

'We cannot allow it, can we, Ned?'

Mary said, 'We'll hide you. We'll tell everyone you've gone, including the children. We'll say you left in the night without warning.'

Will started to object again, but Ned put his hand on his knee to quiet him. 'Hide us where?'

'In the barn,' said Daniel. 'There's hay in the loft where you can sleep. The cattle will provide some warmth. It may even be that you can have a fire if I devise some tale that the cows are sick.'

'No, no. That is too dangerous,' said Will. 'We must give ourselves up. Better still, *you* should give us up, and take two hundred pounds for your trouble.'

For the first time, Daniel looked angry. 'Do you think so little of us? That we'd betray you for thirty pieces of silver?'

'Hush,' said Mary, 'you'll wake the children.'

Ned said, 'Well, I think your plan is sound, if you're willing to take the risk, dear Dan and Mary, and I thank you from my heart for your Christian charity. We can't give up at the first setback, Will. We slept out in the open in winter in Scotland often enough when we were in the army. A month or two in a barn will be nothing in comparison. Our Saviour himself began life in a barn. We'll have the leisure to conceive a plan, and then in the spring we can move on.'

Once Mary had made sure the children were asleep, the officers packed up their belongings and went quietly down the stairs, out of the kitchen, across the yard through the snow to the barn. Mary and Daniel came after them, carrying their bedding, candles, a jug of water and a meat pie for their breakfast that Mary had baked that afternoon. Her mind was troubled, not by fear of the consequences of harbouring so-called traitors, but by the prospect of the endless lies she would now have to tell – to the children, to their neighbours – day after day, sin piled upon sin.

By candlelight they made their way between the dark mounds of sleeping cattle. The place was cold and stank of shit and urine, worse even than a stable. The fumes caught at their throats. Ned climbed the ladder to the hayloft and reached down to take their bags from Will.

Daniel handed up the blankets and pillows. 'I'll come and see you in the morning.'

Returning to the house, Mary noticed that the snow had already blanked out their tracks across the yard, and when she looked back, even their most recent footprints were vanishing behind them. Within a few minutes it was as if the two fugitives had never existed.

In the hayloft, Will piled up the straw and laid out their bed while Ned unpacked their weapons: four loaded pistols, a pair each to go under their respective pillows, and swords and knives placed within handy reach. Then they both crawled beneath the blankets and lay awake, unspeaking, like an unhappily married couple, each with his own thoughts, until the noise of the cattle snoring and shifting in the darkness beneath them slowly lulled them to sleep.

The disappearance of their two lodgers was greeted by the children in different ways. Mary, the eldest, was surprised, but too obedient to question what she was told. The teenage Elizabeth, who had developed an unrequited passion for Will, gave up eating and moped for a fortnight. The three boys were sad for a day or two, then forgot all about them. Only the dog seemed to sense the truth, sitting outside the barn, sometimes whining and occasionally scratching at the door.

In Cambridge, the vanishing of the English officers coincided with the posting of the reward outside the general store. It meant the Gookins' story that they must have taken fright and fled in the darkness was accepted as plausible. Only Reverend Mitchell seemed sceptical. After the morning meeting the following Sabbath, Mrs Gookin felt her voice grow higher and her complexion redder as he questioned her on the details. What time did she notice they were missing? How did she think they had they left Cambridge, on foot or on horseback? Wasn't it strange that they hadn't asked the Gookins for help?

In the barn, the two men barely stirred. These were the shortest days of the year. The light, when it came, barely penetrated the small, dusty windows. The snow was endless – the big flakes falling soft as goose down, feathering the roof, piling up against the timber walls, muffling the sounds of the outside world. They found it easier to escape the cold by staying the whole day in their coats and boots beneath the thick woollen blankets and the piles of hay. Will studied his Bible. Ned stared at the rafters; sometimes he fancied he was already dead and in his tomb. Other fearful creatures slept through the depths of winter – hedgehogs, dormice and the like – why not men on the run? Even when Daniel or Mary came to attend to the cattle and left food and drink for them at the base of the ladder, they often remained where they were.

One day towards the end of January, Bonny's bark announced a visitor. Reverend Mitchell had come to call. He brought with him two thick pamphlets that had just arrived from London, one a record of the trial of the regicides and the other a collection of the final prayers and speeches of those who had been executed. It was the first time that news of what had happened had reached Massachusetts.

'I read these yesterday,' he said, 'and I commend them to you both.' He placed them on the table. 'I believe we should hold a public meeting to discuss the killing of the King.'

Daniel looked at him in surprise. 'You do not think it justified?'

'I am uncertain. I am praying for God's guidance on the issue.' Mitchell stared around the room, rocked back on his heels to peer into the kitchen and eyed the ceiling before returning his attention to Gookin. 'I advise you to do the same.'

'God has already guided me, Jonathan. The killing of a tyrant is no crime.'

'The most learned minds in England disagree with you.'

'Learned minds can still believe wicked things, especially when their own interests are at stake.'

'Even so, we must obey the law.' The minister seemed to be expecting an invitation to sit. When none was forthcoming, he put on his hat and buttoned up his coat. 'Well then, God be with you. Pray be good enough to return those when you have read them.'

Daniel watched him through the snow-stippled window. He did

not go straight back to the road, but stood in the yard contemplating the barn. For a minute or two he watched it, then finally made his way carefully along the slippery path and out through the gate.

'It is plain as day he suspects us of still hiding them.' Daniel picked up one of the pamphlets and read out the title page. '"Rebels no Saints, a Collection of the Speeches, Private Passages, Letters and Prayers of those Persons lately Executed".' He shook his head and suddenly looked so despairing that Mary wrapped her arms around him and drew him close to her. He let out a long sigh. 'And now I suppose I must go and tell Ned and Will that their comrades are dead.'

The officers were awake most of that night, reading by candlelight. The news was both expected and yet at the same time shocking to see in cold print – the brutality and cynicism of the trial, the bestiality of the killings. Ned recited the names of each of the ten who had been executed – Thomas Harrison, John Carew, John Cooke, Hugh Peters, Thomas Scot, Gregory Clement, Adrian Scroope, John Jones, Daniel Axtell and Francis Hacker – and they paused after each and meditated, and at the end Will said a prayer for the repose of their souls: 'Gone to glory, every one.' The description of the slaughter of John Cooke and Hugh Peters on the same morning, the third and fourth to die, was especially vile – Cooke dragged to Charing Cross on a hurdle with Harrison's severed head fixed on a pole in front of him, Peters tied to a railing in a state of drunken terror and obliged to watch Cooke's execution and await his turn. *When Mr Cooke was cut down and brought to be Quartered, one they called Colonel Turner called to the sheriff's men to bring Mr Peters near that he might see it. And by and by the Hangman came to him all besmeared in blood and rubbing his bloody hands together he tauntingly asked, how do you like this Mr Peters, how do you like this work?* To whom he replied, *I am not, I thank God, terrified at it, you may do your worst.*

'Hallelujah,' said Will, 'that the Lord should have granted him courage at the end.'

They had all died bravely, defiantly. General Harrison had even managed to work his arm free while he was being eviscerated and punched the executioner in the head, who quickly cut his throat.

'And yet why did Peters have to die at all?' asked Ned. 'He was a preacher, not a soldier or a lawyer. He didn't sit in judgement on the King or sign the death warrant. We never inflicted such tortures on our enemies. Charles Stuart was killed with a single stroke.'

Will was silent for a minute. 'I should have died with them. The greater the suffering, the greater the devotion it shows our Saviour.' He leafed through one of the pamphlets to the final words of Colonel Jones, the Welshman whose son had sailed to America with them on the *Prudent Mary.* ' "O dear hearts, in what a sad condition are our dear friends beyond the sea, where they may be hunted from place to place, and never be in safety. How much have we gotten a start on them, for we are at the point, and are now going to heaven." That is the truth. They are with the Lord, while we skulk like rats in a barn.'

It was the great divide between them – an argument that by unspoken mutual agreement they always avoided having – that Will blamed Ned for playing the Devil's part by persuading him to flee.

'I'm no coward, Will,' said Ned eventually. 'I hope you know that well enough.' He spoke quietly. 'I'm not afraid of a traitor's death. For all its agony, can it really be much worse than childbirth, which the most humbly born woman endures again and again? And if that is to be our fate, then so be it: I'll gladly march up to

Heaven, I trust as bravely as the rest. But I truly believe that God has chosen a different path for us – to stay alive, to keep the flame and to bear witness. Besides, are we not suffering? Are we not martyrs? John Jones is right. If you weigh it in the scales, it may be that in the end our pain will be heavier than theirs. Theirs is over; they are among the saints who will rule the earth. Ours goes on – and I maintain that our duty is to extend it as long as we can.'

His speech had exhausted him. He lay back on the straw and closed his eyes. He could take no more of trials and hangings. Will did not reply. But after a while, Ned felt him lie down next to him, and a little time after that, his son-in-law's hand reached out and grasped his.

The fate of their old comrades shamed them into activity. Ned borrowed a drill and bit from Daniel and bored a hole in the wall of the hayloft, big enough for him to insert his spyglass. He widened it so that he could manoeuvre the glass sufficiently to command a sweep of the house, the yard and the road down to the river. He used his penknife to whittle a piece of wood that could plug the gap, to keep out the cold. They exercised – press-ups and chest-pulls from the edge of the loft. They kept their weapons cleaned and loaded. They needed to be ready.

CHAPTER ELEVEN

CONSTRAINED BY THE short days and impassable roads of the bitter English winter, Nayler's manhunt languished. Only two reports reached him of individuals arrested on suspicion of being Whalley and Goffe, one from Essex, the other from Kent. But when he sent Nokes on the difficult journey out of London to interrogate the prisoners, both tales proved groundless. Privately, in any case, Nayler was now convinced the regicides were in America. He visited the Customs House on the Thames close to the Tower and arranged with the master there to be notified of all vessels arriving from New England. But it turned out that few captains were willing to hazard the winter storms of the North Atlantic, and out of those ships that did complete the crossing, no one, crew or passenger, claimed to have seen or heard of the fugitives.

And then, in the middle of January, he was summoned by Hyde to Worcester House to be given an unwelcome new task: exhuming the bodies of Oliver Cromwell, his son-in-law, Henry Ireton, and the president of the regicide court, John Bradshaw, from their tombs in Westminster Abbey, and arranging for their posthumous execution at Tyburn on the twelfth anniversary of the King's murder.

He recoiled at the prospect. Of course he agreed the traitors should be removed from the precincts of the abbey before the King's coronation, but why not simply rebury them in some secret grave? He shifted unhappily in his chair. 'That will be foul work, Sir Edward.'

'Since when did that deter you? The idea is certainly not mine, believe me. But Parliament commands it, and really, Mr Nayler,' he added with sudden asperity, 'if you cannot find any more living regicides to bring to justice, you might as well at least employ yourself in hanging the dead.'

Accordingly, a week later, Nayler stood in the draughty central aisle of Henry VII's chapel alongside the Serjeant-at-Arms of the House of Commons, watching the workmen swinging their picks at the stone floor. A crowd of curious spectators was kept back by soldiers. It took about half an hour to open the vault and expose Cromwell's wooden coffin, then lift it from the ground. There had long been rumours that something had gone wrong with the embalming process – that the Protector's body had built up poisonous vapours and exploded and had required a hasty burial; that it was possible, indeed, that the body in the abbey wasn't even his. As the lid was prised off, Nayler covered his nose with a scarf soaked in lavender and camphor and stepped closer.

Beneath the lid was a covering of lead. Once that had been cut away, he could see the shape of a body wrapped in half a dozen layers of greyish cloth. He reached in, rolled them back, and found himself gazing down at the face of Cromwell. The flesh was thin and brownish, stiff, like leather. The jaw had rotted, exposing teeth. But even after more than two years of decay, the size of the bulbous nose and the broadness of the forehead and the remains of the moustache and beard were all immediately recognisable – the wreck of a visage, yet still full of strength and power. A ridge on the skull showed where the embalmers had cut away the top of his head to remove the brain before cementing the bone back in place. There was a chain around his neck with a silver medallion. Nayler averted his face as he reached around the back of the neck and tugged it over Cromwell's head. The inscription was in Latin but easy enough for him to translate: 'Oliver, Protector of the English, Scottish and Irish Republic. Born 25 April 1599, inaugurated 15 December 1653, died 3 September 1658. Here he rests.'

He slowly lowered the medallion back into the coffin, letting the silvery chain pool on the Protector's chest, and took a pace backwards. God knew, he had no love for the man, but it seemed to him that by desecrating his tomb, it was themselves they were degrading rather than their enemy.

'That is Cromwell, no question.'

The Serjeant-at-Arms directed that the coffin should be carried into the main part of the abbey so that the public could inspect the body, at a charge of sixpence each, while the exhumation of the other two regicides resumed. Ireton, Lord Deputy of Ireland, had been in the ground the longest – nine years – and was atrophied, dry and black; but Bradshaw, after only fourteen months, was green, and the stench when the lid was lifted caused the workmen nearest to the coffin to turn away and vomit.

As the short winter's day came to an end, the three corpses were piled into a cart and taken to the Red Lion tavern in Holborn, for a parody of Cromwell's original lying-in-state, with yet more paying customers, despite the stink from Bradshaw, lining up to gawp.

On the morning of 30 January, Nayler rode behind the hurdles as the bodies were dragged through the streets to Tyburn, where a crowd of several thousand waited to witness them being hanged together. As the bodies swung in the wind, the public executioner came down his ladder and remarked, 'I'd cut off Old Noll's prick and balls if they hadn't shrunk so,' at which Nayler turned his back on him. That afternoon, the corpses were lifted down and decapitated – Cromwell's leathery neck required eight blows from the axe – their trunks tipped into a common grave, their heads taken away in a sack to be stuck on twenty-foot poles and hoisted above the law courts in Westminster Hall.

Nayler supervised all of this, and then at dusk went straight to a whorehouse in Milford Lane, where he picked the first woman he was offered – young or old, pretty or ugly, he neither noticed nor cared; all he desired was to lose himself in living flesh. Later that night, in his bedchamber, for the first time in years he did not light the candle beneath Sarah's portrait. He could not bear to look at her, or for her to look at him.

The next morning, he sent word to Nokes that he was sick.

In the days that followed, he stuck to his rooms, stayed mostly in bed, saw no one, had his meals left outside the door by his servant. These periodic fits of black dog had afflicted him since his youth. Sometimes they could last for weeks; a cold, dry, melancholy humour that none of the recommended cures – not laurel broth, or white hellebore, or horse leeches to drain the blood – could ever shift.

One morning, a little over three weeks into his seclusion, he was disturbed around eleven o'clock by a loud hammering at his door. He tried to ignore it. Still the hammering went on. Finally he put a coat on over his nightgown, shuffled across the floor and opened the door a crack. In the dim light of the passage was a tall man, smartly dressed.

'Mr Richard Nayler?'

Nayler squinted at him. He seemed to hear his words from a distance. 'Who wants him?'

'My name is Captain Thomas Breedon, sir.' The man took off his hat and bowed. 'Shipowner and trader with the Massachusetts Bay Company of America, yesterday arrived in London from Boston. The Customs House directed me to the Privy Council, and your secretary directed me to your lodgings. I have a tale to tell you, Mr Nayler, which I believe may be of interest.'

CHAPTER TWELVE

I N CAMBRIDGE, THE snow began to thaw in the middle of February. They could hear great sections of it moving above their heads, sliding off the barn roof and crashing into the yard. Then there was a freeze that kept them under their blankets again. For several days they saw nothing of Daniel Gookin: he had gone to Boston to attend a meeting of the Massachusetts Bay Colony's state council, of which he was an elected member. On the night of Monday the twenty-fifth, soon after they heard him return, it started snowing afresh onto icy ground. Ned lay awake listening to the rustle of it landing, once more deadening and deepening the vast silence beyond the barn. In the stillness of their cocoon the flame of their candle barely flickered, and when – it must have been long after midnight – the dog started barking, he hardly noticed it at first; she sounded as if she was half a mile away.

But there was no doubt: she *was* barking. Suddenly he was alert.

He shook Will awake, then knelt and used his penknife to prise away the piece of wood, and poked his spyglass out into the night.

Four torches, gauzy in the falling snow, were moving in a file along the road and coming in through the gate. He could just make out a couple of figures, their shadows flickering on the snow, one of them carrying the long barrel of a musket.

He turned to Will, who was already on his feet. 'They're here,' he whispered. 'Four at least.'

Will nodded. He handed Ned his pair of pistols, then, taking his own and thrusting them into his pockets, he disappeared swiftly down the ladder, clutching his sword.

Their plan was to split their firepower, give an impression of greater force.

Ned went back to his lookout. The torches were halfway across the yard now. The telescope was useless. He withdrew it, poked one of the pistols into the gap and bent his head next to it. He had the advantage of height, about ten feet of it.

The familiar sensations before a fight. A tightness in his chest, a sharpening of his heartbeat, a peculiar cold calm. Oliver's voice: *Never wait for the attack to come to you, Ned. Always be the one who attacks first, no matter what the odds; rouse the spirit, have faith in the Lord . . .*

The torches were closing in on the barn. He checked himself for a few moments longer, until he calculated Will must have had time to get into position, then took aim at the nearest of the flames and fired. A brilliant flash of powder. A deafening explosion. The smell of singed hair. He saw the torch drop, transferred his second pistol into his right hand, aimed again, fired again, didn't wait to see the result but threw the pistols onto the straw, grabbed his sword and swung himself onto the ladder. There was such a ringing in his ears from the noise of the firing that he could barely hear the crack of Will discharging his own rounds from the door in quick succession. He thought he heard a shot returned from outside.

Terrified cows were struggling to their feet. The barn door had blown wide open. There was a blast of freezing air, and just sufficient light reflecting off the snow for him to make out Will standing beside it, his back to the wall, his sword drawn, discharged pistols at his feet. Ned herded the cattle before him. They scrambled to escape, blocking the door, colliding with one another, spilling out into the snow. He came up close to Will and spread his hands – *where are they?* Will shrugged and shook his head. The two men stood shoulder to shoulder. No sound of shots or human voices came from outside, just the frightened lowing of the cattle.

Ned said quietly, 'How many were there – did you see?'

'Too dark. Five or six, maybe.'

When the last of the animals had escaped and the barn was empty, Ned stepped cautiously into the doorway.

The snow was still coming down heavily. The cows had clustered at the far end of the yard, furthest from the house. Lights moved in the upstairs windows. Bonny was barking. The rest of the yard was empty save for one small winking flame on the ground about twenty paces away. Beyond it, a couple of torches were disappearing down the road towards the river.

They surely couldn't be regular soldiers, he thought, not if they could be frightened off so easily. More likely Boston Royalists or those Scotch scoundrels after the reward.

He kept his sword drawn as he moved through the snow. He lifted the abandoned torch and shone it around. A trampling of panicky footprints, a patch of blood as big as a dinner plate, a smeary trail of scarlet, quite wide, gouged into the snow and already vanishing beneath the heavy fall. He followed the blood a short way until it disappeared, then squatted on his haunches and dug his fingers into the snow, uncovering the red stain. A bad wound, by the look of it. They must have had to drag the injured man away.

Will came up behind him. Ned straightened, wincing at the effort, his joints creaking; he was getting too old for this game, but was exultant as always after a fight. 'We beat the dogs, Will!'

'Aye, but they'll be back. Perhaps even at first light. And there'll be more of them, and they'll be readier.'

Daniel Gookin had emerged from the house carrying a candle, protecting the flame with his hand against the falling snow. He waded knee-deep through the drift towards them. Mary, a coat over her nightdress, watched from the doorway. He called out, 'Are you hurt?'

'Not a scratch,' shouted Ned cheerfully. Will was right, of course. If they stayed where they were, they were dead men. He looked up at the tumbling sky. A freezing gossamer mask of snow began to mould across his face.

The children had been woken by the gunshots and were out on the landing. Mary stood at the bottom of the stairs and kept the kitchen door closed behind her. The colonels heard her telling them it was nothing to be scared of – a hungry wolf prowling in the yard, their father had seen it off – and ordering them back to bed. Ned went outside to check if the attackers were returning, but there was nothing to see except darkness and snow.

After the children had been settled and the cattle driven back into the barn, the officers sat close to the kitchen fire. Steam rose from their damp clothes. The dog lay at Will's feet. They recounted in quiet voices how they had repelled the attack, then listened in silence as Gookin told them of events in Boston. The Massachusetts Great and General Court had spent an entire day discussing their presence in the colony, and although Governor Endecott had refused to put the issue to a vote, it was clear that a majority now believed the situation to be intolerable: that the government in England was obviously firmly established, that it must soon learn the regicides had been enjoying sanctuary in the state, and that the King as a punishment might withdraw their royal charter.

'Governor Endecott asked me to convey his personal regrets, but to warn you he has no choice except to issue an arrest warrant. He'll try to delay it for a day or two so that you can get a head start, and the marshal general promises he'll be less than diligent in his searches. Even so, the colony has become too dangerous for you. Bounty-hunters will soon be the least of your worries.'

Will said, 'Then where are we to go?'

'Somewhere beyond Massachusetts.'

'But where?'

'I think it must be the Connecticut Valley.'

In the silence that followed, the only sound was the crackling of the logs in the fireplace.

'Is that not a great distance away?'

'It is – a hundred miles or thereabouts. But its remoteness is its advantage. Connecticut is Puritan country, much more so than Boston. You'll not find many Royalists there. And I know the state governor, John Winthrop. His late father was governor of Massachusetts some twenty years past. If any man can help you, Winthrop will. Hartford would be the town to aim for.'

Ned said, 'Can we get so far in such weather?'

'It can be done. It won't be easy, mind. At this time of year there's no forage, so it would be necessary to take only one horse, to carry supplies and baggage.'

'We'd need to *walk*?' 'A hundred miles?'

'Yes, but there are some Indian settlements along the trail where we could shelter overnight. The Old Connecticut Path can be hard to follow in winter, but I know it well enough.'

Mary looked at him, alarmed. 'You'd go with them?'

'Who else can guide them? They'd never manage such a distance alone.'

She folded her arms and stared into the fire. Another silence.

'What do you say, Will?' asked Ned.

Will was fondling the spaniel's ears. They were like soft, warm silk. He had a sudden vision of Frances soon after they were married, naked in their bedroom in the firelight. He had to shake his head to empty it from his mind. 'I say I'd like to lie in front of the fire like Bonny here, but God has chosen a harder road for us.' He glanced around at the others. 'I say we have no choice.'

Mary and Daniel withdrew to their room. The colonels collected their possessions from the barn. They reloaded their pistols at the kitchen table, then took it in turns to keep lookout until dawn, one stationed at the window while the other tried to doze in the glow of the fire.

It was during Ned's second watch that the snowfall finally stopped. A spray of stars appeared above the yard, and a bright half-moon. The surface of the snow froze and crystallised; tiny points of ice glittered as if in reflection of the stars. He rubbed his thumb through the frost on the inside of the glass. It promised well for the morning. Better a hard surface for a long journey than drifts and slush and mud. Even so, a hundred-mile march at his age was not a prospect to be relished.

Mary came downstairs and hung a saucepan of meat broth to heat over the fire, then went into the pantry to pack food sufficient for a couple of days. 'We'll need no more,' Daniel had told her. He had unlocked his money chest and produced strings of white and purple clam shells – the native currency. 'I have plenty of wampum. We can buy from the Indians.' She knew better than to try to argue with him once his mind was set. He came into the pantry while she was irritably wrapping a piece of spiced ham, and put his hands around her waist, nuzzled his cheek to hers, his beard rough against her skin. In the morning she knew her face would look as if she had been chapped by the cold.

'You won't get around me as easily as that, Dan Gookin.'

But he did, of course; he always did. She put down the ham and turned and kissed him on the mouth.

The four of them drank the broth by candlelight. Conscious of the children asleep upstairs, they didn't speak much. By the time they were finished, a faint grey light was showing at the window.

Gookin went to the stables to fetch the horse. When he came back, they filled the saddlebags and loaded their belongings, then stood awkwardly in the kitchen until at Will's suggestion they knelt together in prayer. 'Let us comfort one another with the words of the psalm.' He extended his hands, palms upwards. ' "If I ascend to the heavens, You are there; if I make my bed in Sheol, You are there. If I rise on the wings of the dawn, if I settle by the farthest sea, even there Your hand will guide me; Your right hand will hold me fast." O Lord, we commit ourselves to your service and to your care. Amen.'

'Amen.'

They rose, and the three men embraced Mary in turn – Ned somewhat stiff and gruff, Will tenderly, and finally Daniel with a fierceness that almost crushed the breath out of her and which she knew was his way of promising he would return. He whispered, 'I'll be back within two weeks, I swear.' She stood on the doorstep and watched them go. The cold seared her lungs so that it was painful to breathe in deeply. As they passed through the gate, Daniel first, leading the horse, they turned and waved – Will gallantly doffed his hat – then passed out of sight along the road towards the village.

The Cambridge farmsteads were dark with sleep. At the bend, just before the meeting house, the men crossed the frozen creek and followed the trail along the northern bank of the Charles River, their boots crunching through the thin crust of ice and sinking into the snow. After a couple of miles, the sun rose over the frozen landscape, and an hour later, they turned south-west, setting out across the immensity of dazzling virgin white towards the distant forest.

CHAPTER THIRTEEN

THE REGICIDE COMMITTEE of the Privy Council met that same morning in Whitehall Palace, at Nayler's urgent request – Hyde in the chair, Sir William Morice, Sir Anthony Ashley-Cooper and Sir Arthur Annesley all in attendance. They did not look pleased to have been summoned from their other duties by their clerk.

Hyde said, 'Well then, Mr Nayler, here you have us – what is this about?'

Nayler took his usual place at the far end of the table and laid out his papers. His torpor of the past three weeks had vanished. He felt full of energy – dangerously so: he recognised this mood as well. He forced himself to speak slowly and calmly. 'My lords, I am pleased to inform you that I have discovered the whereabouts of Colonel Whalley and Colonel Goffe.'

The news produced no more than a mild stir of interest around the table.

Hyde said, 'Where are they? In England?'

'No, Sir Edward, that has proved to be a false trail. They are in America. To be more exact, I understand them to be living in the settlement of Cambridge in Massachusetts, close to the port of Boston.'

Hyde looked disappointed. 'Then they are not yet in our hands?'

'Not yet, my lord. But they will be.'

'That is hardly urgent news.' Disappointment was turning to irritation. 'Summon us when you have them both in chains, Mr Nayler. Then will be the time for congratulations.' He turned to the Secretary of State. 'Sir William, perhaps you would be so good as to ask Sir Edward Nicholas to draw up an order to the governor of the Massachusetts Bay Colony, instructing him to make the arrests.'

Before Morice could reply, Nayler interrupted. 'I fear the matter is not so easy, my lords. With your permission, may I bring a witness before the committee?'

Hyde glanced at the others. He puffed his cheeks and let out a breath. 'If you must.'

Nayler walked across the corridor to his office. Nokes had left the room, and Captain Breedon was plainly in the act of studying the papers on his desk, although he made haste to step away as soon as Nayler came in. What a rogue he was! Nayler pretended he hadn't noticed. 'The committee will hear from you now, Captain Breedon. Remember what I told you: the facts alone, straight and plain.'

Most men might have felt some trepidation at appearing before the Lord Chancellor of England, a secretary of state and two Privy Councillors. Not so Breedon. He strolled into the council chamber with the confidence of a man about to sell a much-sought-after cargo to a group of eager merchants.

'My lords, this is Captain Thomas Breedon, lately arrived from Boston.'

'Good morning, gentlemen,' said Breedon. 'It is an honour.'

Hyde raised his eyebrows, bemused but polite, and gestured to a seat.

When Breedon was settled in his chair, Nayler said, 'Tell the committee what you told me yesterday.'

And to Nayler's relief, he told it well – how he had sailed from England the previous June carrying, among other news, the names of those regicides whose surrender was demanded by Parliament under the terms of the Oblivion bill; how the ship had docked in Boston on 10 August and how some members of another crew had recognised Whalley and Goffe coming out of a church near the waterfront and walking with various leading Puritans to the house of the Reverend John Norton; how the Scotchmen had come to find him and how he had gone with them and confronted on the doorstep none other than the governor of the Massachusetts Bay Colony himself, John Endecott; how he had read out the order of Parliament and showed Endecott the names of those wanted; how he had seen Whalley and Goffe skulking in the room just behind the governor – 'as plainly as I see you now, my lords' – and how his request that they should be arrested had been rejected with contempt; how he had tried repeatedly in the weeks that followed to force Endecott to do his duty, only to be insulted and called a malignant; how 'the marshal general grinned in my face and said, "Speak against Whalley and Goffe if ye dare, if ye dare, if ye dare"'.

'The marshal general?' repeated Hyde, astonished. 'An official of the Crown, and that is what he told you?'

'Exactly those words, Sir Edward. There are witnesses who will vouch for it.'

'And the governor refused to act? That is an outrage.'

'No, my lord,' interrupted Morice, 'that is treason.'

Annesley said, 'Can you account for their extraordinary behaviour, Captain Breedon?'

'I believe I can, sir.' Breedon adjusted his cuffs and cleared his throat. 'The settlers of New England divide between those who are members of the Puritan churches and those who are not. It is just as great a distinction in America nowadays as that which existed here between the Roundheads and the Cavaliers. The Puritans – not all, but most – are old Cromwellians who refuse to accept the fact of His Majesty's return. Some are even opposed to any longer maintaining a link with England. The most extreme assert that all secular authority should be subordinate to the elders of their church. The Puritans have the loudest voices in government, and it is they who protect Whalley and Goffe.'

'And these regicides, they – what? – they live openly?'

'Quite openly, sir. At the time I left Boston in December, they were lodged in Cambridge, just across the river, where they have been, as I understand it, since the day of their arrival. I am told they receive callers. They visit their neighbours. They meet in church on the Lord's Day. And all the while they boast that if it came to it, they would sign the King's death warrant again.'

'Insufferable,' muttered Ashley-Cooper.

Nayler said, 'You will see now, my lords, why I thought the committee should hear directly from Captain Breedon. If we merely ask the governor in Massachusetts to arrest the traitors, nothing will happen.'

'Clearly so,' said Hyde. He tapped his forefinger against his lips, weighing the matter up. 'Well, thank you, Captain. Your evidence has been most valuable.'

'Is there nothing more I can add?' A crafty look came into Breedon's face. 'In that case, may I most humbly raise the matter of the reward?'

'The reward,' said Nayler firmly, rising and placing his hand on the captain's shoulder, 'will be paid only to those who deliver the bodies of the fugitives to us, dead or alive.' Discreetly, but with a hard grip, he pulled Breedon to his feet and steered him towards the door.

'Your assistance has been noted,' Hyde called after him. 'I am sure some favour can be done in return, can it not, Mr Nayler?'

'I shall see what is possible, Sir Edward.'

Nayler conducted Breedon back to his office. He was relieved to find that Nokes had returned to his desk. 'That was exactly what was required, Captain. If you would be good enough to wait with Mr Nokes, I shall return directly.'

In the corridor, he paused and listened to the murmur of conversation from inside the council chamber. Remember to be calm, he told himself. The suggestion must come from them, not you. He took a breath, stepped into the room, and slipped back into his chair. Morice seemed to be proposing that they should send a warship with an expeditionary force. 'It would not require too many men – fifty at most.'

'Fifty men to fetch back two?' Hyde shook his head. 'That would make us look weak, not strong. It would lend Whalley and Goffe an importance they don't deserve.'

Annesley said, 'Also, if the situation is as difficult as the captain describes, might it not provoke some reaction against His Majesty that could require yet more soldiers to deal with? Before we know where we are, a fight that has been settled in England will be raging again on the other side of the world.'

'Mr Nayler,' said Hyde, 'what is your opinion?'

'I am not a diplomat, my lord, but it would seem to me that officers of the Crown must obey the orders of the Crown or else be removed.'

'Exactly,' said Morice. 'A show of force.'

'Perhaps,' suggested Nayler gently, 'before that stage is reached, we should impress upon the authorities in America the risks they run if they fail to arrest the regicides.'

'And how are we to do that?'

He hesitated, as if the idea was only just occurring to him. 'What if His Majesty himself were to issue a direct order to Endecott and the other officials in New England, naming Whalley and Goffe, and commanding they be taken into custody immediately and sent back to England? Should they fail to obey, it would be clear to everyone that the governors themselves are guilty of treason – and at that point force could be sent.'

There was silence while this was considered. Eventually Hyde said, 'That is feasible.'

'But how would we know whether they were obeying the King's order or not?' objected Morice. 'They have harboured these men for half a year. For all we know, they could do the same for another half-year, while pretending to us they are searching for them.'

Nayler said nothing. He waited. They would arrive at the solution themselves.

It was Ashley-Cooper who reached the obvious conclusion. 'Could we not send an officer of the Crown to convey the King's order to the authorities in person? He would then be on hand to ensure that it was carried out.'

There was another pause, then Hyde laughed. 'Ah, now I see!' He stared down the table at Nayler. 'And pray who might this officer be?' He was impossible to fool.

Nayler stared him out. 'Anyone with some knowledge of the case could go, my lord. My secretary, Mr Nokes, for example.'

'Nokes?' scoffed Morice. 'Who is *Nokes*? Who would take notice of *Nokes*?'

Hyde said, 'I believe Mr Nayler is actually proposing himself.'

'Not at all, Sir Edward,' Nayler protested. 'Whoever goes will be away six months at least. There are still the regicides in Europe to be dealt with. My duties compel me to remain here.'

'Really, sir, don't oblige us to beg you to do it!' Hyde sounded more amused than angry. 'I'm sure you already have a draft of the King's order prepared and know the name of the next ship departing to Boston.'

Nayler did not reply. He had both on the desk in his office.

Annesley said, 'I must say it seems the best plan, if Mr Nayler is willing to undertake the mission.'

Nayler bowed humbly. 'I will do whatever the Council commands me.'

And so the matter was settled: Nayler would sail to America as soon as possible and deliver the King's order to Governor Endecott, and would then remain in New England to make certain it was carried out.

Hyde asked him to wait behind after the others had gone.

'You have some particular animus against these men, Whalley and Goffe.'

'No, Sir Edward.'

'But you do, Mr Nayler, you do. I have watched your face whenever their names are mentioned. I shan't press you on the matter – merely advise you, from long experience, that obsession and good judgement seldom sit well together.'

Over the next few days, Nayler busied himself with preparations. He tried to persuade Captain Breedon to travel with him to Boston, but Breedon had business to do in London; even the prospect of earning the two hundred pounds' reward was not sufficient to induce him to make another voyage across the Atlantic so soon after the last. Instead, he gave Nayler the names of 'two good men, loyal to the King' resident in Massachusetts, whom he might rely upon for help. Nayler booked a single passage on the *King Harry*, due to sail from Gravesend on Thursday 7 March. He packed a trunk with clothes, some good hard cheese, three bottles of French brandy, Sir Walter Raleigh's *History of the World*, and two pistols with pouches of bullets and powder. From the Treasury he drew two hundred pounds in gold and a promissory note that any expenses incurred by the bearer would be paid by His Majesty's government.

All he lacked was the mandate from the King. Unfortunately, the court had transferred to Hampton Court for a week's hunting and His Majesty did not wish to be disturbed. On the night of Tuesday the fifth, the King returned to Whitehall. All the following day, Nayler lingered outside the royal apartments waiting for the mandate to be drawn up, signed and sealed. He allowed himself a fantasy that he might be summoned for a word of good wishes. But when Hyde emerged from his audience, he told him that His Majesty had just now gone to King Street to visit Mrs Palmer.

Eventually the document was delivered to him by a junior clerk from the Secretary of State's office. It was addressed *To our trusty and well-beloved the present governor, or other magistrate or magistrates of our plantation in New England.*

CHARLES R. Trusty and well-beloved – We greet you well. We being given to understand that Colonel Whalley and Colonel Goffe, who stand here convicted of the execrable murder of our royal father, of glorious memory, are lately arrived at New England, where they hope to shroud themselves securely from the justice of our laws; our will and pleasure is, and we do hereby expressly require and command you forthwith upon the receipt of these our letters, to cause both the said persons to be apprehended, and with the first opportunity sent over hither under a strict care. We are confident of your readiness and diligence to perform your duty; and so bid you farewell. Given at our court at White-hall, the fifth day of March . . .

Nayler barely glanced at it before he slid it into its leather case. *Remember it is the office you serve and not the man.* He left the palace without saying goodbye.

That night, he slept badly. The following morning, after he had dressed, he unhooked the miniature of Sarah and held it in his palm. He weighed whether to slip it into his pocket. But Hyde's words had struck home. Perhaps his judgement was becoming clouded. That would never do. This was an official mission, not a voyage of personal revenge. He replaced the portrait on the wall.

His servant was waiting in the passage with a boy to carry out his trunk. Nayler locked his apartment and followed them through the garden to the Thames, where a boat was moored at the pier to take him downriver to Gravesend. It was a fair day for a voyage – some warmth in the breeze, a hint of spring. As they rowed into the middle of the river and caught the current, the city gave way to open country, and he felt his spirits lift.

By mid afternoon, he was aboard the *Prince Harry*, in his tiny for-ward cabin just above the hold, watching the sailors stow his trunk beneath his hammock. They treated him with great politeness – to have a rare private cabin was proof that he must be important – and the first officer relayed an invitation to dine with the captain, which he declined. After they had gone, he found that his chest made a useful step to climb up into his hammock. The deck was barely a foot above his head. He could hear passengers coming aboard, crewmen shouting to one another, barrels being rolled across the planks. The ropes of the hammock tautened against his back and the sides of his body, the canvas enfolded him; he closed his eyes and fell immediately asleep.

He awoke many hours later to darkness. Rocking in his cradle, he listened to the creaking timbers. He had no notion of time.

He had to twist his body to escape the hammock, dangling one leg at a time, lowering his feet until he stood swaying with the motion of the ship. They were at sea. High tide must have risen along the Thames estuary. The ship had cast off while he was still unconscious.

He opened his cabin door and lurched along the gangway. He had to crouch. There was barely five feet of space. From either side came heavy snoring. He had a vague impression of long white bundles suspended in the shadows, like giant chrysalises waiting to mutate. He reached the ladder and grabbed hold of it to steady himself. Looking up through the hatch, he saw a square of stars. Carefully he climbed the rungs to the deck – to the cool night and the wind and the dark: no lights, no trace of land, no crew that he could see, just a sensation of movement as they ploughed their way westwards through the void towards the edge of the world.

PART TWO

CHASE

1661

CHAPTER FOURTEEN

EVEN ON THAT first morning, when their route led straight across the snowbound Massachusetts plain – flat country dotted with great oaks and beeches, terrain no more arduous than an English park in midwinter – Ned struggled to keep pace with the two younger men. His legs ached from pushing through the drifts; sweat froze clammy on his face; his beard became rimed with frost; his heart was an iron ball pounding in his breast. At noon, when they reached the edge of the forested mountain, the going became much harder, the path climbing between tall pines whose bare trunks towered like pillars to a gloomy canopy as high as a cathedral roof.

Gookin entered the forest first, leading their horse. Will followed. Ned lagged in the rear, treading in their footsteps. Every so often they had to stop and wait for him to catch up. As soon as he drew level, he would wheezily assure them he was experiencing no difficulty. The fourth time it happened, he gave up the pretence and accepted Will's suggestion that he should ride. The other two shouldered the extra bags while he swayed in the saddle, humiliated and cursing his old bones.

The path was narrow, not wide enough for a wagon. Occasionally, somewhere in the silent forest, snow dislodged from the high branches and crashed to earth in heavy waterfalls of crystal. Although Gookin had assured them they were following the ancient Indian trail from Boston Bay to the interior, a route he claimed to know well, they seemed to keep doubling back on themselves, and Ned suspected they were lost. But gradually the old soldier in him grasped the cunning of it – how they followed the bank of a river for what seemed a pointless distance until they came to a spot where a tree had been felled to make a bridge across it, or the way huge boulders had been rolled into position to form stepping stones over low-lying land that would be a swamp when it wasn't frozen. The wisdom and labour of hundreds of years – thousands, maybe – was collected in that tortuous negotiation with the obstacles of nature.

Once the light started to fade, Gookin called a halt beside a lake. While the colonels collected firewood, he unpacked a net, found himself a stout branch, and ventured carefully out onto the ice. They stopped their work to watch. As soon as the ice began to crack, he took half a pace backwards and used the branch to smash a wide hole, then cast his net. Ten minutes later, he was on the bank with six fish, writhing against the thin mesh, silvery in the gathering dark. He held his catch aloft in triumph. 'God has created a land of such plenty, a man need only reach out a hand and he will provide.'

They lit a fire, and Will, inspired by the lake and the emptiness, led them in a meditation on the story of Jonah, three days entombed in the stomach of a whale. ' "Then Jonah prayed unto the Lord his God out of the fish's belly, and said, 'I cried by reason of my affliction unto the Lord, and he heard me; out of the belly of hell cried I, and thou heardest my voice.' " '

'Amen.'

'Amen.'

Out of the belly of hell cried I . . . That was right, thought Ned. For all its beauty, that was how it felt to struggle through this cold, unpeopled country.

They wrapped the fish in leaves and stewed them on the hot embers of the fire, and agreed that nothing had ever tasted so delicious. Afterwards, they shared a pipe of tobacco, then Gookin showed them how to make a bed in the Indian way, gathering dead leaves and moss, spreading a layer across the forest floor and stuffing the rest into the net so that it became a thick blanket under which they could all lie close together, to share their bodies' heat. It was surprisingly warm and dry. The fire floated red sparks towards the sky. Animals cried out, invisible in the darkness. They heard a wolf howl, and something large moving through the trees that Gookin said he thought might be a bear. They kept their guns close.

That was the first day.

The morning of the second was mostly spent skirting around the lake. They climbed to the summit of a ridge and descended the other side, emerging from the forest in the middle of the afternoon to discover another great parkland plain. Ned was on the horse again, the other two hunched under the weight they carried. The cloud had not lifted since first light – the sky grey and immense, the wind sharp and cold from the north-west, the flat land silent, like a calm white sea extending miles into the distance, criss-crossed by animal tracks.

Gookin set down his baggage, took out his compass, gestured to his left and set a course due west. The wind began to blow more strongly. After an hour or so, a dark smudge appeared in the snowy landscape a few miles ahead. They halted. Ned drew his telescope from inside his coat and the apparition resolved into what looked to be three long thatched barns. From the roof of each arose a curl of smoke. He dismounted and offered the spyglass to Gookin.

'Indians,' said Gookin, peering at the image. 'Camped in their wigwams beside the river for the fish that rise at the end of winter.'

'Should we change our direction?'

'On the contrary: it was my intention that we should find them.' He handed back the telescope. 'We shall seek shelter with them for the night.' He laughed at Ned's expression. 'Don't look so troubled! They are just as much a part of God's creation as you or I, and in need of our compassion to rescue them from their present state of barbarism and bring them to salvation.'

Still, Ned insisted he would walk the rest of the way, the easier to use his sword and pistols if necessary.

'How did such a savage race come to be in America?' mused Gookin, as they trudged three abreast towards the camp. 'That is the mystery for which I have searched the Scriptures for an answer. Their own legends tell of two young women who waded ashore a thousand years ago, and that the froth or foam of the water touched their bodies, causing them to become with child, that one brought forth a male and the other a female, that the two women died and left the earth and that the son and daughter were the first progenitors of their race.'

Will said, 'What heathen superstition.'

'Indeed. But then the question arises: from which of the sons of Noah *are* they descended? My own conception is that they are the descendants of one of the ten tribes of Israel we read of in the Book of Kings, whom the Assyrian tyrant Salmanasser expelled as captives from Samaria and transported to Asia. The truth will be revealed on the Day of Judgement, when all the hidden things will be made plain to the glory of God. In the meanwhile, we have made good Christians out of many Indians already, and in time we shall make many more. My friend John Eliot, the minister of Roxbury, is even now translating the Bible into Wampanoag, the language of the Massachusetts tribe.'

'That is a mighty task you have set yourselves.'

'Still, we must work to bring them to Christ, as the psalm exhorts us: "Ask of me and I will give thee the heathen for thine inheritance, and the uttermost parts of the earth for thy possession."'

'But you have left out the next verse,' said Will. '"Thou shalt break them with a rod of iron; thou shalt dash them in pieces like a potter's vessel."'

'I don't hold with that at all,' said Gookin, 'although I know some who take such a view.'

With that, he strode on, and no more words were spoken between them until they were almost at the Indians' camp.

The wigwams were surprisingly big, perhaps thirty feet long by fifteen high, and of a rounded elongated shape, like the keel of a ship turned upside down. But they were wretched-looking, Ned thought: bleak, windowless hovels clad in greyish strips of weathered bark, the snow around them melted into filthy slush. The Englishmen's approach had set the camp dogs barking. A pair of scrawny hounds came loping through the snow towards them, and crouched down in their path, growling. The horse shied, forcing them to a halt.

An animal skin covering the entrance to one of the huts was lifted, and half a dozen men dressed in furs filed out, carrying bows and arrows. They stood in a line, motionless, bowstrings drawn back, arrows pointed at the three travellers.

'God help us,' said Ned. 'Look at that.'

Gookin said, 'Wait here. I shall go and speak with them.'

He took one of his bags from the horse and set off towards the encampment, his hand held up in greeting. Ned felt under his coat for his pistol.

'Don't,' said Will. 'We cannot fight them off. There are too many.'

Gookin reached the Indians, set down his bag and raised both hands. He spoke to the tallest of the natives. The bows were lowered. He picked up his bag and followed the men inside.

Ned let go of his pistol. He turned around, scanning the terrain. The contrast with the darkening sky made the snow seem luminous, unearthly. He could hear a river flowing somewhere behind the trees that lay just beyond the camp – in full spate by the sound of it, too fast to freeze. There was nowhere they could run. 'Dear Will,' he muttered, 'what is this land to which I have brought us?'

They waited a long while in the biting wind, and by the time the flap opened again, it was almost too gloomy to make out Gookin. Silhouetted by the red glow of the fire behind him, he beckoned and shouted to them that it was safe. They walked towards him.

'It is all arranged. I have bought us grain for the horse, and two days' food for the journey. We can have shelter and a meal for tonight. Come in out of the cold.'

He lifted the mat. Ned and Will exchanged a glance, then ducked and warily went inside. Gookin dropped the flap behind them.

The effect upon their chilled bodies, and upon eyes that had grown used to the dark, was sudden and overwhelming – the heat from the fire, blazing in the centre of the hut, the soft yellow glow lighting the faces of perhaps twenty Indian men, women and children, all staring at them; the smoky air rising towards the hole in the roof; the smell of roasting fish and maize. The walls were hung with bear and deer skins. The floor was bare earth, but dry and pounded hard. On it stood six large raised wooden platforms similarly draped with skins and blankets. Gookin ushered the two officers towards the fire.

'Admit it, Ned, is this not the warmest you have been all winter?'

'Aye,' Ned conceded, holding his hands out to the heat and looking around him. 'Warmer than any house in Cambridge, that's for sure.'

Gookin said something in the natives' tongue to the tallest Indian, who seemed to be the chief of the group, an imposing figure, sharp-faced, with black hair pulled off his forehead and tied at the back, and deep-set jet-black eyes. He wore a skin over his shoulders and a kind of apron around his midriff; otherwise, he was naked. He gestured to the bed at the furthest end of the hut, where a young woman was feeding her baby, and uttered a few rapid words.

'He says we are to sleep there, and they will bring us food.'

As they approached, the woman covered her breast and slipped away to join the others. Will stared after her. He couldn't help himself. *That heathen girl nursing her child in this savage place is better off than I. How can such a thing be possible?* He briefly closed his eyes. *O Lord, help me to endure Thy plan for us and better understand it.*

Ned set down his bag and lay on the bed. He put his hands behind his head, stretched out his legs and sighed with contentment. 'This will suit us very well. There's more than room enough for three.'

An elderly woman brought them food in wooden bowls – pieces of fish mixed into a pottage of maize and kidney beans and ground-up nuts, very hot, which they had to eat with their fingers, the fish full of small bones that needed to be extracted from their mouths before they swallowed. The taste was strange, and not especially pleasant, but the food filled their bellies and was a better diet, Ned had to concede, than the bread and cheese that had been the usual nightly rations of the New Model Army on the march. Little wonder the heathens looked so fit and lean. Afterwards he licked his fingers and asked Gookin the Massachusetts words for 'fish' and 'good'. He practised the pronunciation, then shouted up to the watching Indians: '*Námás! Wuñne!*' He had to repeat himself a couple of times before he was understood.

Several of the natives laughed and shook their heads. Curiosity satisfied, they turned away to eat their own food, the entertainment of watching the three strange Englishmen over for the evening.

A few minutes later – exhausted, warm, sated – Gookin and the colonels were fast asleep, their mouths agape, the sound of their snoring easily audible at the other end of the wigwam, to the renewed amusement of their hosts.

They walked for the next four days. The further west they penetrated, the milder the weather became and the quicker the snow thawed – not that it made travelling easier, with the mud sucking at their boots and the rivers high with meltwater. They subsisted on the fish they netted when they stopped for the night, and on their bags of *nokehick*, the Indians' parched corn, for which Gookin had bartered a small mirror and four ounces of tobacco: a handful of the grain for each man, mixed with hot water, was enough to stave off cold and hunger. When the wind was sharp, or it started to rain, Gookin showed them how to build a shelter in the Indian way, collecting pine boughs and arranging them in the manner of a miniature wigwam.

On the Friday morning, Gookin suddenly raised his hand and halted them in the forest. 'We are drawing close to our destination.' He pointed to a large flat boulder standing alone beside the path. There seemed no reason why it should be there, other than that it had been dropped from Heaven. That, he said, was Pulpit Rock. From it, ministers had preached to the earliest expeditions of settlers trekking to the interior, and braving the savages who surrounded them, to found their new world (Ezekiel, chapter 37: 'And the heathen shall know that I the Lord do sanctify Israel, when my sanctuary shall be in the midst of them for evermore').

'Consider,' said Gookin, 'what fierceness of faith it took for men and women to travel all that distance from England, knowing nothing of what awaited them, and to walk into this untamed land! Only God's elect possess the spirit to conquer this place.'

And there were other sights he showed them the following day – Black Pond, where the pine and cedar swamps made the water dark as coal, and Crystal Pond, where in contrast it was so clear they could see shoals of fish teeming close to the bottom, as plentifully wondrous as in the Garden of Eden.

It was on the Sunday morning, the sixth day of their journey, after they had been walking for an hour, that they heard a rushing noise in the distance beyond the edge of the forest. They quickened their steps and came out of the treeline to confront a river, more than a hundred yards across, majestic in the wilderness, brown with melted ice and snow, running high against its banks. Twigs and branches swirled past them in the foaming current as fast as a man on horseback and were borne away downstream.

They contemplated it in awe.

'Gentlemen,' announced Gookin, with a modest flourish of his hand, 'the Connecticut.'

It seemed propitious that they should have reached it on the Lord's Day. They knelt and gave thanks. Then Will and Gookin shouldered their bags, Ned once again mounted the mare, and they set off southwards, following the course of the river. A mile or

so further on, over on the opposite bank, the roofs of an English settlement appeared in the distance. Gookin told them it was
Windsor, but on the Connecticut rather than the Thames. When
they drew level, Ned studied it through his telescope – a few dozen
dreary wooden houses, a meeting house with a bell tower, and, on
the river's edge, a ferry. It seemed to him impossible that it might
attempt to cross the Connecticut in full spate, but Gookin assured
him it would, that it was connected to a chain that was laid over
the riverbed and was designed to keep the path to Boston open
even in the foulest weather. Sure enough, a few minutes later, a
man appeared and began to haul the platform towards them.

He was the first Englishman they had encountered in nearly
a week. Unlike the taciturn ferryman on the Charles River, he
was young and inclined to be talkative. But Gookin had already
cautioned the colonels against revealing themselves or their destination. 'I do not know the folk of this part of the state, or their
mood. Remember the price on your heads. It would be best if
you were once again plain Mr Richardson and Mr Stephenson,
as you were on the *Prudent Mary.*' So to each of the ferryman's
questions – how far had they travelled? Where were they headed?
Were they strangers to Connecticut? – they replied in monosyl-
lables, until eventually he gave up the effort and simply hauled
them with strong arms towards the shore. The current swirled
against the ferry's side, occasionally breaking in waves across the
platform. Huddled in his leather army coat, his boots soaked, it
struck Ned for the first time that this would be their lives from
now on – to be suspicious of everyone they met, to remember
always to conceal their true identities, to turn away all enquiries
with a curt yes or no, or silence. How long could they endure it?

They landed on the western bank and paid the boy the fare
he demanded – eightpence for the horse, twopence for each

passenger. At Gookin's urging, they did not linger in Windsor but kept their heads down and pressed on south, trudging along a rutted cart track beside the river for a couple of hours until in the middle of the afternoon they crossed a meadow and reached the outskirts of Hartford. The settlement looked much like Cambridge, only larger and more densely packed with wooden houses, its muddy streets lined with dirty bolsters of compacted snow. Nobody was out of doors. The road branched off from the river and took them up a hill to a large open space in front of a meeting house, from which came the sound of a psalm being chanted loudly. It sounded as if the entire town was gathered inside.

Will said, 'Would that we could join them!'

Gookin shook his head. 'Too great a risk.' He led them away from the meeting house, along a narrower road towards a large dwelling at a junction that he said was Governor Winthrop's. 'He has another farm on the coast at New London, but he is mostly here for state business. Let's hope this is one of those days.'

It was a familiar arrangement – a fenced lot of several acres with an orchard and a paddock, a house with a yard and outbuildings. Gookin took them into a barn where they could wait out of sight. While he went off to the house to look for signs of occupancy, the colonels once more found themselves reclining on straw beside a dozen cattle. Ned pulled off his boots and removed his stockings and tried to wring them dry. His feet were numb. He said, 'Would you mind, my boy?' Will knelt in front of him, tugged off his gloves and tried to massage some warmth back into them.

Presently they heard the gate unlatch and girlish voices in the yard. They both went over to the barn door to peer through the cracks. A couple – Mr and Mrs Winthrop, presumably – had returned with five young daughters, the oldest in her mid teens, all swaddled against the cold. Winthrop was shaking Gookin's hand. It was impossible to hear what he was saying. He put his arm around his visitor's shoulders and steered him into the house. His family followed. The door closed.

A long time seemed to pass. The daylight faded. The barn became gloomy. Ned put on his boots and damp stockings and lay back down on the straw. He closed his eyes, but he was too exhausted to sleep. Will stayed at the door. Presently Ned heard him whisper, 'Someone's coming.' He retreated to the middle of the barn and helped his father-in-law to his feet.

Ned was still brushing hay from his coat as Gookin entered, followed by a stout man in his middle fifties, carrying a lamp. He lifted it and shone it in the regicides' faces, at the same time revealing his own – long and narrow, full of shrewdness and intelligence. His prominent nose, exaggerated by the flickering lamp, immediately put Ned in mind of Cromwell's.

'Governor,' said Gookin, 'allow me to present Edward Whalley and William Goffe.' He turned to the colonels. 'There seemed no point in maintaining the pretence that you are any other than you are.'

Ned noticed that Winthrop did not offer them his hand. 'We are sorry, sir, for putting you in this position.'

Winthrop didn't speak, but continued to examine them

'I've explained the situation to the governor,' said Gookin. He rubbed his palms uneasily. 'Unfortunately, he doesn't think it possible for you to stay in Connecticut.'

In his dismay, Will laid his hand on Ned's arm.

Winthrop set down the lamp and cleared his throat. 'Forgive me, gentlemen. If the risk were mine alone, I wouldn't hesitate. But I have a responsibility to the people of this colony. There's certainly much sympathy for your cause. Even so, I cannot guarantee that some Judas wouldn't be tempted by a reward of two hundred pounds. And that would bring the wrath of the government in England down upon all our heads. You can shelter here tonight – Daniel assures me that no one in the town has seen you – but you must move on before first light. I'm sorry.'

'Move on?' Ned repeated, dully. 'Move on where exactly?'

Gookin said, 'Well, that is the root of the matter. The governor suggests New Haven.'

'And how much further on is that?'

'Another forty miles.'

Will groaned. Ned said, 'Why would we be any safer in New Haven than Connecticut?'

Winthrop said, 'It is an independent colony, founded twenty years ago on strict principles drawn from the Scriptures. They don't acknowledge the King's authority. Indeed, they don't acknowledge any authority save God's. I know the minister there, John Davenport. I was due to send him some medicines in any case. I'll arrange for a local man to guide you.'

Will turned to Gookin in surprise. 'You'll not be coming with us, Dan?'

'I don't know the way so well.' Gookin looked embarrassed. 'Besides, I promised Mary I'd be home within two weeks. You'll be in safe hands with a local guide, I assure you.'

Winthrop did not invite them to sleep in the house, but instead returned with bread and cheese, beer and blankets and a lamp. Gookin, although offered a bed indoors, refused the invitation and insisted on remaining with the colonels, despite their attempts to persuade him otherwise. 'I've shared your hardships this far. I'll not desert you at the last.'

Will led them in a meditation on Matthew, chapter 6: 'Behold the fowls of the air: for they sow not, neither do they reap, nor gather into barns; yet your heavenly Father feedeth them.'

For a final time, the three lay close together for warmth. The other two were quickly asleep, but Ned stayed awake for an hour or more. Although he had said nothing to Winthrop, he knew John Davenport, by reputation at least. His sister, Jane, had lived in his colony for many years. Her husband, William Hooke, had been his assistant. And although she had been careful in what she said – and Hooke himself had always spoken of Davenport as a true man of God – Ned had detected a certain coolness in her attitude towards the founder of New Haven. Now he came to think of it, he remembered that it was Jane who had been the more determined to return to England. He turned the matter over in his mind without coming to any definite conclusion save that they had no choice and should be grateful that the Lord in his unfathomable wisdom seemed to be leading them to the one man in the whole of America who might be willing to protect them.

He woke in the pre-dawn darkness to a lamp being shone in his face. Winthrop was bending over him. He had a man with him, thirty or so, short and broad-shouldered. 'This is Simon Lobdell, a Hartford citizen who knows New Haven well. Simon, these are the men you'll take.' The governor did not offer their names, and something in Lobdell's tight-lipped manner suggested he had been instructed not to enquire who they were.

Ned rose, stiff-limbed, and went through the motions of departure, rolling up his bedding and heaving his bag onto the back of Lobdell's horse, for he was determined to walk this final stretch. And then it was time to say goodbye. It was a formality with Winthrop, but when it came to hugging Gookin, he found that he was weeping, and could not trust himself to say much without breaking down entirely.

'God bless you, Dan, and thank you. And if we do not meet again . . .' His voice cracked, and he had to break off the embrace and turn his back.

'We shall meet again, my friend,' said Gookin. 'Be in no doubt. In this world or the next.'

Ned did not turn around. He raised his hand in acknowledgement and walked out into the yard. He wiped his eyes and listened to Will saying his goodbyes. Presently his son-in-law joined him, then Lobdell emerged and took the reins of the horse, and they followed the clip-clop of its hooves through the gate and out into the street without looking back.

It was difficult to see much in the darkness. The rutted mud had frozen into ridges overnight, hard as iron, that could break a man's ankle if he wasn't careful. They stumbled down the rough road, past the vague shapes of the houses on either side, setting off a barking dog. A light appeared in an upstairs window, and instinctively, despite the night, they pulled down the brims of their hats and bent their heads. Somewhere in the town, a cock was crowing. They descended a hill. The air was cold with damp, the Connecticut invisible, though they could hear it rushing past close by. The road ran near to it and took them away from the town.

After an hour, a greyish gleam appeared in the sky, faintly illuminating a sawtooth ridge of pine trees to their left. That meant they were heading due south, thought Ned. Otherwise, he had no idea where they were. Lobdell's squat, wide shape took form in front of them. The man could be leading them anywhere. They had accepted him on trust. But who was he? He lengthened his stride to catch up with Will, and whispered, 'Is it really possible he doesn't know our names?'

'Why would Winthrop wish to give away our identities?'

'Even so, surely he must guess who we are? Notice of the reward on our heads has reached every corner of New England.'

'You think he would betray us?'

'Why not? He cannot be a rich man, else he would not have taken on this assignment at a few hours' notice. Two hundred pounds would set him up for life.'

Will took his time replying. 'We are cast adrift on a great sea, Ned. We must trust in God.'

'Aye, we trust in God. Of course, at all times. But do we trust in Mr Lobdell?'

There was no answer to that. After a little while, Ned dropped back to his usual place at the rear, and they marched on in silence until the path parted from the Connecticut and they struck across country.

CHAPTER FIFTEEN

THE NEXT THREE days passed much as had the previous six, save that the trail was wider and easier, the snow had melted, and they no longer enjoyed the knowledgeable companionship of Daniel Gookin to ease the journey. They spent the first night in an Indian wigwam with four young men of the Quinnipiac tribe, who sold them fish and showed the colonels how they had caught them – in a weir of stones they had built in the shallow river running off the nearby lake, which gradually narrowed to a V shape and trapped the fish as they ran downstream.

On the second night, they found an empty wigwam beside the trail and ate the last of the *nokehick* Gookin had purchased from the Massachusetts Indians. By late afternoon on the third day, they could tell they were nearing the coast from the seagulls that appeared crying overhead. But Lobdell insisted it was too late to press on to New Haven, since the path ahead was treacherous in the dark – it was the longest speech he had addressed to them – so instead they built a shelter of branches. Will tried his hand at fishing and caught four trout in their net. Afterwards they stuffed the mesh with leaves and moss to make a blanket, as Gookin had showed them, and fell asleep beside the fire.

The following morning, they set off once more at first light, climbing a rocky trail through a pine forest that eventually levelled off and then began to descend quite steeply, so that they were obliged to twist sideways and edge their way down the incline to avoid breaking into a headlong run. They rounded a bend, and suddenly, between the branchless columns of the pines, far in the distance a wide plain came into view, and beyond it a grey sea with scudding white waves stretching to the horizon. Ned called ahead to Lobdell, 'Is that New Haven?' Lobdell half turned, grunted, nodded that it was.

Ned took out his telescope. The town was still some miles away. Even so, it was possible to make out a distinctive grid-like pattern of wide streets and houses grouped together, nestling close to a harbour, quite different to the other settlements they had seen in New England. How had Winthrop described it? *An independent colony, founded twenty years ago on strict principles drawn from the Scriptures.* He liked that notion. He snapped shut the telescope and scrambled down the slope to catch up with the others.

Once they were on the plain, it was clear to see what had drawn the colony's founders to the spot. Bounded by the sea to the south and by ramparts of hills with sheer reddish-brown cliffs to the west, the east and the north, Will declared it reminded him of the plain of Judaea with the holy mount rising above it. There were groves of shrub oaks filled with wild turkeys and partridges. Clear streams ran across a flat landscape dotted with cattle, sheep, pigs and goats, grazing between fields recently ploughed and ready to be planted. A sharp breeze blew off the sea and carried a scent of brine.

Half an hour later, they crossed a wooden bridge with a sluice gate beneath it and entered the town. Lobdell took them on a dog-leg route, left then right, past a whipping post and stocks, to a large corner house on the edge of the settlement, overlooking a creek and a meadow.

'This is Mr Davenport's house.'

It was a veritable mansion, with at least six tall brick chimneys rising above the second storey. He unloaded their bags from the saddle, together with another, which he said contained the medicines from Governor Winthrop for Reverend Davenport, piled them at the side of the road, bade the colonels goodbye, and rode away without another word.

They watched him go until he had rounded the corner. Ned murmured, 'Off to claim his reward, do you reckon?'

'If so, there's naught we can do about it.'

They collected their baggage, let themselves in through a gate and approached the front door. Chickens pecked around a yard. From beyond the meadow came the sound of waves breaking on the shore. The place seemed deserted. Will said, 'Shall we reveal our true selves from the start?'

'Do we have a choice? If he refuses to take us in, we might as well surrender to the King. Because I for one cannot wander this wild country another day longer.'

Ned turned, wiped his hands on his coat, set his shoulders and knocked loudly on the door. From the size of the place, he expected a maid, but after half a minute, the door was opened by an elderly figure who could only have been Davenport himself – garbed in black, with white preaching bands at his collar and a black cap set tight upon a profusion of curly white hair, wispy as thistledown. His face was round and pale and squashed, somewhat pug-like; his eyes bulged behind a tiny pair of green-tinted spectacles. He took in the regicides, glanced at their luggage, and clasped his hands in prayer.

'At last,' he said.

Ned removed his hat. 'Reverend Davenport? We are—'

'Yes, yes, I have already guessed who you are. I have been waiting six months for you to find your way to me.' Davenport reached out and seized Ned's hand in both of his. 'Welcome!' And over Ned's shoulder to Will: 'Welcome, both!' He threw back his head and laughed. 'God be praised that I should have lived to see this day!'

For an old man, Davenport exuded a remarkable energy. He insisted on carrying in their bags himself, called to his wife – 'Elizabeth, come see what the Lord has brought us!' – told them that they must stay as long as they wished – 'Until the Second Coming, which is only five years off, may I be spared to see it!' – and conducted them upstairs. On the landing, Mrs Davenport was standing at an open door with a towel and a bowl in her hands. Behind her, a young man was lying in bed propped up on pillows. The curtains were drawn. A candle lit a dead-white face. 'Elizabeth, John – here are Colonel Whalley and Colonel Goffe, sent hither by God as a gift: may he be thanked and praised for evermore!' He added, confiding, 'My son John is often sickly.'

John raised a shaky hand in greeting.

Ned said, 'Governor Winthrop asked us to bring some medicine for you.'

'That is good of him – very good. He is quite the apothecary. So, you have walked from Hartford? Come, let me show you your accommodation.' Davenport led them along the passage. 'This will be your room, Colonel Whalley.' He threw open a door. 'And yours is next to it, Colonel Goffe. I shall tell the servants to bring up your luggage, and you may divide your belongings later at your leisure.'

The colonels barely had time to register this undreamt-of luxury – a room each for the first time in a year – before Davenport was marching them back along the passage, past his wife, who had yet to speak, and down the stairs. 'I must take you around the town while the weather holds.'

It seemed discourteous to object, although they would have liked nothing more than to rest for an hour or two in their own beds. They followed him out of the house and observed how he strode through the wide streets, acknowledging the townspeople, who uncovered their heads as he passed. As he walked, he spoke of the plan of the new Jerusalem as described in the Book of Revelation: a grid of nine squares, which had been replicated here on a grand scale, the blocks all half a mile wide, with a dozen or so houses in each, and each with its own spiritual leader, chosen by himself. 'For as it says in Numbers, "Every man of the Children of Israel shall pitch by his own standard with the ensign of their father's house . . . about the tabernacle they shall pitch."' He stopped and stretched out his hand. 'And this is our tabernacle.'

By now they had been walking briskly for several minutes, up a slight slope away from the sea, and Ned was out of breath. In the centre of the town, the ninth square had been left untouched – a grassy open space, its dimensions identical, as Davenport explained it, to the sanctuary in chapter 43 of Ezekiel – and in the middle of it stood the wooden meeting house, fifty-two feet square, or thirty cubits, to copy the dimensions of the tabernacle in Exodus. It was two storeys high, with a sharp roof and a lookout tower: 'So that we may still keep watch for Indians while we meet – not that they give us much trouble, poor savages. They know our militia is strong.'

He proposed that next he would show them the harbour, but the sky was darkening, and to Ned's relief, Will asked if it might be possible to save that pleasure for some other time. Davenport, clearly unused to having his wishes thwarted, looked irritated. 'Very well. However, there is one thing more you must see while we are close.'

He led them over the green towards the meeting house. After a hundred yards or so, he stopped and indicated a slab of grey stone. A posy of snowdrops had been laid before it. They bent to read the inscription.

Theophilus Eaton, Esqr. Govr. Dec'd Jan'y 7, 1657, Ætat. 67.
Eaton so fam'd, so wise, so just,
The Phœnix of our world, here lies his dust,
This name forget, N. England never must.

'It was with Mr Eaton that I founded this colony. He was a man of piety and great wealth, all of which he placed in the service of God. Ours were the first houses built here, side by side, to the east of the tabernacle, just where the Bible tells us Moses and Aaron pitched their tents.' He spread his arms wide. 'New Haven is Christ's millennial kingdom. Here he will come in the year of grace 1666, when the saints are resurrected, and here he will reign for a thousand years.'

Ned could not resist asking, 'And which of you was Moses?'

Davenport's eyes widened in surprise behind his green-tinted spectacles. 'Naturally, *I* am Moses.'

From the outset, Ned entertained certain misgivings about their new host, although he kept them to himself. Davenport had been a Puritan minister in London in the 1620s, and then in Holland, but had been ejected from his church in The Hague because of the strictness of his views on infant baptism, which he held should be reserved solely for the children of the Elect: no one else could enter the Kingdom of Heaven. He had emigrated to Boston in the 1630s, fallen out with the church authorities there as well, and sailed along the coast with Eaton and their followers to create New Haven. But Ned could see that Will found his views congenial: like Davenport, he was a millenarian, and believed that in 1666, the Year of the Beast, as foretold in the Book of Revelation, Christ would return to earth. Ned himself did not subscribe to the doctrine, but he knew insufficient theology to argue about it.

Besides, he was beholden to Davenport for his hospitality. He reckoned the mansion must consist of two dozen rooms, maybe more – half of them, as far as he could tell, unused. Davenport claimed his study boasted a thousand volumes. Ned's own chamber looked out to the broad harbour and the distant sea. The ailing John, who never emerged, was the family's only child; at least, no others were ever mentioned. Elizabeth Davenport, tiny and white-haired, flitted wraith-like between the kitchen, her son's room, and the room in which she slept (not with her husband, he noticed). There was a pair of servants, a middle-aged married couple, who lived in their own part of the house, and who shrank back into the shadows with downcast eyes whenever the colonels appeared. The food was poor. The place was cold. There was an odd, unpleasant odour. Despite the number of chimneys, fires were seldom lit. Taken altogether, it was a strange household.

Three days after their arrival, on the Lord's Day, Davenport took them to the crowded meeting house, where to Ned's surprise, he introduced them by their real names. He quoted Hebrews, chapter 23 – 'Be not forgetful to entertain strangers; for thereby some have entertained angels unawares' – and preached a sermon full of dread and terror: 'For the torments of the devils, and punishments of the damned in Hell, and all the plagues inflicted upon the wicked upon earth, issue from the righteous and revenging justice of the Lord, and he doth own such execution as his proper work.'

Afterwards, on the green, he summoned the leading citizens of the town to meet his eminent guests, among them Nicholas Street, who had replaced William Hooke as assistant minister and headteacher at the town's school, and William Jones, the grave young man who had sailed over with the colonels on the *Prudent Mary* and whose father had been executed the previous October for signing the King's death warrant. They had got to know Jones well during the long weeks at sea. He was newly married to Hannah Eaton, daughter of New Haven's co-founder, and had moved into Eaton's house – the only mansion larger than the Davenports'. When Ned tried to offer his commiserations for the loss of his father, Jones held up his hand to stop him. Like Will's, his voice had a Welsh lilt.

'No need to mourn. I'm told he was arrested whilst walking quite openly in Finsbury Park. He made no attempt to escape. My mother writes that he embraced his fate on the scaffold like a groom on his wedding night, and now he is a saint. I shall meet him again in due course.'

Street said, 'And how long do you intend to remain in New Haven, Colonel Whalley?'

'For as long as you will have us, Mr Street. We have no plans, except to survive and to serve the Lord. I still have hopes of a political change in London.'

Will said, 'We are willing to work, of course.'

'Did you have occupations before you joined the army?'

'We did,' said Ned, 'a draper and a salter, although all we've known for nigh on twenty years is soldiering.'

'But that is a skill you can practise here,' said Davenport. 'We have great need of experienced soldiers. You must train our militia.'

There were encampments of the Quinnipiac tribe all around New Haven – in the hills to the north; along the eastern shore of the wide inlet that formed the town's natural harbour, where they maintained an ancient burial ground; and at Oyster Point, to the west. As a precaution against attack, every male citizen of the colony between the ages of sixteen and sixty – some three hundred men in the town alone – had been issued with a gun, powder, flint, four fathoms of matchlock, twenty-four bullets and a sword. Four cannons and a chest of pikes were stored in the meeting house. Each man was obliged to give up six days a year for training. By chance, the next was fixed for Wednesday of that week.

The two colonels fell naturally into their former roles in the New Model Army. Will oversaw the pike- and musket-men, instructing them in drill and target practice. Ned lectured on tactics to the cavalry in a meadow just outside the town. To sit again on a horse, to draw up a line of riders, to pass in front of them, to look each man in the eye – it brought back memories of the first winter of the Civil War . . .

The grey afternoon in October '42 when he had been ditching on his farm in the flatlands of Essex that ran down to the Thames estuary – poor land: he never made a go of it – and horsemen had appeared low on the horizon who turned out to be Oliver and his eldest son, also named Oliver, and his brother-in-law, Valentine Walton, come to urge him to join the cavalry regiment that Cromwell was raising in Cambridgeshire to fight the King.

The way Katherine had pleaded with him not to go, following him around, carrying the baby while he packed his bag – *you're two years past forty, you know nothing of soldiering, you will be killed for certain, you will leave me a widow with four little ones to look after and no money to do it.* 'Besides, your cousin Cromwell is half mad, you've said it often enough yourself' (this spoken quietly, with a glance at the window, beyond which Oliver sat impatiently on his mount).

The months of training in Ely, living under the Cromwells' roof, with Oliver and Betty and their six children, the seriousness of purpose and yet the laughter, the twice-daily prayers and the Scripture study, the endless interviewing of recruits, and Cromwell's fiery speeches: 'I will not deceive you that we fight for "King and Parliament" nor any suchlike nonsense, and I tell you now that if the King chances to be in the body of the enemy that we are to charge, I shall discharge my pistol upon him as at any other private person, and if your conscience will not permit you to do the like, I advise you not to list yourself in my troop or under my command.' Oliver did not care if the men who joined him knew how to fight: that could be taught. What could not be taught, and what he wanted most, was godly men, men of faith and discipline, who were prepared if needs be to die: 'For the man who is willing to die will always be your master.'

Ned looked out across the meadow of New Haven and saw exactly such men now. He demonstrated the tactics of the Ironsides' cavalry charge as Cromwell had developed them. The advance to be made in three lines. The troops in the first line to be at close order, every left-hand man's right knee to be locked under his right-hand man's left ham. The charge to be at a fast trot. No man to fire his pistol until he came within horse's length of the enemy. After firing, throw the pistol in their faces and fall on them with the sword. And then – the stroke that had transformed the balance of force on the battlefield – after sweeping through the enemy's line, halt, turn, and charge again.

He knew of course that such tactics were not fitted for New England, where the numbers of cavalry were so few and the enemy was likely to be merely Indians. But he was so caught up in the past, he performed the manoeuvres anyway, and the farmers and blacksmiths and shepherds of New Haven watched him in wonder, this legendary grizzled old soldier reliving his prime. When he had finished, they gave three cheers for Colonel Whalley.

'By the grace of God,' he said, much moved, 'if we had but two hundred friends such as you who would stand by us, we would have no fear of anyone, Old England or New.'

Perhaps that was what they should do, he thought that night, smoking a pipe in his room, looking at the glittering pathway of the bright moon reflected on the waters of the harbour: stop running away, raise a fresh New Model Army in America, proclaim a republic and stand and fight the King. And such was the false sense of security engendered by the atmosphere of New Haven, surrounded by like-minded people and far removed from the dangers in Boston, that he actually gave the idea serious consideration, to the extent of drawing up a list of forces that would be required. It was only later that he recognised the folly he had fallen into, a human trait he had long observed: that merely because one wishes to believe in a thing, it does not follow that it is true.

One evening over supper, Davenport described how the colony was administered. Under Mosaic Law, only those judged predestined to be saved could become members of the church, and only members of the church could vote or hold office. And as it was Davenport who judged who was predestined, and as he possessed the absolute power to excommunicate any whom he judged to have fallen short in their devotions, he effectively controlled the government. 'Ours is a theocratic state, the only colony in America in which the secular authorities must defer to the divine.'

'Would that we had imposed the same strictness in England when we had the chance,' Will said. 'If we had, we would not be here now.'

Ned considered it perhaps the most foolish remark he had ever heard his son-in-law make. Even Oliver would never have attempted to impose such a policy. But in keeping with his determination to avoid disagreement, he merely observed mildly that perhaps there was a difference between a community of a few thousand souls, who had emigrated precisely because they shared the same faith, and a diverse nation of several millions.

Nevertheless, there *was* an acting governor of the New Haven colony, and on Tuesday 26 March, nearly three weeks after the colonels' arrival in the town, the man who was unhappily discharging that responsibility, Mr William Leete, arrived at the Davenports' house with sobering news. He was a mournful-looking lawyer, not yet fifty, and he had ridden over from his home in the nearby town of Guilford, carrying with him a copy of the warrant that Governor Endecott had finally been obliged to issue in Boston for the arrest of 'the detestable regicides, Whalley and Goffe'. They passed it from one to another in dismay.

Davenport said, 'Endecott has no jurisdiction in New Haven. We shall ignore it. Let Massachusetts and Connecticut bend the knee to the King if they like. We acknowledge God alone.'

Leete rubbed his hands unhappily. 'You are right in principle, as always, Mr Davenport. But those states are established by royal charter, and ours, at present, is not – and if it becomes known that we are harbouring two men who signed the King's death warrant, it never will be.'

'We've existed here for twenty years without need of any charter.'

'For most of which time England was a commonwealth and the government sympathetic. Now I fear matters are very different.'

Davenport took the warrant, slowly tore it up and let the fragments flutter to the floor. 'That is what I think of Endecott and his warrant, and of Charles Stuart, for that matter, both first and second. Has Boston sent any men to carry out these arrests?'

'Not so far.'

'You see? They do not dare!'

'But they will come, Mr Davenport,' said Leete quietly, 'sooner or later. If not men from Boston, men from London. And brave and well armed though it is, our militia will not be sufficient to withstand them.'

'Oh William.' Davenport shook his head sadly. 'William, I am starting to fear for the state of your soul.'

Ned raised his hand. 'Might I say a word, as one of those who is the source of all this trouble?' The realisation of his own stupidity was almost as great a shock to him at that moment as the peril of their position. 'Our mistake – my mistake – was to move around New Haven so openly. We should have been more prudent – used false names, or better still stayed hidden out of sight until this hue and cry had died away.'

'You say that now!' said Will.

'I do say it now, Will, and I agree I should have said it earlier – we both should have said it. But we were worn out from our journey, and our instincts weren't as sharp as they ought to have been. Plainly we cannot continue to live here. So the old problem remains: where are we to go?' As he spoke, he sensed the outline of a plan beginning to form in his mind. He hesitated. 'Now I think of it, perhaps I do have a notion of what to do – the ghost of a notion, anyhow – although it would not be without risk; to you gentlemen as much as to us.' He stopped.

'We are not afraid of risk,' said Davenport. 'Go on.'

The colonels left New Haven the following morning on a pair of horses lent to them by Davenport, laden with all their baggage. Before they exited the town, they made a point of riding right the way around the green, saying thanks and farewell to everyone they recognised. A few people called out to ask where they were going. They did not answer directly, just shouted back that it was time to move on, 'perhaps to other shores'. When, soon afterwards, they were seen to set out along the westerly coastal road, it was naturally assumed that they must be heading for the Dutch colony, perhaps to take ship at New Amsterdam for Holland.

They travelled without a guide: the fewer who were in on the secret the better, and the trail, though winding, was at least easy to follow along the shoreline, the sea always breaking on the rocks to their left, the dark pine forest stretching away to their right. After ten miles, they came to the town of Milford, part of the colony of New Haven. They stopped at the general store and bought a few items from its owner, Micah Tomkins – a net, a knife, a small axe, a cooking pot – asked the distance to New Amsterdam, made some general conversation with the other customers concerning the weather and the state of the road, then left. On their way out, they noticed, pinned up on a board, the bulletin offering a reward for their capture. It was obvious from the way some of the men in the store stared at them, standing in their old buff-coloured leather army coats, that they had been recognised. Good.

They returned a little way along the road, dismounted, and led their horses into the forest for about a mile until they found a small clearing next to a stream. Here they collected wood, lit a fire and roasted some pieces of mutton, stuffed the net with leaves and moss, and lay down to wait. Will read his Bible. Ned smoked his pipe.

Around seven, when the sun went down, they packed up their camp and stamped out the embers of the fire. Their walk back to the road was accompanied by the sounds of the forest settling down for the night, the haunting cries of the whippoorwills and the croak of bullfrogs. The twisting coastal trail was hard to make out in the darkness. Their horses, unable to see, kept refusing to go forward, so that in the end they had to dismount and lead them. The waves crashed against the rocks. Even Ned, whose steady temperament was not usually prone to such fancies, sensed the Devil all around them.

It must have been midnight by the time they reached New Haven. A tiny scythe-blade of moon barely lit the wide grassy street. They passed thirteen houses, all in darkness, before they returned at last to Davenport's, where a candle lit an upstairs window. Nobody saw them go inside, and they did not venture out again for another five weeks. As far as the town was concerned, they had gone.

· CHAPTER SIXTEEN

R ICHARD NAYLER SAILED into Boston Bay on a sunny
afternoon on the last day of April, at the end of an eight-
week crossing of the North Atlantic.

Insofar as he had been able to picture his destination, in between
bouts of seasickness during that interminable and detestable
voyage, he had imagined a kind of primitive trading outpost of
timber buildings, with a wooden jetty and a bare church filled
with long-faced Puritans. It had been a surprise, therefore, to pass
a stone fortress protecting the harbour entrance with a battery of
thirty cannon, to proceed down a channel between large ships at
anchor, and to be confronted by a vista of wharfs and cranes and
warehouses stretching for half a mile. Behind the port, handsome
houses of red brick slid into view, with two large churches, the
entire settlement overlooked by a second fortress on a hill. And
beyond all that, receding into what seemed an infinite distance,
lay the plains and forests and rivers of the colony. He clenched the
gunwale of the *Prince Harry* and for the first time felt a sweat of
alarm at the task he had set himself.

Nor was his suffering quite finished yet, for no sooner had he stepped ashore than he quickly had to plant his feet apart to steady himself against the shock of the motionless earth. The impact travelled up his legs. The New World seemed to sway and dance around him. He bent over, hands on his knees, and vomited onto the quayside. After half a minute of spitting out bile, he straightened, wiped his mouth with the back of his hand, and looked to see if anyone had been watching. But the bustle of unloading and disembarking continued without a glance in his direction.

He squinted and tried to take his bearings.

A balmy day. An unusual brightness of light playing across the sparkling water. Vivid greens and blues. The cries of unfamiliar seabirds. A smell in the air he couldn't quite place – a strange, sweet spiciness.

England, and yet not England.

O my America! my new-found-land . . .

Once he felt reasonably sure he would not be sick again, he pulled his notebook out of his inside pocket and consulted the list of names Captain Breedon had given him in London. He found the address he wanted and repeated it to the sailor who had agreed to act as his porter. The rooming house occupied the central part of a terrace along a narrow street close to the harbour. A crowded public chamber was filled with tobacco smoke. Twenty men much like Breedon – merchants by the look of them, captains and shipowners – sat huddled at tables set with jugs of beer and wine. Several turned to look at him as he entered – the opening of the door having disturbed the motionless layers of smoke and sucked them towards the street – then went back to their pipes and their business.

The owner, a runtish cross-eyed man named Shadbricke, at first insisted he had no private rooms available. But when Nayler announced that Captain Breedon had sent him, and laid a gold coin upon the counter, Shadbricke (having tested it with his teeth) suddenly remembered that he did after all have an empty lodging. It was small and high up in the attic, but the door locked, and he wouldn't have to share it with anyone else. He wasn't asked to provide his name. The sailor carried his trunk on his back up the winding, narrow staircase; Nayler tipped him a shilling, locked the door behind him and lay down on the hard wooden bed.

The blankets were dirty and stank of stale bodies. He could hear rats rustling in the roof. He did not care. He felt his strength and confidence returning. These people could be bought – that was his discovery of the day. The land might be huge and strange and mostly Puritan, but it was pulsing with energy and greed. And he had money – plenty of money. He would catch his prey with gold.

Over the next several days, Nayler kept to his room and had his food and drink brought up to him. He needed to recover from the voyage. He also did not wish to show his face in public and so invite the sort of gossip that might alert Governor Endecott to the presence of a mysterious new arrival from England. He paid the potboy who served his meals to deliver two letters that had been written in London, at his request, by Captain Breedon to the pair of his Boston associates he had recommended. To each of these letters Nayler added a note in his own hand inviting the men to meet him at his rooming house at four o'clock on Friday afternoon. Each replied by return that they would be honoured to attend.

He felt it would give a poor impression of the seriousness of his mission to entertain them in his squalid chamber, so just before the appointed hour, he locked his door, descended to the ground floor and took a table in the corner close to the fire where he could keep an eye on the door. The room was gloomy, quieter than it had been on the day of his arrival. He asked for a lighted candle, three tankards and a jug of wine.

Breedon had already told him something of the men he was about to meet. Thomas Kellond was the younger of the two. Born to wealth in Devon, he had come to America to increase the family fortune. He owned a ship, a ninety-tonner, which he had named the *Charles*, an act that gave a fair clue to his politics. He was the first to arrive. Nayler recognised him from his age – 'middling twenties', according to Breedon – his fine clothes and the fact that he was alone. He rose and beckoned the young man over.

'Mr Kellond, is it?'

'Indeed. And you, I take it, are Mr Nayler?' Kellond spoke with a soft West Country burr.

'I am, sir.' They shook hands. 'Sit, please. Now then, will you take a drink with me?'

'It is a little early – but yes, why not?' He eyed the third tankard. 'You are expecting someone else?'

'Captain Thomas Kirke. Do you know him?'

'I do. Indeed, here he is.' Kellond gave a tilt of his chin towards an older man who had just come in and was standing in the doorway, looking about the room. He was around sixty, tall, stout and slightly bow-legged, with a ruddy, wind-blown face. Breedon's information was that Kirke had fought in the war on the King's side and had risen to the rank of colonel, then fled to New England when Cromwell took power. 'He's a solid fellow and knows the country well – better than does Kellond. You could not ask for two more devoted adherents to the Royalist cause.'

Kirke's gaze lighted on Kellond and he came across to join them. The three shook hands. Nayler said, 'Take the seat closest to the fire, Captain Kirke.' He finished pouring the wine. 'We should drink a toast. He raised his tankard. 'To the King.'

'The King.'

They drank. Nayler winced. The wine was sour. 'Well then, let us settle straight to business.' He looked around to make sure he would not be overheard. 'As our mutual friend Captain Breedon has explained in his letters, I am an officer of the Privy Council, charged with bringing to justice those criminals still wanted for the murder of the King's father. I've come from London with an order signed by His Majesty directing Governor Endecott to proceed at once to discover and arrest Colonel Edward Whalley and Colonel William Goffe. You've heard of them?'

Both men nodded. Kellond said, 'Their presence here has brought shame upon the whole colony.'

Nayler went on, 'Doubtless then you're also aware that Mr Endecott and the marshal general, Michelson, have been – how shall we put it? – *less than diligent* in their efforts to apprehend the traitors. Rather than go directly to the governor and give him a further opportunity for delay – and perhaps even to appoint a search party sympathetic to their cause – it's my intention to raise a group of reliable men to hunt down these murderers myself.' He leaned forwards. 'I would like you two gentlemen to organise and lead the chase.'

Kirke's eyes shone. He thumped the table. 'By God, the dogs must be made to pay!'

A man nearby turned to stare at them.

Nayler lowered his voice. 'For this service, I'm authorised to offer you a payment of fifty pounds each, a fifty-pound bonus if the regicides are caught, and the grant of two hundred and fifty acres of good farmland.'

The two men looked at one another. Kirke took a swig of wine and licked his lips. 'Well now, this is a formidable undertaking you are proposing, Mr Nayler, even at such a price. Might there be space for some improvement? Could we not share the reward money, perhaps?'

'I'm not here to haggle, Captain,' said Nayler. 'That's my offer, take it or not. If it's insufficient, I'm sure I'll find others to accept the commission for half the price. I'm told the Scotch are very agitated, against Whalley in particular.'

'Not so fast, sir,' said Kirke with a smile, 'not so fast. No need to take offence. Remember we are businessmen. Our instinct is to bargain.' He exchanged another look with Kellond, who gave a slight nod. 'Very well, out of our loyalty and devotion to the King, we agree to your proposal. But we must be defrayed for all expenses.'

'Agreed.'

'It won't be cheap.'

'I understand.'

Kellond said, 'Where are the colonels to be found?'

Was the fellow simple? wondered Nayler. 'If I knew that, Mr Kellond, I'd not be sitting here making such a generous offer to you. My intelligence is that they were last seen living openly in Cambridge, but that was some time ago. Doubtless they've moved on since.'

'I know for a fact that they have,' said Kirke. 'There was an attempt to take them one night in February – a raggedy, ill-thought-out affair, which the villains saw off easily enough by firing pistols. When our side went back to try again, there was no sign of them. Naturally, the Gookins deny all knowledge.'

'The Gookins?'

'Daniel and Mary Gookin. Theirs is the house where the colonels stayed, close to Harvard College. Gookin is a man of some prominence locally. He held office under Cromwell in England.'

Nayler took out his notebook and made a note of the name. He remembered Nokes saying that Gookin had sailed from England on the same ship as the colonels.

Kirke drained his wine and waited for his tankard to be refilled. 'My guess is they'll have headed west. The Puritans are very strong in Connecticut.'

'Connecticut.' Nayler wrote that down as well. He didn't care for how much Kirke was drinking. Who were these men – a simpleton and a toper? Was this the best that Breedon had to offer? 'What about New Haven? I know Whalley has a connection with the colony through his brother-in-law.'

'That's certainly a place to look – in New Haven they're fanatics against the King. They might also take a chance on the Dutch colony in New Netherland – the Calvinists there care neither for the English nor the King.'

Nayler asked Kirke to draw a map in his notebook showing where the places were and the distances between them. After that, the discussion got down to practicalities. How many men might it take to overpower two professional soldiers who were armed and desperate? Kirke suggested six at least. 'You said we were to lead the search, Mr Nayler. Will you be coming with us?'

'Of course. But I'll stay in the background. This should be a wholly New England affair.'

'And may I ask, sir – are you handy with a weapon?'

'I fought at Naseby. I carry a wound. But I can still use a sword and pistol.'

Kirke regarded him with respect. 'I was at Naseby myself. That was a bad day for England.'

'It was, Captain. And Whalley and Goffe were both there. So let us avenge our fallen friends.'

In the end, they settled on a hunting party of eight – the three of them, plus a guide ('I know just the man,' said Kirke, 'he has

Indian blood') and four others, to be paid five pounds each for their services. Nayler suggested they hire Scotchmen, as it seemed they would be up for a fight. The hunters would travel on horseback in order to cover the distance as fast as possible. Kellond undertook to provide the mounts and weapons, although Nayler warned him to be discreet: it was important that no inkling should reach the regicides in advance and give them time to move on – another reason why he didn't intend to approach the governor until they were ready to leave.

By six, their business was complete. They drank a final toast to the ruin of the King's enemies and agreed to reconvene at the same place and hour the following Monday. Just before Kirke and Kellond left, Nayler asked them where he might find the Gookins' house.

The next morning, Nayler sent the potboy to arrange with the ostler for the hire of a horse, and an hour later he was riding out of Boston along the road beside the Charles River. He was conscious of breaking his own strict rule by showing his face out of doors, but he reasoned that amid the thousands who lived in the town and the hundreds more passing through, he was unlikely to be noticed. Besides, his curiosity was irresistible. He wanted to see the place where Whalley and Goffe had stayed. The Gookins' house was the first genuinely attested link to them he had found after nearly a year of searching.

It was noon by the time he reached the bridge over the Charles. He stopped halfway across, his eye caught by a long, narrow boat with six men hunched over their paddles, heading towards him from upriver. An Indian canoe. He recognised the description from Raleigh's book – a vessel carved out of a single tree trunk. It flashed beneath him so rapidly he barely had a chance to register the bronzed, muscled figures – naked, as it seemed to him – and then they were fifty yards downriver, sped along by the current.

He transferred his gaze to the opposite bank, to the settlement of wooden houses dominated by a much grander building. That must be Harvard College, where they produced the stern young sectaries who spread their dour religion across New England. A strange country this, he thought, where two such conflicting races and philosophies, heathens and fanatics, existed side by side. What good could ever come of it?

He rode on to the end of the bridge, across low marshland divided by a creek, up the road towards the first house on the right, which Kirke had told him was the Gookins'. It had been his intention to walk his horse slowly past it, complete a circuit of the town and then return to Boston. But as he drew level, a well-built man in shirtsleeves and a leather jerkin came out of the barn carrying a bundle of hay and stopped to look at him. Their eyes met.

'Are you lost, friend?'

Nayler drew up his horse. He could not resist the opportunity. 'I'm looking for two acquaintances of mine, Mr Richardson and Mr Stephenson.'

'There are none of those names here.'

'You are Mr Gookin?'

'I am, sir.'

'Then you might know them better as Colonel Edward Whalley and Colonel William Goffe.'

Gookin shook his head. 'Those two have long gone.'

'How long ago?'

'December, I believe.'

'December? Yet that is a full six months after they were declared wanted men by Parliament.'

'News from Parliament reaches us very slowly.'

'In truth, were they not still here in February? I'm told there was a fight.'

'There's no proof that was them. Most probably it was vagrants sheltering in the barn. I know nothing more of the business.'

'Vagrants armed with pistols? Come now, Mr Gookin – is it not an offence against your faith to lie?'

Gookin lifted his burden, smiled, and gestured with it towards Nayler. 'You see I must get on. Good day to you.'

Nayler felt his anger rising. He tried to staunch it, but the condescension of that smile was infuriating. 'You must give up where they are, sir, otherwise you too will be found guilty of treason by reason of harbouring them – and the penalty for that is not pretty, let me assure you.'

'Who are you? You say you are acquainted with the colonels? How?'

'From a Christmas Day some years ago. They'll not remember me, but when you see them next, you may say that I have not forgotten them. And I shall find them.'

He had said too much. He pulled hard on the reins, turned his horse around and trotted back down the slope towards the river, cursing his short temper.

He locked himself away after that, sent the potboy out to buy him whatever the booksellers had to offer on the history of America – he returned with Maverick's *Brief History of New England*, which proved to be most useful – and then set about writing the various letters he needed to begin his expedition. Between times he met Kellond and Kirke, followed the progress of their recruitment and provisioning, and authorised the settlement of various accounts. He also drafted a handbill to publicise the reward money on offer for the capture of the regicides 'dead or alive' – he liked that phrase: he asked for it to be set in a particularly large type – and had it taken to Stephen Daye, the colony's printer, with an order for two hundred copies.

A little over a week later, on the morning of Tuesday 7 May, when all was at last in readiness, he donned his best suit of clothes, retrieved the royal mandate from beneath his bed, and set off to visit Governor Endecott. He stopped a passer-by and was told he would find him in the State House, the grand new public building close to the Boston First Church. The ground floor was an enclosed market crowded with stalls, thick with the smells of fresh fish, herbs and spices. Chickens squawked in a cage. A flight of wooden stairs led up to the chamber where the State Court met. At the top, a secretary asked him to give his name and business, to which Nayler replied that he had come from London and what he had to say was for the governor's ears alone. The man went away and returned to say Mr Endecott would see him, but only briefly.

The room was large and airy, with high mullioned windows on all four sides that let in a good clear morning light. At the end of a long table, surrounded by papers, ink, pens, sealing wax and a lit candle, in his accustomed Elizabethan lace collar and black cap, sat Endecott.

Nayler removed his hat. 'Good day to you, Governor.' He bowed. 'My name is Richard Nayler, clerk to His Majesty's Privy Council, lately arrived from England on the *Prince Harry*, under instructions from the Lord Chancellor and the Secretary of State to present you with this mandate in the name of the King.'

He laid it on the table and took a step backwards.

Endecott poked the royal seal with a mittened forefinger. He was plainly discomfited. 'Please be seated, Mr Nayler.'

'Thank you, sir, but I am happy to stand.'

Endecott stared up at him, half blind. With his hollow, hairy cheeks and sucked-in toothless mouth, he might have been a hundred.

'As you wish.'

He held the document very close to his eyes. ' "To our trusty and well-beloved the present governor, or other magistrate or magistrates of our plantation in New England . . ." ' His head moved back and forth. 'This concerns Colonel Whalley and Colonel Goffe?' He peered more closely. ' "Our will and pleasure is, and we do hereby expressly require and command you forthwith upon the receipt of these our letters, to cause both the said persons to be apprehended." That is very princely language, sir. Very princely. But we have already set the matter in hand.' Nayler watched impassively as the governor searched among his piles of papers until finally he pulled out the document he wanted. 'I issued a warrant for their arrest two months ago.' He pushed it across the table.

Nayler read the title. *Minute of the Council of New England, directing the Secretary to issue a warrant to Edward Michelson to make diligent search for the apprehending of Whalley and Goffe. Boston, 1661, March 8.*

He replaced it on the table and pushed it back. 'May I ask, sir, what has been the effect of this warrant?'

'As yet they have not been found.'

'How many men have you sent out searching?'

'I have sent messengers to all the towns in New England.'

'Messengers? Such men are hardly to be caught by messengers.' Nayler opened his case. 'I have taken the liberty of preparing a new warrant, which may bring a little more urgency to the matter.'

He stepped forward and placed another document in front of

the governor. Endecott's hand hovered over it, as if it was dangerous even to touch it, but at length he picked it up.

This business with his eyes, thought Nayler. It's all a trick. He
can see as well as any man. But it buys him time.

He was starting to lose patience. 'You will see it appoints two
citizens of the Massachusetts Bay Colony, Captain Kirke and Mr
Kellond, to lead a search party. You know the gentlemen?'

'I do know them, and I do not care for them.'

'Well, I have interviewed them and found them suitable.'

'You have *interviewed* them, sir? Pray, how long have you been
in Boston? You say you arrived on the *Prince Harry* – that has been
at anchor a week, at least.'

'That is correct.'

'And in all that time you have not done me the courtesy of
announcing your presence?'

'Read the warrant, Mr Endecott. It's addressed to all the magistrates of New England. It will explain the position better than I.'

For a moment, he thought the governor was about to hand it
back and order him to leave. Instead, after working his toothless
jaw in irritation for a few moments, he began to read aloud again,
in a tone of mounting anger and disbelief. ' "To desire them to
have thorough search made for Whalley and Goffe, and if found
to bring them into the Massachusetts jurisdiction, impressing
sufficient men well accoutred and horse to enable them to do
so. To make diligent enquiry what Whalley and Goffe have been
doing, and where they have been, so that the King may have a
true account thereof. To give bills for their expenses, which will be
discharged by the Treasurer. All military commanders, constables,
and other officers and inhabitants, are to be aiding and assisting
them, as they will answer for the contrary at their uttermost peril.
In case Whalley and Goffe be gone into the Dutch jurisdiction,

they are to deliver the letter and enclosure to the Governor there and request he will deliver them up . . ." ' He looked up. 'You wrote this?'

'I did, with the authority of the Privy Council.'

Endecott laid down the warrant and stared over Nayler's shoulder. Eventually he muttered, 'We shall obey, of course. But all this will take us time to organise.'

'No more time is necessary. It is done.'

'Done?'

'We have the men, the horses, the supplies and the weapons. All that is required is your signature.'

'And when do you propose to begin?'

'Today. I mean to leave no time for word of our expedition to reach Whalley and Goffe ahead of us.'

'And if I do not sign?'

'Then we will go ahead in any case. I shall report back to London, and His Majesty will draw his own conclusions about the loyalty of this colony and its ruling officers.' Nayler pulled out a pile of letters from his case. 'All these will also require your seal and signature. Perhaps you'd care to summon your clerk?' He smiled. 'I think now I will take up your kind offer of a seat.'

Kellond and Kirke were sitting downstairs in the rooming house when he returned. Nayler patted his document case. 'I have it all. The warrant signed and executed. Letters from Endecott to the governors of Connecticut, New Haven and Plymouth, enclosing a copy of the King's mandate. They are ordered to assist us. He's even signed a letter to Stuyvesant, director of New Netherland, requesting the cooperation of the Dutch.' He laughed, he could not help it; the old man's reluctance had been so comical. 'He tells them all he "doubts not they will faithfully discharge their duty to His Majesty as is desired". I swear it cost him blood to write it. Come, let's not waste another moment.'

He fetched his money, sword and pistol from upstairs, paid Shadbricke half a sovereign to keep his room until he returned – how long he would be away he could not say – and walked with the others to the harbour.

By now it was mid afternoon. The hunting party had been waiting all day, along with their horses, arms and supplies, in a warehouse belonging to Kellond. As Nayler entered, the men were sprawled on bales of wool, playing dice. It was the first time he had met them. Kirke made the introductions, beginning with their guide, John Chapin – trim-bodied, sharp-faced, with jet-black hair and eyes: Nayler could see why he was rumoured to have some Indian blood. The four Scotsmen, all taken prisoner after the Battle of Dunbar in 1650, were in their early thirties: John Stewart, who had spent some years as a forced labourer in the iron foundry at Lynn until he had been purchased and set to work as a blacksmith in Springfield; William Mackwater, also from the Lynn ironworks; Niven Agnew, who had been sent to the sawmills in Maine, where he had lost two fingers of his left hand; and John Ross, who had laboured for nine years in the graphite mine near Sturbridge.

Nayler shook hands with each of them. He liked the look of their leanness, their sinewy muscled arms, and especially the hatred in their eyes. They were like a pack of hungry hounds. 'So,' he said, 'are you men all eager for the chase?'

A ragged chorus of 'Aye, sir.'

'Good, because so am I.'

Never had he felt more alive. He could not stop laughing. He swung himself up onto his horse. Kirke pulled open the door. Chapin went first, then Kellond, Nayler and the Scotsmen. Kellond locked the warehouse behind them and spurred his mount to catch up. They clattered over the cobbles as people turned to watch, out of the harbour, up through the streets of Boston, and when they reached the open country, they turned westwards – my life tends ever westwards, thought Nayler – the sun in their faces, across the plain towards the dark line of the forest.

CHAPTER SEVENTEEN

ONLY EIGHT PEOPLE knew the secret of the colonels' return to New Haven: the three members of the Davenport family; the Davenports' two servants; the assistant minister, Nicholas Street; William Jones, the son of the regicide; and Governor Leete.

Yet they had lost their peace of mind, and the first few days were worse even than winter in Cambridge, which at least had been quiet. Now, if they heard a distant gunshot, doubtless fired by some hunter in the woods, they imagined it to be the beginnings of a raid; the sound of more than one horse in the road had them reaching for their pistols. They stayed in their rooms most of the time, and for exercise walked up and down the passageway in their stockinged feet to be sure of not making a noise. Davenport invited them to browse the shelves in his study, which was on the same floor and full of improving religious tracts, but these were more to Will's taste than Ned's.

Because of Davenport's pre-eminence in the colony, there were too many visitors in the habit of dropping by unannounced for them to risk venturing downstairs during daylight. The only time to which they could look forward was nightfall, especially the hours around midnight, when the town was asleep and it was safe to step out into the Davenports' lot, feel the fresh air on their faces, inhale the smell of the springtime honeysuckle, and listen to the chaffing of the night birds and the constant rustling movement of the sea. But gradually the tediousness of their predicament began to weigh upon them more than its peril, and after the first week they became bolder. Sometimes, in the early hours of the morning, they risked hurrying across the road – it was precisely sixty feet wide, whether for some Biblical reason or not Ned didn't dare enquire, in case he invited another of Davenport's lectures – where they could walk through the minister's large meadow to the shore and look at the lights of the lobster traps.

Their lives, without them being conscious of it, became semi-nocturnal: retiring to bed just before dawn and sleeping until noon, when their dinner was brought up to them.

There is nothing more calculated to expose a person's true character than enforced proximity, and the more Ned saw of Davenport, the less he cared for him. The minister's moods could veer three times in a day - sometimes in an hour – between brooding silence, manic high spirits, and tyrannical rage, his shouts resounding from one end of the mansion to the other. It was a necessary part of his duties to hand out punishments – Ned understood that: he had ordered his fair share of floggings in the army. But Davenport seemed to take a peculiar relish in passing judgement on offenders, imposing fines and imprisonment, confinement in the pillory, and whippings. Under Mosaic Law, which applied throughout the colony, the Sabbath began at sundown on Saturday and extended right the way through until dawn on Monday, during which time all work and travel – except to the meeting house – was forbidden. It was easy to break the law inadvertently, and there were plenty willing to inform on their neighbours. And if that was not sufficient, Davenport was also always on the lookout for witchcraft as a cause of illness or crop failure; twice women were brought to the house to be questioned.

At least once a week, Mr Street and Mr Jones would call on the colonels in the middle of the afternoon, often together, and the four men along with Davenport would pray in the study and discuss texts from the Scriptures. It was during one of these meetings that Ned became aware that the unpleasant smell that often permeated the house seemed to be emanating from Davenport himself. None of the others appeared to notice, so he merely took care to sit as far from the minister as possible, and to lean forward over his Bible, with his hand covering his nose and mouth, giving an appearance of intense concentration.

Increasingly his mind took refuge in the past. He would lie on his bed with some theological tome or book of sermons resting unread on his chest and relive the tumultuous episodes of his life, so vastly different to his present non-existence. The things he had seen! The battles and sieges, the feasts with the King at Hampton Court, and then His Majesty's trial and execution, the eviction of Parliament at gunpoint, the splendour of the Lord Protector in Whitehall Palace and Hampton Court, Cromwell's death . . .

It was while he was indulging in one of these waking dreams that it occurred to him that he might better pass the endless crawl of time by writing them down. But would that not be sinful vanity? Who cared about the life of Edward Whalley apart from Edward Whalley? A memoir should have some usefulness.

And then he was struck by an altogether better notion.

After turning it over in his mind for a while, he walked down the passage to Davenport's study and knocked on the door. The room was empty. The desk, beneath the window, was the kind a schoolmaster might use. He raised the lid, took one of the sheets of paper upon which the minister composed his thunderous sermons, picked up a pen from the rack, dipped the nib in the inkwell, and wrote:

Some Memories of the Life of
His Highness, the Late Lord Protector,
Oliver Cromwell
by his cousin
Col. Edw. Whalley

That was as far as he got. He had scarcely lifted his pen from the paper to compose his thoughts when he sensed Oliver at his back, leaning over his shoulder, demanding to know what impertinence was this?

'People ask me about you all the time,' he muttered.

Then let the damned fools ask, but leave me be!

The voice was so real he felt the hairs rise on his scalp.

He folded up the paper and left the study. He wondered if he was going mad.

But the following afternoon he was back, and this time he did not hesitate, but charged full tilt at his objective as if he were leading a cavalry troop against the enemy.

I was born in the Year of Our Lord 1598, the second son of Sir Richard Whalley of Kirkton Hall, Nottinghamshire, of which county my father was the Member of Parliament, and brought up in the Puritan faith. My mother, Frances Cromwell, the younger daughter of Sir Henry Cromwell of Hinchingbrooke, Huntingdon, was sister to Robert Cromwell, the father of Oliver, who was born in the same year as myself.

He paused. So far, so good. These were plain facts, indisputable. He liked facts. As long as he was dealing with facts, he was comfortable. He dipped his pen in the inkwell. The nib scratched across the page.

The closeness of our families, our shared religious beliefs and the nearness of our ages made possible a familiarity of relations that began in boyhood and lasted for more than fifty years.

Again: facts. But now it became harder. To set down the long summer days at Hinchingbrooke – fishing, climbing trees, playing ball and hide-and-seek with the cousins – seemed trivial, and he decided to skip over them. It was some time before he felt able to continue.

I am often asked what he was like. In body, he was tall – only two inches below six feet – well compact and strong; I have seen him carry an anvil for twenty paces and lift a cart trapped in a rut, such feats of strength as he liked to demonstrate when he was younger. His head was large, his complexion ruddy, his eyes bright, his hair thick and long. For books in those early days, he cared but little. His interests lay all outdoors – riding, hunting, hawking, wrestling. He knew more of horses than any man I ever met. His temperament was fiery but mixed with an odd tenderness for any creature in distress, be it animal or human. He wept often and was prone to melancholy.

That would do well enough. Time for more facts.

When I reached the age of sixteen, in the Year of Our Lord 1614, I was sent by my father to study at Emmanuel College,

Cambridge, renowned for its Puritan learning, and the following year Oliver became an undergraduate at Sidney Sussex College, barely half a mile away, also most devout. I saw him often.

Various scenes came into his mind: Oliver fighting with some town boys in the marketplace, Oliver gambling in an upstairs room of the Rose Tavern, Oliver lying with a local girl on the banks of the River Cam while Ned kept watch . . . But none of that must ever be mentioned, otherwise he would do the work of the scurrilous royalist pamphleteers for them.

His pursuit of his studies was not always diligent. After a year, he left Cambridge without taking his degree, although this was not for any want of application. Rather, his father had died, and it was necessary for him to return to his family to support his mother and his sisters. I stayed at Emmanuel and graduated. It was not until several years later that I discovered that my father – whose profligacy and lack of judgement had squandered our family's fortune – had borrowed £600 from Robert Cromwell and was unable to repay it. It was this debt, and the deficit it left in Robert's estate, that required Oliver to give up his degree and take charge of the family's farm. Yet never once did Oliver mention it, and when I discovered the true situation, and swore to him that I would repay the sum, he refused my offer absolutely, saying the debt was my father's, not mine.

He had never told anyone this story before. Even now, forty years later, writing it down, he felt his face burn with shame. But if the reader was to understand Oliver's character – why men would follow him, no matter what – it was too revealing an episode to exclude.

He proposed next to describe how after Cambridge, in their early twenties, he and Oliver had lived in neighbouring streets in the same parish of the City of London. But when he dipped his pen in the inkwell, he found he had drained it. Where would he find more?

There was none that he could see in the small compartments that lined the back of the desk. The pair of drawers above his knees was locked. However, by chance one afternoon as he was passing the open door, he had seen Davenport hide the key, tucking it between two volumes on the nearby shelves. He saw no reason to trouble him about a mere pot of ink, so he retrieved the key. The first drawer contained nothing except paper and sealing wax. But the clink of glass when he started to pull open the second was more promising. It was crammed with coloured bottles, of dark green and dark blue, neatly labelled. There was also a little wooden box containing a very thin brass tube, about six inches long, with a small funnel at one end. A catheter, was it? Curious, he held the bottles up to the window. They were not ink. Some of the names he did not recognise, but two he did: mercury and guaiacum. There could hardly be an officer of any army in Europe, obliged to deal with rampant soldiers during a campaign, who would not have recognised the standard treatment for gonorrhoea.

He stared at them. The sickly son, the absence of other children, the separate rooms – all was suddenly explained. Davenport must have contracted the disease many years ago, before he even came to America, either in London or The Hague.

Quickly he put the bottles back, locked the desk and replaced the key. Gathering his manuscript, he checked the passage was clear, then hurried back to his room.

Man was born in sin. He struggled. He erred. He fell. All this Ned understood.

And often – he understood this too – those who inveighed the loudest against the temptations of the Devil turned out to be those who had most grievously succumbed to them; indeed, they preached so loudly precisely because of their knowledge of human weakness. Such examples were perhaps more complicated than mere hypocrisy. In any case, he had seen too much to be shocked for long.

Still, he found it hard to meet Davenport's eye when he met him the next afternoon for their Bible study. And he detected a corresponding unease in the minister. He wondered whether in his haste he could have failed to return the key to its exact hiding place, or perhaps he had left the medicine bottles slightly out of order. Whatever the truth, it was plain that Davenport suspected his secret had been discovered, because soon afterwards he suggested that the time had come for the colonels to leave.

'You have been here nigh on eight weeks,' he explained, sounding uncomfortable but determined, 'and while we would be happy to entertain you for as long as you wish, questions have begun to be asked at the store regarding the amount of food we are ordering – nearly twice what it was before. I have spoken to William Jones, and he is happy to take you under his roof for a spell. Hannah is heavy with their first child, but they have many rooms they do not use. Then you may either return here or take a turn at Mr Street's.'

So much for the offer to stay until the Second Coming.

'We understand,' said Will, although he could not conceal his surprise, 'and we thank you for your hospitality. It is a debt we can never repay. When do you wish us to leave?'

'We thought tonight.'

Will looked even more taken aback. 'As soon as that?'

'If it is to be done, it is best done quickly, and tonight there will be little moon, so there is less risk you may be seen when you move across the street.' Davenport did not look at Ned.

After he had gone, Will said, 'It seems a mighty rush. Have we done something to offend him?'

'But there is logic in what he says,' replied Ned. He was not sorry to be moving. He had not been able to bring himself to tell Will of his discovery: his son-in-law took a less forgiving view of human frailty. 'He is right about the moon. It will only get brighter over the next fortnight, and if rumours are already spreading, the danger increases the longer we remain.'

Sunset was at eight, but light lingered in the sky till nearly ten, which was the hour when Jones appeared. No one in the household had stayed up to see them off, apart from Davenport, who shook their hands and told them he would visit them in a day or two. They picked up their bags and stepped outside. The door closed behind them. Their departure was very different to their welcome, Ned thought.

Will whispered, 'This is very handsome of you, William.'

'Think nothing of it. Are you ready? It is only a short walk, a few hundred paces.'

They stumbled in the darkness into the road and turned left. The massive Eaton residence, with its profusion of chimneys, was dimly silhouetted by the sliver of a crescent moon. Suddenly Jones stopped. A lamp was weaving along the track towards them. He whispered a warning, crossed the road and opened the gate to the nearest house, and steered the colonels through it. 'Lie low.'

They crouched down on the grass behind the fence and listened as Jones greeted whoever was carrying the lamp.

'Dennis Crampton, is it?'

'Mr Jones. You're out late.'

'I've been with Mr Davenport.'

'Is that so?' Crampton hawked and spat. 'Now there's a man you're welcome to!' He sounded drunk.

'You're far from home, Dennis. Are you fit to travel?'

'I'm lodging with John Thorp. Will you share my light? I can see you to your gate.'

'Thank you, no. I'll linger here and take the air a little longer.'

'As you like.'

Crampton moved on. A minute later, Jones leaned over the fence. 'That was bad luck.'

Will said, 'He does not care for Mr Davenport.'

'He ordered him a whipping for his drinking. I thought he had moved to Guilford.'

They came out into the road. Ned glanced over his shoulder and saw the lamp again, bobbing to and fro. 'He's coming back.'

Jones swore. He seized one of Ned's bags. 'We'd best make a dash for it.'

They half walked, half ran, almost falling, until they reached the mansion's gate. Jones pushed them into the yard. Ned was wheezing, had a pain in his side; he doubled over to catch his breath. 'Has he seen us?'

'I reckon not,' said Jones, 'but it's no matter. He's a fool and a drunk and nobody pays him any account.' He opened his front door. 'You'll be safe here.'

CHAPTER EIGHTEEN

THERE WERE TIMES, especially at the start of their journey, when Nayler felt the vastness of America would defeat them. No sooner had they traversed one endless vista of forests and mountain ridges, plains and lakes, than another opened up before them. How were two men determined to hide ever to be discovered in such a silent, unpeopled wilderness? But by the second day, he began to view it differently; not so much as a land but as an ocean, with an archipelago of tiny settlements stretched across it: stepping stones of civilisation surrounded by hostile nature. Unless the colonels proposed to live with the Indians – unthinkable, surely – their hiding places were peculiarly limited, and the risk of exposure correspondingly much greater than it might appear. The Christian population of New England was only some thirty thousand; London's alone was nearly half a million. The regicides might have done better to have stayed at home.

If he was to succeed, what he needed most was the element of surprise. His abiding worry was that Endecott might have dispatched a messenger to warn the regicides a few hours before he and his party set out. It was never far from his thoughts, even though John Chapin, their guide, assured him there was no other trail to the Connecticut River except the one they were following, and that none of the Indians they had met had reported a lone rider ahead of them. He nevertheless insisted they go on each day until after sunset, to cover every last possible mile, despite the protests of Captain Kirke that it was too dark and dangerous to continue. Wherever they stopped, however remote, he pinned up a copy of his reward handbill – *DEAD or ALIVE* – reasoning that some hunter or traveller might see it and spread the word. At dawn, he was always the first to rise, going round the camp and shaking the others awake. He was aware of the resentment building against him among the Scotchmen, whom he overheard complaining that they had merely exchanged one form of slavery for another, and even in the mild-mannered Kellond and Chapin, who warned that their horses were becoming exhausted.

Still, they obeyed, that was all that mattered to him, and in the middle of the afternoon of Friday 10 May – only three days after setting out from Boston, having ridden more than a hundred miles – they reached the Connecticut. Rather than let the men briefly rest and savour their achievement, he consulted Chapin as to what lay ahead and announced that they must move on immediately to the ferry at Windsor. Wearily they saddled up again. An hour later, they were across the river, and sitting with wooden beakers of ale in the cramped downstairs room of a little inn beside the general store – all apart from Kellond and Kirke: Nayler had sent them with the warrant to find some figures of authority to question about the regicides. While he waited for them to return, he pinned up two of his reward notices in the store and the inn, and handed more out to the customers.

Kellond and Kirke reappeared around six o'clock to report that neither the minister nor the church elders would admit to having seen Whalley or Goffe but conceded that they had heard rumours of the pair being observed in Hartford.

'How long since?'

'Two months,' said Kellond, 'or thereabouts.'

'You believe them?'

'I do,' replied Kirke.

'And you, Mr Kellond?'

'I agree.'

'Good.' Nayler drained his ale and stood. 'Then Hartford it is.'

A loud chorus of complaint arose from the Scotch, especially John Ross, the former graphite miner and the most sullen of the four.

'But there are rooms here, Mr Nayler,' objected Kirke, with an eye on the jug of beer, 'and only a couple of hours of daylight left. Rather than sleep another night in the open, we could rest the horses and move on in the morning.'

'We must move on now. Otherwise you may be sure some Puritan spy will be speeding down the road ahead of us.'

For a moment nobody shifted, and Nayler wondered if he had a mutiny on his hands, in which case he wasn't sure what he would do, so far from home in this alien land. But then Chapin spoke up in his support. 'We shall have to walk the horses, Mr Nayler. Another hard ride would finish them.'

'Very well, we shall walk the horses,' he said gratefully, 'and we shall spend the night in Hartford, where I promise you we shall seek food and shelter – and wine,' he added, with a look at Kirke.

The captain held his gaze for a moment, then nodded. The crisis passed. Five minutes later, they were on the road again.

*

John Winthrop the Younger – fifty-five years old, a man of science and business as well as of faith, three times annually elected governor of Connecticut Colony – was seated at the kitchen table in his house in Hartford with his wife, Elizabeth, and the five youngest of their nine children: Mercy, Sara, Margaret, Martha and Anne. They had just finished supper, and Winthrop was reading to them from the New Testament when he heard the sound of horses coming to a halt in the street outside. He glanced at the window. A soft, dark purple light. Dusk.

Loud knocking came at the door.

Elizabeth said, 'Who can be calling at this hour?'

'I wonder.' He knew, though; he knew even as he rose to his feet. He had been expecting this moment for weeks. 'Why don't you take the girls upstairs?'

And when he opened the door, he saw at once that he was right: two men on the step with their hats removed politely; a third standing behind – Indian blood, by the look of him – holding their horses' reins; five others mounted, staring down at him, all filthy and unkempt from long days' travelling, all armed.

'Good evening, Governor,' said the elder of the two men. 'I am Captain Thomas Kirke, and this gentleman beside me is Mr Thomas Kellond. We are sorry indeed to disturb you at so late an hour, but we have come from Boston on urgent business.'

Winthrop stalled for time. 'Not so urgent that it can't wait till morning, surely?' The pair hesitated. 'Come back tomorrow – as early as you like. We'll speak then. I'm just away to my bed.'

But as he started to close the door, one of the men on horseback called out, 'We'll speak now, Mr Winthrop, if you would be so good.'

'And who are you, sir?'

'My name is Richard Nayler.'

'And are you from Boston also, Mr Nayler?'

'No, Governor, I have come from London.'

'From London?' Winthrop detected authority in his voice and manner, and a certain menace. Now it was his turn to hesitate. 'Well then, Captain Kirke and Mr Kellond,' he said reluctantly, 'you had best come in.' He opened the door wider. 'And you too, Mr Nayler.'

They spread out their documents on the kitchen table – the warrant, the King's order with the royal seal, the letter from Endecott. It was more serious than Winthrop had anticipated. He had considered the matter for more than two months, had prayed to God for guidance, and had made up his mind what to do. 'So, you are in pursuit of Colonel Whalley and Colonel Goffe?'

Kirke said, 'We have intelligence that they were seen in Hartford at the beginning of March.'

'Not to my knowledge.'

'They may have been travelling under false names – Richardson and Stephenson.'

Winthrop made a pretence of trying to remember. 'Richardson and Stephenson . . . Yes, now I think of it, I believe those do sound familiar.'

'You met them?'

'I recollect I did.'

'They stayed in Hartford?'

'No, they merely passed through.'

'On their way to . . . where?'

God forgive me, thought Winthrop. 'I believe to New Haven.'

The man from London, Nayler, who had plainly been longing to speak for some while, could contain himself no longer. 'Come now, Governor.' He smiled unpleasantly. 'Do you expect us to believe you had no notion who they were? The most wanted men in America, with a reward of a hundred pounds apiece on their heads? They come to see you, in flight from justice, and you allow them to proceed on their way? Wittingly or not, you were aiding and abetting traitors.'

'I am very sorry, sir. It is my custom to take men at their word. For example, you tell me you are Richard Nayler, and I believe you, although I have no proof you speak the truth.' Winthrop was pleased to see that that froze the man's smile. He continued in an emollient tone. 'They asked directions to New Haven, which I provided. I am happy to order a search of Hartford at first light, if you demand it, but I am confident you will not find them here. That is the extent of Connecticut's involvement.'

Nayler, no longer looking amused, came back at him. 'I find this hard to credit, sir. Were they alone, or did they have a guide?'

'They were alone.'

'Two men who do not know America – one of them past sixty – travelling on their own across rough country from Boston, in winter? It defies all credibility. How did they find their way?'

'With difficulty, I should imagine. I assume that's why they stopped to ask directions.'

'Directions to New Haven, you say? To the town or to the colony in general?'

And now came another calculated lie. 'My recollection is that I directed them to Guilford, the nearest town.'

'Your recollection? When we catch them, we shall question them most closely about the help they have received in New Eng-land, and we shall see if their story tallies with yours.' Nayler turned to the younger of his two companions. 'Gather up the papers, Mr Kellond. There's no point us wasting another minute here. It seems we must move on to Guilford.'

Kirke said, 'Thank you for your time, Governor. We shall let you get to your bed.' He glanced anxiously at Nayler, then back at Winthrop. 'I wonder, could you direct us to a suitable inn?'

After they had gone – Nayler leaving behind a dozen of his reward notices, with instructions that they should be displayed across the town – Winthrop sat alone at the table with his hands resting on the family Bible bequeathed him by his father. He examined his conscience. What would the old man have done? It was a grievous sin to lie. It was also a grievous sin to betray one's friends. Yet somehow, in the interests of Connecticut and its future, he had contrived to do both in the same evening. Such dissembling, he supposed, was a necessary part of statesmanship. How else could he protect his people from the vengeance of the Crown, and yet try to gain a little time for the colonels by throwing their pursuers off the scent? Soon he would have to make the long journey to London and plead Connecticut's case for a royal charter.

When Pilate saw that he could prevail nothing, but that rather a tumult was made, he took water, and washed his hands before the multitude . . .

He thought of Nayler, with his growth of beard, his false smile, his exhausted staring eyes and mud-spattered face and clothes. The man had seemed half crazed. It made him feel doubly sorry for Whalley and Goffe. He certainly would not care to be hunted by such a Fury.

He took the reward notices over to the kitchen fire and fed them one at a time to the flames.

Nayler passed a sleepless night in Hartford's only inn, trapped on a narrow bed between Kellond and Kirke. Every hour of inactivity was a torture to him. Soon after five, the sun rose, and he with it, and by six he had his men on the road again. By starting so early, he was fairly confident no one could have left the town ahead of them. It was Saturday 11 May.

Chapin knew the way to Guilford. The settlement lay on the coast, he said, some thirty-five miles due south, and the path turned out to be tortuous, strewing all manner of natural obstacles in their way – dense forest, swamps, cliffs of reddish rock, a wide stream they had to walk beside for a mile or two until they came to a fording place, where they had to dismount and lead the horses across, wading up to their thighs in chilly, fast-flowing water. The horses were the problem – panting unhealthily, twisting their heads, sometimes wandering off the path like drunks and crashing into the undergrowth. The first collapsed under Mackwater around noon with foam at its mouth, and Chapin had to take out his pistol and shoot it. A second, Niven Agnew's mount, dropped stone dead an hour later. After that, they were all obliged to go on foot, with the result that it was late afternoon by the time they arrived at Guilford.

It was a small settlement, not nearly as prosperous as Cambridge – a few decent stone-built houses scattered amongst what were mostly little more than wooden hovels; unlikely, Nayler thought, that the regicides would have chosen to stay in such a place, where they would have been so conspicuous. Nevertheless, he ordered pistols drawn and loaded, and he was pleased to see how the prospect of action at last concentrated the minds of the Scotchmen. They walked their horses along a muddy street to the meeting house, carefully scrutinising every face they passed, and Kirke demanded of an elderly man who was standing on the green that they should be taken to the town's chief magistrate. By six o'clock, Kellond and Kirke, with Nayler in the background, were gathered in the parlour of the governor of New Haven, Mr William Leete.

Nayler recognised immediately the fussy mannerisms of a fellow lawyer. Before he would even consent to read the warrant and letters, Leete sent a servant to fetch the town elders so that he might consult them. That took the best part of another hour. When, around seven, half a dozen granite-faced Puritans had assembled, all formally dressed in black and wearing identical flat-topped black hats, Leete seated himself at his desk, took out a pair of spectacles, carefully adjusted them on his nose, and slowly began to read the King's mandate aloud. ' "To our trusty and well-beloved the present governor, or other magistrate or magistrates of our plantation in New England . . ." ' He stopped and frowned. 'Well, that is plain wrong to begin with. There is no such office as "the governor of New England". This mandate has no legal force.'

Kellond and Kirke swung round to Nayler in bafflement.

'Let me see that.' He leaned over Leete's shoulder. It was true that the grammar could be clearer, but the intent was obvious enough. This was simply a town clerk's legal pettifogging. 'You are wrong, Mr Leete. The reference to "the present governor" is well separated from the words "New England".'

'That does not alter the meaning.'

'It does most certainly alter it. You are reading it in such a way as to suggest there is a comma after "magistrate or magistrates". In that case I grant you there would be an error in the drafting. But there is no comma – look.'

For the next few minutes they argued back and forth about the legal weight of the comma, until Nayler thumped his hand on the desk. 'For God's sake, sir! I have not come three thousand miles to debate syntax! Read the rest of the mandate and the other letters and let us finish this business before the day ends.'

'Very well, I will continue to read the document,' said Leete mildly, 'but that does not mean I concede the point. I repeat, there is no "governor of New England". Ours is an independent colony.'

He removed his spectacles, polished them, replaced them on his nose, and continued.

Time passed. The governor's voice droned on. As the light began to fade, he called to a servant for candles. Nayler stole a glance around the crowded room. By now there must have been a dozen spectators at least, with another gathering of their sombre womenfolk standing outside in the yard, watched by the Scotch with their pistols drawn. Men came in and out as they pleased. It would be easy for one to slip away and warn the regicides. Their chances of taking the colonels by surprise were waning by the minute.

'Enough, Mr Leete,' he said wearily at last. 'Enough. This is not a public entertainment. Either send these people away or let us withdraw to some place where we may speak in private.'

'There is nothing I have to say to you in private that I would not say in front of my friends.'

'Nevertheless, a word with you alone, Governor, if you please.'

The governor sighed. 'Very well, if that is what you wish.'

He gathered up the documents and led Nayler into a small adjacent room shelved with legal and religious books. Nayler closed the door and leaned his back against it. 'Let us speak frankly, Mr Leete. Our views in general may differ, but our interests in this particular matter collide. I mean to find these regicides, and you – if you are a man of sense, which I take you to be – wish to avoid the wrath of my masters in London. I understand you have to put on a display of reluctance for those gentlemen out there, but you must know times have changed, and if New Haven wishes to become a colony recognised by the Crown, it must yield to the King's authority.'

'It is not as simple as that, Mr Nayler.'

'It is simplicity itself. We are both servants of His Majesty. All I require from you are eight fresh horses, for which I shall pay the full price, and your authority to conduct a search of the colony, and we'll be on our way.'

'You must give me more time.'

'I have wasted too much of it already.' Nayler opened the door and went back into the crowded parlour. 'We are leaving,' he said to Kellond and Kirke.

'Not so quickly, Mr Nayler,' said Leete. 'If you would allow me to finish. I cannot give permission for a search of any part of the colony without the approval of my fellow magistrates.'

'And how long will that take?'

'Two days.'

'Two days!'

Leete allowed himself a thin smile and pointed at the darkening window. 'The sun has gone down. The Sabbath has begun. No business can be undertaken until Monday morning.'

Nayler closed his eyes. He swayed slightly. 'Then at the very least I demand we have the horses.'

'Impossible, sir. Under Mosaic Law, nothing temporal can be transacted until first light on Monday. In any case, all travel further than two miles is forbidden unless it is to attend an act of worship.'

'What is this Mosaic Law? The King's government recognises no laws save those passed by Parliament. Wasn't that the cause for which you people fought the war?'

A stern figure standing by the window said, 'The war was fought for liberty of conscience, sir, and here in New Haven we exercise that liberty by observing the Law of Moses, as written in the Book of Exodus: "Abide ye every man in his place; let no man go out of his place on the seventh day." In the Scriptures, a man is stoned to death merely for gathering sticks on the Sabbath. Even if our governor here were to issue an order to the contrary, you'll find no man in Guilford willing to transact with you till Monday.'

The men around him growled assent.

'That's right.'

'Well said.'

Nayler did not trust himself to speak. He pushed his way out of the parlour and into the yard to see for himself. The evening sky was still full of light, but the roofs of the wretched wooden houses opposite were outlined by the red glow of sunset. He clenched his fists. Tricked and stalled by Puritan madmen! Would to God he had the means to arrest them all for treason, and burn their damned town to ashes around their ears. Behind him, in the yard, he could already hear Kirke enquiring of the locals whether Guilford had an inn.

CHAPTER NINETEEN

I N NEW HAVEN, the colonels had just finished supper and were spending the final hour before bed in their adjoining rooms, apart from one another, Will reading the Bible, Ned smoking a final pipe of tobacco. By that Saturday evening, they had been resident under the Joneses' roof for exactly twelve days.

It was a tiny household for such a large mansion, consisting just of William, his wife, Hannah – ten years his junior and ready to give birth at any time – and a maid and manservant considered trustworthy enough to be let in on the secret of their guests' identities. The colonels had been obliged to give up their habit of taking the night air: the Joneses' house, which was set a little further back from the sea than the Davenports', had neighbours on three sides who could see into the property from their upper storeys. Otherwise, their routine was unchanged – reading, exercise along the passageway, and twice-weekly discussion of the Scriptures.

It was around nine when they heard an urgent knocking at the front door. Both men looked up. But such callers were not unusual, and after a few moments, they returned to what they were doing. A minute later, they heard Jones running up the stairs. He went straight into Ned's room, out of breath, in a panic.

'There's a search party in Guilford, come from Boston to arrest you.'

Will appeared in the doorway behind him. Ned rose to his feet. Despite expecting it for so many months, now that it had happened, the thing felt unreal. 'How many men?'

'Eight. All well armed. They have a mandate from the King himself, and letters from Endecott demanding assistance.'

'When did they arrive?'

'Two or three hours since. Leete will try to hold them up. But the messenger says they look a wild crew, capable of anything. We've no time to waste. Your bags are packed?'

The colonels nodded. It had been a precaution ever since their return to New Haven.

Jones went over to the window and peered out into the evening. 'The question is, where should you go?'

Ned said, 'We should make for the hills. We're used to sleeping in the open.'

'You can't tonight. Till Monday morning, you can travel no further than two miles.'

Ned had forgotten about the rule. He had never encountered such a custom in England, however strict the community. 'But *two miles* . . . ?' He broke off, shook his head, incredulous. 'Two miles is hardly a safe distance.'

'Nevertheless, it is the law.'

'And we really must observe it?'

'Of course we must,' said Will. 'How could you think otherwise?'

'But surely this is Jewish bondage? Why must we?'

'There is perhaps a place,' said Jones. 'A ruined mill, the other side of town. That cannot be above two miles distant. I'll show you the way and help carry your bags.'

'Could we not hide our belongings here?' Ned had a sudden sense where this was heading.

'The house is certain to be searched. Besides, I fear you may not be able to return.' Jones went out into the passage, stopped and turned. He had tears in his eyes. 'Forgive me. I must consider Hannah and the baby.'

Will touched him on the arm. 'We understand. You have run risks enough already.'

Jones hurried back downstairs. Will returned to his room. Ned packed away his pipe and gathered up his memoir of Cromwell. If there had been a fire, he would have burned it, but he could hardly leave it behind for their enemies to discover, so there was nothing to do except bring it with him. He took a last look at the room. He doubted they would know such comfort again, not with eight men on their trail. He felt an abrupt welling-up of self-pity, which he suppressed at once. The Lord gave, the Lord taketh away. He must not question it.

A few minutes later, they were slipping out of the gate and into the wide grassy street.

Jones led the way with a lamp. The moon was curiously veiled by cloud, gleaming through the misty layers in a series of reflected circles, like a torch shone down a well. There was a wind off the sea, but no rain: that at least was a mercy. They covered the half-mile to the green without encountering a soul, then cut across it at a diagonal, passed Eaton's gravestone and the meeting house and then entered the street that separated the north-west division of the town from the north-central. Candles glimmered in a few of the windows on either side, but most of the households were already asleep. Once they were clear of New Haven, there was nothing ahead but wind and darkness, and that eerie moonlight falling softly over the landscape.

They stumbled along a winding track across open country. After half an hour or so, they reached a wood. Owls hooted in the trees, and they briefly glimpsed one, huge and white, swooping silently across the track like a ghost. Ned could hear a stream nearby. Jones halted and raised his lamp. 'This is the place.'

It was impossible to make it out at first – a small stone-built dwelling, abandoned years before and since reclaimed by nature, covered in ivy and brambles, with tall weeds poking out of the shattered windows. A broken door hung off its hinges. Inside, the floor was strewn with rubble. The wind moaned through the gaps in the roof. Jones set down his lamp and used a taper to light a second. 'I'm sorry,' he said. 'At least you should be dry for a night or two. I'll return on Monday.'

After he had gone, they gathered together a few green branches and damp pieces of broken furniture and lit a fire in the hearth. But the chimney must have been blocked by birds' nests and the room soon filled with smoke so thick it made their eyes water. They had to stand outside until it cleared.

'Such a desolate, haunted spot,' said Ned. He could imagine them crouched inside, their pistols aimed through the gaping windows as their pursuers closed in on them through the trees. He thought it looked exactly the sort of place where a pair of desperate outlaws might make their last stand.

CHAPTER TWENTY

UILFORD'S INN, SO called, was barely more than a
wooden shack in the middle of the settlement – a single
windowless room with a table and chairs in one corner
and straw mattresses spread across an earth floor. The owner,
Goodman Bishop, citing the Book of Exodus, informed them on
their arrival, regretfully, that the cooking or serving of food after
sundown on Saturday was forbidden ('the Lord hath given you
the Sabbath, therefore he giveth you on the sixth day the bread
of two days'). Accordingly, he laid out on the table plates of cold
food and pitchers of water that he said would have to last them
until Monday morning, when he also undertook to return with a
pair of horses to replace the two that had died. For these facilities,
he extracted an excessive payment, in full, and in advance.

After he had gone, Stewart and Mackwater lit a fire in the yard
and cooked the last of the fish they had caught two days earlier
from a pond beside the Old Connecticut Path. Nobody spoke
much during the meal. Kirke took nips of brandy from a flask
he did not offer to share. Once they had eaten, the Scotchmen
started playing cards. Nayler sat apart from the others, with his

back propped against the wall of the shack, smoking his pipe and brooding. Finally he went over to where Chapin was sitting with Kellond and Kirke.

'How far is it to New Haven, Mr Chapin?'

'Sixteen miles.'

'That is not so far. If we were to set out at first light, we could walk it easily before noon.'

Kellond said, 'We could. But we would break their law, and when we arrived, we would have no authority to search.'

'Our guns would give us the authority.'

'They have a strong militia,' objected Kirke. 'Their guns would outnumber ours twenty to one. And New Haven is a proper town, not a miserable piss-hole such as this. Where would we begin?'

'At the house of John Davenport, the minister.'

'Davenport will not let us past his door. And what evidence do we have that Whalley and Goffe have even been there?'

'By God, you are a feeble crew,' muttered Nayler, loud enough for the Scotchmen at the fire to look up from their cards. He got back to his feet and returned to his place, and there he stayed, smoking his pipe, trying to see a way through, while the others retreated indoors to sleep. The worst of it was, the fault was not theirs but his alone: he knew it. He had not anticipated such stubborn recalcitrance. Perhaps Secretary Morice had been right. To settle this business, it would be necessary to send a military expedition. Except it would require not fifty men, but five hundred. He shuddered at the prospect of reporting his failure to Hyde.

The evening breeze blew away the cloud. The stars came out. The fire collapsed into glowing embers. The only sound was the occasional crack as a fresh piece of wood caught alight and sent sparks fountaining into the darkness. Snores emanated from inside the hut. He could not face going in. He spread his coat across the ground and shortly after midnight fell asleep.

The next morning, he awoke with a plan. It was not much, but it would be better than wasting an entire day in enforced idleness.

For once, he let the others sleep on, until he heard a drum being beaten outside the meeting house to summon the citizens to their first assembly of the day. Then he went around and roused them, gave each man a couple of the reward notices and a few pins and told them to put them up somewhere prominent – a street corner, outside the Guilford store, on the gatepost of Leete's house: any place they might be seen. He took one himself and walked through the deserted town to the meeting house. He could hear the Puritans inside, chanting a psalm, and he took great pleasure in placing a notice against the door and quietly tapping in the nails with the heel of his boot.

Soon after they had all returned to the inn, Kellond produced a Bible and suggested that Nayler should lead them in prayer.

'I am no priest,' said Nayler. 'Let each man pass the time according to his conscience.'

He went inside and lay down on one of the straw mattresses. It was a long time since he had been in a church. The last time had been when he had dug up Cromwell's corpse from the chapel in Westminster Abbey. He had no belief in God – Puritan, Anglican or Catholic – though he was not such a fool as to expose the fact. To maintain his position in society, he would mouth the appropriate words like everyone else. He listened as Kellond began to recite the Lord's Prayer, and to his surprise he heard the others all join in, including the Scotchmen, whom he had expected to resume playing cards. He felt a sudden exultation in his singularity. Well, damn the world for its superstition. He entertained himself by imagining the faces of the Puritans when they emerged from their meeting and discovered their Sabbath laws had been broken by the posting of the notices. Would their religion permit them to tear them down, he wondered, or would such activity count as labour?

' "Ask and it shall be given to you," ' intoned Kellond, ' "seek and ye shall find . . ." '

When their devotions were over, the young Royalist came into the dormitory. 'You did not join us, Mr Nayler.' His voice was reproachful; he was a conventional man.

'I prefer to concentrate my thoughts on the task in hand.'

'And do you really believe your offers of reward will bear fruit, even in a community such as this?'

'Why not? Behind their long faces and black garb, their minds teem with lust and avarice, the same as other men's. Would you care to take a wager on it, or will your conscience not permit gambling on the Lord's Day?'

'I doubt that anyone, in this colony especially, will wish to be seen a Judas.'

'I agree, they will not wish to be seen, which means they will come when they are least likely to be observed, either this afternoon, when the town is at its second prayer meeting, or tonight, when it is dark. Or they may not come at all. I am by no means certain. You should take the bet.'

Kellond was silent. 'You are a cynic, Mr Nayler,' he said eventually, and went outside.

Nayler dozed. In the middle of the afternoon, he was woken by the drum sounding again. Not long afterwards, he heard a click as the fence gate was unlatched, then voices in the yard. He got to his feet as Kellond and Kirke came in, accompanied by a man in his thirties, very thin and ragged-looking in his threadbare

Sabbath clothes. He took off his flat-crowned hat and lingered in the background, twisting the brim in his hands.

Kirke said, 'This fellow says he has information for us.'

'You are a wise man, sir,' said Nayler. 'May we know your name?'

'He won't give it,' said Kellond.

Nayler shook his head. 'I fear that will not do. If we are to trust you, we must know who you are.' Their visitor glanced nervously over his shoulder at the men in the yard. 'I assure you, on my honour, it will go no further than the three of us.'

Finally, the man said quietly, 'Dennis Crampton.'

'Good, Mr Crampton.' Nayler pulled out a chair from the table. 'Come. Sit and have some dinner. We have not been left much, but what we have, we shall willingly share.'

He had seldom seen a man so hungry. He allowed him time to fill his stomach. He wanted him to feel comfortable in their company. And gradually, between mouthfuls of bread and cold meat, Crampton told them his history – born in Devon, emigrated to New England at the age of twenty, pitched up in New Haven, married but childless, his barren wife accused of witchcraft on account of her supposed envy of neighbouring mothers and dead of a fever while still under suspicion ('the gossip broke her'); how he had lost his way in life ('I freely confess it, gentlemen') and been whipped on the orders of Reverend Davenport for being drunk on the Sabbath (a charge he vehemently denied), how he had lately come to Guilford in the hope of employment but found the place no better than the last. He wiped his mouth on his sleeve. 'I have great need of that reward money, sir. It would set me on my feet again and pay for my passage back to England.'

'And you shall have it, Mr Crampton,' said Nayler, clasping his hand on the man's bony knee, 'you shall have it if you can lead us to Whalley and Goffe. Now.' He pulled out his notebook and a stub of pencil. 'To business.'

'Well, I have seen them with my own eyes, sir, drilling the militia in New Haven, on which occasion Colonel Whalley declared that if he and Goffe had but two hundred such men who would stand by them, they would fear nothing in Old England, nor in New England neither.'

'He said that?'

'I watched him muster the cavalry and heard him with my own ears.'

Nayler made him repeat the exact words. He wrote them down. ' "Two hundred such men . . ." You hear that?' he said to Kellond and Kirke. 'They plot another rebellion against the King.' He turned back to Crampton. 'And are they still in New Haven?'

'The folk that live there will tell you not, but I know different.'

'Go on.'

'They lodged with Davenport for several weeks from the start of March, then left for New Amsterdam to take ship for Holland, or so it was said. But it is my belief they returned soon after and hid themselves beneath his roof again.'

'You have some evidence for that?'

'In April, Davenport's servants laid in ten pounds' worth of food above their normal order from the New Haven store.' He sat back proudly.

Nayler made a note. 'So they may be still at Davenport's even as we speak?'

'That I cannot say. I know for a fact they sometimes moved across the street to the house of Mr William Jones, the son of the regicide, because I saw them one night when I was staying with John Thorp – very late, when no one was about.'

'You saw them after they were supposed to have gone to New

Amsterdam?' Nayler leaned forward. 'That is an honest fact? The truth now – no exaggeration.'

'Yes, sir, I believe I did, though they hid at my approach.'

'When was this?'

'Less than a fortnight since.'

Nayler closed his notebook. That was clever, to lay a false trail. They were cunning. But he was more cunning. 'Gentlemen,' he said, 'I do believe we have them.'

CHAPTER TWENTY-ONE

I N A CORNER of the ruined mill, the colonels spent the Sabbath out of sight, praying and studying the Bible. From time to time, Ned went over to the window to check no one was lurking outside, as much to alleviate the boredom as anything else. Bees hummed between the purple heads of the weeds and flew away, heavily laden with amber beads of pollen. He craved a pipe of tobacco, but he knew Will would disapprove. Towards the end of the afternoon, he suggested they should stretch their legs.

Will frowned at him in disapproval. 'But we have walked our allotted two miles. It would be an offence.'

'An offence against whom? God or Mr Davenport? I do believe them to be quite separate entities, even if Mr Davenport tends to forget the fact.'

'Now you are blaspheming.' Will went back to his Bible. 'You walk if you wish. I shan't move until first light.'

For a minute or two Ned stayed where he was, then he stamped outside, muttering under his breath.

Will did not live in the real world, that was his trouble. He never had. Ned could see him now – gaunt, pale, Christ-like, not yet thirty, with his long dark hair and beard, ranting from the pulpit at a meeting of the army in Putney back in '47. His speeches, always very popular among the men, had teemed with visions and prophecies. He had even had the nerve to lecture Lieutenant General Cromwell on his imperfect understanding of God, so much so that Cromwell had demanded he apologise (which he did, before the whole congregation, very meekly).

But Cromwell, with that odd sentimental streak of his, had taken a shine to him: 'That young man has the power of the Spirit in him.' And so Ned had made the mistake, a year or so later, not long after the King's execution, when their regiments were both quartered in London, of inviting him home to dinner after church, only to observe Frances – then barely sixteen – making eyes at the handsome officer all afternoon. Katherine had thought it a good enough match – Will was by this time a colonel – but Ned, not keen to have a Fifth Monarchist for a son-in-law, had made it a condition, when Will had asked for his permission to marry, that they wait two years, until the campaign against the Scotch was over. And now here they were, a decade later, and it was not Frances who had ended up yoked to him till death us do part, but Ned Whalley!

He walked a little way along the path, then went down to the stream. He pulled off his boots, rolled up his trousers and stood in the water, inhaling the peace of the wood, the scent of pine resin, the cooing of the pigeons, the gentle splash of the flow over the stones. Midges swirled above the surface, like dust thrown into a shaft of sunlight; occasionally a fish rose to a mayfly. It was foolish to linger in such a spot, less than an hour's walk from New Haven, when there was a search party in the neighbourhood. They should at the very least get up into the hills, which rose less than a mile away, where they would have the advantage of height and be able to see their enemy approaching. He toyed briefly with the idea of setting off alone, but that he could never do – he was ashamed for even thinking it.

He sat on the bank and let his feet dry, put on his boots and went back to the mill. But his son-in-law was still sulking, and no more words were exchanged between them until the sun had set and they lay down to sleep.

At dawn on Monday, Goodman Bishop, the Guilford innkeeper, turned up as promised, leading the two fresh horses Nayler had paid for – money was money, after all – and an hour later the search party was on the road. Crampton tried to wheedle his way out of coming with them, but Nayler was insistent: he must join them to point out the houses of Davenport and Jones, otherwise there would be no reward. He told him brusquely to stop complaining and mount up behind Mackwater, the smallest of the Scotchmen.

The track wound through a forest of pine and scrub oak, the sea sparkling through the trees to their left, taking them over steep ridges and shallow streams and alongside brackish lagoons. They passed a couple of big Indian settlements, where crowds of natives were standing on the shoreline watching the nets being cast. Around nine o'clock, on the opposite side of the estuary, the harbour of New Haven came into view. They were held up for a half-hour waiting for the ferry to fetch them, but as soon as they were across, they mustered on the quayside, drew their weapons and rode at a fast trot towards the town. People watched them in alarm. As soon as they reached the first corner, Crampton called for them to stop. He slid down from his horse and came up to Nayler.

'That there is the Davenport place,' he said, indicating a large house facing towards the harbour, 'and that bigger one up the street to the right is Jones's. And now, sir, may I have my money?'

'You shall have your reward when the traitors are dead or in chains. Wait here and guard the horses. You too, Mr Chapin.'

Nayler dismounted and gave Crampton his reins. The others gathered round him on foot. He surveyed the spacious properties. By God, they did themselves well, these prosperous Puritans: they lived like lords. 'Which one first, I wonder?'

Kellond said, 'Do we not require a warrant from the governor before we search?'

'We cannot wait for that.'

Kirke said, 'Davenport's is the closer.'

Nayler nodded. It was as good a basis for a choice as any. 'Davenport's it is then. Mr Stewart and Mr Ross, will you take up a position at the rear and make sure no one escapes?' He cocked his pistol.

With a sword in his left hand and his gun in his right, he led Kellond and Kirke, Mackwater and Niven across the road and through the gate. His heart was thumping, but he felt quite cold and calm. At the door, he said, 'Captain Kirke, will you do the honours?' He took a step backwards and trained his gun on the entrance. Kirke hammered with his pistol butt on the heavy studded door. After half a minute, when no one had appeared, Nayler called out to him to open it.

He pushed past him and entered first, his finger tight on his trigger. So excited was he – so certain he had cornered his prey – he almost let off a shot at the black-garbed figure coming down the stairs. But at the last moment he saw that it was the minister and lowered his pistol. He mounted the stairs two at a time. Davenport was shouting at him in outrage. Nayler shouldered him out of the way. He reached the landing and walked rapidly along the passage, opening the doors on either side. In the first room he surprised an elderly woman, her startled white face turned towards him, and in the next a young man in a nightdress. The other chambers were all deserted. He worked his way back along the passage, stopping to search under the beds. Nothing. He returned to the landing.

'How is it with you, Mr Kellond?'

Kellond shouted up the stairs, 'All clear down here, Mr Nayler!'

Nayler grabbed Kirke by the elbow and turned him round. 'We're in the wrong house!'

They clattered down the staircase, past Davenport – who was kneeling in the hallway with his hands clasped, praying loudly – and out into the street. They ran around the corner. It took them less than two minutes to reach Jones's house, and this time Nayler didn't even bother with the formality of knocking. He flung open the door and headed upstairs with Kirke and Mackwater at his heels, but even as he mounted the steps, the place sounded hollow, and he could feel his hopes evaporating with every stride. It was the same story as at the Davenports' – empty rooms, undisturbed beds, no evidence the regicides had ever been present, except perhaps in one room, where the faintest trace of stale tobacco smoke lingered to mock him. Jaw set in frustration, he went back downstairs. An elderly couple and a heavily pregnant woman were being guarded by Niven at gunpoint. Ross and Stewart converged from opposite ends of the hall.

'Any sign?'

'Only these three.'

He turned on the pregnant woman. 'Where is William Jones?'

She was trembling violently. 'He is not at home.'

'That I can see. Where is he?'

She gasped and fell back against the wall. Her eyes swivelled upwards, turning the sockets marble white, and if instinct had not propelled him forward to catch her, she would have toppled in a dead faint onto the stone floor.

Jones was at that moment running through the wood as if Beelzebub himself was on his tail.

Ned, sitting in the mill house on his spread-out coat, whittling a stick with his penknife, heard the cracking of twigs outside. He and Will both seized their pistols, but before they were even properly on their feet, Jones was in the doorway – scarlet-faced, breathless, barely able to stammer out his words.

'They've come for you.' He leaned against the broken door frame, panting, doubled over. 'They're at the Davenports' now.'

'Did anyone see you leave?' asked Ned.

'I couldn't say. I think not.'

The colonels hoisted their bags.

'Where to now?' asked Will.

'The hills,' said Ned. 'It'll have to be.' And then, to Jones: 'Thanks for the warning. You'd best get back before you're missed.'

'There's a farmer I know, a little way on.'

'Can we trust him?'

'I believe so. I'll take you.'

Now here is peril, thought Ned as they hurried out onto the path. This is how we die – running from pillar to post, forced to put our trust in strangers, each one less known to us than the last. But what else was there to do?

The morning was turning hot now. As the ground became steeper and they climbed in their heavy army coats towards the cliffs, they began to sweat. A cottage built of stone appeared ahead, and the figure of a man in white shirtsleeves chopping logs. The rhythmic blows of the axe mingled with the sound of woodpeckers and twittering birds.

Jones said, 'Wait here. I'll speak with him.'

Ned dropped his bag and sank gratefully to the forest floor, legs stretched out. He looked over his shoulder at the path behind them. It wound through the trees and dipped out of sight. He listened hard but could hear nothing that suggested pursuit.

'Take heart,' said Will. 'We've been in tighter scrapes.'

'If so, I'd be obliged if you could name them.'

Will laughed at that, and after a few moments Ned joined in. He lay full length on his back and felt the sun on his face, glad to at least be out in the open. He wondered who they were, these eight men on their trail. By God, if he was to die, he'd like to take a few down with him.

Jones returned with the farmer. His rolled-up sleeves showed muscled arms, brown as leather, and a long scar on his right arm from his elbow to his wrist. He looked as if he had been in a fight or two. The colonels stood. Jones said, 'This is Richard Sperry. Richard, these are the friends I spoke of.'

Sperry nodded but did not offer his hand.

Jones said, 'He'll show you a place where you can shelter. I'll return as soon as it's safe.' He embraced them both, and with a final 'God be with you' set off back to New Haven.

'We are—' Will began, but Sperry cut him off.

'I know who you are. Best not speak of it. The less I know, the fewer lies I'll need to tell.'

He set off without another word. They lifted their bags onto their shoulders and followed him – first to the yard of his cottage, where he collected his axe and a weighty coil of rope, and then for about a mile along the path, climbing ever steeper, until abruptly he left it and led them into the gloom of the forest. There was a strange thundering noise that gradually became much louder, and through the trees they saw a waterfall, plunging a good forty feet over the edge of a rust-coloured cliff face into a pool that fed a stream.

Sperry said, 'Stay here.'

He looped the rope around his neck, tucked the axe into his thick leather belt and began to climb the cliff, swinging from foothold to foothold, weaving back and forth as he ascended the sheer rock. Ned put his hand to his forehead to shield his eyes from the sun and followed his progress. 'By heavens,' he muttered, 'does he mean for us to follow him?'

Sperry reached the top and vanished over the edge. A moment later, he reappeared and began paying out the rope. He shouted down, 'I'll start with the bags.'

They tied Ned's first, and Sperry hauled it up quickly, banging it against the rock. He took the next bag, and then called down to Will to tie the rope around his waist. 'Don't be afeared, I have you.'

Ned could not bear to watch, but then he thought he must, to see how it was done. There was no careful seeking-out of footholds. Will went up straight, leaning out at an angle from the cliff, his hands clutching the rope, as if he were walking along the ground. Near the top, his boot slipped, and Ned cried out, certain he must fall. But the rope held, and after dangling for a few moments, Will leaned out once more and finished his ascent.

Sperry paid out the rope again. Ned was sure he could never manage it. If it came to it, he would sooner die fighting with his back to the wall of rock than be killed in a fall. He shouted up, 'No, I cannot. I am too old, and too heavy.'

Will called back, 'We can hold you, Ned. So long as you are tied tight, you cannot fall.'

'Come on, Colonel,' shouted Sperry. 'I fought at Marston Moor. If you can beat a king, you can beat a bit of rock.'

A veteran, thought Ned. That explained the scar – a pike wound, probably. It put things in a different light. He'd never lost face in front of his men. He'd be damned if he'd do so now.

He tied the rope around his stomach, fixed it with a triple knot and felt the line tauten. He grabbed it in both hands, hauled himself up, and began to climb. With every third or fourth step, the soles of his boots slipped against the smooth rock, but somehow, leaning back, he managed to maintain his purchase. The last part was the worst – swaying out in the breeze over the sheer drop. He made the mistake of looking down, and that almost did for him. But then he closed his eyes and scrabbled the final couple of steps, and Will leaned out and grasped his wrist and dragged him to safety.

He crawled on his hands and knees away from the edge. He stood and brushed away the dirt on his coat and surveyed the spot. A wide ledge, maybe thirty paces across, extending like a roadway in either direction, strewn with boulders and bushes and small trees, to one of which the rope was anchored. Another wall of rock behind them, with a cleft in it as wide as a man and twice as high, which looked as though it might lead to a cave. A cascade of water into a clear pool. And a view, magnificent, across the forest to the plain, with New Haven's grid of streets plainly visible, and the harbour, and the sea beyond it stretching to the horizon.

Sperry said, 'The cave is dry, though the wind does howl when she blows off the sea. There's a track to the top, but hard to find. You should be safe enough.'

'Shelter, water, aspect,' said Ned. 'It is the perfect place.'

'I'll leave the rope and send my lad later with food in a basket, which you may haul up. Don't show yourselves – it's best he doesn't see you.'

Before they could properly express their thanks, he was gone, shinning down the rope.

'This will do us very well,' said Ned, 'for a night or two, at least, or even longer if needs be.' He climbed up onto a boulder. 'We can keep a good lookout from up here.'

He extended his spyglass and trained it on New Haven. Groups of figures were moving purposefully through the streets towards the south-east corner of the town, where Jones and Davenport lived. He watched them for a while, trying to make out what was happening. Whatever it was, it looked like trouble.

By the end of the morning, Nayler's mission was mired in difficulty, and the situation, far from progressing, was turning ugly.

Hannah Jones's waters had broken, and she had gone into labour and been taken upstairs. Word had spread through the town that an outrage of some kind had been committed, and twenty or more citizens – several of the menfolk armed with their militia swords and pistols – had congregated in the yard. Davenport was conducting a prayer meeting in the street, appealing to God to protect mother, child and community (' "And let them make me a sanctuary, that I may dwell among them . . ." ').

In the middle of all this, Governor Leete had arrived with another sombre magistrate of the colony – Mr Joseph Crane, from the nearby town of Branford – and was angrily demanding an explanation.

Nayler stood with Kellond and Kirke and the rest of his search party on the side of the road, between the Jones and Davenport houses. He had ordered his men to put away their weapons to avoid further provocation. Crampton had disappeared. Nayler was attempting to mollify Leete.

'We had good intelligence that Whalley and Goffe were in one or other of these properties. It was necessary for us to act upon it quickly.'

'You had no legal authority.'

'Is the authority of the King not recognised in this part of his dominions? Really, Mr Leete, I am bound to say, you have done everything in your power to frustrate us.'

'And I am also bound – by the laws of this colony.'

Davenport, who had come over to listen to their argument, joined in. 'The sole authority in New Haven is God.'

Nayler had already taken the minister's measure – pious one minute, imperious the next; the worst kind of hypocritical religious despot. He lost his temper. 'Do you deny, sir, that the regicides lived under your roof? You cannot! The whole town knows it. They drilled the militia and preached sedition.'

'They did indeed lodge briefly with me, and if you had treated me with courtesy, I would have explained the facts. I had no knowledge of any warrant for their arrest, and by the time I learned of it, they had left.'

'To take ship at New Amsterdam?'

'So it is said. They were seen in Milford, on the road to New Netherland.'

' "So it is said"! What manner of reply is that? These men are wanted for the murder of the King.' He swung back to Leete. 'I demand the right to search the town.'

Leete said, 'Before I have the authority to draw up such a warrant, I must first have the agreement of Mr Crane here, and of two other magistrates, Mr Gilbert of New Haven and Mr Treat of Milford.'

'And where are they?'

'They are sent for.'

'I swear this colony has more magistrates than people.' Nayler looked over Leete's shoulder, at a man hurrying down the street from the northern part of the town. He seemed to be a notable figure. People were taking off their hats, murmuring to him, patting him on the shoulder. 'Who is that person?'

Davenport said, 'That is William Jones, whose wife you so cruelly abused.'

'Jones? The son of the regicide? And where has he been all this time?' Nayler left the group and strode up the street. 'Mr Jones! A word, sir, if you please.'

Jones halted at his gate. 'I shall speak to you after I have seen my wife.'

From inside the house came the sound of a baby crying. They both glanced at the open upstairs window. Nayler felt an unexpected surge of relief. He had not wanted a miscarriage on his conscience – that would have been the bitterest of ironies. He seized Jones by the arm. 'I insist you answer my questions now.'

'You have no right, sir.' Jones shook himself free, and disappeared inside, and when Nayler moved to follow him, his path was blocked by two burly men in Puritan dress. He turned away, went back down the street and beckoned to Kellond and Kirke to join him.

'That Jones – whose traitor father I caught and hanged last summer – has just spirited away the regicides, I'm sure of it.'

'But we searched the house,' objected Kirke. 'There was no trace of them. How could they have moved so quickly?'

'Perhaps they left while we were detained in Guilford, and he has just returned from warning them.' Suddenly he glimpsed what must have happened. 'This ban of theirs, on travelling over the Sabbath – it would have applied to Whalley and Goffe, would it not? They'd not have been permitted to go further than two miles. Jones came from the north just now.' He looked at the cliffs beyond the town. 'That's where they are. I feel it in my bones. Mr Chapin!' he shouted to the guide. 'Do you know those hills at all?'

'A little.'

'Take us there.'

'And the town?' asked Kellond. 'Are we not to search it?'

'There must be a hundred houses here, and we are only eight men. It'll take us days, we'll find nothing, and our quarry will all the while be up there, laughing at us.' Nayler could not bear the thought of being mocked, of being defeated by these wretched people. He could sense the regicides slipping through his fingers. He called out to the Scotchmen, 'Mount up. We're moving on.'

As the four men moved towards their horses, Leete hurried to intercept him. 'You must not search till I have spoken with the magistrates.'

'Speak with your magistrates, sir, and when I return to London, I shall speak with the Privy Council, and then we shall see whose speech has most power in this colony.'

He swung himself up onto his horse, dug his heels into its flanks, and set off up the street, followed by the others. The towns-people outside Jones's house briefly tried to block their way, but he galloped straight at them, scattering them like bowling pins, and the way ahead was clear – to the green, the meeting house, and the road to the distant hills.

Watching through his spyglass, Ned observed the party of riders moving through the town. He continued to watch them until they disappeared into the wood. He lowered the telescope. 'I count eight men, doubtless coming our way.'

'They are unlikely to discover us up here.'

'Even so . . .' he clambered down awkwardly from the boulder, 'we should put away that rope and hide our bags.'

Chapin went ahead of the rest. Occasionally he dismounted to inspect the track. They would halt to watch him as he prodded the leaves and twigs and put his face close to the ground. But each time he looked up and shook his head. He stopped again at the ruined mill and went inside. When he emerged, he said, 'There was a fire lit.'

'How recent?' asked Nayler.

'It's cold. I cannot say.'

He looked back at the path. 'Do you reckon we've come two miles yet?'

'Aye, just about.'

He took off his hat and wiped the sweat from his face. He felt the sting of a mosquito on the side of his neck and clapped his hand to it then inspected his palm, a trace of his blood amid the black smear of its corpse. He rubbed it off on his leg. 'So they could have rested here over the Sabbath and then moved on this morning? By God, we're only two or three hours behind – so close I swear I can almost smell them.'

They set off again. After a while, they reached a stone cottage. Nayler jumped down from his horse, drew his pistol, went forwards and knocked on the door. It was opened by a woman with a baby in her arms and another child clutching her skirt. She was drab and beaten-down-looking, her frizzled brown hair already threaded with grey.

Nayler said, 'Is there a man of the house?'

'He's hunting with our boy.'

'My name is Nayler. We are officers of the Crown, on the track of criminals. You will permit a brief inspection, to make sure you're safe.'

He went straight in without waiting for a response. Mackwater and Kellond followed him, while Kirke and the other Scotchmen headed for the outhouses. The search took no time. There was nothing to see except evidence of a hard life – rough home-made furniture, wooden plates, plain whitewashed walls. On a peg on the back of a door hung an old buff coat, New Model Army issue. Nayler felt the thickness of the leather between thumb and forefinger.

'Your husband fought with Cromwell?'

She did not reply.

'What is his name?'

'Richard Sperry.'

Nayler made a note. He went out to the others. 'The colonels passed this way – they must have done, if they were heading for higher ground. The farmer here is an old Roundhead. My guess is he must be helping them.' Their expressions were sceptical. He could see they were becoming exhausted and disheartened. 'Cheer up, lads! We must press on. Mr Chapin?'

They toiled on up the track behind their guide as the day grew hotter, the climb steeper, the mosquitoes hungrier. Nayler began to feel as though the peaceful emptiness of the forest was taunting him. Chapin no longer bothered to stop and look for clues. A perilous narrow path, winding up the side of the cliffs, drew them westwards until they came out onto the summit of the ridge of hills, the plain of New Haven spread beneath them. Without waiting for Nayler's command, the men dismounted and threw themselves down in the shade of the scrub oaks and passed around a gourd of water. There was insolence in the action, he thought – insurrection, even.

'Well, we are here, Mr Nayler,' said Kirke, 'as you commanded, on the ridge. Now what do you intend?'

He lifted his leg and swung himself out of his saddle but remained standing. 'To rest a while and then continue.'

Kirke looked around at the others, as if seeking their support. 'To what purpose, might we ask? You could put an army up here for a week and they'd still find nothing.'

'That is not the spirit of our enterprise, Captain Kirke. We have a commission; we must discharge it.'

'Aye, but as it stands, we are chasing the uncatchable.'

'That's right,' said Stewart, the Springfield blacksmith. His compatriots nodded.

Kirke continued, his tone becoming more defiant, 'If the colonels live rough in open country, then their arrest is a different task entirely to the one you set us back in Boston – impossible, in fact.' Further nods of agreement. 'Would it not be more profitable to return to New Haven, give out your posters, see what intelligence we may gather, and then follow their trail towards New Amsterdam? Davenport says they were seen in Milford. That should be our next stop.'

'But surely that is a false scent? If it really was their plan to board a ship to Holland, don't you think they would have taken pains to keep it secret? Instead, they told the entire town of their intention, then made sure they were noticed in Milford.' It was so plain to him at that moment, so entirely obvious, he was amazed they could not grasp it. 'You may embark on a wild goose chase, Captain Kirke, if that is your preference, but I shall search for them here.'

It was a mistake to have made such an offer. He wished at once he could take it back. But he was hot and vexed, and his leg was aching, and he realised too late that he had in effect given them permission to abandon the search.

'Very well,' said Kirke quickly, with his merchant's eye for clinching a good bargain before it was snatched off the table. 'That's what we shall do, if the others all agree?'

They did – even young Kellond, who was the most obedient of the party; even the dogged Chapin, who said sorrowfully that he felt the trail had now gone cold.

As they mounted to return to New Haven, Kirke called down from his saddle, 'We shall meet up with you in the town later, Mr Nayler. Or on the road to New Amsterdam, if you care to follow us. Otherwise, we'll await you in Boston. God be with you.'

Nayler sat in the shade with his head in his hands and listened to their descent – the whinnying of the horses, the scrabble of stones running down the slope, the murmur of their voices – and then the silence of the ridge closed over him and he felt utterly abandoned. It took all his willpower not to go after them.

Very well then – alone.

He stood, checked his pistol, tucked it into his belt, remounted and rode slowly along the ridge, stopping now and again to take out his spyglass and scan the canopy of trees beneath the cliff. He moved cautiously, conscious that if by some extraordinary stroke of luck he found the regicides, the odds had abruptly shifted in their favour. Even so, he was not afraid. Death held no terrors for him: he could imagine that when the moment arrived, he might almost welcome it.

He came to a spring that fed a stream and stopped to let his horse drink. He got down himself and cupped the fresh cold water, gulping it, splashing his face and tipping it over his head. The stream ran a little distance then poured over the lip of the ridge. He walked alongside it to the edge of the cliff and looked down at the wide ledge, some twenty feet below, where the water tumbled into a pool.

After watching it for a few minutes, he tied his horse to one of the stunted oaks and picked his way between the boulders and bushes until he thought he saw a promising spot. He sat, and gently eased himself over the edge until his feet were dangling, then turned and began to descend. A couple of minutes later, he dropped onto the ledge.

He drew his pistol from his belt, cocked it, and moved forwards. There was a cleft in the rock, partly obscured by bushes. At first he walked past it, thinking it no more than a shallow fissure, then he checked himself and went back. It was deeper than he had realised, but narrow – he had to twist to squeeze his body into the gap, and edged along with his head turned to one side, his chest rubbing against the rock. The aperture widened slightly, and he was in a passage. Not that he could make out much. It curved to the right, and once he had moved further from the opening, he could see nothing at all. The roof was high: he reached up but couldn't touch it. He stood listening. A silence as profound as the darkness.

He brought up his pistol and held it at arm's length, aiming it into the black emptiness as he ventured towards the interior. Now it seemed limitless. He could no longer feel the walls. He stopped again to listen, but all he could hear was his own heartbeat. Slowly he turned full circle. He felt entirely disorientated, adrift in space. Suddenly he couldn't breathe. I am dead and in my tomb, he thought. Oh Sarah, Sarah, I have gone mad, and this is where my madness has brought me.

Arms flailing, he lurched in a panic towards where he imagined the wall must be. He banged his shoulder against it, clung onto it for a few moments while he recovered his nerve, then felt his way along the rock, around the corner, back towards the narrow entrance and the blinding crack of light.

Behind him, at the far end of the cave, their guns still cocked and pointed, the colonels stood motionless in the absolute dark.

CHAPTER TWENTY-TWO

I T TOOK NAYLER much longer to climb up from the ledge than it had to clamber down. He had to work his way crab-wise across the cliff face in search of footholds, jamming his toecaps into narrow cracks and clutching at protruding roots, some of which came away in his hand. But his strength was all in his upper torso, in those wrestler's arms and shoulders that compensated for his weakened leg, and eventually, dripping sweat, he reached the clifftop. After sitting a while to recover his breath, he untethered his horse and hauled himself into the saddle. The mare seemed to know her own way back, which was just as well, carrying him along the ridge and down the steep track to the forest floor. He barely registered Sperry's farmhouse as he passed it, nor the ruined mill. His black dog loped beside him.

By the time he reached New Haven, the sun was sinking; the shadow of the meeting house stretched far across the green. After the disturbances of the morning, the settlement was quiet. A couple strolled by arm in arm, taking the evening air. He asked them for directions to the inn.

As he had anticipated, the men of his searching party were gathered downstairs drinking wine and ale.

'Mr Nayler,' cried Captain Kirke, raising his glass, 'did you have much joy?' He was smirking.

'Never mind that. Have you conducted a search of the town?' Those who knew Nayler of old would have taken notice of his dead-calm tone.

'We still lack a warrant.' The captain took another swig of wine.

'Is that so?'

'It is.'

'You have drunk enough, I think.'

'I shall drink as I wish.'

'Not while I am paying you.' Nayler stepped forwards and calmly knocked the glass from his hand. Kirke swore and started rising to his feet. Nayler swung his fist and punched him on the side of his head, very hard – hard enough to send him sprawling to the floorboards, where he groaned and tried to sit up and then fell back again.

Sucking his skinned knuckles, Nayler glanced around at the other men, daring them to intervene, and when no one met his gaze, he climbed the stairs to the dormitory and lay down on the first bed he saw. He turned his face to the wall, and there he remained as night fell, until he heard footsteps and Kellond's voice. 'Mr Nayler, sir?' His tone was nervous, respectful. 'Governor Leete has come to talk to you.'

'Tell him to go away.'

'He says he has news of the warrant.'

'I have retired for the night.'

'He is most persistent.'

Nayler groaned, rolled over and put his feet to the floor.

Downstairs, Kirke was slumped over a table, apparently asleep, his head resting on his folded arms. Nayler was confident he would have no further trouble from that quarter: even the Scotchmen were sitting well apart from him, as if he had the plague. Leete stood in the doorway.

'Governor Leete,' said Nayler. 'You wish a word?'

'In private, if you please.'

'You sing a different song, sir. I thought you had nothing to say to me that couldn't be said in public?'

'Even so.'

The two men went outside. The quiet was unearthly. Nayler wondered how they could stand it. No wonder they were all half insane.

'I wish,' sighed Leete, 'that I were the humblest ploughman, that I might be spared these responsibilities.'

'I'm sure that no one forced them upon you. Do you have the warrant?'

'I have hopes of obtaining one tomorrow.'

'In that case, you do not have it.' Nayler turned to go, but Leete caught his arm.

'It is not my doing, Mr Nayler. It is the magistrates. Reverend Davenport has them under his influence. Yet I have great hopes that good sense will prevail in the morning – great hopes.'

'Too late, sir. Too little and too late. I no longer wish to search this place. There is no point to it. The birds have flown. You have played me for a fool, sir.' He could feel his rage welling up again. 'And now you shall pay the cost. And of one thing you may be certain. When the royal charters are issued, there will be a state of Massachusetts, and there will be a state of Connecticut, but there will never – never, as long as a king sits on the throne of England – *never* will there be a state of New Haven. Your little land of Moses here is finished. I bid you goodnight.'

★

The search party quit the town the following morning – not early, as there now seemed little point, but only when the sun was well up – and rode along the coast to Milford. There, Nayler remained outside the general store while Kellond and Kirke (the captain now mild as a lamb) interrogated its owner, Micah Tomkins. He confirmed that the regicides had stopped by in March, and had bought a few objects and provisions before riding off in the direction of New Amsterdam. He claimed not to have realised who they were until after they had gone. At Nayler's insistence, despite the lack of a warrant, the store was searched – its outbuildings as well as the nearby house – but nothing was found. He did not expect otherwise: he only ordered it because Tomkins protested his rights so loudly and because he was sure the man was part of the conspiracy; the Scotchmen made sure to break a few items.

After two days' hard riding, they reached New Amsterdam and went directly to the fort to see its director general, Peter Stuyvesant. He was sixty, ill-tempered – had lost a leg in the Indies to a Spanish cannonball – but lacked the military resources to refuse a request from the English, who far outnumbered the Dutch. He stamped across his office on his wooden peg to greet them, read the royal mandate and Endecott's letter with a businessman's thoroughness, and undertook, in his correct but thickly accented English, to have all the vessels in the harbour searched. He also issued an order that anyone travelling under the names of Whalley and Goffe – or Richardson and Stephenson – should be prevented from leaving. More than that he could not do, he added apologetically, without authorisation from his masters in Holland, and as the Dutch government had turned down all requests to arrest those regicides sheltering within its borders, he did not hold out much hope.

'And have you heard reports of Whalley and Goffe,' asked

Nayler, 'or anyone who might be them in disguise, coming into your territory?'

'No, sir, I have not.'

'You see?' said Nayler, turning to Kellond and Kirke with a smile of bitter triumph. 'It was a false trail.'

After the meeting, they rode down from the fort to the Monhatoes docks, with a letter of authorisation signed by Stuyvesant, and while the others went from ship to ship to interview their captains, Nayler – who regarded these formalities as a waste of time – sat on a capstan on the harbourfront, smoking his pipe, half listening to the gruff Dutch voices all around him. It was a warm afternoon – a clear blue sky, seagulls crying over the water, the buoys riding high on the choppy tide. Beyond the ships anchored in the channel he could see the flat grey ribbon of Long Island, a few houses and a windmill outlined against the sky. The fort was very lightly defended, he noticed, compared to Boston. No more than twenty cannon. He must remember to report that.

The noise of the gulls and the play of the light reminded him of his arrival in America, when he had been so full of misplaced hope. What a fool he had been. He thought with sudden longing of London and its fine buildings, and of his chambers in Essex House and his office in Whitehall Palace; of the familiar English countryside of tightly clustered villages and stone churches and small fields narrowly hedged. He even recalled with fondness the stink of the Thames at low tide and the sewage along the Strand.

A few minutes later, Kellond and Kirke appeared, the younger man carrying a ledger. To his surprise, their expressions were triumphant. 'You have made a discovery?'

'We have,' said Kirke. 'Perhaps it was not such a false trail after all.'

Kellond handed Nayler the leather-bound volume. He clamped the pipe between his teeth and balanced the book on his knee. He opened it at a page marked with a sheet of paper.

'What is this?'

'The cargo manifest of the *Vleigende Draeck* – the *Flying Dragon*. The customs master allowed us to borrow his record book to show you. She sailed on April the third for Rotterdam, carrying tobacco mostly, and twelve passengers. The seventh and eighth names are of interest.'

Nayler looked down the list.

Edw. Richardson.

Wm. Stephenson.

He grunted, cocked his head. 'But this is too neat, surely?' Even so, he held on to the ledger and frowned at the names.

Kirke said, 'True. But then what evidence do we have that they did *not* take ship on the *Flying Dragon* but instead returned to New Haven? Nothing, save the word of Dennis Crampton, the only man who claims to have seen them – a proven rogue with a grudge against the town. And where is Crampton? He vanished as soon as Leete arrived in New Haven.'

'Yet Leete and the magistrates did not behave like men with nothing to hide.'

'They had very much to hide,' said Kellond. 'Their involvement in the escape is plain. Maybe they wished to make sure all trace of the regicides had been removed before we searched. Or perhaps they were not sure that Whalley and Goffe had got away, and wanted to give them more time.'

Nayler thought this over. 'It is possible,' he conceded. He handed back the ledger. 'But I am not convinced. The whole thing is most likely a trick designed to persuade us to give up the search.'

'You mean to continue?'

'Most certainly. I shan't rest till I have them in my hands or I know for certain they are dead.'

Kellond and Kirke exchanged glances. 'Forgive us, Mr Nayler,' said Kellond, 'but there is a ship in harbour, sailing to Boston tomorrow.'

'What of it?'

'We had it in our minds that we might join her, in preference to travelling home by land – there seems little left for us to do here.'

Nayler thought how shifty Kellond looked. He had an inspiration. 'And would this ship, by any chance, be named the *Charles*?'

'As a matter of fact, yes.'

'The same name as your family's vessel? Well, there is another neat coincidence. Now I understand your keenness to reach New Amsterdam.' He tapped his pipe on the side of the capstan and blew down the stem to clear it. He recognised defeat. 'I agree, the trail here has run out. We might as well abandon it. But on one condition: you say nothing of this manifest. I do not wish to give those Puritan governors any fresh excuse to do nothing. You agree?'

'We agree.'

The following afternoon, leaving Chapin and the Scotch to make their own way home with the horses, the three men sailed for Boston.

You have eluded me this time, thought Nayler, as he stood at the gunwale and watched the shoreline recede. But I have raised such a hue and cry against you that if you are still here, I believe your lives will be quite wretched. You cannot hide for ever. I shall have you one day.

Already in his restless mind he was plotting a visit to Holland, and if that failed, another expedition to New England.

★

Nayler was correct. From the time of their near encounter in the cave, the colonels' lives had indeed become quite wretched, almost as if a curse had been put upon them.

Because of their fear that the intruder might be lurking outside and could pick them off with a pistol as they emerged, they stayed in the darkness, risking the occasional whisper.

'How many were there?'

'Only one, I think . . .'

'Has he gone?'

'I'm not sure . . .'

'There might be others close by . . .'

'He could have heard us and gone for help . . .'

By the time they decided to risk squeezing back through the crevice into the open air, it was dusk. If Sperry's son had tried to bring food, they had missed him. The pool at the base of the higher waterfall at least gave them plenty to drink. Searching for firewood in the fading light, Ned found a small axe – Indian, by the look of it – and in its honour they called their refuge Hatchet Harbour and gave thanks to God for their deliverance. But their relief was short-lived. They decided they dared not light a fire lest it be seen from the town, glowing in the night sky like a comet. And the narrowness of the entrance made the cave feel like a trap, so they slept out under the stars.

Sperry's son appeared as promised on their second afternoon and called up to the ledge in a piping voice. They lowered the rope and hauled up a basket, but when they opened it, they discovered only a meagre portion of bread and cheese, which they devoured at once. On the third morning, they heard a man's shout. They let down the rope, and Sperry scaled the rock face. His first question was whether anyone had passed by, and they told him about the man who had come into the cave and stood listening in the darkness. Will said he could not have been more than twenty paces from them. They could even hear his breathing.

'Doubtless that would be Nayler,' said Sperry, 'come all the way from London to find you, or so it's claimed.'

'Who is he?'

'A terror, I can tell you that. He put the fear of God into my wife.'

'Is he still in the town?'

'He's taken his search party towards New Amsterdam. But Mr Jones says he's made the whole of New England unsafe for you by his threats of punishment and the posting of reward notices. Jones asks me to tell you that you must keep away from the towns until he advises otherwise.'

'But we cannot stay here for ever,' protested Ned.

'Not here. I know a better spot.'

They gathered their possessions and followed him along the ledge until he found the place he was looking for, where they adopted the same procedure as before – Sperry climbed the cliff, threw down the rope, hauled up their bags and then helped each of them ascend in turn.

The second place offered some improvement on the first. It was not so much a cave as a heap of half a dozen massive rocks – like a pagan temple, thought Ned, a natural Stonehenge – that formed a shelter roughly forty feet square and twenty high, with a tunnel between two of the giant boulders and a ledge high above the ground on which they might sleep. It was well screened by surrounding trees, yet when they scrambled to the top, they found it offered an even more commanding view than the last, not only of the town and the sea but of the sweep of forest to the north.

Sperry said, 'There is a stream further down you may fish, and plenty of wood for a fire – so long as you light it on the other side, it cannot be seen from the town. The Indians call this Dead Man's Rock and believe it to be a place of evil spirits, so they will not disturb you. You have your pistols?'

Ned patted his pocket.

'I advise you keep them by you. There are wolves and bears and mountain lions that might disturb you – a shot should scare them off. I'll send my boy with food when I can. He'll leave a basket you may empty after he has gone and which you may then put out again for him to collect. Keep out of sight. Mr Jones promises he will come and fetch you when it's safe to move.'

'And when might that be?' asked Will.

Sperry shrugged. *Who knew?*

They realised from the start that they could not rely on sufficient food from Sperry's son to stave off hunger – the family, it was obvious, had barely enough for themselves – and so they were forced to apply some of the Indian methods they had learned on their journey to the Connecticut. They fished the stream with the net they had bought in Milford, stewing their haul in leaves in the embers of the fire as Gookin had showed them, and when the catch from the net proved inadequate, they built one of the natives' stone weirs that funnelled the fish into a narrow trap. They collected edible plants they recognised from their old forced marches in England – dandelions, white mustard, shepherd's purse – and American berries and fungi they did not know and that they had to test for poison by putting a tiny amount on their tongues. Once, despite their precautions, Ned suffered terrible stomach spasms and Will made an emetic out of charcoal and water. Ned spent most of that day vomiting over the latrine he had dug with the hatchet fifty paces from their shelter.

At night they sometimes heard wolves howling quite close by, and lay sleepless on their net blanket, their fingers on the triggers of their pistols.

One day at dawn, in the middle of their second week of this existence, Ned woke to see a deer sniffing around their campfire. Very quietly he raised his gun and shot her in the flank. She staggered a few paces, then went down, and he finished her off with the axe. They gutted her and cut her meat into cubes, which they boiled. Then they made a frame of branches and dried her skin.

On some days in June the weather was insufferably hot and they had to burn green wood to smoke away the insects. At other times the wind howled around their exposed position and the rain blew in off the sea with such force it was impossible to escape the wet. They stripped off their damp clothes and Ned cut wide belts from the skin of the doe, which they wore as a kind of apron. As time went on, they found it more comfortable to live in this Indian style of dress; their exposed bodies blistered and then turned brown in the sun. Their hair and beards grew long – Will laughed and told Ned that his greyness gave him the appearance of Methuselah – but however often they bathed in the stream, it was impossible to rid themselves entirely of lice.

Dear God, thought Ned one afternoon, watching Will standing in the water almost naked, still as a statue, with a spear he had made to try to catch fish, we are Christian gentlemen no longer. We have turned into savages, save we lack their bodily grace and competence.

They talked endlessly of their predicament and what they could do to relieve it. Could they try their luck in a different town? But if New Haven was no longer safe, where was? Besides, they had only the haziest notion of the local geography. They could head to the coast and follow the path to New Amsterdam. But that was the direction in which the mysterious Nayler and his search party were said to have gone. The Dutch might be more hospitable, but the colonels had no grasp of their language, and little money: as such obvious strangers, it would surely be only a matter of time before they were betrayed for the reward. Perhaps, suggested Will, they should simply give themselves up. But Ned recoiled from that. 'God has sent us this trial for a reason. It is our duty to endure it.'

They prayed first thing in the morning and late in the afternoon. Will kept careful track of the days by scratching marks on one of the rocks, and on the Sabbath they passed much longer hours in meditation, Will reading aloud from the Bible with a rocking motion that he said aided his concentration. He returned often to the story of Christ's forty days and forty nights in the wilderness, as related in the gospels of Luke and Matthew: how Jesus had fasted and gone hungry, and how the Devil had appeared to tempt him.

One afternoon in the sixth week of their isolation, Will came down from the ledge clutching his Bible. His dark brown eyes, which emaciation had made seem larger than before, were unusually bright with excitement. Ned was poking the embers of the fire in preparation for cooking their meal.

'I believe at last I grasp the meaning of it, Ned.'

'What meaning is that, Will?'

'God has set us up here in this wilderness – amid the stones and the high mountains, exactly as he did Christ – as a test, so that we may be taught that we must live by faith alone, not bread and worldly temptation.' He recited from memory. ' "Then saith Jesus unto him, Get thee hence, Satan: for it is written, Thou shalt worship the Lord thy God, and only him shalt thou serve. Then the Devil leaveth him, and, behold, angels came and ministered unto him." ' He counted the scratches on the stone. 'Our fortieth day and night are reached the day after tomorrow, on the twenty-third of June – the Lord's Day.' He rechecked his calculation. 'Yes, I am sure of it. Today is Friday, so it is this coming Sabbath.'

'What is?'

'The end of our test – the day we should leave the wilderness, as our Saviour did, and return to the world of men.'

'And go where?'

'To the meeting house in New Haven to proclaim our faith.'

Ned was used to his son-in-law's sudden bouts of fervour. He always tried to treat them with respect: had not Oliver himself declared that Will had the spirit of Christ within him? But this was too much.

'It would be madness to do such a thing. We must wait for word from Jones that it is safe to move.'

'No, you are wrong. What if Jones never comes? We must have faith in God's plan for us.'

'God also gave us the sense not to thrust our hands into a fire merely out of faith that we would not be burned.'

They argued until nightfall – their first serious dispute since they had come into the wilderness – and as they settled down to sleep, Ned realised to his dismay that Will intended to go down to the town regardless of whether he joined him or not. The thought of being left entirely alone appalled him. He lay awake for a long time, trying to decide what he should do, and when at last he fell asleep, his dreams were restless. He imagined the Devil was coming after him, a beast with yellow eyes that made a sound like nothing he had ever heard before – an unearthly deep-throated, hollow growl that stiffened all the hair on his body.

He opened his eyes to discover that an animal had crept up onto the ledge and was crouching no more than six feet away, silhouetted by the pale light of a thin moon and the field of stars. By the trembling of its hindquarters, he could see that it was preparing to spring. For an instant he was too frightened to move, but then his mind was suddenly very clear, and he felt along the edge of the mattress for his gun.

The slight movement must have provoked the creature. Just as he was bringing up the pistol it leapt at him. He felt its heavy weight land on his chest and smelled the hot stink of its breath even as he pressed the barrel against its fur and muscle and pulled the trigger. The explosion half deafened him. He was aware of Will yelling and the thing lying on him – dead or alive he could not tell – then he was struggling to sit up and shouting for help. Will grabbed hold of it and together they heaved it off the ledge and heard it fall heavily to the ground.

He lay back panting. Will asked him if he was injured and he replied that he believed not. All the same, he did not move but lay with his eyes wide open, his second pistol, cocked and loaded, resting on his chest. Will did the same.

At first light they climbed down from the ledge to inspect the corpse. It was not the Devil but a mountain lion, a female. In Ned's mind it had been huge, but in the grey dawn she proved to be almost puny, no more than a yard long, and very skinny, with protuberant ribs and a small head. Her upper fur was tawny, her stomach pale and matted with dried blood where the bullet had penetrated – straight into her heart by the look of it. Half starved, thought Ned, like us. He felt a sudden pang of pity.

Will pointed to his right shoulder. 'You're wounded.'

Ned looked at the top of his arm. Red puncture marks, inflicted by teeth or claws; not much blood, but they would leave scars – a few more to add to his collection. He went down to the stream to bathe the wound. He knew that Will would say it was a sign from God that they should move, and would produce some Biblical reference as proof – which he duly did, from Proverbs: 'The young lions do lack, and suffer hunger, but they that seek the Lord shall not want any good thing' – but it wasn't that which changed his mind. He knew now that he could not possibly live in this lonely spot with all its dangers and hardships without his son-in-law. They had come this far together, and they would go on together – as the Bible had it, *even to the end.*

To observe Mosaic Law, upon which Will continued to insist, it was necessary for them to get within two miles of the meeting house by sundown. The obvious solution was to head back to the ruined mill. They could not countenance descending two cliff faces, especially not with Ned's wounded arm, which meant they would have to walk the long way round. Ned gutted the lioness, then cut what little flesh there was into small pieces and put it in a pot to boil. While he waited for it to cook, he stretched the skin and tied it to the frame, just in case they might be forced to return.

It did not seem to matter how long he boiled the lion meat. It remained tough and hard to chew, although the gamey taste was rich enough, like wild boar. He stuffed what they did not eat into his bag for their dinner. Then they dressed in their English clothes, stamped out the fire, and set off.

They walked west along the ridge for several miles until the land began to descend, then turned south through the forest, keeping track of their direction by the position of the sun. When the path began to level out, they turned east. It was hard going in the heat, especially in their leather army coats – the rough terrain twisting underfoot, the mosquitoes, the big flies whose bite was vicious enough to draw blood. But their weeks living outdoors had hardened them; their months of travelling had taught them how to pick up a trail. Late in the afternoon, they reached Sperry's farmhouse. They briefly debated whether they should call on him, but decided against it; the place looked empty in any case.

They arrived at the mill just before dusk. Ned was too exhausted to do much more than chew a few pieces of cold lion meat, then he spread out his coat and fell asleep.

The following morning, they hoisted their bags onto their shoulders and set off again. After they had gone about a mile, they heard the meeting house bell ringing in the distance, and by the time they entered the town fifteen minutes later, the wide streets were deserted, the citizens all at prayer. As they marched across the green, Will striding ahead, Ned had a premonition that they had made a terrible error, and when they entered the meeting house and the packed assembly turned to stare at them, he knew it for a fact.

Their appearance – both the fact of it and the way they must have looked after almost six weeks in the forest – drew exclamations of shock. Davenport was in the pulpit, midway through his sermon, and for perhaps the first time in his long career he seemed to be briefly rendered speechless. After a few moments, with the murmur of conversation growing louder, he stepped down and walked towards them, making shooing movements with his hands, as if they were a pair of wild animals that had wandered in from the forest. Governor Leete and William Jones rose from their places at the front, and the three men herded the colonels outside. Jones turned and closed the door, then swung back to them.

'In the name of God,' he said quietly, 'I thought I told you to stay in hiding until I gave the word. Why have you come back?'

Will tilted his chin in defiance. 'We have passed forty days and forty nights in the wilderness, and now it is written that our test is over, and the angels shall come and minister to us.'

'Where is it written that your test is over?' demanded Davenport.

'In Matthew, chapter four.'

'That is not the meaning of the passage.'

'I believe it to be so.'

'Do you presume to teach me Scripture?'

'No, sir.'

'Do you claim you are Christ, Colonel Goffe? If so, that is the gravest blasphemy.'

For the first time, Will looked uncertain. 'I do not mean to contend that either of us is Christ, merely that we humbly follow his example as revealed in the Scriptures.'

Leete was shaking his head in disbelief. 'Your return puts us in a most dangerous situation. The whole of New England has turned against our colony since you left. Mr Davenport here is in grave jeopardy of arrest – and Mr Jones and I with him.'

Ned said, 'We are sorry—'

'We have given our assurances to the Crown authorities that we know nothing of your whereabouts – and yet here you are. And the whole town has seen you.'

'Go,' said Jones, and he too made the terrible shooing gesture, which Ned would ever afterwards remember as the moment they were expelled from human society. 'Go now. We shall say you came down from the hills to surrender yourselves and you are on your way to Boston.'

'But this is not Christian,' protested Will.

Ned took him by the arm. 'Come, Will,' he said gently. 'They are our friends. We cannot ask more of them than they are able to give.' He turned to Jones. 'We can last out the summer in the open. But once the weather starts to change . . .' He could not bring himself to finish the sentence.

'We'll see what can be done,' Jones said. 'You have our word. I'll come to you when we have a plan. Now leave, please.'

Will looked set to argue further, but Ned pulled him away. After a few paces, he ceased to resist, and together they set off across the green. When they reached the road, Ned looked back. The three men were still watching them. But a minute later, when he looked again, they had gone inside.

The colonels were to spend another fifty-six days in the wilderness, each one carefully scratched into the rock by Will, along with the dates of the full moons – 11 July, 9 August. But for his meticulous record-keeping, they would have had no notion of the passage of time as the days merged into one another.

They made snares to catch rabbits, and fashioned a bow out of a branch of hickory, stringing it with fibres they wove from nettle stems and fashioning arrows of birch that they tipped with flint heads and flighted with feathers. It saved ammunition, its manufacture passed the time, and it proved surprisingly effective in bringing down deer. They did not starve. Indeed, their diet of boiled and roasted animal flesh, stewed fish, berries and edible plants made them, if anything, healthier than before. It was only the prospect of autumn and winter that frightened Ned: he was sure they could never survive cold weather in such an exposed position. They began scouting around for a better cave, penetrating further into the forest each time.

It was on one of these expeditions that they encountered Indians. Will saw them first – three figures, all male, standing perfectly still in the trees. After half a minute, during which the two sides stared at one another, Ned raised his hand in greeting, whereupon the Indians turned and disappeared into the forest. They never saw them again. But from that moment, they sensed they were under observation. It added to their unease. One night they heard something that might have been a bear sniffing around their campfire, close to their store of food, and in the morning found their larder empty. It was the feeling that their survival was entirely contingent on this unremitting struggle that began to tell on them – that hostile animals, and possibly humans too, were watching and waiting for them to make a slip, and that when they did, they would be finished. The days, filled with activity, were not so bad, but as the nights grew longer, their minds conjured up more and more anxious imaginings. The land in the darkness was noisy, empty, haunted. Every bird cry, howl and rustle evoked evil spirits. Ned wondered if they were going mad.

On a Monday afternoon – the nineteenth day of August, according to Will's calculations – Ned, atop the highest rock, saw through his telescope four figures approaching on horseback. No, there only were two men on horseback: the other two horses were riderless. And they weren't Indians. They were Europeans. He watched them for a while, then called down a warning to Will. Lowering the spyglass, he wiped the sweat from his eye. Next time he looked, he saw that the men were Jones and Sperry.

There was no time to change back into their English clothes, so they met them as they were, Will with their bow slung over his arm, Ned with the lion skin draped across his shoulders. He could see the shock in Jones's eyes – not just shock, indeed: revulsion.

The visitors stared around the camp at the drying fish and deer hides, the open pit where they had flung the bones of the animals they had caught. The wind, coming from the north-east, shifted slightly and carried the stink of their latrine.

'The time has come,' said Jones, 'and none too soon by the look of things. We have found you a place for the winter.'

'Where are we to go?'

'Gather your belongings. You'll see.'

It took them an hour to clear up the camp and pack their bags.

Ned could not bring himself simply to abandon all the tools they had made, the bow and arrows, the spear, the drying frames and the hatchet they had found. He dug a hole and buried them, along with their fishing net.

The route that Jones and Sperry had chosen took them along the ridge and then down into the forest, but rather than heading south, they continued south-westwards in a great arc that meant they avoided New Haven. Towards the end of the afternoon, they stopped at the edge of the treeline to eat, and waited until the sun was setting before they moved off again. Wherever we are going, Ned thought, they mean for us to arrive in darkness.

They crossed another of those wide plains that resembled an English park, dotted with large trees, and gradually it became apparent that they were approaching the coast. A small settlement emerged out of the dusk, and it wasn't until they reached the coastal road and night had fallen that Ned realised they were in Milford, at Micah Tomkins' store. Jones knocked, and Tomkins appeared with a lamp. He did not invite them inside, but checked over his shoulder nervously and after a brief handshake conducted them across the yard to an outbuilding. In the gloom, it wasn't possible to make out much – barrels, sacks, lengths of timber. He shifted a few things, lifted a trapdoor and held his lamp above it.

'It's dry at least. You should be safe down there. I'll return in the morning.'

He gave the lamp to Will, who thanked him and at once began to descend. Ned peered into the shadows – he did not care for the look of it, but he was hardly in a position to complain – and after a brief hesitation followed him down a ladder to a stone floor. Above their heads, the trapdoor dropped.

PART THREE

HIDE
1662

CHAPTER TWENTY-THREE

THE FOLLOWING SPRING – AT eight o'clock on the morning of Sunday 2 March 1662 to be exact – four men in their middle to late fifties, each carrying a Bible and all wearing the sombre dress of a Puritan on the Sabbath, were to be observed walking together through the City of London. There was some defiance in the action: under the laws of Charles II's government, the maximum number of Puritans permitted to gather at any one time was five; more than that was considered a conventicle, punishable by imprisonment. Their appearance was legal, but only just.

Accompanied by peals of bells from the city's churches, they made their way north from the river along Coleman Street, turned right into Swan Alley, a lane of merchants' houses, and stopped before a tall, narrow dwelling that seemed to have been squeezed into the terrace as an afterthought.

Frances Goffe was pouring a glass of water for her Uncle William when she heard their knock. As usual, the old minister was bent over his papers. He said, without looking up, 'That will most likely be my visitors. Would you let them in? You may find them of interest. They have newly come from America.'

America. 'Do you think they may have news of Will and Father?'

'It's very likely.'

She hurried down the passage, smoothing her skirt and straightening her hair, and opened the door. The most senior of the four men looked at her for a moment, then gave her a grave smile.

'Do I have the honour of addressing Mrs Goffe? Mrs Frances Goffe?'

She was not so far gone in her excitement as to forget her caution. 'May I ask who wishes to know?'

'Forgive me.' He touched the brim of his flat-crowned hat. 'I am John Winthrop, governor of the colony of Connecticut. This is Major Robert Thompson of Guilford in New Haven, Captain Scott of Long Island, and Mr Nathaniel Whitefield, also of Guilford. We are here to see Reverend Hooke.'

'Come in, please. My uncle expects you.' She stood aside to let them enter, quickly checked the street to see if they had been followed, then showed them into the parlour.

She lingered on the threshold, hoping for the chance to ask some questions, but Uncle William said firmly, 'Thank you, Frances. You may join your aunt now. Please close the door.'

It was too cruel, she thought, to shut her out from their conversation. Nearly two years had passed since she had last seen Will or her father. In all that while she had received no letter from either, apart from that scribbled note of Will's. She had been forbidden to write to them, despite her tearful entreaties, even when her mother died: it was considered too great a risk. She tried to overhear what the men were saying, but she could make out nothing, and eventually she went upstairs to Aunt Jane and the children.

Richard was almost two now, the image of his father traced

upon his face, and walking so determinedly they had been obliged to put a gate across the top of the stairs to prevent him tumbling. Betty and Nan were still prone to sickness, but Judith was sturdy, and Frankie was a help with the little ones, although it was not much of a life for a girl of ten, cooped up in a borrowed house and wearing cast-off clothes given by members of the church. Not that Frances's own were any better. People were kind. They didn't ask questions. Yet she knew they whispered about her behind her back – not just the wife but the daughter of a regicide, fugitives who would be hanged, drawn and quartered if they were caught. It was another reason to keep the children indoors: she wanted to shield them from the truth as long as possible. Money was scarce. She had to take in laundry and work as a seamstress to make ends meet.

Aunt Jane had Dickie on her lap. The Bible was open on the table; she was waiting for Frances to join them before beginning their discussion. Frances held Judith's hand and tried to concentrate, especially during prayers, but her thoughts kept returning to the men in the parlour, and when, after a couple of hours, she heard the door open and the sound of voices, she excused herself and ran downstairs to intercept them.

The group was just emerging. She could tell at once that harsh words had been exchanged. Major Thompson and Mr Whitfield, the Guilford men, had their backs turned on Mr Winthrop, whose hands were spread helplessly, as if he had been appealing to them and they had rejected whatever he had been saying. 'Friends, friends,' said Uncle William plaintively, following them into the hall, 'we must not fall out among ourselves. Intolerance is the sin that has brought us to our present sorry state.'

'No, sir,' said Mr Whitfield, 'rather it is an excess of toleration that has been our ruin. Plainly there is nothing more to be said.

God be with you, Mr Hooke. And Mr Winthrop – may God guide you to a better understanding.'

Whitfield, Thompson and Scott all left. Winthrop stared after them, shaking his head. 'You see how it is, Mr Hooke – quite hopeless.' He sighed. 'Well, I thank you for your efforts. Now we must see how matters play out.'

He was moving towards the door when Frances called from the stairs, 'Mr Winthrop, before you leave, I beg you – do you have any news of my husband and my father?'

He halted and turned. 'We have told all we know to your uncle.'

'But would you tell me, sir? Forgive me, it has been so long without a word.'

Hooke said, 'I shall tell you later, child.'

'Have you seen them? Are they in good health?'

'Frances!'

'It's no matter, Mr Hooke,' said Winthrop pleasantly. 'Yes, Mrs Goffe, I have seen them. A year ago. They passed through Hartford. And yes, they were well – tired from travelling, but otherwise in good spirits.'

'And now? Where are they?'

'Somewhere in the colony of New Haven, I believe. Their exact location is a secret, known only to a handful. It is safer that way.'

'Are their lives very hard?'

'They're among friends, Mrs Goffe, and as far as I know they're alive. That is something. The rest is in God's hands.'

'If you see them, will you tell them I am well, and the children also? That we pray for them every day, and live in hope that we shall be reunited?'

'If I see them, I'll be sure to tell them.' Winthrop smiled and touched the brim of his hat. 'Good day to you both, and God be with you.'

His smile died as soon as he was in the street. If there was one thing he knew for certain, it was that he would take care never to see the colonels again. The last he had heard, they were said to be living in a cave. If so, how could they have survived the winter? Poor fellows, he thought. Poor fellows, they would be better off dead.

Hooke ordered Frances to join him in the parlour. She started to apologise, but he did not seem to be listening. He sat with his back to her at the small table he used as a desk, where he composed his 'intelligencers' – forbidden to preach, he now devoted most of his energy to letters that were really miniature newspapers, full of facts and rumours he had picked up in the city, which he dispatched to Puritan communities outside London, on the Continent and in America. They lived like rebels, underground. He had been working on his latest dispatch all week. His pen moved swiftly across the paper.

'I fear,' he said, 'that your father and your husband have been the cause of grave disagreement among our friends in New England. The men of New Haven, Mr Davenport in particular, have been open – it seems too open – in their hospitality and obstructed the official search. Now the talk is that the colony will be dissolved by the King. In that event, its settlements will most likely be absorbed by Connecticut. The New Haven men seek reassurance from Governor Winthrop that he will not agree the transfer. I was asked to act as honest broker between the two.'

'And Mr Winthrop will not give such reassurance?'

Hooke shook his head. 'He will not. He has come to London to arrange a new charter of his own. He says that to refuse to obey the King's decision will put Connecticut under suspicion.'

'And what do you say?'

'I see both sides. It's an abiding weakness of mine. Now . . .'

he finished writing and blew on the ink to dry it, 'Mr Thompson tells me that a connection of his, one Samuel Wilson, a merchant, is sailing to Boston tomorrow. He is of our faith and willing to take the risk of carrying messages. I have written a digest of news for Mr Davenport, and just now added a postscript regarding this morning's meeting – guarded, but he will guess the meaning. Would you be so good as to deliver it to Mr Wilson? He has a house close by the river. I would go myself, but I am often followed, and my legs are not so nimble.' He folded the pages into a package and sealed it with wax. 'Here is Wilson's address. I shall go and give Jane the news of her brother.'

Frances went to fetch her coat from the kitchen, and when she returned, her uncle had gone. The thick letter bore the inscription *Revd. John Davenport, New Haven.* Samuel Wilson's address was in the parish of St Peter's and St Paul's Wharf. She turned the piece of paper over in her hands. Here was a thread, however tenuous, that might link her to her husband. The temptation was irresistible. She sat down at the desk, took another sheet, dipped her uncle's pen in the inkwell, and let the nib hover over the blankness. It could be no more than the barest whisper of love – no details of their true condition, nothing that might betray where they lived, or who had sent it, or even to whom it might be addressed. On the latter point, she would have to trust to Mr Davenport's discretion.

My dearest heart, she wrote, *God has set us apart, but by His mercy the children are all well, & by His infinite grace I have faith we shall one day be reunited.*

She paused and thought of adding a line for her father, giving him the news that her stepmother was dead – it had been a mercy, she wanted to tell him – but she could not find the words, and saw no point in adding to his miseries.

She folded the sheet in four and sealed it with a drop of wax.

Then she broke open the letter to Reverend Davenport. Inside was a bill of exchange for twenty pounds, collected from local Puritans. They could have done with that money themselves, though naturally she did not begrudge it. She slipped her own letter into the middle of the eight closely written pages and resealed the packet in four places with her uncle's signet ring. She scrutinised it carefully. No one could ever tell it had been tampered with.

She heard a sound above. Her uncle was descending the stairs. Quickly she replaced everything on the desk as she had found it, then took the letter and Wilson's address and went out onto the street.

The merchant's house was little more than a mile away, close to the river near Blackfriars. She asked directions from the verger at the church of St Peter and St Paul, and half an hour after leaving Hooke's study, she was knocking on Wilson's door. He was younger than she had expected, dressed in Puritan black. Behind him she could hear children laughing. For some reason the sound reassured her.

'My uncle asked me to give you this to carry to America.'

He glanced at the name on the letter and grimaced. 'I shall need to keep this most particularly hidden.'

'But you will do it?'

'I shall. I gave my promise.'

'God bless you. You are a good man.'

He seemed surprised by the passion with which she spoke. 'Will you come in for a moment?'

'No. Thank you, but I must get back to my own children.'

She was nearly halfway home when she realised that the stout woman in a brown dress and dark green bonnet whom she had registered at the end of Wilson's street was no more than fifty paces behind her. She ducked into the church of St Mary-le-Bow, walked briskly up the nave and out again through the chancel door, along the street and left into Old Jewry. The woman was still trailing her, but further back. Frances turned into a courtyard, ran across the cobbles, found an unlocked door and crouched in the passage behind it. Did it mean that Wilson was being watched? Or was it her uncle they were after? In which case, should she go back to Wilson and warn him she might have led trouble to his door?

She waited for the best part of an hour, until the church bell tolled twelve, then decided to risk emerging. There was no sign of the woman in the narrow lane. She took a long way back to Swan Alley and kept regularly checking over her shoulder, but it seemed she had thrown off her pursuer.

She told Uncle William what had happened as soon as she got home. He seemed unconcerned. He ran great risks to keep the faith alive. He accepted the dangers; so would Wilson. 'It is in God's hands,' he said.

CHAPTER TWENTY-FOUR

O N THE SAME Sunday that Hooke met the four men from America, Richard Nayler sailed to Rotterdam.

Four days later, on the evening of Thursday 6 March, he was crouched by the window of an upstairs bedroom in the Dutch town of Delft, his telescope trained on a flat-fronted white-washed house just across the canal. It was a little after six, the sun just setting, shadows creeping across the damask wall coverings. Seated behind him in a high-backed wainscot chair was Sir George Downing, His Majesty's ambassador at The Hague. Downstairs were half a dozen English soldiers, armed but in civilian dress, who had arrived surreptitiously at intervals throughout the after-noon from the *Blackamoor*, a ship of the Royal Africa Company, owned by the Duke of York, that lay moored in Rotterdam har-bour about six miles to the south.

Downing yawned. 'What if they do not come?'

'They will come,' said Nayler, adjusting the focus slightly so that he could scan the street. 'I have read their letters. Affection is their weakness, believe me.' It was an article of faith for him.

'Imagine missing your wife so much you would be willing to

risk your life to see her.' Downing's voice was incredulous. He started to laugh.

Nayler hated him.

He had returned to London from Boston at the end of July, resolved to intensify his enquiries into those regicides still at liberty on the Continent: if Whalley and Goffe were among them, he would hear of them soon enough. When he made his report to Hyde – now Earl of Clarendon – on the failure of his mission in America, and raised the possibility that his quarry might have fled to Holland, Hyde told him of Downing's recent reappointment as ambassador. 'Write to him. You will find him anxious to assist.'

'*Downing* is at The Hague?' Nayler was astonished. 'But he was Cromwell's man in Holland.'

'Exactly. And now he is ours. Between you and me, he came over to us secretly while the King was still in exile, and proved a most useful spy. He is another of those former Parliament men now anxious to show his zeal. Don't look so shocked, Mr Nayler. Scruples do not suit you.'

And Downing did indeed prove effective in tracking down the regicides – there was no denying it – precisely because of his history. Reared in Salem, Massachusetts, one of the first to graduate from Harvard, a chaplain in the New Model Army before entering government service, he had maintained friendly contact with his exiled former colleagues, who still trusted him. His reports, passed on to Nayler's intelligence committee, teemed with names and places. Of the thirteen signatories of the King's death warrant still at liberty, he gathered reliable news of six. John Hewson, a former cobbler, who had lost an eye fighting with Cromwell's army in Ireland, had recently died in Amsterdam: he could be crossed off the list. Miles Corbet, an elderly lawyer, was living in Holland between Zwolle and Kampen. The other four – Valentine Walton, Cromwell's brother-in-law; Sir John Barkstead, former Lieutenant of the Tower of London; John Dixwell, and Colonel John Okey, who had been Downing's commanding officer – were all in the town of Hanau, near Frankfurt.

In Germany they were out of reach. But if they could be lured to Holland, they might be captured.

Downing provided the names; it was Nayler who devised the trap. There was a merchant in Delft he knew named Abraham Kicke, who acted as postmaster for the regicides, passing letters between Barkstead and Okey and their wives in England. Nayler read the letters before they were delivered and was struck by the tenderness of their tone. At his suggestion, Downing offered Kicke a bounty of two hundred pounds a head if he would propose that the two men came to his house to meet their women-folk in secret. 'The promise of seeing their wives again will lure them, gentlemen,' Nayler assured his committee. To bait the trap further, Downing also promised Okey safe passage across Holland.

The rendezvous was fixed for the first week of March, although Mrs Okey and Lady Barkstead knew nothing of it and remained in England.

At seven, the bells of Delft rang out in graceful tinkling chimes and by half past, Kicke's house was fading into the darkness, save for a lamp in a downstairs window. Perhaps they would not come, suggested Downing. In which case, said Nayler, he would return the next night, and the next, for as long as it took. Behind him, the ambassador shifted in his chair and sighed.

Suddenly, from around the corner to the right, two shadows appeared – close together, walking quickly, bulky figures, doubtless armed. They passed in front of the lighted window and stopped. A few moments later, an oblong yellow glow briefly showed their outline. They stepped over the threshold, and the door closed.

Nayler, squinting through his telescope, said, 'They're here. They've gone inside.'

'How many?'

'Two.'

Downing came and stood next to him, resting his hand on Nayler's shoulder. He had a jowly face and a heavy body; his clothes smelled of roast mutton. It took Nayler an effort not to shudder. A few minutes later, a candle appeared in a top-floor window.

'That's the signal,' said Downing. 'I'll tell the men.' He started to move away.

'Wait,' called Nayler, refocusing his spyglass. 'There is a third.'

On Nayler's instructions, Kicke had extended an additional invitation, to Miles Corbet, living just outside Amsterdam, asking if he wished to meet his comrades. And here he came, by the look of it, as Nayler had anticipated he would, unable in his loneliness to resist – a stooped figure walking from the opposite direction to the others, moving slowly as befitted a man of nearly seventy. The door opened to admit him, and he too was swallowed up in the darkness.

'Now?' asked Downing.

His eagerness to betray his friends was something else Nayler found insufferable.

'Let them shed their coats and pistols, Sir George, and take a cup of wine. It will be their last, after all.'

They waited another half-hour before going downstairs to gather the men. One soldier carried a sack of hand and leg irons; another had a lantern on the end of a pole. Downing drew his gun; Nayler did the same. Together the raiding party stepped out into the empty street. As they crossed the little bridge over the canal, Nayler felt the familiar tension in his chest.

By arrangement, Kicke had left the front door unlocked. Downing pushed his way to the front of the arrest party. He meant to take the credit, Nayler thought: his dispatch to Clarendon was probably already drafted. Downing turned and put a finger to his fleshy lips. The men moved silently into the hall. From the room to their right came the sound of voices. When they were all assembled, Downing turned the handle and threw wide the door.

The regicides were sitting with Kicke by a blazing fire, drinking beer and smoking pipes. The expressions of shock and terror on their faces as the soldiers poured in and they recognised Downing were to be fixed in Nayler's memory for a long time. The elderly Corbet fell to the floor and had some sort of seizure, his bony frame jerking and rattling on the polished boards like a marionette; it was difficult to attach the manacles. Within five minutes, it was over. Looking at the prisoners as they were led away, Nayler felt – for this one night at least – some brief relief from the nagging torment that he hadn't managed to do the same to Whalley and Goffe.

It was to be several days before Nayler had the chance to interrogate the prisoners.

As word of their capture spread, a crowd of local sympathisers gathered outside the prison. A petition for their release was laid before the courts. It took all of Downing's bullying guile, and some hefty bribes, before the extradition warrant was approved and the captives were transferred to Nayler's custody. At two o'clock on the following Tuesday morning, they were escorted by the English soldiers through the deserted streets to a barge and rowed to the *Blackamoor* in Rotterdam, where they were taken down to the hold and placed in chains in separate cabins. The next morning, the ship weighed anchor, and Nayler went below decks to inspect his haul.

Miles Corbet he scarcely bothered with – a spindly lawyer, a committee man, he had not fought in the Civil War and had spent most of Cromwell's regime as an administrator in Ireland. He claimed never to have met either Whalley or Goffe, apart from in Westminster Hall at the King's trial and afterwards in the Painted Chamber, where the death warrant was signed. Nayler was inclined to believe him.

Barkstead and Okey were a different matter.

As Lieutenant of the Tower, Barkstead had been notorious for his harshness and avarice, and as Deputy Major General in London he had imposed a rigid Puritan regime, demolishing the Globe theatre, rounding up hundreds of prostitutes and exiling many to America, pulling down all the maypoles, closing the Bankside bear garden, and forbidding the traditional merriment of Shrove Tuesday. The soldiers knew all about him and had treated him roughly: his face was puffy from repeated beatings and his nose looked to be broken.

More interesting to Nayler was the fact that Barkstead had risen to the rank of colonel in the New Model Army and had fought alongside Whalley at the siege of Colchester in the summer of '48, when the surrendering royalist commanders, Sir Charles Lucas and Sir George Lisle, had been given a summary trial. Barkstead, Whalley and Henry Ireton had all been involved in passing their death sentence. When General Lucas had protested – 'It was never known that men were killed in cold blood before' – Whalley was said to have responded, 'Sir, I shall answer you for that,' and had reminded him of the fourteen surrendering Roundhead soldiers who had been hanged at Woodhouse in Wiltshire. The exchange had been extensively reported in the Royalist press. 'After this, six dragoons with firelocks discharged at him; and after his falling, Sir George Lisle having kissed him, was also shot to death.'

Barkstead claimed to have no memory of the incident.

'But Whalley was a friend of yours?' Nayler had brought in a three-legged stool to sit upon, so that he might question him in comfort. Barkstead was chained to the ship's hull.

'He was.'

'When did you see him last?'

Barkstead thought it over. 'Two years ago.'

'Where is he now?'

'I cannot tell you.'

'Cannot, or will not?'

'Cannot.'

'I have evidence he came to Holland last year.'

'If he did, I have no knowledge of it.'

'Perhaps you have forgotten. I can call in some of my men to stir your memory.'

There was a flash of fear in Barkstead's eyes, but then the old soldier within the broken frame braced himself. 'You may beat me all you wish. My answer will not change. Colonel Whalley's whereabouts are unknown to me. I am only glad to hear that he is still at liberty.'

Nayler briefly considered administering the beating himself, then decided it wasn't worth it. He picked up his stool and lamp and went to the next cell, where Colonel Okey was huddled in the corner. Okey had commanded the regiment of dragoons at Naseby that had helped turn the battle in Parliament's favour. He must have known Whalley well. Nayler decided to try a different tack. He placed his lamp on the floor and sat on the stool. 'Now, Colonel Okey, how goes it with you?'

'As well as it can for a man who has been foully betrayed by one he trusted.'

'I can well understand your feelings. Downing is a rogue with the morals of a whore. I am sorry for what he did to you.'

'Can you "well understand" it? I doubt it. That man was my chaplain. He lodged in my house. I raised him up from nothing.'

'It saddens me to see you in this state.' Nayler leaned forwards. 'I could ease your conditions – perhaps allow you up on deck to take the air.'

'You wish to make a bargain with me? Spare yourself the effort. I have nothing to offer in return.'

'Just a little information is all I require. Colonel Whalley and Colonel Goffe – these men were friends of yours?'

'Goffe not really – too much the radical and the mystic for my taste. But Ned Whalley I knew well.'

'Tell me of him.'

'A good officer. Cromwell's man through and through. That was both his fortune and his curse.'

'In what way his curse?'

'He traded his judgement for his position. He became Cromwell's creature. Did you know he was one of those who urged Oliver to become king? That was how rotten the Commonwealth became.'

'He is in Holland, I believe.'

Okey stared at him for a moment, then started to laugh. 'Now I see your game. Downing was my Judas, and I am to be the same for Whalley. And all so I can go up on deck and put some colour in my cheeks before I am hanged and quartered.'

'But he is said to be on the Continent. If so, he must have tried to seek you out.'

'I last saw Ned Whalley hiding in a ditch near Daventry when General Lambert was captured and the republic died. That was nigh on two years ago. Since then – nothing. Although I tell you frankly, Mr Nayler, I would not betray him even if I had seen him last week, so you may take that answer as you will. Now perhaps you would leave me to my prayers. I have a long journey to make to meet my God, and not much time to prepare for it.'

Nayler contemplated him with reluctant respect. They were hard men even in their present pitiful state. Little wonder they had won the war. Once again he picked up his stool, but this time on his way to the upper deck he ordered the commander of the guard to allow each of the prisoners half an hour of fresh air, under strict supervision.

The *Blackamoor* dropped anchor in the Thames estuary at Gravesend on the morning of Sunday 16 March. Mr Pepys of the Navy Board, on Hyde's orders, sent a barge to meet it, and the three regicides were transferred to the vessel's enclosed cabin at the stern. The gilded benches inside were upholstered in crimson velvet, for the comfort of the officers of the Admiralty. Corbet, Barkstead and Okey in their chains made incongruous passengers. The guards sat in the forward open section with the sailors who were manning the oars. The blades dipped. The barge moved off. After a few minutes, Nayler found the spectacle of the prisoners, and even more the clink of their fetters whenever they moved, so depressing that he went outside to join them.

They reached the Tower at dusk. The regicides were pushed and hauled up the green-slimed steps beyond Traitors' Gate, and as Barkstead passed him, Nayler couldn't resist remarking that he supposed that for him it was a homecoming, 'although to less comfortable apartments than you were used to, I fear'. Afterwards, the barge let him off at the jetty of Essex House, and he strolled through the gardens to spend the evening in his chambers.

The next morning, he went direct to Whitehall Palace, where Samuel Nokes was clutching a file and waiting to congratulate him. After Nayler had taken his seat at his desk and described the arrests, Nokes said, 'And did you discover any intelligence regarding Whalley and Goffe?'

Was it his imagination, or was his secretary gently mocking him? 'No, Mr Nokes, I did not, although I fancy from your smile that you may have done.'

Nokes opened his file. 'Do you recall the merchant, Samuel Wilson, we suspected of carrying secret messages between the Puritans in London and America?'

'Of course. I was the one who ordered a watch be put on him.'

'Whilst you were in Holland, I discovered that his ship was about to sail and arranged for it to be searched. We discovered a great many subversive newsbooks, religious tracts and suchlike hidden in the cargo. Wilson is now in custody and swears he had no knowledge of them or where they came from.'

'And how does this concern Whalley and Goffe?'

'There was also this.' He laid a thick letter in front of Nayler.

'Reverend Davenport,' said Nayler. 'Now there is a piece of work.' He skimmed the pages – a litany of complaints about government oppression of the Puritans, and various items of tittle-tattle hostile to the King – until he reached the end. 'Signed "D. G.". Who is he?'

'The meaning of the initials is unclear. But judging by the contents, he is a Puritan minister, advanced in years, who at one time lived with Davenport.'

'William Hooke?'

'That is my belief. He describes a meeting with Governor

Winthrop and some prominent men from New Haven two Sun-
days ago that seems to have gone badly. And you might care to
look more closely at the very last part.'

The writing was tiny, the lines crammed close together to save
paper, but easy enough to decipher. *I pray, salute my relations you
mentioned in one of your last, & acquaint them with as much of this
as you think fit. Tell them our friends here are well.*

Nayler looked up at Nokes. 'His relations? That would be Whalley and Goffe?'

'Almost certainly. Whalley is his brother-in-law, Goffe his
nephew by marriage. The "friends" most likely include Frances
Goffe. Folded into the letter was a second message.'

He handed over the note with, most unusually for him, something like a flourish. It was in a very different hand – uneducated,
almost childish.

'One of our agents reported that a woman visited Wilson's
house the day before he was due to sail. She was described as in her
twenties, thin and poor-looking. But clearly no fool – she eluded
our agent, who lost her in the city.'

'Frances Goffe,' said Nayler. He raised the note to his nostrils
and sniffed it. Sarah used to sprinkle her love letters with perfume,
but Frances's paper had no scent. Of course, it wouldn't: she was
a good Puritan wife.

'Do we know where she is living?'

'She was in Swan Alley with the Hookes, but they must have
got wind of Wilson's arrest. They have moved again.'

Nayler struck the table in frustration.

He dealt briskly with the correspondence that had piled up in
his absence and went next to Worcester House to see the Lord
Chancellor to report on the events in Delft. When he had finished,
he added, 'And we have fresh intelligence that Whalley and Goffe

are still in America, almost certainly in New Haven, still living under the protection of Davenport and his friends.'

'I thought you said they might be in Holland?'

'I believed there was a chance. But it seems we must direct our efforts back to America.'

'What do you propose?'

'I have come to the view that Secretary Morice was correct. The task demands a full expedition. No more reliance on a local search party. We must sail to New Haven and take the place to pieces until they agree to give them up.'

'*We?* Who would command this adventure?'

'I would go again myself, if you would permit me, only this time I would stay until the job was done.'

'Whalley and Goffe,' groaned Hyde. 'Whalley and Goffe. I have warned you once already. You are in danger of becoming a bore on the matter. When these three regicides from Holland are done with, we shall have executed thirteen men.' Nayler started to protest, but Hyde raised his hand. 'It is enough, Mr Nayler. The temper of the times has changed. People are growing sick of the spectacle. We are in danger of turning murderers into martyrs. If Whalley and Goffe fall into our hands, naturally they must pay the price the law demands. But I absolutely forbid you to waste any more of the country's resources on this fruitless endeavour. I make myself clear?'

'Of course, my lord.'

But even as Nayler bowed his way out of the room, his fertile mind was turning over the matter of Whalley and Goffe and how he might devise some fresh means to ensnare them.

The date of the triple execution was fixed for 19 April – a Saturday, to ensure the largest possible attendance. By early morning, the slopes around Tyburn were filled with tens of thousands of spectators and the usual attendant entourage of stallholders offering beer and rum, oysters and pastries and the like. Parents lifted children onto their shoulders for a better view. Nayler supervised, and it did not look to him as though there was much waning of enthusiasm among the London crowd for blood and gore.

The numbers were so huge that the sledges bearing the condemned men could not get through and they had to walk the last part of the way to the scaffold – Okey first, then half an hour later Barkstead, who got the loudest jeers, and finally Corbet. The prisoners clambered up onto the cart beneath the scaffold, their wigs were removed, and the nooses were put around their necks. The braziers heating the iron implements shone merrily in the spring sunshine. They made their speeches – Okey taking a final swipe at Downing ('one who was formerly my chaplain that did pursue me to the very death') and urging the crowd to support the King – then Barkstead cried out, 'Lord Jesus, receive our souls!' as the horse was smacked on the hindquarters, the cart trundled forwards, and they were left swinging in a row.

But crowds are curious creatures, with their own distinctive character – no two alike, in Nayler's experience. As the executioner started on his butchery, a strange silence fell over Tyburn, and Nayler saw that Hyde was right: people were indeed sick of it. They started to drift away long before the quartering and the boiling of the heads. And the following day, when the various parts of Okey's body were returned to his family for a Christian burial in recognition of his repentance, an immense throng turned out for the funeral in Stepney, so large that the service had to be abandoned for fear of civil disorder and his remains were secretly interred within the precincts of the Tower.

The following Monday, when Nayler walked to the Privy Council corridor, Hyde was already waiting for him.

'Did I not warn you this might happen? We had to move His Majesty to Hampton Court yesterday for his safety. No more executions. Henceforth, if we locate a regicide, we should dispatch them by other means.'

Nayler looked at him in surprise. 'You wish me to send assassins overseas to kill them?'

'Why not? As long as it cannot be traced back to us.'

Nayler continued to convene his intelligence group throughout that spring and summer. News of the seizures of Barkstead, Corbet and Okey had driven the exiles into a frightened silence. Two more were reported by Downing to have died. Valentine Walton, who had been married to Cromwell's sister and who had ended his days scraping a living as a gardener, had revealed his identity with his dying breath. Thomas Challoner, it turned out, had passed away in Middelburg more than a year earlier. That left only seven of the signatories of the death warrant still alive: Edmund Ludlow, living in Vevey in Switzerland under the pseudonym Edmund Phillips, and William Say, also in Vevey, both protected by the Swiss canton of Berne; Michael Livesey, said to be somewhere in Rotterdam; Daniel Blagrave, sighted in Aachen, in Germany; and Whalley and Goffe in America. The whereabouts of John Dixwell, former governor of Dover Castle, were no longer known.

Fifty-two expunged out of fifty-nine, whether by execution, natural causes or life imprisonment, with just one man – Ingoldsby – pardoned, was a respectable tally. Still, Nayler chafed at the thought of a job not yet done. He spent hours contemplating his chart of regicides, now black with crossed-out names. The Lord Chancellor was right: assassination was the only realistic means of erasing the rest. However, although that might be possible on the continent of Europe, which teemed with English agents and former soldiers looking for employment, where would he find such men in America? The more he considered the problem, the more convinced he became that Whalley and Goffe could be dealt with only by a military expedition. But Hyde would never change his mind and countenance such a costly venture simply to hunt down the two colonels – so what could be done?

The answer came to him one July night when he was lying in bed, unable to sleep because of the heat.

The Duke of York.

The king's brother, not yet thirty, was always trying to find some means of making money, and if there was a chance of military glory into the bargain, so much the better.

Nayler contrived to run into him in the House of Lords the following day, where the duke liked to lounge on the Woolsack, yawning his way through debates. He had a voluptuary's face – long and pale as a midnight moon, with a wide, soft mouth and a permanent expression of bored contempt. As he rose to leave the chamber, Nayler stationed himself at the door and bowed deeply. 'Your Royal Highness . . .'

The duke paused and turned a hooded eye upon him. 'Ah yes, Mr . . .'

'Nayler, Your Royal Highness.'

'Nayler?' The duke looked as if he had been up half the night. The royal mind worked slowly. 'Our regicide-hunter-in-chief?'

'Indeed, sir.' Another bow.

'And how does that business proceed?'

The royal personage walked on, followed by his usual coterie of hangers-on. Nayler slid in beside him. 'It is mostly completed,

ROBERT HARRIS

sir. Only a handful remain at liberty. A few on the Continent, and those two in America . . .'

In the time it took to walk the length of the corridor, Nayler managed briefly to describe his visit to New England and the frustrations he had encountered.

'Shocking,' said the duke, sounding unconcerned.

'Shocking, sir, to meet such obstruction from the King's subjects. And then there are the Dutch.'

The duke paused at the door to the courtyard. A flicker of interest. 'What about the Dutch?'

'Their harbour at New Amsterdam seems to have been used by the regicides. But the Dutch settlers think only of money. The whole colony is very prosperous, and an obstruction to our own expansion. Yet it is very lightly defended.'

'You have seen this?'

'When I visited the governor in his fort, I counted only twenty cannon. Their militia is very small.'

'Interesting.' The duke rewarded him with a slight smile, as if bestowing a coin. 'Well, good day to you, Mr . . .'

'Nayler, Your Highness.'

Nayler watched him walk across the courtyard. He had planted the seed. He would have to see if it grew. In the meantime, he would continue to press for information on the whereabouts of Frances Goffe and the Hookes, but yet again they had vanished, protected by the Puritan network in the City of London.

Frances was to remember the hot months of that summer as the worst she and her family had endured since Will had fled.

As soon as they heard of Samuel Wilson's arrest, they had loaded their possessions onto a pair of handcarts, and she and her children and the Hookes had removed themselves in haste from

Swan Alley to yet another hiding place, in West Harding Street in Holborn, just north of Fleet Street. Their new lodgings were meaner than the last – two bedrooms for the eight of them in a damp terrace halfway up a gloomy alley barely fifty paces long. The drinkers in the nearby alehouses used it as a latrine. As the weather warmed, the sewage stank. Betty and Nan fell ill again. Frances left Aunt Jane to look after the children and found work as a tobacco cutter in a warehouse on the river. It was hard to maintain a cheerful facade in front of the little ones, not least because of her guilt that she had helped bring this disaster upon them.

She had confessed at once to her uncle that she had slipped a message into his letter to Davenport. He had been angry, but not for long. He made her recite exactly what she had written. 'If you did not use any names, I cannot see it matters.' He had even made a joke. 'Imagine it, Frances – your love note in the hands of the Privy Council.' Outwardly he seemed undaunted. While she worked and Aunt Jane minded the children, he continued to compose his intelligencers, although he did not now dare to address them directly to Davenport – a marked man – but rather sent them to another old friend of his, Reverend Increase Mather of Boston's North Church.

And then one day towards the end of August, just after she had returned home exhausted from the tobacco factory, he took her aside. He had his hands behind his back and looked unusually stern.

'Uncle?' she said, fearful that something might have happened to one of the children. 'What is it?'

'Nothing bad.' His face broke into a smile. 'You have received a letter.'

He took his hands from behind his back and produced a small sheet of paper, folded.

She hardly dared ask the question. 'Not from Will?'
He nodded.

The moment had been so much desired, and so long in coming, that for a few seconds she wasn't sure what to do. She knew that she needed privacy. She took the letter and carried it out into the street. Her hands were shaking so badly she could barely open it, and the familiar handwriting trembled before her eyes.

May 29th 1662

My dearest heart, so much has happened since we parted, & so many adventures have befallen me, that I scarce know what to write, & besides I have little time for composition as the messenger cannot wait & I did not expect this chance. But know that I am well, & your beloved father also, who sits beside me now & bids me send his fondest wishes. O, my dearest love, God's plans for us are the deepest mystery, and this separation from you & the little ones is most hard to bear. Yet I cannot but believe & know there is a meaning to it. 'It is the Lord's mercies that we are not consumed, because his compassions fail not. They are new every morning: great is thy faithfulness.' (Lamentations 3:22) Write to me if your relations think it safe, for I long to hear all. I exist only in the hope that one day we shall be together, & I shall see your sweet face, & then all will be explained, for it is truly said there is nothing covered that shall not be revealed; neither hid that shall not be known. My love, farewell.

She read it again and again, and from that night onwards slept with it under her pillow.

CHAPTER TWENTY-FIVE

O N THE DAY that Frances received Will's letter, the two colonels had been living in Micah Tomkins' cellar for exactly a year. They were not prisoners as such – they were free to leave whenever they wished – but Tomkins had made it plain that while they remained in his safe keeping, they must abide by his rules, and these amounted to imprisonment. For twenty-three hours out of twenty-four, they were obliged to remain underground. The hour when they were permitted to emerge was always during darkness, after the household – Tomkins and his wife, Mary, and their two young daughters – and indeed the whole of Milford, was asleep. Then they were allowed to exercise in the yard and venture as far as the orchard. Often, when the nights were fine, they couldn't bear to return, and stayed out for longer, only creeping back to their hiding place at dawn.

The cellar was beneath a storeroom that lay between the house and the general shop. It was high enough for Ned to stand erect and measured twenty feet by twenty, as they well knew, having paced it often enough. There was a kind of enclosed iron box with a flue, which Tomkins had built himself, where they could light a fire in the winter. (He explained the smoke to his neighbours by saying he was smoking meat.) There was a table, a plain wooden chair each, and a bed, which they shared. In the corner stood a slop bucket where they could relieve themselves; they carried it upstairs at night and emptied it into the cesspit. The cellar extended two feet beyond the storeroom at one end, and here there was a metal grille that admitted some daylight and fresh air, although this had to be closed by shutters on the outside when there was rain or snow. It was their habit on sunny days to sit beneath it and look up at the blue sky, or on clear nights to watch the stars.

Tomkins was a serious fellow, sombre to the point of sullenness, and it was clear he took no pleasure in his role as host. He brought them their food and drink every day as a Christian duty: at least, because he owned the town's store, it was easy for him to hide the fact that he was feeding extra mouths. Thankfully, his was not the only face they saw. Davenport and Jones both rode over from New Haven occasionally for prayer meetings and to deliver news from the outside world, much of it provided by William Hooke in London and now sent via Increase Mather:

The Solemn League and Covenant has been burned at the hands of the Hangman . . . The Marquess of Argyle was beheaded and at his death showed much resolution and courage . . . It is ordered by Parliament that Lord Monson, Sir James Harrington & Sir Henry Mildmay (who sat as judges of the late King) shall be degraded of their honours & titles, & shall on each anniversary of the King's murder be drawn upon sledges with ropes about their necks, from the Tower of London to the Gallows at Tyburn, their faces besmeared with blood, there to stand for six hours, thence to be carried back to the Tower, and to remain prisoners during their lives . . .

So much for mercy to those who had surrendered themselves and recanted.

Some men of the Milford community were also in on the secret of the colonels' presence – Roger Newton, the minister, and Robert Treat and Benjamin Fenn, both magistrates – all joined them from time to time. Tomkins' wife and daughters they never once set eyes on, although the girls used the storeroom for spinning, and the colonels often listened to them singing as they worked. The childish songs brought tears to Will's eyes. They could also hear customers coming to the store, standing outside and gossiping. It was diverting to eavesdrop on the trivia of the wider world, although the easy voices, heedless of the presence of the two fugitives, also emphasised their isolation.

They passed the time in part by reverting to their former occupations. Ned cut cloth and stitched the animal skins Tomkins had traded with the local Indians. Will smoked and salted meat and fish. Their produce was sold in the store, and after Tomkins had deducted the cost of their food and fuel, he insisted on paying them the balance, so that they even began to accumulate a little money.

Those who have not endured the misfortune of confinement for a long while in a small space naturally suppose that the days must drag by slowly. But those who have suffered the experience know that the contrary is true. When each day becomes the same as the last, there is nothing for the mind to catch onto. Time becomes formless. The days slip by, indistinguishable from one another, fast merging into weeks and months. Instead, by some strange compensatory trick of nature, it is the nights that are most vivid, filled with startling dreams, which in Ned's case were almost invariably of the past. He would wake, sweating and exhausted, to find himself alone, Will having taken himself off to sleep on his blanket, unable to endure his father-in-law's tossing and turning.

Amazingly, they rarely argued. Each had become so familiar with the other's moods, they knew the warning signs and learned to keep silent. So when Will was irritable, Ned understood that it was because he was thinking of Frances and the children, and avoided any topic that might provoke him. And when Ned withdrew into his own thoughts, Will guessed he was remembering Cromwell, and the circumstances that had raised him once so high and now cast him into these depths.

All public assemblies are utterly broken, & those who meet in private are watched, & many of them hauled to prisons, & how soon I may be taken I know not . . . The Glory is departed, & evil come upon the people of God, to the utmost. The rage of the enemy & the sufferings of the Saints increases more and more . . . Our friends in England are in great doubt & much in the dark what to do, whether to fly or stand & abide the issue . . . Prince Rupert is made constable of the Tower . . .

They learned of the deaths of Barkstead, Okey and Corbet, and of their bravery on the scaffold, which caused Will to launch into another bitter lament about their folly in fleeing to America. 'Look at us, imprisoned in a cell without freedom or honour, when if we had had the courage of our martyred friends, we would now be with God . . .' Ned wanted to point out that the three men had also fled to escape punishment, and had only died martyrs because of their own carelessness, which hardly seemed more honourable to him, but he managed to master his tongue.

Dwelling on the executions, Will lapsed into a melancholy that lasted for several weeks and was only ended in November, when Davenport paid another visit. He came alone and seemed greatly aged and depressed. A dispatch had arrived from London with the news that a royal charter had been agreed with Winthrop, and that all the territory of New Haven was now to come under the jurisdiction of Connecticut. 'Can it really be the will of God that the laws of Moses should vanish from this land?' He was utterly perplexed by the workings of the Almighty, so much so that it was only when their scriptural study was over and he had set one foot on the ladder to leave that he suddenly remembered another reason for his call.

'Forgive me, Colonel Goffe. I did clean forget. You have a letter from England.'

Will waited until Davenport had gone, then carried the letter over to the part of the cellar beneath the grille, where there was just enough weak winter light for him to make out Frances's awkward hand. Like him, she was conscious of not being properly educated. It was one of the bonds between them.

My dearest Heart, I have been exceedingly cheered by your precious letter.

Through mercy, I and your little ones are in reasonable health, only Betty and Nan are weakly, and I fear will be lame a little, the others are very lusty.

I do heartily wish myself with you, but I fear it may be a means to discover you, as it was to Colonel Barkstead and Colonel Okey, and therefore I shall resist attempting any such thing for the present, hoping that the Lord will, in his own time, return you to us. Let us comfort ourselves with this – even if we should never meet in this world again, yet I hope, through grace, we shall meet in heaven. My dear, I know you are confident of my affection, yet give me leave to tell you, you are as dear to me as a husband can be to a wife, and if I knew anything that I could do to make you happy, I should do it, if the Lord would permit it, even to the loss of my life.

As for news, my uncle Burket is dead, and my mother is with him. My brother John is gone beyond the sea, but I know not whither. Henry and Edward, the same.

My dearest, my aunts and many others are very kind to me, so that, through mercy, I have no want of food and clothes, though in a mean way. Though it is an unspeakable comfort to hear of your welfare, yet I earnestly beg of you not to write too often, for fear of the worst. They are very vigilant here.

And now, my dear, with 1000 tears, I take my leave of you, and recommend you to God, who neither slumbers nor sleeps and who, I hope, will keep you, and my dear friend with you, from all your enemies, and in his own time return you to your family. Which is the daily prayer of your affectionate and obedient wife till death, F.

Many friends here desire to be remembered to you. Richard and the rest of your dear babes that can speak talk much of you, and long to see you. My humble duty to my dear father and tell him I pray for him with my whole heart; but I am so bad a scribe I dare not write to him. Pray be private and careful who you trust.

He read it through again, and then went back to the sentence 'my uncle Burket is dead, and my mother is with him'. It was a shy way to convey such terrible news, almost in passing, but he knew it was a testament to her faith: after years of illness, Katherine Whalley was at peace with God; it was not to be lamented.

He glanced across the cellar at Ned, who was leaning forwards in his chair, watching him eagerly.

'Come then, Will,' he said. 'What does she say?'

'You should read it for yourself, Ned.'

He gave him the letter and put a consoling hand on his shoulder. Ned looked up at him sharply, his expression suddenly fearful.

After he had finished reading, he sat back in his chair, staring into the distance, the letter still clutched in his hand.

Will said, 'I am so very sorry. She was a fine lady, filled with God's grace. She suffered much, and now it is over.'

A silence.

'Well, there it is,' said Ned.

That night, when they went up as usual to take the air, Ned wandered off in the direction of the orchard. Will let him go alone.

A sea fog had rolled in off Long Island Sound. In the damp November dark, the apple and pear trees stretched out their bare branches – in lamentation, or so it seemed to Ned. Images of her, so long suppressed, moved through the mist around him – the young Katherine Myddleton as she had been at nineteen, when he took her as his second wife after Judith had died in childbirth; the worn-out Katherine he had left behind on the farm in Essex, with four young children – two of Judith's and two of her own – when he went off to the war; the radiant Katherine who had been feasted by the King at Hampton Court when Charles had been his prisoner and it still looked likely that a deal would be struck; Katherine the fashionable matriarch, presiding over the household in King Street in the days of plenty, when they were part of the Protector's ruling circle and found themselves rich and feted; and the stricken Katherine who had unexpectedly become pregnant in the twentieth year of their marriage, and who had almost bled to death when the baby was lost and had never recovered her health, neither in body nor in mind. So many Katherines, none of them ever to be seen or held or whispered to again; so much regret.

He sank to his knees in the chilly New England orchard and wept.

That winter – their second in Milford, their third in exile – was as bitterly cold as their first in Cambridge. Snow fell and the shutters over the grille had to be kept closed. In the semi-darkness, they huddled around the firebox and tried to work by candlelight with frozen fingers. No more letters came. It was perilous for a ship to attempt the North Atlantic in the stormy season. They also heard from Davenport – who had heard it from Increase Mather – that William Hooke was in hiding following the interception of a letter and could no longer write to New Haven directly.

Will continued to keep track of time by making a record of the days, and one morning announced it was Christmas. He said gloomily, 'Doubtless in England it is once again a time of drunkenness and godless feasting.' Then he brightened. 'Do you remember that day in 'fifty-seven when we surprised that secret Mass in Essex House?'

Ned looked up from his needle and thread. He remembered it well. The Council of State had become alarmed at the way its ordinance banning such popish festivals was being ignored, and had ordered the army to crack down hard. It had been Will's idea to raid the Marquess of Hertford's private chapel and catch them in the act. Ned had not been especially enthusiastic, but had gone along with it to humour his son-in-law. 'We certainly gave those arrogant cavaliers a fright! Do you recall that impudent fellow who tried to argue with us – the one we ordered to be arrested?'

'Hertford's secretary,' said Will promptly. 'Nayler.'

'That's it – Nayler.' Ned went back to his stitching, then looked up again. 'Was that not the name of the government agent Sperry said was leading the search for us?'

'Was it?' Will shrugged. 'The name is not uncommon. It's unlikely to be the same man.'

'True enough.' But it preyed on Ned's mind all the same. Hadn't the man's wife started bleeding from her womb and had to be carried out of the church? He remembered the awful contrast between the redness of her blood on the flagstones and the mortal whiteness of her face: she had looked the same as Katherine had when she suffered her haemorrhage the previous year. He wondered what had become of her. *Nayler*. Yes, that was right. He was a terror, Sperry had said.

It was too cold to go outside to exercise that evening. After supper, Ned lit another lamp, and while Will lay on the mattress studying the Bible, he sat at the table, opened his old army bag and took out his papers.

Some Memories of the Life of
His Highness, the Late Lord Protector,
Oliver Cromwell
by his cousin
Col. Edw. Whalley

He hadn't looked at his book for more than a year and a half. But now his mind was so filled with images of the past, he felt his head must burst if he did not relieve the pressure by releasing them onto paper. Besides, he knew at last to whom his memories might be of interest – to Frances, upon whom his career had brought such disaster. The thought that his daughter did not dare write to him because of her poor script appalled him. He had always been too hard on her. He would make up for it. He would not write her a letter; she would have a book.

Although I had been born and raised a gentleman, by the time I came of age my father's estate was bankrupt through his profligacy. He lived entirely on what he borrowed. At the age of nineteen, my expectations vanished, and I was sent to London to be apprenticed to the trade of tailor.

For seven years, I was in servitude, in an occupation not of my choice, but with the consolation of having a sober, godly master. He in turn was blessed with a fine and sensible daughter – your mother, Judith – to whom, with his warm approval, I was married. I am sorry you cannot remember her. She was gentle, kind and modest; her spirit lives on in you. By one of those coincidences that marked our lives, Oliver married in the same year Elizabeth, daughter of Sir James Bourchier, a leather merchant in the City, and we saw much of one another before he returned to farm in Huntingdon.

Despite his happy union with Betty, swiftly blessed with children, Oliver was afflicted by an intense melancholy, often-times laid low with ailments, more imaginary than real, and with a deep conviction, often expressed to me, that he would certainly die before he was thirty. He drank more than was good for him, gambled on cockfights, was over-ready with his fists in the taverns, and less than diligent in his attendance at prayers. Shortly after I finished my apprenticeship, and was admitted to the Guild of Merchant Taylors, and set up business on my own, he disappeared entirely from his home. His friends searched for him anxiously over several days, fearing the worst, but in vain.

And then, a week later, by God's good grace, he turned up at our door in London – the same Oliver, and yet transformed. (This was before you were born.) There was a brightness in his eyes, a burning fire; I know no other way to express it. Our Lord and Saviour had come to him and rescued him from the hellish pit into which he had fallen. 'Oh, I have lived and loved in darkness,' he said to me. 'I have been the chief of sinners. I have been blind, but now I see. I have placed my life in His hands and henceforth I shall walk in the light of God's will, wherever He may direct me.'

What the revelation was, and where and how it had been granted to him, I never did discover, but he spoke the truth. He was reborn and henceforth he prospered. He had changed, and, although we could not guess it then, by the fire of his faith he would change England.

It cost Ned several days, and much crossing-out and rethinking, just to compose these few paragraphs. But what did it matter? Time was the one commodity he did not lack. Often he put his manuscript aside for days or weeks before returning to it. He would daydream for hours over a sentence. For every memory he set down, he recalled a dozen more, a hundred. The hopelessness of his commercial ventures he preferred to forget. The woollen trade was poor, prices low. The Dutch refused to accept his finished cloth. Twice he had to flee his creditors. He leased a farm called Longhouse Place on the Essex marshes bordering the Thames estuary and attempted to reclaim the adjoining land by drainage, and failed at that as well. But what business was it of posterity to know all this? It was humiliating to recall.

He thought often of Judith. Her father had died young. Her inheritance soon ran out, swallowed up in Ned's failed schemes.

She gave birth to two children, John and Frances, and died before she was thirty trying to give him a third. He met Katherine soon afterwards. She was the daughter of an Essex neighbour, local gentry – her grandfather, Sir Thomas Myddleton, had been Lord Mayor of London – and she married him for love: the tall, well-born widower in his thirties, a gentleman struggling alone to bring up two young children. But if she had also hoped for prospects, she was to be as disappointed as he was. All he could offer her was flat, unproductive, mortgaged land, looking out to the salt marshes and the sea, and when the King imposed his ship tax – that most detestable levy, raised to fund his popish policies – Longhouse Place tipped over into bankruptcy.

Thus Edward Whalley at the outbreak of the Civil War, in his forty-fourth year, on the day his cousin Cromwell came calling to invite him to join his regiment: fallen in society yet educated above his station, disappointed with his lot, frustrated by the world as it was ordered, devout in his Puritan faith, physically strong from his toil on the farm, restless for adventure, fervent in his detestation of the King's government; fearless, really – a revolutionary in embryo.

'What is it you write, Ned?' asked Will one evening. 'Whatever it may be, it goes very slowly. It cannot be letters, for we are not able to send any, and even if we were able, you never do so.'

'It is merely a diversion, to pass the time. A few recollections, nothing of any consequence.'

'I should like to read it. May I?'

'Perhaps. One day. When it is finished.'

But for some reason, he did not want Will to see it, and he guarded it carefully, folding the pages each night and hiding them at the bottom of his bag.

★

The truth was, there were many episodes he did not care to describe, especially to his daughter. That first winter of the war, for instance, when they roamed around the eastern counties, arresting Royalist sympathisers and seizing money to send to London. They rode into Suffolk, to Lowestoft, took about thirty malignants prisoner and turfed the popish priests out of their livings. Then they went to Cambridge – Ned had not been back since he was an undergraduate – demanded all the colleges' gold and silver plate, and when none was forthcoming, locked up the masters and the vice chancellor in their rooms. In St Mary's, the university church, they rode their horses up the nave, seized the Book of Common Prayer and tore it to pieces, and Cromwell attacked the wooden carvings in the chapel with his sword, chopped them up and burned them before the altar. That was in March. In April they fell upon Peterborough Cathedral – took axes to the organ, smashed the stained-glass windows, destroyed the altar and the altar rails and the brasses, burned the library and the archives and the rood screens, stabled their horses in the Lady Chapel . . . They left that massive medieval structure as bare as Micah Tomkins' cellar. He remembered how some of his troopers found the priests' vestments and put them on and cavorted around the city. They were crusaders in a rage of pent-up holy fury, and he wondered now, looking back on it, if that had truly been God's work. But Oliver had gloried in it – he could see him now, his red face redder still in the glare of the burning books and ancient timber, the light dancing in his dark eyes. What they really wanted was to kill some Royalists – 'That is our business,' said Oliver, 'to slay the enemy' – and in May they got their chance.

It was not a battle – a skirmish, merely, with no artillery, two miles outside Grantham in Lincolnshire. A couple of thousand on the enemy side, cavalry, foot and dragoons, who emerged out of the summer dusk, drums beating, flags flying; and roughly a thousand under Cromwell's command, about half of them his own regiment and the rest a very poor and broken-down lot of local men. For half an hour, the two little armies faced one another and exchanged musket shot, and then, with darkness coming on, Oliver lost his patience and despite the unfavourable odds ordered a charge.

It went exactly as they had practised it all winter – an advance at a fast trot in three lines, Ned in the first line with his legs locked around those of the men on either side of him, his pistol drawn. He felt not the slightest fear, only the power of God surging through him – they sang a psalm as the charge gathered pace, although it was hard to hear it above the thunder of the hooves – and suddenly the enemy line, which had seemed a long way away, was very close. He fired his pistol and hurled it at the head of the nearest Royalist, then drew his sword as they crashed through the line, slashing blindly at the figures on his right. Their momentum carried them a hundred yards or so. They halted, wheeled – this the enemy, now tending their wounded, did not expect – and charged them again from the rear, and what had been an orderly formation broke into a panicking mob of desperate men intent only on running away. Ned spurred his horse and set off in pursuit, and that was when he made his first kill, catching up with a man, leaning out of his saddle, and swinging at him with his sword, the blade chopping into the side of his neck. There was a spurt of blood. He didn't stop to see who he was – he was young, he thought, and small – but galloped after the rest until they melted away into the dark.

He wrote on steadily throughout that year – 1663 – and into the next, emptying Tomkins' store of his stock of paper and obliging him to send to New Haven for fresh supplies, while above the cellar the seasons changed. Only one letter came to Davenport in all that time from Reverend Hooke, very guarded in its language, describing, as if it had happened to someone else, the incident of the seized intelligencer. *You will know how his letters miscarried, & into whose hands they fell, upon occasion whereof he is obscured & cannot write to you as formerly . . . I understand also that your friend has some relations not far from you, known to you, who would be glad to hear he is well, & he the like of them.* There was no further letter from Frances, although Will prayed for one daily. It was clear that conditions in London were dangerous. *The people of God are very sad, not knowing what to do or whither to go . . .*

Ned felt the isolation less keenly than his son-in-law. His body might be trapped in the cellar, but his mind was soaring through the England of twenty years before, reliving the glory days of the war, when Cromwell's Ironsides swept all before them – more and more certain, as victory followed victory, that they must be doing the Lord's work.

There was Gainsborough in Lincolnshire, two months after Grantham, when they fought up and down the sandy slopes pitted with rabbit warrens – terrible ground for cavalry, yet with God's help they maintained their formation, and when the Royalist general, young Cavendish, came down off the high plateau with his regiment and charged the retreating Parliamentary troops, Cromwell gave the order and they set off after him, forcing him down into a quagmire. Cavendish, only twenty-three, son of the Earl of Devonshire, became trapped. Whalley and Major Berry cornered him. Berry, the Shropshire ironworks clerk, dismounted, waded through the marsh, and stuck him with a fatal thrust under his ribs that made him squeal like a pig.

Then there was Boston, two months after that, where Cromwell had his horse shot from under him and was nearly killed, but was saved by the grace of God. A hundred enemy soldiers were drowned in the ditches of the Lincolnshire Fens. And there was Marston Moor in Yorkshire the following year – the greatest battle ever fought on English soil: forty-two thousand men engaged – when Whalley, now a colonel, commanded the cavalry that broke Prince Rupert's line. The noise and stink of three and a half thousand horse thundering across the thick grass and broad slopes of the moor. The precision with which Cromwell's troopers drew up after their first charge, wheeled and charged again. The flower of the King's army cut down – four thousand enemy slain, for the loss of a mere three hundred on the Parliamentary side.

And finally there was Naseby the next summer, on the flat lands of Northamptonshire, where early on that June morning, with skylarks singing in alarm overhead, Oliver rode over to Ned with a huge grin – he often laughed and smiled before a battle, so sure was he of victory – and gave him the honour of leading the first charge against Sir Marmaduke Langdale and his fifteen hundred northern horse, who were already beginning to move up the slope towards them. 'God will work his wonders, Ned, for the children of men.' That had been a hard fight at close quarters, amid the furze bushes and rabbit holes, after they had discharged their pistols and set about hand-to-hand fighting with their swords. He had killed so many of the enemy by this time they had become a blur, and he reckoned he dispatched another three or four that day, and at the end of the battle, exhausted and bloody, for the first time he felt no exhilaration, but only weariness with the whole business of war.

It was not so much the battle that disgusted him as the massacre afterwards, not only of the retreating soldiers, but of a hundred or more women discovered sheltering in the Royalist camp. Ned looked into it. There was no rape, thank God – there was never any report of rape committed by the New Model Army in the entire course of the war – but there was mutilation as well as slaughter. The men claimed the women were Irish papists, or whores, or witches, or all three, but Ned suspected they were merely the wives of Royalist soldiers, travelling with their men. They might have been Judith, or Katherine.

He raised the matter with Oliver, but General Cromwell, as he now was, merely said such things happened in war, they should not have been on the battlefield, and it should never be mentioned again. The King's army was entirely broken, that was all that mattered, and they had good reason to believe the war was over. 'Naseby was none other than the hand of God,' said Cromwell, 'and to him alone belongs the victory.' Ned arranged for the women to be buried in a mass grave. Unable to find the words to express his feelings, he left the incident out of his memoir.

Outside the cellar it was late summer – hot, still, close – the rolling boom of the thunder over Long Island Sound and the flicker of lightning through the iron grille like harbingers of some approaching battle.

CHAPTER TWENTY-SIX

T HAT AUGUST OF 1664 saw Nayler restlessly on the move again, travelling under the false name of Richard Foster, jeweller – first to Paris, where he delivered various secret messages from Hyde to the English ambassador, Lord Holles, thence to Geneva, where he spent the night before embarking on a coach journey around the northern shore of Lac Léman to the Swiss city of Lausanne, arriving on the afternoon of Wednesday the tenth and taking lodgings in an inn, L'Auberge Saint-Gabriel, overlooking the lake.

He would not normally have involved himself in something as risky as a murder, but the mercenaries he had hired had so far proved singularly ineffective. They had bungled an earlier attempt to assassinate General Edmund Ludlow in his home in Vevey, further along the lake. Protected by the canton of Berne, Ludlow was now doubly on his guard and out of reach. Unable to abide the thought of another failure, Nayler had decided he had better take control of matters himself. Besides, it had been unusually hot in London, there was an outbreak of fever, the court had left for the summer to join the King in the country, and he was bored.

The three would-be killers came to the *auberge* that evening – James Fitz Edmond Cotter, Miles Crowley and John Rierdan (or 'Riordo', as they called him) – all Irish Royalist officers in their thirties, fallen on hard times, keen to perform some service that might restore their fortunes. They were an ungainly trio: clumsy, sweating in the heat, with broad freckled faces and atrocious French accents, immediately conspicuous as foreigners. Nayler groaned inwardly as soon as he saw them across the terrace approaching his table. But in this kind of affair, he had learned it was necessary to work with such tools as came to hand.

Their victim was to be Sir John Lisle, aged fifty-four, the lawyer who had managed the King's trial, who had sat next to the president of the court throughout the hearing and the drafting of the sentence, and who was now living under the pseudonym of Mr Field. He had not served as a judge himself, or signed the death warrant, but he was attained for treason for his role in proceedings – a secondary figure compared to Ludlow, but worth the effort and the risk.

It was Cotter, the leader of the three, who outlined the plan. After observing Lisle's movements for several weeks, they were confident that he would walk to church the following morning, accompanied by two bodyguards. Cotter and Rierdan would deal with the guards, while Crowley would shoot Lisle with a specially chosen weapon. Crowley had an object hidden under a blanket that he now laid on the table, partly unwrapped, and surreptitiously showed to Nayler – a short musket known as a musketoon, with a barrel like a trumpet, that discharged half a dozen bullets at once. Nayler regarded it with dismay and glanced around the crowded terrace.

'For pity's sake, Mr Crowley, put that thing away.' After the gun had been replaced under the table, he said, 'You will need to get very close to him if you plan to use a musketoon, otherwise you will injure half the congregation.'

'Oh, we shall get close to him, Mr Nayler,' said Cotter. 'You need have no worry about that.'

But Nayler did worry. He lay awake for half the night worrying. Their planned ambush was much too public for his liking. He even considered leaving the town at first light. If an official of the Privy Council was discovered directing an assassination on foreign soil in a neutral country, it would cause a diplomatic outrage. In the end, he decided it was his duty to see it through, and when he rose the next morning, he loaded his pistol and slipped it into his pocket.

The church of Saint-François stood in the middle of Lausanne, about a mile from his *auberge*. To reach it demanded a stiff climb through crowded, winding streets. A bell began to toll. He emerged from an alley into a cobbled square, the church on one side, shops on the others, outside one of which – a barber's – lurked Cotter, Crowley and Rierdan. Absurdly, despite the summer weather, they were all wearing cloaks. Worshippers were walking purposefully towards the church door. Nayler searched the crowd for someone who might be Lisle, and spotted him immediately – he was as conspicuous as his waiting murderers – a portly figure in a periwig, wearing the robes of an English lawyer, with a burly companion on either side.

Almost at the same instant as Nayler saw him, Cotter and the other two recognised him as well. They left the barber's and walked briskly across the cobbles, coming up behind him, opening their cloaks and pulling out their weapons just as he reached the church door. The brass barrel of the musketoon flashed in the sunlight, its flared end inches from Lisle's back. There was a terrific bang that lifted a flock of pigeons and sent them flapping across the square. Lisle's arms went up. The blast propelled him forwards and he landed heavily, face down on the church steps. His bodyguards tried to draw their pistols, but Cotter and Rierdan had them covered. They aimed their guns and shouted a warning at the same time as they started backing away. A woman screamed. Cotter called out, in his appalling French, *'Vive le roi d'Angleterre!'* and then all three turned and ran, out of the square and down a side street to their waiting horses.

A crowd was gathering around the victim. Nayler crossed the cobbles to join them. He pushed his way through to get a better view. Lisle lay motionless on his stomach on the stone steps, his wig knocked askew, blood pooling beside him. In the small of his back was a ragged crimson wound the size of a dessert plate, like a dish of raspberries, pulsing blood. His bodyguards rolled him over. There were exclamations of horror. The old lawyer stared blindly at the sky, slack-mouthed. Nayler stayed long enough to be certain he was dead, then turned away and slipped between the gawping spectators.

No one tried to stop him. For the first time since his arrival in Switzerland, he felt a certain lightness in his step. If all had gone to plan, Cotter, Crawley and Rierdan should at this moment be boarding a boat to spirit them away to Geneva. One more of the King's murderers justly killed. And the Duke of York's expedition to capture New Amsterdam should be making land in America any day now. With luck, by the end of the summer he would be able to cross out the names of another two.

CHAPTER TWENTY-SEVEN

THE THIRD ANNIVERSARY of Ned and Will's incarceration in Micah Tomkins' cellar arrived that same week in mid August. In the stifling heat, the colonels had both taken to wearing only their underclothes. Ned spent the day at the table, writing his memoir, struggling to put in order all the sieges he had taken part in during the two years after Naseby – Bridgwater, Sherborne, Bristol, Dartmouth, Banbury, Exeter, Oxford, Worcester . . . Even though the King's army had been destroyed in the field, there had seemed no end to the pockets of Royalist resistance. Will salted mutton in preparation for the winter. The confined space was thick with the smell of blood and fat and the buzzing of flies.

Neither man remarked upon the date. What was there to say? There was nowhere they could go, nothing they could do. They could only pray for circumstances to change.

That night, after Tomkins had brought them their supper, they waited until it was past midnight, when the air was cooler, and then went up the ladder, through the storeroom and out into the yard. The night was very still and clear, a brilliant half-moon, the summer sky awash with stars. It was easy to see their way across the road and down the narrow path that led to the sea, about a hundred yards distant through the pines. Long Island Sound extended like a dappled silver lake beneath the moon. The waves breaking on the shore made a sound no louder than an intake of breath, followed by a long withdrawing sigh. They found a patch of sand between the rocks, took off their boots and clothes, and waded naked out into the water.

For the next hour they swam, taking care not to be carried too far along the shore by the current. Not a word passed between them. The night felt too sacred to disturb by talk, as if they were in some immense cathedral, very close to God. Afterwards, they lay down on the sand and stared at the stars until they fell asleep. When Ned awoke, he sucked his arm to taste the salt, then rummaged through his pockets for his telescope and trained it on the moon. It was bright enough to make out the mountain ranges and craters. A shooting star fell to the horizon. He followed its trajectory and let the spyglass play across the darkness, very slowly, right to left.

He saw the dark shadow of a ship.

He lowered the telescope in shock and sat up straight, then put it back to his eye. For a moment, he could see nothing, but then he found it again. About a mile distant. A big vessel, high in the water: a three-decker, triple-masted, with four large sails to each mast and a huge flag trailing at the stern, moving slowly through the calm night, silhouetted by the moon. She was no cargo boat. She was a warship. And she was not alone. There was another just behind her, and another, and – dear God! – another.

He shook Will awake and handed him the telescope. 'Four men-o'-war,' he whispered. 'Heading west.' He pointed to the horizon. All were plainly visible now.

Will stared at the flotilla for half a minute.

Ned said quietly, 'Can you make out the flag?'

Will squinted again, adjusted the focus. 'She's English, no doubt about it.' He returned the spyglass. 'That's a military expedition.' In the moonlight his face was pale and grim. 'Could it be they're looking for us?'

'It's possible.'

'They really want us so much they'd come all this way?'

'Perhaps.' We can run to the edge of the world, Ned thought, and still they will never give up. 'We should get back.'

When Tomkins brought them their food later that morning, they told him about the ships. The news threw him into such a panic he forgot to be angry, even though they were forced to confess that the only reason they had spotted the flotilla was because they had gone down to the sea.

The following afternoon, he returned with Reverend Davenport.

Without preliminaries, Davenport announced, 'An expedition of English warships has arrived in Gravesend Bay. Four men-o'-war with four hundred soldiers.'

Ned said, 'Where is Gravesend Bay?'

'The furthest end of Long Island.'

'Do we know their purpose?'

'They first made land at Boston three weeks ago to re-provision. They showed their orders to Governor Endecott. They are commissioned by the Duke of York to force the surrender of New Amsterdam – and to capture you.'

They would have liked more time to prepare, but Tomkins was insistent. He couldn't be certain that in the last three years someone in the town hadn't glimpsed them one night, especially if they had made it a habit to disobey his instructions and venture beyond the orchard. The two-hundred-pound reward was still on offer. If they were discovered on his premises, he would be hanged. He wanted them gone by morning.

'And where are we to go?' asked Ned.

'Now,' said Davenport uneasily, 'there is the question.'

They discussed it for only a short while before reaching the inescapable conclusion that the only option was their old refuge in the rocks above New Haven.

'I shall inform William Jones,' said Davenport, plainly relieved that they had not asked to return to his house. 'We'll try to bring you provisions when we're sure it's safe, and in the meantime, I'll endeavour to arrange a new hiding place for the winter.' He sighed and shook his head. 'But exactly who will take you in, given all this, I cannot say. It will have to be somewhere far from the sea.'

After their visitors had gone, Ned sat slumped in his chair opposite Will. The prospect of yet more weeks spent living in the wild, with no end in sight, was dreadful to him. He was sixty-five. His old wounds ached first thing every morning and last thing at night. He was not sure he could survive it. Eventually he said, 'I know I've always been the one who's urged us to flee, but now I wonder if we wouldn't do better to surrender ourselves.'

'Surely you don't imagine they would show us mercy?'

'No. Our fate would be the same as Okey's and the others'. But we'd be taken back to London for execution, where at least we'd have a last chance to say goodbye to our families. And we'd show manly resolution and have the martyrs' deaths you've always craved.'

Will did not reply immediately, then he reached for his Bible and searched for the passage he wanted. ' "We are troubled on every side, yet not distressed; we are perplexed, but not in despair;

persecuted, but not forsaken; cast down, but not destroyed." St Paul to the Corinthians.' He put his hand on Ned's and looked at him intently. 'Another year – at most a year and a half – and all will be well, I promise you.'

'How can you know that?'

'Because I have discussed it often with Mr Davenport, and it is foretold. In the Year of Our Lord 1666, Christ will return, and the rule of the saints will be established here in America. You were right. We must keep the faith, Ned, as Paul instructs us – run the race and finish the course and live to see God's kingdom here on earth.'

He spoke with such conviction, Ned briefly felt his spirits strengthen. Will had Oliver's knack of always being able to put his finger on something in the Scriptures to justify following his instincts. Nevertheless, when it came to cramming everything into his bag, and it was clear that he must leave behind either his memoir or something else to make room for it, he chose to discard his Bible. He told himself they did not need two, and that he would share Will's.

They sat with their bags between their knees and waited in silence.

As soon as the sky had darkened above the grille, the trapdoor was lifted, and Tomkins descended to escort them out. Although Ned had longed to escape the cellar, now that it came to it, he felt a twist in his stomach at the thought that he would never see it again. It was not just the idea of living rough he recoiled from: it was the outside world. Stupid old fool, he reproached himself, living in the darkness you have gone as soft and white as a grub. He refused Tomkins' offer of help, gave a brisk speech of thanks, shouldered his bag and climbed the ladder. Behind him, Will lingered to deliver a more elaborate farewell and say a prayer for the Tomkins family. A minute later, the colonels were out on the road, walking eastwards in the moonlight, trying to put as much distance as possible between themselves and the English ships before daybreak.

It was their good fortune that the last week of August and the beginning of September 1664 saw a waxing moon over New England. It cast a bluish glow across the plains and woodlands, bright enough to create sharp shadows. They walked until the birds awoke and started singing and the sun began to rise above the trees. About a mile short of New Haven, they turned off the coastal road and used their swords to cut a path through the undergrowth into the dense forest. In a clearing surrounded by massive pine trunks, they rested and ate the bread and cheese Tomkins had provided for their journey, then slept as well as any men can who know four hundred soldiers are searching for them. As darkness fell, they resumed their trek.

They skirted the edge of New Haven, its roofs clearly visible in the moonlight, and picked up the familiar trail that led north. They reached the abandoned mill, exhausted, early in the morning and lay on their coats amid the weeds debating whether to alert Sperry to their presence. Years had passed since they had last seen him. Who could say whether he would be willing to help, or even if he was still to be trusted? They decided against it.

On the fourth day, they arrived at their old home among the rocks. They scouted the area roundabout, but could find no evidence it had been visited. The weir still stood in the stream, exactly as they had left it. After half an hour of scratching his head and digging holes without result, Ned found the place where he had buried their tools and net. As the sun went down, they lit a fire and stewed the fish Will had caught, their first hot food for nearly a week. Perhaps it was merely the effect of a full belly, but that night as they settled down to sleep on the ledge, Ned had a curious sense of well-being – of happiness, almost. They were still together, and in good health. They were one step ahead of their pursuers. By God's good grace, they would survive.

Within a day, it was as if they had never left. Their lives settled back into the familiar routine of hunting, trapping and fishing, gathering berries, leaves and fungi, skinning and drying hides, sleeping with their pistols cocked, listening to the wolves. At first light, Ned would climb to the top of the rocks with his telescope and scan the immense vista, starting with New Haven and the sea three miles distant and then swivelling clockwise – the English farms on the plain, the woods leading to Sperry's cottage, the ridge, the great expanse of forest to the north, the ridge again and back to the sea.

The full moon rose on Monday 5 September. As it waned, the weather turned – blustery winds and drenching showers, shorter days, chillier nights. Ned stitched together the skins of the rabbits they had snared to make a blanket, which they stretched out on the rocks to dry when the rain stopped. They used the hatchet to fell a couple of trees and kept a log fire going throughout the night. On the nineteenth and the twentieth there was no moon, even though the sky was clear, and on the twenty-first, Ned sat up late, waiting for the sliver of the new moon to appear. When it finally rose above the horizon towards Long Island, he found himself murmuring a prayer of thanks until he came to his senses and stopped. Next he would be worshipping the sun and stars.

One morning at the beginning of October, standing on top of the rock, his eye was caught by a curl of smoke rising from the forest to the north. It was too far away for him to make out any detail. He called down to Will to join him.

Will studied it through the spyglass. 'Could it be the soldiers' camp?'

'More likely Indians.'

'The trees are on fire – look.'

He handed back the telescope. Bright orange flames were spreading across the canopy of leaves. Further in the distance, more smoke was rising from a second fire. They had heard of the Indian custom of burning the land when autumn came, but had never witnessed it, and for the next hour they watched awestruck as the conflagration spread. The sea of roiling flames threw up an immense pall of smoke and ash that dimmed the sun to a brown disc and eventually blotted it out entirely. The northern wind blowing in their faces carried an unearthly roar and the smell of scorching wood.

Towards evening, a crimson glow spread across the sky. It was still light enough for them to be able to see one another's faces at midnight, and they feared the fire might force them to flee their camp. But that night there was a heavy rain, and in the morning the flames were mostly out. Only a few isolated tall pines continued to burn like brands in the blackened, ashy landscape.

'Armageddon,' said Ned eventually.

'Not yet,' replied Will. 'But it is coming.' He spoke with a certain relish.

One consequence of the fire was that the forest animals were driven up onto the ridge, filling the colonels' traps and snares with squirrels and rabbits. Will brought down a starving deer with their bow and a home-made arrow.

It was starting to get cold now. Winter was approaching. Twice they woke to find their coats and blankets rimed with frost. Ned fashioned two pairs of mittens out of deerskin. He reckoned they had food enough to last two months. It wasn't hunger but the weather he feared most. Will would probably survive it; he was sure he himself wouldn't last long in the snow. He made up his mind what he would do when the time came: creep out of the camp one night when Will was asleep and walk until he dropped and fell asleep in the cold. He had seen plenty of soldiers succumb to the Scottish winter. It was not such a bad death, and it would give Will a better chance if he was on his own, without an old man to worry about.

In the third week of October, two English warships appeared in New Haven Bay.

The colonels watched through Ned's spyglass as they sailed down the harbour channel and dropped anchor. After half an hour, both frigates lowered a pair of longboats crammed with soldiers. They were too far in the distance to make out numbers. It was only possible to tell they were soldiers at all by their red coats, which merged into single splashes of colour, vivid on the dark water.

Will said, 'How many men to a boat, do you reckon?'

'A couple of dozen?' Ned was guessing.

'Then perhaps a hundred or so in all.' He collapsed the telescope. 'What would you do in their place?'

'If I was going by the book? I'd start with the town. Post sentries on the roads to stop anyone entering or leaving while every house is searched. Then I'd move out into the country.'

'And as you're not a dull fellow?'

'I'd do it the other way round. Post sentries to seal the town but begin with the country, hope to drive us towards New Haven.'

'So what should we expect them to do?'

'We should obey the first rule of warfare – assume that your enemy's not stupid.'

They spent the rest of that day and the whole of the next

morning clearing their camp – filling in the latrine, replacing their tools in the hole Ned had dug three years earlier, burying their bags and food and logs, covering the traces of their fire – so that by the time they had finished, there was no evidence of their presence except the marks Will had scratched on the rocks to record the passage of the days during their first summer: there was nothing they could do to erase those. Then they walked into the nearby woods and used Sperry's old rope to climb a massive oak, its lower branches wide and straight enough for them to each lie full-length, head to toe. They kept their swords and pistols with them in case it came to a fight.

Showers overnight soaked them to the skin. By morning, Ned's teeth were chattering with the beginnings of a chill.

In the afternoon, through his fever, he heard men's voices. Lifting his head, he saw four redcoats emerging along the ridge from the west, carrying muskets with plug bayonets fitted to the ends of the barrels. They circled the great rocks, prodding at the ground and the nearby undergrowth. They halted. One of the soldiers climbed up to the highest boulder, took out a telescope and scanned the surrounding trees. His vantage point was higher than their hiding place. Ned pressed his cheek to the rough bark and clamped his jaw tight shut to stop it rattling. Someone shouted, 'Captain, look here!' Ned raised his head again and risked a sideways glance. The officer had put away his telescope and was clambering down to inspect something. It sounded as though they had discovered Will's calendar. Their conversation became more animated. Ned listened to them removing their bayonets, priming their muskets. They advanced towards the trees and passed in single file directly beneath the oak.

The sounds faded. After a few minutes, Will whispered, 'D'you suppose they've gone?'

'I doubt it. There's barely three hours of daylight left. They'll most likely return the way they came so as not to get lost.'

'Should we try to take them?'

It was tempting. But if four men went missing, the rest would surely come in numbers looking for them. 'Only if they see us.'

A gunshot echoed through the woods. Instinctively Ned pressed his head down again. Two more followed in rapid succession. Shouts. The noise of bodies crashing through the undergrowth, then a long silence. Ned hardly dared to breathe. Finally he heard voices again – angry now, an argument. The soldiers passed back below them.

'I'm telling you I saw something!'

'Aye – a ghost.'

'Last night's rum, most likely!'

Someone laughed. The first man continued to protest. Their voices faded.

The colonels stayed in the tree till nightfall.

By this time, Ned was shaking so much it was hard for him to climb down. He went and lay on the ledge while Will dug up some skins to wrap him in, brought him a cup of water and some cold meat. They continued to speak in whispers and dared not light a fire in case the soldiers were camped nearby. O Lord, prayed Ned, forgive my weakness. I cannot endure it. Let me die tonight.

But the next morning, he was still alive.

For three days the fever continued. He was conscious of Will tending him as if he were a child. On the fourth morning, he woke without a temperature. Beside him, Will was snoring. He managed to stand, and walked unsteadily across to the trees to relieve himself. Afterwards, he felt much better – the wonderful euphoria that follows an illness. He took his telescope and carefully climbed to the top of the rocks. A milky mist was rising off the plain, but the sea was clear, lit by the sunrise.

The harbour channel was empty. The warships had gone.

That afternoon, they had their first friendly visitor for two months.

William Jones brought them provisions – freshly baked bread, cheese, ham, beer and tobacco. The Welshman seemed almost surprised to find them still alive. He apologised for leaving them alone so long. He said it had been judged too risky to venture out of the town with so many soldiers in the area. He sat on the lowest rock with the colonels, and while he watched them eat, he told them what had been happening.

Stuyvesant had surrendered the Dutch colony to the English expeditionary force without a fight. New Netherland no longer existed. New Amsterdam had been renamed in honour of the King's brother. It was now New York. Once their military mission had been accomplished, the redcoats had searched for the colonels in New Haven, Milford, Guilford and the surrounding countryside. They had treated himself, Reverend Davenport, Mr Leete and the magistrates with considerable roughness, which suggested they had come armed with good intelligence. But they had discovered nothing. Frustrated, they had set sail back to Boston the previous day.

'Meanwhile, we have not been idle on your behalf. Funds have been raised among your friends in America. Mr Hooke has also sent money collected in London. A new refuge has been prepared for you both.'

Ned was smoking his pipe, savouring the taste. 'This is for the winter?'

'No. This is to be permanent at last.'

'In a cellar? An outbuilding?'

'No. In a house, with a family. Richard Sperry will return tomorrow with horses. He'll guide you.'

'Horses?' Ned had assumed they would be returning on foot to New Haven. 'Where are we to go?'

'Hadley, Massachusetts.'

He glanced at Will, who shrugged. 'We've not heard of it.'

'Nobody has, that's the beauty of it. Hadley's a new community, eighty miles north of here on the Connecticut – the farthest point of English settlement in the whole of America. It's all arranged. You are to lodge with the minister, John Russell, an old friend of Mr Davenport's. There are only some fifty families in the entire place. No one will disturb you there. As far as the outside world is concerned . . .' Jones smiled and opened his hands, as if releasing a bird at the end of a conjuring trick, 'you will have ceased to exist.'

CHAPTER TWENTY-EIGHT

PERRY CAME WITH the horses soon after dawn the next morning, and they left at once, taking as many of their possessions as they could carry, leaving the rest behind without bothering to conceal them. Whatever their fate, Ned promised himself, they would never return to the rocks.

They trekked through the burnt-out forest with handkerchiefs tied around their faces to protect them from the ash thrown up by the horses' hooves. Here and there, curls of smoke rose from fires still burning underground. Yet it was amazing to see how many trees had survived. Already green shoots were beginning to spread across the blackened earth. Now they understood why so much of New England had the appearance of English parkland. By nightfall they had reached the Connecticut River.

The following day they pressed on northwards. In the clear late-autumn light, the forests were a profusion of reds and golds, interrupted occasionally by large patches of black, like holes burnt in a Turkish carpet. Occasionally they spotted the Indians' camps in the distance. After a detour through the woods around Hartford to avoid being seen, they returned to the river at Windsor – the first time they had showed themselves in public for years. To see a dozen faces at once, gathered around the ferry station, was disconcerting. Beneath his coat, Ned kept his hand on the butt of his pistol. No one paid them any heed. Once the ferry had taken them across, they stuck to the path, with the river always on their left, and ended the day camped about five miles south of Springfield.

At sunset on the third day, they finally reached a sweeping bend in the Connecticut, in the crook of which nestled a tiny settlement. That, Sperry announced, must be Hadley, although he could not be certain: he had never been this far north before. He told them to wait out of sight while he went in search of Reverend Russell.

It was a beautiful spot. They could see that even in the gathering dusk – a meadow with pine trees, huge willows along the riverbank, a mountain forest beyond, a pair of eagles circling very high. But the very remoteness of it, and the silence, was haunting, melancholy. Ned studied the hamlet through his telescope. 'Such a small place,' he said. 'They must live in fear of attack.'

'So far from the rest of humanity,' replied Will, 'is it any wonder?'

An hour later, when it was almost dark, Sperry returned. 'Mr Russell is ready to take you in. The town seems already asleep, so there's no risk of being seen.'

'What sort of a man is he?' asked Ned.

'A fine Christian gentleman, Colonel. You'll like him.'

'So I hope, if we're to spend the rest of our lives with him.' He meant it good-humouredly, but the words came out with a slightly desperate edge.

'Only a year,' corrected Will, 'until 1666. And then we shall be saved.'

They remounted and followed Sperry along the track, across the meadow, towards the town.

There was just sufficient light to make out the shapes of the timber houses on either side of the wide grassy street. Each stood in its own fenced lot with a wide distance between them. They rode on for several minutes, past a dozen properties, a few with candles in the windows, until they came to a large house on a corner. Sperry dismounted and opened the gate. The colonels climbed down from their horses and led them by their reins into the yard, where a man with a lamp was waiting – tall and broad-shouldered, long-haired, in the prime of life. He shook their hands with a hard grip more like a soldier's than a minister's.

'John Russell. Thanks be to God for your safe deliverance.'

On the night of their arrival, Reverend John Russell was thirty-eight. Born in Ipswich, England, and brought to Massachusetts when he was a child as part of the Great Migration of religious independents opposed to the policies of Charles I, he had been only the fourteenth student to graduate from Harvard. Like his friend and mentor Davenport, he had fallen out with the more moderate Puritans in New England, particularly on the issue of baptism for all infants whose parents desired it – a lack of strictness that he opposed – and had led his congregation out of Wethersfield, Connecticut, to form a new community in Massachusetts, far from the interference of the church authorities.

But here, Ned was glad to observe, his similarities to Davenport ended. He had four young sons: John, aged fourteen, born to Russell's first wife, Mary (later killed like so many first wives by childbirth); and a further three boys by his second, Rebecca – Jonathan, nine, Samuel, four, and a baby, Eleazer, barely one year old and still being nursed by his mother. The household was completed by two black slaves in their twenties, Abraham and Martha, a married couple, bought at auction in Rhode Island and taught the tenets of the Christian faith. They slept in one of the outbuildings, their bondage briskly justified by their master on the grounds that the Bible condoned the taking of slaves from among the heathen: 'I assure you, there would be many more slaves in England if they were as short of labour as we are.' Russell had none of Davenport's dreamy fanaticism. He could handle a gun, an axe, a hammer, a plough and a Bible with equal dexterity. He had built his house with his own hands and had modified it over the past month to accommodate his expected guests.

The main part of the dwelling, where the family had their chambers, was to the north. Added onto its south side was a newer wing, some forty feet long by twenty, with a hall and a parlour on the ground floor, positioned either side of a staircase and a large fireplace. As soon as they had unloaded their bags, Russell shepherded them up the stairs. On the upper floor he showed them two good-sized bedrooms, where candles had been lit. 'These will be entirely for your own use,' he told them. 'And now look at this. I finished it last week.'

He opened a door onto a narrow connecting passage running behind the chimney between the two bedrooms. It exuded a smell of fresh paint and sawdust. Halfway along, he pulled up a couple of loose boards. He beckoned them to come and see, and shone his lamp over a ladder leading down into the darkness. 'There's a small chamber hidden behind the chimney on the ground floor. If anyone comes looking for you, you can conceal yourselves there.'

'Most ingenious,' said Ned. That is the hole where I shall crawl to die, he thought.

After Russell had withdrawn for the night, promising to introduce them to the rest of the household in the morning – 'You may rely on them to keep your presence secret' – the two colonels sat on one of the beds.

Will said, 'He is truly a man of God. One can sense it.'

'He is,' replied Ned wearily, 'no doubt.'

'Then what could be more perfect? We have shelter, food, company, space, a hiding place, a room each. We even have windows.'

'That is true.'

'And yet you are not content?'

Content? Ned wanted to cry aloud. How can we be content? We are at the very edge of civilisation! Do you not understand? This is the end of our wandering. We shall never see England again. He longed for his house in Whitehall, for Katherine and his sister, Jane, for Frances and his grandchildren, for the noise of King Street, for his friends and comrades, for Cromwell and the army, for his old life at the centre of events. 'Forgive me,' he said. 'I am just very tired.'

It was agreed that they would keep to their rooms and take their meals separately from the rest of the household to minimise their contact with the children and avoid any questions about their identities and the reasons for their presence. At dusk they were permitted to go out into the Russells' eight-acre lot for exercise, providing they took care not to be seen. But the houses were so widely spaced, and with winter coming on there were so few people lingering outdoors, there was little danger of that. The first snow fell in November, the wind sweeping down off the mountain and across the freezing river, and Ned was sure he had never known such cold.

The only other person in Hadley let in on the secret of their presence was the town's magistrate, the deacon of the church and Russell's effective deputy, Peter Tilton. He was a Warwickshire man originally, a few years older than Russell, quieter but of a similar stamp. He came over to the house twice a week, on the

Sabbath and on a Thursday, to pray with the colonels and study the Bible.

At the beginning, they slept a lot, recovering from their exhaustion. In December, Will asked to be given useful employment, and was set to work chopping firewood in the barn, releasing Abraham to work in the fields. Both Ned and Will found the notion of slavery unchristian – for every verse in the Bible that was supposed to justify it, Will could cite two or three that said the opposite – and shortly afterwards, so that Abraham could come in again from the cold, he volunteered to go back to his old trade of salting meat. There was no general store in Hadley, nor even yet a meeting house. Families bartered goods with one another: cloth for firewood, firewood for meat, meat for corn . . . If anyone was curious as to why the Russells suddenly had a surplus of salted pork, it was never mentioned. The priority in winter in that remote spot was simply to stay alive.

Ned spent the days huddled close to his fire, a blanket over his knees, a tray on his lap upon which rested the manuscript of his memoir. He had nothing to do except write, and he had a premonition that not much time remained to him. Yet for hours that winter he simply stared at the burning logs, sometimes listening to the Russell boys throwing snowballs in the yard. Fighting the Civil War came more readily to his temperament than describing it. But surely if he had found the courage for the one, he must be able to summon the resolution for the other? He glanced at the window, the snow piling on the sill, and thought about those terrible dragging winters of the mid forties, when victory seemed forever to elude them. How could he explain it all to Frances – the steps that had led inexorably to the King's execution and the destruction of their lives together? Finally his pen began to move again.

In the winter of 1646–7, General Cromwell was afflicted by a fever so severe it was thought likely to prove fatal. He told me afterwards that he gladly received the sentence of death, that he might thereby learn to trust in the Lord, for all things of the flesh are lighter than vanity.

That spring, I was with the army, encamped at Saffron Walden, when news arrived that Parliament had voted to disband half the regiments. My men, unpaid for many months and suspecting their cause was about to be betrayed, raised a petition of grievances. Every regiment felt likewise, and a great meeting of their delegates was held in St Mary's church to which General Cromwell and other army leaders came to hear the men's complaints.

He stopped. It was in the crowded pews at Saffron Walden that he had first set eyes on Will, then a captain in Colonel Pride's regiment of foot. He had been among the most militant of the protesters, mingling demands for the impeachment of their opponents in Parliament with apocalyptic descriptions of God appearing to him in a dream, demanding not negotiations but the destruction of the King. Ned could hear him now, chopping wood in the outhouse. How fortunate the man who never knew doubt.

After hearing the views of the army in St Mary's, and promising his support for their demands, General Cromwell returned to London. At the end of May he invited me to a small private meeting at his home in Drury Lane. The King was living under Parliamentary supervision at Holdenby House in Northamptonshire. Fearful that they might reach an agreement with him and use it as a further pretext for disbanding the regiments, General Cromwell proposed that the army should take His Majesty into its own custody.

Who had been present? Ireton, certainly, by now married to Cromwell's daughter, Bridget. The preacher Hugh Peter. John Thurloe, Oliver's secretary. Perhaps half a dozen more officers were praying for guidance in the next-door room. He remembered Betty Cromwell coming in and out with plates of food and jugs of beer. Pipes being smoked. Mutinous, dangerous talk.

Cornet George Joyce had five hundred men near Oxford. He was like-minded. He could seize the King.

An order was drafted.

Ned had drawn Cromwell aside. 'You cannot do this, Oliver.'

'Why not?'

'Because you do not have the authority.'

'You are a milksop. What is the point of winning fight after fight if Parliament loses us the war?'

'Fairfax is commander-in-chief, not you.'

'Fairfax is a lion on the battlefield – I'd follow him into hell – but in politics he's a dormouse. He'll thank me for forcing the decision on him.'

At the conclusion of the meeting, I returned to the army, now at Newmarket. A few days later, I was summoned to see General Fairfax. He had just received a message that the King had been forcibly removed from Holdenby by Cornet Joyce and was being brought to Newmarket.

'Your cousin is behind this.'

An awkward moment for Ned, standing at attention in front of the commander-in-chief, his helmet in his hand.

'General Cromwell must answer for himself, Your Excellency.'

He ordered me to proceed with my regiment at all speed to intercept him and to ensure His Majesty was well treated and given the chance to return to Holdenby.

He had come upon Joyce's column the following afternoon, on the road about four miles west of Cambridge. Joyce was a young hothead, still in his twenties, well puffed up by the fact that he had the King of England in his custody. Ned showed him Fairfax's order. 'I'll take over from now on, Cornet.'

'You're welcome to him, Colonel.'

'You'd better introduce me.'

As they walked along the halted column, Ned said, 'What's his mood?'

'He's polite enough, if you handle him firmly.'

Ned had never seen the King before. He seemed a tiny figure, surrounded by his attendants, seated on his big horse, gazing bemusedly around him at the summer country hedges, filled with creamy hawthorn and pink dog roses.

Joyce announced, without preliminaries, 'This is Colonel Whalley, Your Majesty, sent by General Fairfax to ensure your safety.'

Ned removed his helmet and bowed. The King stared down at him for a moment, then extended his hand. Ned hesitated. He detested the man, yet Charles was still his sovereign. He was also, although he took care not to show it, nervous. He stepped forward, took the royal hand, and kissed it – very soft and white and delicate it had been, like a lady's hand. Sitting now in his snow-bound bedroom at the frontier of civilisation, he could hardly credit the memory.

Dear Frances, you may imagine my feelings. I made myself known to the King, conveyed General Fairfax's compliments, said that I was at his disposal, and stood ready to conduct him back to Holdenby, to which he replied firmly that he preferred to go on to Newmarket, as Cornet Joyce had promised him, and meet the leaders of the army. His answer was unexpected and placed me in a quandary. The day was ending, and it would be necessary for me to find shelter for the King in a suitable place while I awaited fresh orders.

He had stood, uncertain, in the lane.

'Might we offer a suggestion, Colonel Whalley?' The King seemed amused at his predicament.

'Your Majesty?'

'Childerley Hall is quite close by. Sir John Cutts died a few months back, but we are sure Lady Cutts will be honoured to entertain us.'

Honoured or not, the widow Cutts had little say in the matter, as a regiment of cavalry poured onto her estate. That evening, Ned stood at his bedroom window and surveyed the deer park, in which five hundred of his troopers were bivouacked, their horses grazing on the short grass, with sentries posted at the park gates and at every door of the house, while the King kept to his own suite of rooms.

The following day, the Sabbath, after Ned had attended a prayer meeting under the trees with his men, and the King had observed his own devotions in private with his chaplain, he had been invited into the royal presence.

The King repeated his desire to press on to Newmarket as quickly as possible; he preferred to negotiate with the army than with Parliament. Ned asked him to wait until he had received a reply to the dispatch he had sent to Fairfax, requesting further instructions.

On Monday, Fairfax, Cromwell and Ireton rode up to the house with their bodyguards. Fairfax kissed the royal hand; Cromwell and Ireton conspicuously did not. After the interview, which was polite but cold, Cromwell took Ned for a walk in the garden. 'See how cunning he is? He pretends to be amenable, while all the time he plots to drive a wedge between us and Parliament. Stay by his side as much as possible. Pay him all due respect. But in the name of God make sure he does not escape.'

My child, you will surely find it hard to picture your old republican father with the King of England, and yet I saw him almost every day for the next seven months – far more than anyone else on the Parliamentary side during the whole course of the war. What a curious mixture he was – good-humoured one minute, haughty the next. He seemed to observe the world through a thick pane of glass, set apart from other mortals. I can remember only one disagreeable occasion. That was on the day when he was visited by an officer who wished to return the ensigns of the Order of the Garter belonging to the late Prince of Orange. As they walked back and forth, it seemed to me that they were engaged in some manner of secret conference, but when I tried to inter-pose myself, the King pushed me away with both his hands and raised his cane as if to strike me on the head.

My orders were to keep him always within easy reach of the army, for ease of negotiations and in case some attempt was made at rescue. Finally, when the army reached the outskirts of London, the King returned to his former home at Hampton Court. Here he was allowed to receive his friends and younger children, to have his old servants around him, and to ride about the royal park as he pleased. He met often with Cromwell to discuss a lasting settlement that would preserve the peace – that would allow him to retain his throne, guarantee the rights of Parliament, and permit liberty of religious belief. Some characteristics of the King appealed to Oliver – his obvious love for his children, his deep religious feeling, even his refusal to bend his principles, whatever the personal cost. Indeed

He stopped.

Indeed . . .

Indeed . . . what?

Indeed, His Majesty had privately hinted he might create Oliver an earl and give him command of the nation's army once a constitutional settlement had been reached. Imagine it – Cromwell the Earl of Ely, and Betty a countess!

Indeed, relations became so dangerously friendly that one evening in September, after the King had been playing with his children and Ned was escorting him back to his private apartments, he deigned to engage him in a personal conversation.

'Do you have a wife, Colonel Whalley?'

'I do, Your Majesty.'

'And children?'

'Four, sir.'

'You should bring them here. We have fifteen hundred rooms and no longer a court worth speaking of, so it's certain we have space. Speak with Sir Jack.'

Sir Jack was Sir John Ashburnham – handsome, rich, dim, former Groom of the Bedchamber, the King's closest courtier.

Naturally, Ned did no such thing. But a day or two later, Ashburnham sought him out and told him that His Majesty had commanded him to invite Mrs Whalley and her children to stay at Hampton, 'if that would be agreeable to you?' He was also commanded to say that the King would like to invite the colonel and his wife, 'and General and Mrs Cromwell, and General and Mrs Ireton' to dine with him.

And so, the unbelievable had happened – unbelievable at the time, even more so at nearly twenty years' distance – that after months apart, Ned and Katherine had been reunited on the freshly laundered, lavender-scented sheets of some courtier's apartment in a deserted wing of the palace, and he and the creator of the Ironsides had later sat down with the King to be formally feasted. A grand table, with chairs along one side, faced out to the large hall, where courtiers stood watching the spectacle. Betty Cromwell had been seated on His Majesty's right, Katherine on his left. Bridget Ireton – Oliver's eldest daughter – had been placed further along the table, next to Ned. Oliver was next to Katherine. On Ned's other side, however, was an empty seat: Henry Ireton had refused to come.

Your mother looked most beautiful, the King was charming to her, the wine and food were of the highest quality, the evening convivial . . .

When word of it reached the army, only seven miles from Hampton, along the Thames at Putney, there had been outrage, whipped up not least by the young and radical – and now Lieutenant Colonel – William Goffe.

That night, after supper, they sat in front of the fire in Ned's room and smoked their pipes as snow fell in the darkness outside. Such silence.

Ned said, 'I was thinking today about the army's debates at Putney.'

'Were you ever present? I thought you were always at Hampton with your friend the King.' A slight bitterness in Will's sarcasm, even after all this time.

'I was there at the beginning. I still remember your speech on the first day.'

'Did you approve?'

'It was . . . fiery.'

'I spoke as the Lord directed me.'

The army leadership had assembled in the Putney church, St Mary's, to determine what their policy should be – Cromwell presiding. Will had marched up to the pulpit like a man going into battle. He declared that their victories had shown that God was 'throwing down the glory of all flesh', that he had been granted a vision in a dream that they should not be negotiating with the King at all, that 'a voice from heaven has come to us, that we have sinned against the Lord in tampering with his enemies'. His words had been met with a roar of approval. It was for this that Cromwell had demanded – and received – an apology.

At the end of the first session, Ned had walked with Oliver away from the church, and made some comment about the ugly mood.

'Ugly? By God, it is! And angry – and perhaps with some justice. It was a foolish vanity to have allowed ourselves to be publicly feasted. Henry was wise to have had nothing to do with it. Did you hear I have been threatened with impeachment? I have even been warned of a Leveller plot against my life.' Ned had never known him so troubled. 'The army is God's instrument. In its temper we catch the echo of His voice. If we cannot bring the army to our sense, we must go to theirs. You had best get back to Hampton tonight, and I shall see what may be done with our friends here tomorrow.'

Ned leaned forwards and poked the fire. 'I meant no offence, Will. Oliver always respected you for your godliness.'

'But we were right,' said Will fiercely. 'We could never have reached agreement with Charles Stuart. We should never have even tried.' He gave Ned a suspicious look. 'I wonder sometimes what you are putting in that book of yours.'

He finished his pipe and went back to his room.

For two weeks the army debated in Putney, seeking guidance from God, while I remained at Hampton. I received reports most days of how strongly the mood ran against the King. At the conclusion of their deliberations, on November 11th, General Cromwell sent me a letter which he directed me to show him. I have reason to remember its exact words – 'Dear Cos. Whalley, there are rumours abroad of some intended attempt on His Majesty's person. Therefore, I pray have a care of your guards, for if any such thing should be done, it would be accounted a most horrid act.'

I made haste to show the letter to the King that afternoon. I told him, on my word of honour, that I was sent to safeguard not to murder him, that he could be sure no such thing would be done on my watch, and that I would die at his feet in his defence. For this he thanked me. 'You have always treated our person most respectfully, Colonel Whalley.'

I increased the guard as ordered, but in truth it would have required four or five hundred soldiers to secure every entrance of such a vast palace, and I had barely a quarter of that number.

It was the King's habit to spend Thursdays – which day this was – writing letters to be sent to foreign parts, emerging from his bedchamber between five and six in the evening, afterwards going to prayers, and following that to supper, before retiring for the night. It was a blustery, rainy evening, a high storm raging. At five, I came into the room next to his bedchamber and asked his servants for the King. They told me he was still writing. At half past five, and then at six, I enquired again. At seven, with my fears increasing, I told one of his bedchamber men, Mr Mawle, that I wondered if the King might be ill and asked him to go into his room. He replied that the King had given him a strict command not to disturb him, that he dared not disobey, and besides the door was bolted. I looked in at the keyhole to see if I could perceive His Majesty but could not.

When it drew towards eight, I went to Mr Smitheby, Keeper of the Privy Lodgings, desiring him to go along with me the back way, through the garden – where I had sentinels – and up the stairs, from chamber to chamber, till we came to the room next to His Majesty's bedchamber, where we saw his cloak lying in the middle of the floor, which much amazed me.

Now I ordered Mr Mawle to go in. He said he would do so, but that I must stay by the door. I said I would and did. Mr Mawle immediately came out and reported the King was not there. We all went in, and someone said, 'It may be that the King is in his closet.' Mr Mawle went to check, and presently replied, 'He is gone but he has left a letter for you.'

Ned could taste the dryness in his mouth as he relived that moment – how he had read the King's message thanking him for his service ('I assure you it was not the letter you showed me today that made me take this resolution but rather must confess I am loth to be made a close prisoner under pretence of securing my life'), how he had ordered parties of horse and foot to search the park in the wet and windy darkness of the November storm, and had sent immediate dispatches to Fairfax and Cromwell alerting them to the King's escape.

Oliver had arrived from Putney at midnight. To Ned's surprise, the general was calm, cheerful even. Once he had heard a full account, he put a consoling arm around his shoulders. 'Don't take it too hard, cousin. It was an impossible task we set you – to hold him a prisoner yet let him live freely in this great place. Besides, it may work to our advantage. He has betrayed our trust, showed the kind of man he is, and relieved us of the burden of these negotiations. In the matter of Charles Stuart, we can all be Levellers now.'

'And what if he succeeds in fleeing abroad?'

'So much the better – we shall be rid of him. But I doubt he'll get that far.'

Of course, he had been right. Like so much else in his reign, the King's escape was rash in conception and slipshod in execution. Fleeing the grounds of Hampton Court, he met by prearrangement Ashburnham and two other loyal supporters, Sir John Berkeley and William Legge. The four at once rode south through the royal forest towards the coast, the King swearing he knew the way. But on that foul night they became lost, and by daybreak had proceeded only as far as Sutton. His Majesty then proposed they make for Southampton, but Ashburnham admitted no ship had been arranged to carry him to France. Accordingly, they diverted to Lymington, and sent word to the governor of the Isle of Wight, Robert Hammond, whom the King believed to be a loyal supporter. Hammond agreed to receive him, but upon his arrival confined him in Carisbrooke Castle and sent word of his prisoner to London.

Later, we discovered the full extent of Charles Stuart's treachery. He had made a secret agreement with the Scotch to invade England and restore his position. He also wrote to the Queen in France that he did not consider himself obliged to keep any promises extracted from him under compulsion, and that 'he should know in due time how to deal with the rogues who, instead of a silken garter, should be fitted with a hempen cord'.

That was the kind of man he was. Do you wonder, daughter, why we had to kill him? There would never have been peace as long as he lived.

Ned looked up. The day had dwindled into darkness. Shadows clustered in the corners of the room.

He did not want to write any more. It was troubling to disturb the sediment of the past, to stir up old fears and suspicions. That letter of Cromwell's, for example, which he had told Ned to show the King – it occurred to him now that it might have arisen less from a desire to warn the King of his peril and more from a calculation that it would provoke him into trying to escape. In which case, did it mean that Cromwell had been willing to risk exposing his cousin to humiliation – perhaps to a court martial, possibly even a firing squad – purely in order to extricate himself from his negotiations with the King and restore his relations with the army?

He blew on the ink to dry it, put the thick pile of pages back in his bag, and lay down on the bed. He closed his eyes. One could never be sure with Oliver. Ambition and godliness, self-interest and the higher cause, the base metal entwined with the gold.

CHAPTER TWENTY-NINE

A FEW DAYS LATER, an event occurred that was to change his relations with Will.

It was the middle of the afternoon, the bitterest day of the winter so far, a hard, light snow – tiny flakes whipping like musket pellets in a blizzard across the dead white fields. Will had been driven indoors by the cold and was in his room. Ned was at his own window. It looked south, as did Will's, across the yard and the street to the distant houses. He was watching the snow, his mind as blank as the view, when a figure emerged, struggling along the side of the road, obviously male, his head bent against the wind, a burden of some sort across his shoulders. He stopped at the Russells' gate and looked up at the house. Ned drew back out of sight. When he looked again, the man was through the gate and approaching the door.

He grabbed his pistol from beneath his pillow and strode along the passage. Will was lying on his bed, staring at the ceiling. He sat up as Ned entered. Ned put his finger to his lips, warning him not to speak. 'There's a man come,' he whispered, 'a stranger.' He beckoned to Will to follow.

They went into the passage and lifted the planks. Ned descended the ladder to the earth floor. Will climbed down a few rungs, reached up and replaced the boards, then came down the rest of the way to join him. It was the first time they had been forced to hide. They had no candle. Pressed close together in the warm darkness behind the chimney, they stood and listened to the murmur of voices, indistinct through the heavy brickwork. Presently they heard the clump of footsteps going up the stairs. The heavy feet passed above their heads and stopped. The planks were lifted. John Russell's head appeared.

'You have a visitor.'

Ned said, 'Who is he?'

'He gives his name as James Davids and claims to know you both. He'll say no more till he sees you.'

'Is he genuine?'

'I believe so. He says he's come from Holland.'

'*Holland?*'

Will said, 'How does he know we're here?'

'He was told by our friends in Boston, which makes me think he speaks the truth. They must trust him, although the letter he brought from them is naturally circumspect. They sent him with a guide.'

'What do you say, Ned?'

Ned thought it over. 'If he knows we're here, any harm is already done. But I know of no one named James Davids.'

'Nor I. It sounds a made-up sort of name.'

They climbed up out of the chamber, brushed the dust from their clothes, and followed Russell downstairs – Will first, eager with curiosity, Ned behind with his pistol, more wary.

The stranger stood warming himself at the fire, an old leather sack at his feet. He had the look of a vagrant – a narrow, half-starved face, blotchy with cold, and long, straggling hair and beard, just starting to turn grey. He took off his hat. 'Colonel Whalley! Colonel Goffe! How glad I am to find you both alive!'

As he moved towards them, hand outstretched, Will said in a tone of astonishment, 'I believe I recollect your face,' and after a moment or two, beneath the havoc wrought by the past six years, Ned dimly recognised him too – Roundhead colonel, wealthy gentleman, Member of Parliament, judge at the King's trial, and fellow signatory of His Majesty's death warrant – John Dixwell.

That evening, after Dixwell had cleaned himself up and put on some old clothes belonging to Reverend Russell, the four men sat down to supper in the parlour and he told them something of his adventures. When the monarchy had been restored in the summer of 1660, he had at first promised to turn himself in under the terms of the Act of Oblivion. But he had delayed the date of his surrender, pleading ill health, and used the time to sell some property. Then, carrying enough money to live comfortably, he managed to slip out of England to Rotterdam. From there he went to Hanau in Germany, where he stayed for a couple of years within walking distance of Valentine Walton, John Barkstead and John Okey. He had almost been caught in the same trap as Barkstead and Okey, but something about the invitation to Delft had made him suspicious.

'I told them they were fools to go, but Okey trusted that serpent Downing. When I heard what had happened, it was no surprise to me. I knew then I had to get out of Hanau.'

He moved on to Switzerland, to Lausanne, to see Edmund Ludlow, who had assured him it was safe. Then Ludlow had nearly been kidnapped by some Irish adventurers, and John Lisle, living in the next town, was shot dead in the street, and so he had abandoned Switzerland and headed back to Holland. But then came the capture of New Amsterdam, and everywhere suddenly there was talk of a war between England and the Dutch. Deciding that, as an Englishman, in such an event he would be too conspicuous, he had taken a ship to Boston, arriving in December, and now here he was.

Ned said, 'It seems that wherever you go, disaster follows.'

Will laughed, shaking his head. 'Come now, Ned, that's unfair. John merely showed prudence.'

John . . .

From the start, Ned did not care for Dixwell. There was something about him – a smugness in the way he talked, a certain condescension, although Will did not seem to notice it, hanging on his every word. Ned guessed he was about ten years younger than himself, ten years older than Will. He had been MP for Dover at the outbreak of the Civil War, and had been given the rank of colonel, although he had never fought in a proper battle, at least not that Ned could recall. What he did remember was that Dixwell had voted in the Commons to put the King on trial, and had sat as judge, but then like many others had tried to avoid signing the death warrant. He was one of those MPs Cromwell had hauled out of the chamber on the day before the execution, marching him to the room where the warrant lay on the table and thrusting the pen into his hand.

Still, Ned tried to adopt a more friendly tone. 'So how long will you stay with us, Colonel Dixwell?'

'That depends upon the goodwill of Mr Russell.'

'You are welcome as long as you wish to remain,' said Russell.

Dixwell said, 'I am confident of a great change in our fortunes in 'sixty-six, when the Lord is come in glory and our cause will be restored.'

Ned said, 'You will stay as long as that?'

'If I am permitted.' Dixwell glanced at Russell, who nodded. 'It will be a glorious day to share together.'

'Amen,' said Will. 'God came to me in a dream last night and showed me a vision of a world on fire, with a great light coming down from Heaven, and a man walking through the flames unscathed, clad from head to toe in white. Our Lord and Saviour, come to save us.'

There was a silence as they considered this.

'Can it really be so certain?' Ned blurted out. 'I am no authority on the Scriptures, but the prophecy seems to me conjectural. If 666 truly marks the end of days, should not the Second Coming have occurred in Saxon times? It seems a long time for you to wait for something that mayn't happen.'

'Forgive my father-in-law,' said Will. 'Sometimes I think he has the makings of a Presbyterian.'

Offended – a Presbyterian, him? – Ned excused himself abruptly and went upstairs to bed. He knew his behaviour was sulky, childish even; that he was turning into one of those querulously stubborn old men he had despised in his youth. He would apologise. He lay awake for an hour or two, presuming that Will, when he came up, would shift along the passage to share his room, and surrender his own to Dixwell. Instead, when at last he heard them mount the stairs, the two men retired together. He fell asleep to the sound of their murmured conversation.

The next morning, he said, with a forced smile, 'You are very thick with Colonel Dixwell.'

'We thought it best that John should share with me, for as long as he decides to stay.'

'As you wish.'

'You are offended?' Will put a concerned hand on Ned's arm.

'I thought the arrangement would suit you. You keep to your room more than I do mine. It means you may write your book in peace.'

'I have it in mind to abandon my book.'

'Why?'

'It is not pleasant always to dwell so much in the past.'

'But how else will you pass the time? At least I am still able to work.'

It was not meant unkindly. Still, Ned flinched. There it was – the unspoken spoken at last. He was in his sixty-seventh year, his old wounds aching, his muscles shrunken on his thin arms: a burden, too old to do much now except sit in his room with his memories.

'Well, I suppose that's true enough.'

He stood at the window and watched the two younger men walk across the yard to the barn.

My dear and only daughter, I must speak now of the execution of the King, the act which brought us to our present unhappy state.

Following His Majesty's recapture and close imprisonment on the Isle of Wight, the Civil War – which we had thought won – flared up anew, and for a time, our position looked quite hopeless. A huge Scottish army was mustering in the north, to come to His Majesty's rescue. Our counsels were divided, between those in Parliament who still believed a settlement with the King was possible, and the bulk of the army which believed Charles Stuart was Satan. Royalist uprisings spread across the country. In May 1648, General Cromwell and I parted, he to the west, to suppress the King's forces there, and I to the east, to help perform a similar task in Kent and Essex.

The fighting of that summer and autumn was much crueller and more desperate than anything that had gone before. His mind recoiled at the memory. Such things as he had never expected to see in England. Crops and barns and windmills set on fire to starve the enemy countryside. Colonel Shambrooke shot through the body with a poisonous bullet that had been boiled in vitriol. At Chelmsford, the bodies of twenty Royalists laid out in a row, all gentlemen, with their fine clothes and white skin, all shot in the back of the head. At Colchester, his troopers had thrown a grenade into the enemy's gunpowder store and blown more than a hundred men to pieces. The Royalist commanders, Sir Charles Lucas and . . . what was the other one called? Sir George Lisle, that was it . . . both shot in the castle yard after a drumhead trial despite having surrendered. So many good men lost.

To understand what followed, Frances, you had to know what it was like.

After General Cromwell had beaten the Welsh at Pembroke, and then the Scotch at Preston, the forces of the New Model Army converged on London determined to settle the matter of the King once and for all. I arrived along with the main force on Saturday 2nd December. We occupied the palaces of Whitehall and St James, sleeping in the royal apartments, the state rooms, the servants' quarters – wherever a man might lie. On the following Tuesday, despite the presence of many thousands of soldiers, the Commons passed a motion to continue negotiations with the King. Seeing there was no possibility of such an assembly ever agreeing to bring His Majesty to trial, the Army Council decided to exclude all those Members of Parliament who had voted in favour of a settlement.

It was Will's regiment, commanded by Colonel Pride, the most radical in the army, that had been given the honour of surrounding the Commons chamber. Will had been in the thick of it, dragging off forty MPs who dared to protest to a holding prison in a nearby tavern, and turning back more than twice that number at musket point when they came to take their seats. Ned had helped in the task, carrying away that prating windbag William Prynne, with his earless skull and twisted face.

You may wonder – many did; I did myself – at the action of an army that had gone to war in the name of Parliament now treating it more roughly than the King had ever dared. But we knew that God was with us. How else could we have won so many victories? We were sure it was his work we were doing.

Even so, he had argued privately with Cromwell about their methods. Surely there must be simpler ways to dispose of the King than the full panoply of a trial. His Majesty had tried often enough to escape. Give him the opportunity to try again, then shoot him as he fled: would that not be just? But Cromwell retorted that the Lord's work was not to be done in the dark. The people should see Charles Stuart charged with his crimes and justly punished according to the law. He was confident the King would be utterly humiliated. Ned was not so sure.

Six weeks later, the King was brought to London under heavy guard and imprisoned in a house on the Thames, within the precincts of Westminster, which was an armed camp. Ned was among the panel of one hundred and thirty-five commissioners – officers, MPs, lawyers – appointed to be judges. The trial was fixed to start at Westminster Hall, the largest space in England, on the afternoon of Saturday 20 January.

From the outset, looking out across the vast building, ringed with soldiers, crowded with hundreds of spectators, he was uneasy. Only half the judges' seats were occupied; the rest were too frightened to attend. When the roll call was taken, General Fairfax was found to be among those missing. People whispered: where was he? A woman called out from the public gallery, 'He has more wit than to be here!' Few recognised her, but Ned did: Lady Fairfax.

After that, it played out exactly as he had feared. He knew Charles Stuart better than any of them. The moment he came up the steps into the hall, that slight figure, flanked by soldiers commanded by Colonel Hacker, Ned could see he was entirely unbowed. The King was not provided with a lawyer. He had not been told the charges against him. He took his seat and glanced around him with his usual mixture of detached curiosity and contempt. He scanned the judges' benches – apart from Cromwell and Ireton, men almost entirely unknown to him – and for a moment his eyes rested briefly on Ned before dismissing him with a flicker of disdain and moving on. When John Cooke, the prosecuting attorney, began to read the indictment, accusing the King of breaking his coronation oath and making war on his own people, Charles reached over and tapped him on the shoulder with his cane to interrupt him, and when Cooke took no notice, he struck him hard enough for the silver head of the cane to fall off and roll across the flagstones. He waited for someone to retrieve it, and when no one did, he picked it up himself.

Bradshaw, the president of the court, asked him how he wished to plead.

'First, I would know by what power I am called hither – what *lawful* authority.' His voice was clear and firm. 'There are many unlawful authorities in the world, thieves and robbers by the highway. Remember, I am your King, your *lawful King* . . .'

He refused to enter a plea until he was told the legal precedent for the court, and as there was none, he put them all on the defensive – so much so that when he was taken away at the end of the afternoon, there were even shouts of 'God save the King!'

He behaved in the same fashion when they assembled on Monday afternoon, and again on Tuesday. It was no longer the King who was on trial, but the army and its legitimacy. A change of tactics was required. On Wednesday morning, the judges voted in private to exclude the accused from the court and to hear the prosecution witnesses in his absence. On Saturday morning, they found him guilty behind closed doors. In the afternoon, he was brought back to Westminster Hall to receive the verdict. Bradshaw asked him if he had anything to say before sentence was pronounced. Still refusing to recognise the army's court, he asked to address a joint meeting of the Lords and Commons. Bradshaw refused, at which point an extraordinary scene occurred. An MP, a nobody named John Downes, who was sitting two places along from Ned, called out, 'Have we hearts of stone? Are we men?'

Shaking off the restraining hands on either side, he struggled to his feet. Cromwell, on the bench immediately in front of him, turned round, frowning. 'What's wrong with you, man? Are you mad? Sit still and be quiet!'

'No, sir. I cannot be quiet. Even if I die for it, I must object.'

Bradshaw nervously adjourned the court and the judges retreated to their chamber, where Cromwell railed against Downes for his cowardice. But two or three other judges spoke up in his support. 'Could we not at least hear what His Majesty has to say? He must have in mind some offer which might settle the peace of the nation?'

'God's teeth, can you not see? It is merely another trick of his! We have not come so far to turn back now! You are milksops . . .'

For half an hour, Cromwell thundered at them, until their resistance weakened and cracked, like some fortress under siege, whereupon they all trooped back into Westminster Hall – apart from Downes, whom they left behind in tears – for sentence to be pronounced.

'. . . that the said Charles Stuart, as a Tyrant, Traitor, Murderer and a public enemy, shall be put to death, by the severing of his head from his body.'

The King said calmly, 'Will you hear me a word, sir?'

'You are not to be heard after the sentence,' said Bradshaw. 'Take him away.'

The King looked astonished. 'I may speak after the sentence . . .' And for the first time, as the guards moved in to lead him away, his composure broke. 'By your favour, hold! The sentence, sir – I say, sir, I do—'

The remainder of his words were lost in a welter of shouts from the soldiers – 'Execution! Justice! Execution!' – as he was marched down the steps out of sight to await his fate.

Ned sat back in his chair, exhausted. He had a sharp, stabbing pain behind his eyes and a tingling in his arms. He had not thought about the events of the trial for many years – never, in fact, in any detail. He waited for the symptoms to pass, as they always did. What else could he remember? That the following day, Sunday, was a day of prayer and meditation. That on Monday, the death warrant was laid out on a table in the Painted Chamber, and he had walked over with Cromwell from Whitehall Palace to sign it (Oliver had requisitioned one of the finest bedrooms in the royal apartments). A dozen or two of the judges were already waiting, warming themselves at the vast fire. It was a perishingly cold day. There was a Turkish carpet spread across the table. Bradshaw signed first, then Lord Grey, the only nobleman among them, then Cromwell, who was in high spirits – he flicked ink onto the face of Henry Marten, who flicked him back. Then Oliver handed Ned the pen and he signed it next, in fourth place, and added his seal with the family crest of three spouting whales. He did so without a qualm. The punishment was just. It was God's will. Only the trial had been a mistake. He gave the pen to John Okey. He remembered also that Will was there, fresh from visiting the King, standing at the fire describing how he had tried, as an act of compassion, to convince Charles Stuart to pray with a couple of Puritan ministers he had taken along with him: he had been dismissed without a word.

By the middle of the morning, they had about three dozen signatures. 'Not enough,' said Cromwell. Ned went with him down to the door of the Commons chamber to haul out the MPs who were trying to evade their duty. 'Those that are gone in shall set their hands. I will have their hands now.' Cromwell went in to fetch them. Dixwell was one. The wretched John Downes was another: Cromwell walked him to the Painted Chamber with his arm around his shoulders, telling him this was his chance to redeem himself in the eyes of God and his comrades.

Ned set off soon afterwards to walk up King Street and attend to the preparations for the execution the next day – the erection of the scaffold, the demolition of part of the Banqueting House masonry so that the King could step onto the platform, the fetching of 'the bright execution-axe' from the Tower of London – so many details: he couldn't remember them all now. It took him until late into the night. Early the following morning, he went back to Cromwell's room. Harrison and Ireton were lying asleep on the bed. Cromwell was already up, with the death warrant and the order for the execution lying on a table and the three colonels who were meant to supervise the beheading – Hacker, Axtell and Huncks – gathered around him. At the last minute, Huncks was refusing to go through with it, and Cromwell was calling him 'an awkward, peevish fellow'. Doubts, doubts, even at that late stage . . . But Ned was resolute. It was like a cavalry charge: head down, link legs with the men on either side, full tilt at the enemy.

I returned to the Banqueting House to make sure there was no chance of some attempt at the last moment to rescue the King. I was present when he went out to meet his death. He brushed by me but did not seem to see me. I was told he wore an extra shirt on that cold day, so as not to be seen to shiver. He died very bravely I must say that.

Could a bad life be redeemed by a good death? Standing at the open window, he had caught the King's last words: 'I go from a corruptible to an incorruptible crown, where no disturbance can be, no disturbance in the world.' He watched the axe descend, heard the groan of the crowd, saw the severed head held aloft. Afterwards, they had stitched it back on to the torso so that the corpse could be displayed in an open coffin in St James's Palace to foreign ambassadors and other dignitaries, to prove that Charles Stuart was dead.

He looked back over what he had written. *He died very bravely* . . . That was not quite right. It was more than bravely: it was serenely, almost cheerfully. He must have known that by his demeanour at the trial and on the scaffold, he had won a victory over his enemies at last. It was only then that it occurred to Ned that the King had died exactly as the regicides had many years later – in the absolute certainty that he was right.

CHAPTER THIRTY

NAYLER'S OFFICE AT the end of the Privy Council corridor was these days very quiet. Mr Nokes had asked to be excused from his duties as his secretary and had gone to work for Sir William Morice. The members of the intelligence committee had drifted off to more urgent business. As autumn turned into winter, and still no word came from America, Nayler sat most days alone, forgotten as it seemed to him, the only sound the hissing of his coal fire. One of the few diversions was the appearance of a comet over London in the week before Christmas, which he went up onto the roof to observe. And then, on the penultimate day of January 1665, on the anniversary of the King's execution, he was summoned to see the Lord Chancellor.

Sir Edward Hyde – Nayler could not get used to his new title – was still in his old room in Worcester House, still surrounded by the usual wall of papers and immobilised by gout, his swollen legs propped up on cushions, his great barrel of a body even fatter than before, despite his frequent diets and purges. His hands over the years had twisted into red and scaly claws. He gestured with one of them to the seat beside him, and when Nayler was settled, grasped the document that lay before him and held it up between his thumb and palm. He had to tilt his head slightly to one side parrot-fashion to read it.

'We have received a dispatch at last from Colonel Nicolls in Boston, reporting the outcome of his mission to New England. It seems the Dutch have been subdued without the necessity to fire a shot – God be praised. New Amsterdam is now New York, and His Royal Highness may expect an income of some thirty thousand pounds per annum.'

'Congratulations, my lord,' said Nayler. 'That is a great triumph.' He didn't care a fig about New York. He wanted only to know about Whalley and Goffe.

'Is it such a triumph? We shall soon have a war with the Dutch that will cost us two million a year.'

Nayler squirmed in his chair. He had put nothing in writing, had been careful to keep clear of the actual planning of the expedition, was almost certain that Hyde was unaware that the initial suggestion had come from him – but with the old man, one never knew.

'You will doubtless wish to hear news of the regicides. As ordered, Colonel Nicolls commissioned a thorough search for colonels Whalley and Goffe.' Hyde glanced up from the document. He paused, prolonging Nayler's agony. 'Nothing.'

'Nothing, my lord?' Nayler slumped in his chair. Now that the blow had fallen, he realised he had been expecting it. Somehow he would have known in his bowels if Whalley and Goffe had been killed. 'Nothing – absolutely?'

'They searched in all the places you suggested. Nicolls interviewed this man Gookin and came away in little doubt that he is part of a network of Puritans who are shielding the fugitives. He even believes he may have invested money on their behalf. But he felt there was insufficient evidence to arrest him.'

'So they have defeated us?'

'If you count it a victory to live three thousand miles from home, fearful of every stranger, unable to show your face out of doors. I would not call it such.' Hyde laid down the dispatch. 'Well, there it is. I have decided the time has come to dissolve the regicide committee. We rarely meet in any case. I am sure your talents can be better employed elsewhere.'

Nayler braced himself. He had half expected this as well. He had served his purpose. He would be dismissed.

'I had you in mind to be my private secretary.'

He stared at Hyde, too surprised to respond.

'Mark you, you would have to give up this obsession with the colonels in America. I have made enquiries. I know the reason for it. To lose a wife in such a way is most dreadful. But that business is finished. You must accept it.' Hyde adjusted the position of his leg and winced. 'You will not turn me down, I hope?'

'No, my lord. I should be honoured.'

'Even so, you may wish for more time to consider it. My influence nowadays stands lower than it did. I have many enemies, in particular Mrs Palmer, or Lady Castlemaine as we must learn to call her. They have the King's ear, while I am old, and ill, and always tired. This war we shall soon have with the Dutch will not be easy, and next year is the one to which the millennialists attach such significance. You do not hold with such superstition, I assume?'

'It is just a year, like any other.'

'But many thousands believe otherwise and will be alert for portents, such as that comet, which was held to be a prodigy. A febrile mood can bring its own Armageddon. Be warned – you may be yoking your fortunes to a falling star.'

'I still accept, my lord, most humbly and willingly.'

'Then I suggest you move your apartments here to Worcester House. I often work late at night, and it would be convenient to have you close. Shall we say tomorrow?' Hyde reached out his twisted hand for another document and began to read, then looked up, apparently surprised to find Nayler still present. 'There is something else?'

'No, my lord.'

To be private secretary to the Lord Chancellor of England – now that was something, that was a prize, even though it was true what Hyde had said: his power was waning. He had made a great enemy of the King's mistress, now Lady Castlemaine, by objecting to her appointment as Lady of the Bedchamber to the Queen, which he held to be grossly insulting to the King's wife. He was also building a vast house close to St James's Palace, said to be grander than the royal residence, which was taken as a sign of his ambition: as Charles's numerous children were all illegitimate, Hyde's granddaughter, Anne, remained second in line to the throne. Still, as Nayler walked along the Strand towards the Privy Council offices, his imagination swam at the prospects opening before him.

Beneath the window of the Banqueting House from which the King had stepped to his death sixteen years before, little bunches of such meagre flowers as England could produce in January – snowdrops, witch hazel, winter heather – had been laid in tribute. A group of pilgrims prayed across the street.

Nayler went through the courtyard of Whitehall Palace, up the stairs to his room, and sat at his table. He lifted the pouch from around his neck, took out the fragment of handkerchief stained with the martyred King's blood, and kissed it. He had the comfort of knowing he had fulfilled his vow as best he could. He studied the chart of the regicides, still propped up on its easel, as an artist might contemplate a finished painting. It was a mass of black lines. Nearly all the names were scored through. After a while, he put away his relic, unpinned the chart and rolled it up. Then he emptied his safe and started sorting through four and a half years' worth of papers, making a pile of those he wished to have sent to Worcester House. Deciphered letters, agents' reports, notes of interrogations, signed confessions, pleas for mercy, anonymous denunciations, receipts, accounts – most of these he burned on his fire.

He found a file marked *Wm. Goffe* and took out the note the colonel had sent to his wife: *God will protect us, for He makes all things right on Earth. Pray for me, as I pray always for you; the greatest gift He has bestowed upon me. I will come back to you again as soon as I am able.* Insufferable, canting Puritan! He carried the message over to the fireplace, knelt before the grate and held it towards the flames. He watched the furthest edge of the paper brown and curl. For a few more moments he stayed like that, the taste of failure suddenly bitter in his mouth, until his fingers began to burn, at which point he thought better of it, snatched it back and put it with the other documents to go to Worcester House.

Beyond the mullioned window, although he did not yet know it, England's Armageddon was beginning.

A couple of miles to the north-east, in Holborn, Frances Goffe was hurrying home. She had heard no word directly from Will for more than two years. He was safe, but in a different place, that was all she knew.

She had just passed the church of St Giles in the Fields when she noticed that the crowd ahead of her had diverted its course, like a stream flowing around a boulder. People were choosing to walk in the deepest filth in the middle of the street rather than go

close to the wall on the opposite side. As she drew level, jostled
by the bodies around her, she saw what it was they were avoiding: a house, standing isolated, its door and windows boarded
up, a red crucifix a foot high painted on the planks. There was a
message, also daubed in red, the letters dripping like blood from
a cut: *Lord have mercy upon us.* Someone told her the family were
locked inside.

The Goffes and the Hookes still lived in the same cramped,
narrow house in West Harding Street, only ten minutes' walk
away. As soon as Frances got in, she told Uncle William about the
boarded-up building and the red cross and the imprisoned family.
She knew what it meant, although she had never seen it before.
There had not been plague in London in her lifetime. Hooke
said, 'The Book of Revelation tells us that the apocalypse will be
heralded by four horsemen – Death, War, Famine and the Antichrist. This is Death.'

She ran upstairs to the children.

From then on, she started to buy the weekly bills of mortality,
on sale for a penny, that the parish clerks compiled, listing all the
local deaths and their symptoms. 'Black swellings', or some such
phrasing, was the thing to look for. Another woman died of it
in February. In April, there were two more. By the end of May,
there were a hundred a week. It was a hideous sickness, a folk
memory of horror – agonising sweats and headaches, dark lumps
in the armpits and groin, vomiting, diarrhoea – the body turned
to liquid; fatal in three quarters of cases. She kept the children
close indoors, made them rinse their mouths with warm water
and vinegar and chew the tobacco leaves that she stole from the
factory, hidden under her skirt – anything that it was rumoured
would ward off the evil. For the first time, she was glad that Will
and her father were on the other side of the world.

At the beginning of June, she was working in the warehouse on the Thames when an unearthly continuous boom came rolling down the river. She went out onto the muddy bank, where a crowd had gathered to listen. It seemed to emanate from the east and might have been mistaken for thunder, except that it was almost ceaseless, with only occasional lulls and then a fresh eruption. It could be heard everywhere in London. It pursued her home, past the boarded-up houses, along streets now so deserted by the fleeing population that grass was starting to grow across the mud and filth. Uncle William, who had been to the precincts of St Paul's to pick up news from the booksellers in Paternoster Row, announced that it was the sound of a great battle being fought out at sea between the English and Dutch fleets.

'The second horseman – War. It is the beginning of the end of days. We must have courage to live through it, so that we may see our Saviour come clothed in glory, to restore the saints to earth.'

The battle lasted four days. On the English side, ten ships lost and a thousand men killed; on the Dutch, four ships sunk and fifteen hundred dead. Both countries claimed victory, but everyone knew the English had come off worse.

By July, deaths from the plague were running at nearly two thousand a week and people said the country was cursed. By September, the weekly tally of dead was seven thousand, and Frances gave up reading the bills of mortality. She lay awake at night and listened to the handcarts trundling down the street, the mournful cries of 'Bring out your dead' as the corpses were piled up and taken away to the mass graves. During the day, the funeral bells tolled ceaselessly, until there was no one left to ring them and gradually they stopped. Uncle William, who seemed to have no fear of infection, went out at all hours, despite the pleas of his wife. He visited the pit at Aldgate. 'Forty feet long,' he reported, 'half as broad, and twenty deep – as deep as they could go before it filled with water.' The scale of the calamity seemed to give him satisfaction. The shops were empty. People were starving in the streets, lying dead in the gutters. The third horseman – Famine.

Frances could not understand it. 'If this is the start of our Lord's return to earth, why does he punish the righteous as well as the ungodly?'

'Look upon it as the agonies of childbirth, my dear – a necessity to be endured so that something new may be born.'

'There speaks a man,' said Aunt Jane in a rare flash of irritation, and he at least had the grace to fall silent.

The Lord Chancellor had gone to the country to be with the King and the rest of the court, but Nayler stayed at his post. He took a few precautions on the advice of one of Hyde's doctors – swallowed a daily mixture of nutmeg and honey, drank fortified wine from Spain – but otherwise moved about his business as usual, wearing the new green velvet coat that he had commissioned to celebrate his appointment as private secretary. He arranged for the first Wednesday of every month to be a solemn fast day to pray for deliverance from the plague. He met with the Lord Mayor to set a curfew of nine o'clock at night. He attended a council of war on board the warship *Prince* to discuss the shortage of sailors caused by the plague, and reported to Hyde, who was by then with the King and Parliament in Oxford, on the troubling state of the war with the Dutch. Worrying reports reached him that Hyde had given the King another stern lecture on the immorality of the court and had blocked some of Lady Castlemaine's attempts to pay off her debts from the privy purse. He ordered the temporary shutting-down of all the building work in Clarendon House – it seemed hardly appropriate when so many were dying and starving. He worked from dawn until late at night, and for the first time in more than five years, whole weeks went by when he never once thought of the regicides.

Frances had been certain that some of them at least would die. Frankie and Judith were healthy enough, and Richard now a robust boy of five – those three might survive it. But Betty and Nan were often ill even in normal times, she herself was worn out and hungry – her ribs poking out beneath her second-hand clothes – and her aunt and uncle were showing all the infirmities of old age. And yet when winter came and the dying stopped, she found to her surprise that the household was intact, and everyone was still alive.

In February, the intelligencers announced that the King and court, after a seven-month retreat to the safety of the country, had returned to Whitehall.

But now it was 1666, the fateful year, and Uncle William was full of grim prognostications. Frances was secretly shocked by the relish with which he seized on any disaster. In June he came back from Paternoster Row with a smile to report that the English fleet had suffered another defeat after a second four-day battle with the Dutch. He studied the bills of mortality to see if the summer heat might bring a resurgence of the plague, and seemed disappointed when it didn't.

And then, at the beginning of September, on the morning of the Sabbath, came the final horseman – the Antichrist, clothed in fire.

Frances woke to find a strange red light shining brightly through the shutters, too vivid for the dawn. She tiptoed past the children and went downstairs and out into the street. The whole neighbourhood seemed to be up and in their nightclothes. Sparks were raining down on them like fireflies. The eastern sky was a lurid, feverish crimson. She ran indoors to wake the household, hammering on her aunt and uncle's door, rousing the children. They all went out together. It was starting to get light now. Flakes of ash like black snow were mingled with the fire drops. Richard ran around screaming with laughter. Frances was frightened his hair might catch fire. She scooped him up and retreated to the doorstep.

Uncle William was exultant. He raised his hands to the flaming sky. ' "Is not my word like as a fire? sayeth the Lord; and like a hammer that breaketh the rock in pieces?" '

'Listen,' said Aunt Jane. She cupped her hand to her ear.

In the distance they could hear the roar of the inferno.

Uncle William insisted they had their Sabbath prayer meeting as usual, gathered around the kitchen table. He combed his Bible for references to fire – of which, Frances noticed, there were a great many: the Scriptures that morning seemed to consist of nothing except fiery portents – but when they had finished their discussion and sung a psalm, she could sit still no longer. She pulled on her boots and announced her intention of going to check on the extent of their danger.

Hooke protested that he should be the one to go, but she considered him too old, and suspected he might become so enraptured by the spectacle he would forget all about them.

'No, Uncle,' she said firmly, 'I shall do it. You wait here with Aunt Jane and the children.' To her aunt she added quietly, so as not to frighten the little ones, 'Perhaps you might pack up whatever food we have, and anything of any value. I'll return directly.'

She made her way eastwards through the winding streets, then south to the river at Blackfriars. No church bells were sounding anywhere that Sunday morning, either in the city or beyond the

ROBERT HARRIS

walls. There was only that terrible constant roar. People were fleeing towards the Thames, pushing handcarts, carrying as much as they could manage, babies in arms crying, old folk stumbling to keep up. A warm wind blew into her face and carried a smell of scorching timber. The air shimmered with tiny sparks. Occasionally a larger piece of flaming debris whirled overhead. It was obvious the fire was advancing westwards towards them. There was no need to go further. She turned and pushed her way back through the crowds, against the tide of panic, towards the house.

Nayler, working in his office even though it was the Sabbath, heard news of the fire from his manservant around eight in the morning. He went immediately to the roof of Worcester House to look for himself. About a mile away along the Thames, a great cloud of black smoke was rising above the city. At first, he could see no flames, but then a large soft yellow ball billowed up out of the darkness and exploded into the smoke. Soon after that, he noticed a fringe of brilliant orange creeping worm-like along the crowded houses lining London Bridge. The sight was so sinister and outlandish that he briefly doubted the evidence of his own eyes. But then he came to his senses, with a jolt of shock, and ran downstairs to find the Lord Chancellor.

Hyde was in his wheelchair, being pushed towards his private chapel, Lady Clarendon walking alongside him, his servants behind. He seemed unable to grasp the significance of what Nayler was telling him.

'But there are fires every day in London.'

'Not ones such as this, my lord. It has reached the bridge.'

'What would you have me do about it?'

'Call a meeting of the Council – or as many members as can be found.'

366

'On a Sunday morning?' He tapped the side of his wheelchair in irritation. 'Find out more and bring me a report when I have finished my devotions – which, by the by, you should observe yourself more often.'

Shifting from foot to foot with anxiety, Nayler bowed. 'My lord.'

He commandeered a coach from the courtyard and had himself driven along the Strand as far as Blackfriars, where they were halted by the crowds and the wall of heat. On the steps close to the river, a man was on the ground being beaten by a group of youths wielding cudgels. They looked set to kill him. Nayler jumped out of the carriage.

'Who is this? What is this?'

One of the attackers turned, out of breath. 'He's a Frenchmen – they set the fire!'

Another said, 'It's a popish plot!'

'Let him go.'

'On whose authority?'

'The Lord Chancellor of England.' They stared at him, mulish, stupid. 'You don't believe me? See, there's Lord Clarendon's carriage, with his crest upon the door.'

With a final couple of kicks and a shower of spit, they backed away

Nayler seized the Frenchman by the arm and pulled him to his feet. 'Run,' he said, 'and don't open your mouth until you're out of the city.'

He climbed back into the coach. 'Worcester House,' he ordered the driver. 'As fast as you can.'

It took Frances and her family until mid afternoon to reach the river. They were met by pandemonium. By now, the fire was barely half a mile away. Above the nearby houses, billows of black smoke and shooting flames; beneath the rain of sparks, thousands of people crammed along the Thames and milling around a jetty. Frances plunged into the crowd, dragging the children after her, the Hookes struggling in the rear, until she reached the front of the queue. Money had lost its value; the boatmen charged whatever they could get. She had to hand over half their savings to buy places on a coal barge that was ferrying passengers to safety. Uncle William and Aunt Jane were helped aboard. Frances lifted the children down, then scrambled after them. The boat was crammed and seemed to her to be lying dangerously low in the water. As they crouched in the coal dust and the boat pushed off, the wind whipped water over the side.

The rowers had to struggle against the tide to reach the opposite shore. At Bankside, they picked their way between families sprawled exhausted on the grass above the mudflats until they found a patch of waste ground where they could sit. From here they had a clear view across the river to the fire. It seemed to be a living thing – devilish, malevolent, climbing the church steeples and sheathing them blood red, arcing between buildings and across streets, moving relentlessly westwards. Above the roar came the crash of buildings collapsing. A huge cloud of smoke hung over the city. As the daylight faded and night came on, the sky was lit from beneath by a fierce red glow, bright enough for Uncle William to stand and read his Bible. He declared that they were witnessing the destruction of Sodom and Gomorrah. People gathered as he began to preach.

'But the fearful, and unbelieving, and the abominable, and murderers, and whoremongers, and sorcerers, and idolaters, and all liars, shall have their part in the lake which burneth with fire and brimstone: which is the second death . . .'

Someone shouted, 'Be quiet, old man!' Others cried for God

to save them. An argument began. Frances reached out her arms and drew all five children in close to her, and started to recite the twenty-third psalm. ' "The Lord is my shepherd; I shall not want. He maketh me to lie down in green pastures . . ." '

They stayed there for the next two days, warmed at night by the fire, which warded off the early autumn chill, managing to survive on the food they had brought with them and what little Frances was able to buy. They watched barges carrying away the property of the wealthy and heard the explosions near the Tower and at Whitehall as the soldiers demolished houses to make a fire break. Their great hope was that the River Fleet, which flowed only a hundred yards from West Harding Street, might stop the flames. But on Tuesday morning, the conflagration vaulted across it as if it was nothing more than a ditch.

Throughout all this, the massive steeple of St Paul's Cathedral, encased in wooden scaffolding as it was undergoing repairs, rose intact above the fire and smoke. On Tuesday evening, however, Uncle William cried out and pointed to the serpents of flame that had scaled the poles and were slithering across the roof. The lead began to glow red hot, and an hour later they watched the huge edifice collapse, followed a few moments later by a terrifying cannonade of tumbling stones.

' "The Lord is my shepherd . . ." '

On Wednesday morning, Frances woke with the dawn, her clothes drenched with dew, and stood to discover that the worst of the fire appeared to be over. A view that since Sunday had been a shifting panorama of every shade of red – crimson, vermilion, scarlet – was now static, mostly black and grey, with flickering patches of orange light where there was still something left for the flames to consume. In a hundred places, where once there had been church steeples, ghostly thin towers of smoke were rising.

At four o'clock, the wind dropped, and they decided it was safe enough to set off back to Holborn and find out if anything remained of their home. Frances used the last of their money to pay their fares on a barge. They landed opposite Farringdon Street. Most buildings were either gone or gutted; those that remained looked to be on the point of collapse. Fires still burned beneath the surface. The ground was hot under their feet, littered with blackened bricks and spars of timber turned to charcoal. Their shoes sank into the soft warm ash. For the first time, the girls began to cry. Only Richard still treated it as an adventure. She had to cling on tight to his hand to stop him running into the exposed houses, where shadowy people, covered in soot – owners? looters? – were searching through the wreckage.

They turned in to what remained of Fleet Street. It seemed impossible to Frances that their house could have survived. Penniless, homeless, hungry – what were they to do? They would starve to death in the street, like the beggars in the plague. Half the buildings on Fetter Lane had also gone, but the devastation was not quite so complete as elsewhere, and she prayed, as she had never prayed before, not even for Will, that their home would still be there. She could not bear to look herself. She whispered to Frankie to run ahead and check. And for the rest of her life, she would never forget the smile on her daughter's face when she returned to say that it was a miracle: West Harding Street had been spared.

Nayler had scarcely slept since Sunday morning – sweating, soot-streaked, running hither and thither on behalf of the Lord Chancellor, trying to give the impression his master was at the centre of events. It was the King himself who had convened the Privy Council. Its senior members had all been allotted districts of London to supervise. But Hyde was too immobilised by his arthritic, gouty legs to attend the meeting or do anything other than sit fretfully in Worcester House and fuss about the loading of his valuables into a boat. Nayler had spent most of the past three days acting as his intermediary with the King and the Duke of York as they took command of the fight against the fire in the absence of General Monck, the Duke of Albemarle, who was with the fleet. It was universally agreed that this had been the brothers' finest hour – directing operations from their saddles and from the royal barge, ordering the demolition of buildings to create fire breaks, showing themselves in public, ignoring the risks, steadying morale. Now, late on Wednesday afternoon, they were setting out again on horseback from Whitehall Palace for yet another tour of inspection. Nayler went with them, hoping to put in a word for Hyde.

'And how is the Lord Chancellor, Mr Nayler?' enquired the King, suddenly turning round. 'We have been so occupied we have scarcely had time to think of him. He is safe, I hope?'

'He is well, Your Majesty.'

'Well rested at least, I should think.'

'I would not say that, Your Majesty. He is only sorry his infirmities have prevented him from joining you. But he has been at his post throughout.'

'I am most grateful for his services.' And then, almost as an afterthought, 'But he does need a rest – a long rest.'

The King trotted forwards to ride beside his brother, leaving Nayler with the uneasy feeling that his master's reputation after the fire was rather like one of the magnificent old buildings in the city: apparently still intact, but tottering.

Uncle William sat at the table with his Bible open. It was not a miracle, he corrected them: it was God's plan, as foretold in

Revelation. From the ashes of the Whore of Babylon, the Commonwealth would rise again, an earthly paradise.

Frances went out to look for food, carrying a candlestick hidden under her coat in the hope of making a trade.

In Fleet Street, there was a commotion – a troop of horses at the end of the shattered highway, the blast of a trumpet, a flash of blue and gold in the distance. People emerged from the ruins to see what was happening. From the direction of Whitehall, escorted by a guard of cavalry, two fine gentlemen appeared on horseback, doffing their hats to the survivors. There was a wave of cheering, shouts of 'God save the King!' She drew back against the wall as they passed with their attendants. The taller of them even smiled at her. The King of England with his brother, the Duke of York, the hooves of their high grey horses raising clouds of powdery ash.

She didn't recognise Nayler, and he most certainly didn't notice her among such a multitude.

As she watched them disappear in the direction of the City of London, the sounds of acclamation followed them like the wash from the prow of a boat, and it seemed to her that her uncle was wrong – that the usurpers were not to be so easily humbled, nor the rule of the righteous so swiftly restored.

CHAPTER THIRTY-ONE

F LATTENED BY TIME and distance, the ripples of these great events did not reach Hadley until roughly four months after they had occurred.

It was only in October 1665 that Ned and Will and Colonel Dixwell heard that the war with the Dutch had begun with a defeat at sea – a cause for celebration among men hoping to hear of divine punishment of the Old Country.

They then had to wait another three months, until January 1666, before gradually coming to appreciate the severity of the plague. This did indeed sound like God's punishment. But when Reverend Russell read out the letter from Increase Mather, with its long list of London parishes and their dead – St Botolph's, Aldgate, St Sepulchre, Newgate, St Ann's, Blackfriars and all the rest – only Dixwell was exultant. The sombre expressions of Ned and Will seemed to take him by surprise.

'Why so long-faced? Consider the date. Surely this is the wrath that heralds the Second Coming?'

Ned, whose opinion of Dixwell had not improved, said, 'It is easier for you to be joyful, Mr Dixwell, with a wife in Kent. But these are the districts where our families were living when last we heard.'

Privately Ned prayed for the plague to abate, even if it was divinely sent, and gave thanks later in the year when they learned that it had. By then, the death toll was said to be over a hundred thousand – one Londoner in four – and when Will heard the number his face turned pale. What were the chances that Frances and all the children had escaped unscathed? He longed for a letter saying they were safe, but none came.

The year went on in an agony of apprehension, hoping for the disasters foretold in Revelation, yet dreading what they might be.

It was not until the end of December 1666, in the last few days of that portentous year, that word of the Great Fire finally spread to the banks of the Connecticut. The colonels handed round Reverend Mather's digest of intelligence. Thirteen thousand houses destroyed, eighty-seven churches, and St Paul's Cathedral. Exactly the same parishes were affected as had been visited by the plague. Nobody could say how many hundreds had died: most of the victims had been reduced to cinders. It was as if God in his infinite wisdom had decided that those few square miles of London were the fulcrum of all the evil in the world. And yet it was reported that the King had emerged a hero.

'Why are Charles Stuart and his wicked court in Whitehall spared,' asked Ned, 'while the righteous within and without the city are visited by disaster? Is this the deliverance for which we have waited?'

'Their turn will come,' prophesied Dixwell.

'But when? And in the meantime, what are we to do except pray our families are safe?'

'Are you questioning God's plan?'

'Perhaps I am, for I confess it makes no sense to me.'

Three faces – Russell's, Will's and Dixwell's – stared at him in shock.

Will said, 'You no longer believe this is the year of the Second Coming? Even though the fire in London exactly matches the vision in my dream?'

Not for the first time it struck Ned that his son-in-law had entirely lost his reason. 'I thought you predicted that the Second Coming would be here in New England.'

Will hesitated. 'That was Mr Davenport's opinion.'

'Well, if this is indeed the year, there are few days left of it. So we shall know soon enough.'

On New Year's Day 1667, Ned rose at first light and threw open his shutters. And yes – of course! – the world was still there: the yard, the road, the distant houses, silent and unchanging. No Saviour clad in white from head to toe would walk through Hadley that morning – or any morning, for that matter. Looking out from his window, he felt he had been granted a glimpse of a great truth, one that had been whispering at his conscience for many years: that God was not to be pressed into service merely to suit the needs of men, however righteous they believed their cause to be; that such presumption was itself a sin. He felt both despair and a bitter vindication.

That evening, the three of them began their supper in silence.

'Perhaps,' said Dixwell eventually, 'there is some fault in the calendar, which may be traced back to an error made centuries ago, and the reckoning of the year is not correct. Or it may be dated as the lawyers do, from Lady Day in March.'

Ned made a noise, something between a splutter and a groan. 'So we must wait yet another three months?'

Will said, 'The letter about the fire was written at the beginning of September. How can we know what has happened since? It may be that England lies in ruins and the Lord has indeed come.'

'The fire is out,' said Ned. 'The letter said so. Or do you think there has been another since?'

'You must not lose faith, Ned.'

'*Lose* faith? I have no faith left in your prognostications. I do not believe that in the next few weeks our Saviour will return to earth. It is a nonsense, based upon a wishful reading of the Scriptures – a delusion believed by few except fanatics, and I am sorry that I ever listened to it.'

A long pause followed, like the quiet after an explosion. Then, without a word, Dixwell rose from the table, opened the door and went outside. Will bowed his head. His lips were moving. He is praying, Ned thought – is it for Armageddon or my immortal soul? After a minute, he lifted his head and gave his father-in-law a terrible look – full of anger and reproach: such an expression as Ned had never seen from him before – then followed Dixwell out into the yard.

Ned assumed that he had gone to calm Dixwell down and fetch him back. But time passed and they did not reappear, and after an hour he gave up waiting and went upstairs.

Later that night, Will came to Ned's door. He did not enter, but stayed on the threshold. 'John is leaving.'

'When?'

'As soon as it is warm enough to travel.'

'To go where?'

'He is not certain. He thinks New Haven.'

'But it is not safe.'

'He thinks it is.' Will's tone was cold, metallic. 'He points out that he did not make our mistake when he arrived in Boston and use his real name. The authorities are unaware of his presence in

America – they seem to think him still in Holland. He has money. He plans to purchase a property and live under his pseudonym of James Davids, posing as a settler newly arrived from England.'

'Still, it is far too great a risk.' Ned swallowed hard and got to his feet. 'I shall go to him and apologise.'

'He does not want your apologies. He wants nothing more to do with you.' Will paused, then added quietly, 'He has asked me to go with him.'

'Will – you can't!'

'Why? Because you need me here for company?'

'No, because your face is too well known in New Haven! The reward . . . It is a certainty you'd be caught.'

'He says he will conceal me beneath his roof, and that in time it will be safe for me to venture out. The place is bigger than Hadley, and less remote, with a greater chance of congenial company.'

'Congenial? In what way congenial?'

'People who think as we do.'

'You mean who share the same delusion?' Suddenly Ned could stand it no longer. 'Go then, if it's a comfort to you. Go! It doesn't matter to me. I've done my best to protect you.'

'Is that truly what you think you've done? *Protected* me?' Will was shouting now. 'Do you not see the truth even yet? Stubborn old man, you've led us both to ruin!'

He turned away. Ned slammed the door after him.

Dear Frances, one question troubles me. It was not Charles Stuart alone we meant to kill that January day, but monarchy itself. Cromwell said, 'We shall cut off the King's head with the crown still upon it', and that is what we did. Our intention was that England should be a righteous republic, and that no kings or princes, lords or bishops should ever again interpose themselves between the people and Almighty God. The principle was a fine one; I believed in it then and believe in it still, despite our present afflictions. But here is the question which I cannot answer. If the victories God gave us were proof we were doing His work, how are we to interpret what has happened since? Has he withdrawn his favour from our cause, or

He hesitated, then finished: *were we in error all along?*

Ned kept to his room after that terrible New Year's Day and wrote. If he passed Will or Dixwell on the stairs, they turned their heads, and he did likewise. They still met at their twice-weekly prayer meetings with Reverend Russell and Peter Tilton, but their conversation was limited to discussion of the Scriptures, and no one mentioned the Book of Revelation.

He wrote by daylight and by candlelight. He wrote about Cromwell in the years after the King's execution – about the turbulence in the army when the Levellers mutinied (some of Ned's own troops among them), demanding free elections and votes for all men, and how Cromwell had had the leaders shot by firing squad to reimpose discipline. He described how he had stayed behind in London responsible for security while Cromwell went off to Ireland with a terrible gleam in his eye to punish the rebellious Catholics, a punitive expedition of slaughter he had been glad to miss. He wrote about the campaign against the Scots and the battle at Dunbar, when they had been trapped against the sea, and how he had led the cavalry charge to break their perilous encirclement, and how he had been wounded. He described the last great battle of the Civil War at Worcester, when the Royalists had been routed and he had been wounded again. He wrote about Oliver's triumphal return like Caesar to London trailing four thousand prisoners – he was 'His Excellency the Lord General' now, granted the use of Hampton Court by a grateful Parliament, as well as the palace known as the Cockpit in Whitehall. And then the happy years that followed: his house in King Street with the children, Frances's marriage to Will, the confiscated Royalist estates he had been granted, the wealth and years of plenty. He so exhausted himself in the act of re-creation that sometimes he looked up and was surprised to find himself not in one of his fine residences but in this silent prison chamber. How high he had risen, and how low he had sunk.

Will's voice nagged at him. *Stubborn old man, you've led us both to ruin . . .*

February came and the weather turned warmer. Early one morning, when he was sitting at his fireside, he heard voices in the yard beneath his window. He used the poker as a walking stick, both hands grasping the handle to help him to his feet. Outside it was a warm day, spring-like, birds singing, the last of the snow melting on the roof, trickling into the yard and gurgling into the brook beyond the fence – a day full of promise. Dixwell was wearing his heavy coat and boots, his bag beside him. Russell was with him, dressed for outdoors, and so was Will, in his old army coat. Their voices carried up to him, indistinct. He caught his own name and they glanced up at his window.

He pulled back his head sharply so as not to be seen, and the action seemed to snap something inside him. His heart was beating sharp and fast. He felt a pain across his chest and arms, like an iron band, tightening. Would Will really leave without a word of farewell? He leaned heavily against the wall. His head drooped. He heard the door slam, and the latch of the gate lift and fall, and then there was nothing except the twittering of the birds, the drip of melting snow, the hammering of his heart. He could not move. He felt that if he tried, he would collapse.

Presently the pain began to subside, and he caught the sound of footsteps coming up the stairs. He lifted his head.

'Will?'

Supporting himself on the poker, he shuffled across the room and opened the door. Will was on the landing.

'You did not go?'

His son-in-law could not bring himself to look at him. He briefly shook his head. 'You are right. I am trapped. For ever. With you.'

Cromwell in a rage with Parliament, which is not a proper Parliament at all, merely the spavined rump left after the exclusion of members who wouldn't vote for the King's trial. It talks and it talks, and it does nothing. Cromwell says again and again, 'Was it for this we fought the war?'

Cromwell, on an April morning in 1653, in his plain black clothes and grey worsted stockings, restlessly pacing one of the grand reception rooms of the Cockpit, is told that Parliament is rushing through a bill to extend itself indefinitely. He stops, stupefied. He summons six files of musketeers from his own regiment, and with Ned and Will in tow, and without even pausing to put on proper clothes, storms down King Street to Westminster, bursts into the Commons chamber, sits fuming for a quarter of an hour, then launches himself to his feet and starts striding up and down the aisle like a madman, kicking out in his soft leather house shoes, pointing to this member and that, calling them whoremasters, drunkards, godless cowards, corrupt buffoons.

'Perhaps you think this is not parliamentary language? I confess it is not, neither are you to expect such from me. You have sat long enough. I will put an end to your prating. You are no Parliament. I say you are no Parliament. I will put an end to your sitting.' He shouts, 'Call them in!' and Ned, who is standing at the door, steps aside to make way for the musketeers, who pour into the chamber where Oliver points at the Speaker. 'Fetch him down!'

As Speaker Lenthall is dragged from his seat, the moderate Henry Vane cries out, 'This is not honest! It is against morality and common honesty!'

Cromwell turns on him. 'O Sir Henry Vane, Sir Henry Vane, the Lord deliver me from Sir Henry Vane!' He seizes the mace from the table in front of the Speaker's chair. 'What shall we do with his bauble?' He throws it to Will. 'Here, take it away.' When the chamber is empty, he locks the door, pockets the key, marches back up King Street to the Cockpit, where the leaders of the army are waiting, and throws the key down before the stunned officers. 'When I went there, I did not think to have done this. But perceiving the spirit of God so strong upon me, I would not consult flesh and blood.'

And that is that. Oliver becomes Lord Protector, moves into Whitehall Palace, from now on is addressed as 'Your Highness', travels in a coach-and-six with ten footmen, has a throne to sit upon whenever he appears in public, and is England's military dictator – her king in all but name.

I asked what duties he wished to set me. He replied that my task was to keep him alive so he could complete the work God had given him. It was not an easy business. I cannot count how many plots there were to kill him – to poison him, shoot him, blow him up – nor the number of ambushes laid between Whitehall and Westminster and on his route to Hampton. He never went out of doors without his lifeguard of forty-five troopers and a loaded pistol in his pocket. Oddly, the nearest he came to death was by his own hand. The Duke of Oldenburg, hearing of the Protector's love of horses, sent him a gift of six magnificent Friesland greys which he took to Hyde Park. After dining under the trees with a group of us, he insisted on hitching them all to his coach and driving them as a team. He whipped them too hard, the hot-spirited stallions became unruly, somehow his foot got entangled in the reins, and he was thrown and dragged along the ground some distance, causing his pistol to discharge in his pocket. We carried him unconscious back to Whitehall Palace where he lay in bed three weeks. It is my opinion his health never fully recovered, for he scarcely knew a day thereafter without some illness – colic, the stone, tumours, catarrh, and a tertian ague which had plagued him since the campaign in Ireland.

Cromwell had the power, but to what end? Each time he tried to restore Parliament, it antagonised him, and he dissolved it. The army was divided, the country sullen. He lived in a trap of his own making. Ned could picture him now, wandering restlessly from room to room in his palace, and along the leads of the roof. He realised finally who it was he reminded him of – that other semi-prisoner, Charles Stuart.

In the summer of 1658 at Hampton Court, his daughter Eliza-beth died of a canker. Never had I seen him more distraught. He retired to his bedchamber and had me read to him that passage of St Paul that had sustained him when his son died: 'I have learnt in whatever state I am therewith to be con-tent . . . I am instructed both to be full, and to be hungry, both to abound and suffer need. I can do all things through

Christ that strengtheneth me.' He was too ill to attend Elizabeth's funeral. His thoughts were all of death. We moved
him to London, to St James's Palace, further from the river,
where his physicians said the air was healthier, but to no
avail. (Afterwards the doctors found his spleen was full of
suppurating pus; we were wrong to hope of any recovery.)
On the night before he died, Secretary Thurloe summoned
me and Will to act as witnesses at his bedside. He was asked
to make a sign if he still desired his son, Richard, to succeed
him. He raised his hand slightly. Then the doctors bade us
leave. It was the last time I saw him.

Ned's own strength was weakening fast now. His life, his wounds
were catching up with him. He found it hard to write. Some days
he could barely get out of bed. He put away his manuscript. One
morning he woke to find Oliver looking down at him.

'Get on your feet, you milksop.'

'I cannot, Your Highness. I lack the strength.'

'What is this "Your Highness"? Surely I am plain Oliver to you,
and have been since we were boys.'

'Really? As I recall, you were always most particular about your
title, even in private.'

'Ha! You think I desired that bauble? But if we learned nothing
else, it was that the people of England will not follow a committee. They still hankered after a king, and by the grace of God I
was the next best thing.'

'And you would have had yourself crowned, if sufficient of the
army had agreed.'

'True, but I never wanted it.'

'Yet you named your son to be your successor, just as if you
were a king.'

'It is all a nonsense, Ned. There is only God's will.'

'You cut off the King's head and left us a void. Richard was never fit to be Lord Protector. You must have known it. What were we to do, Oliver? Oliver?'

But he had gone.

Will stood in his stockinged feet on the landing outside Ned's bedroom door. He could hear his father-in-law muttering to himself. He tried to decide whether he should go in. Relations between them had been so bad for so long, he was fearful of the harsh words he might receive. He did not wish to make matters worse. On the other hand, he was worried. The old man seemed to be in a fever of delirium. He reached his hand towards the door handle. But suddenly the muttering stopped. Slowly he retracted it. Best to let him sleep. He would find some other opportunity. He tiptoed away.

Ned was playing a game of hide-and-seek with Oliver among the huge pink rhododendrons in the gardens of Hinchingbrooke when he heard the creak of floorboards on the landing.

'Will, is that you?'

His words sounded in his ears like gibberish.

It took him three or four attempts to roll over onto his side, and then he struggled to put his feet to the carpet. With an effort, he pushed himself up off the mattress and just about managed to stand. His head ached so much he was almost blind. He took a few tottering steps through the fog towards the door, and stood swaying for a moment before he crashed full-length.

PART FOUR

KILL
1674

CHAPTER THIRTY-TWO

S EVEN YEARS LATER, in the middle of August 1674, very early
in the morning, an hour before sunrise, Colonel William
Goffe stepped out of the Russells' house carrying a bulging
canvas sack.

It had been a long, hot summer. Already a mist was rolling in
off the Connecticut, bearing the promise of another warm day. He
inhaled the river's particular vapour – cool, slightly musty – then
crept to the gate and craned his neck to check both ways along
the street. There was just enough light for him to be sure it was
deserted.

He hoisted his sack over his shoulder, wincing as the metal
inside shifted and clinked, quietly unlatched the gate, turned left
into the wide grassy road, and left again, and hurried down the
side of the highway towards the edge of the settlement.

Beyond the fence at the end of the Russells' lot, immediately
to the east of Hadley, lay what the locals called Pine Plain. Isolated tall trees like the masts of ships at anchor poked above the
thin white haze. It was a relief to be getting away from the town,
however briefly. He would have liked to savour the sensation of

freedom, the spring of the grass beneath his boots, the spreading light of the approaching dawn, but he had no time. He walked on quickly – fifty-six years old now, but still trim and fit, his long grey hair pulled back off his forehead and secured in a ponytail, his thick grey whiskers hiding the lower part of his face. Almost no one apart from the Russells and their household had set eyes on him for almost a decade. He felt himself forgotten, a relic from another age. If anyone had passed him, they might have thought him a grizzled sailor recently stepped ashore after a long voyage. Only the paleness of his skin might have caused them to wonder – that, and the unmistakable light of religious zeal in his dark eyes, and the bulge of the pistol he carried in his pocket.

It took him a quarter of an hour to cross the plain and reach the edge of the forest. There he had to slow his pace to follow the path in the grey light, even though he knew the way, stepping from boulder to boulder, planting his feet carefully on the mossy trunk that lay across the stream. Something moved in the trees to his right – a deer, probably; if it had been an Indian, he never would have heard them. Another ten minutes brought him to the Norwottucks' camp, a dozen big huts just visible in the gloom, spread along the shore of the lake. He knew there were more wigwams beyond, about fifty in all. Mist was rising off the water here too, like steam from a boiling cauldron, mingling with the smoke drifting from the roofs. A dog barked as he drew nearer. There was a smell of cooking maize.

The woman with whom he always dealt was squatting in her usual place. Her age was a mystery to him. Her face was unlined, her hair black. He guessed she was about thirty. He did not know her name. They never spoke. He knew that Norwottuck meant 'in the midst of the river' and was the native name for the bend in the Connecticut now occupied by Hadley. They communicated by signs and occasional pictures they drew for one another in the dirt. A large circle had been her way of telling him that he should always come at the time of the full moon.

He bowed politely and squatted opposite her. She offered him a platter of the Norwottucks' corn porridge, which he did not want or have time for but which he ate as quickly as he could without appearing rude. He opened his sack and took out his wares – tools, mostly, which he had ordered from Hartford: hatchets, knives, hammers, a chisel, a small saw, a brass kettle. She inspected them with care, holding them up and turning them round, testing the sharpness of the blades against her thumb. Then she counted out her side of the bargain – two dozen beaver pelts of good size and quality. He knew better than to haggle: the only time he had tried, she had stood and walked away, and he had been obliged to run after her and press his hand to his heart in a show of apology, to the amusement of the watching men. Whoever she was, she was not to be swindled. He put the skins carefully away in his sack, drew a circle in the dust and held up his fore- and index fingers. He would come again in two full moons. She nodded.

As he left, the usual group of men stood watching him. But today there were no smiles. They had muskets, he noticed, which it was forbidden for the English to trade with the native Americans. He nodded as he passed them. They stared back – hostile looks, it seemed to him – yet the Norwottuck were supposed to be friendly. Halfway along the path, he sensed they were following him. He put his hand in his pocket for his pistol and kept checking over his shoulder. There was no one he could see. Still, that meant nothing, and it was a relief to come out of the forest and onto the plain, where the mist wasn't thick enough to hide an attacker. He lengthened his stride, with only occasional backward glances,

and by six, just as the sun broke over the trees behind him, he was
safely home in Hadley.

After he had stashed the skins in his room – they would fetch a
good price when he sent them to the fur traders in Boston – he
went across the landing to deal with Ned.

His first task of the day, as always, was to check he was still
alive. He touched his cheek. The old man's eyes met his. 'God
bless you, Ned. Good morning.' In response came a slur of sound.
'Let us give thanks to the Lord for another day.' He put his arm
beneath Ned's shoulders, pulled him upright, then lifted him off
the bed and supported him as he shuffled over to the commode.
A quick inspection showed he had not soiled himself during the
night, always a good start. He pulled Ned's nightshirt above his
wasted legs and guided him into position, then stood behind him,
his elbows hooked under his armpits to support him. While he
waited for the morning piss to start, he sang, in that fine voice of
his, made by God for chanting psalms:

> Ned, Ned, lies in bed,
> His legs don't work and nor does his head.

The silly little rhyme, composed in the early days, had always
amused Ned. Most of the time he seemed to understand what was
said to him, even though he could not speak. He smiled. A drool
of spittle leaked from the corner of his mouth, and Will pulled
out a handkerchief and wipcd it away.

This has been their routine for the past seven years.

After the morning visit to the commode, Will dresses him. In a
practical sense, this is pointless, since the old man won't be leaving the room, but it saddened him too much to see Ned, once

so particular about his appearance, lolling around all day in his nightshirt. He has to do everything for him – wash him with the Russells' greasy home-made soap of lye and tallow, spoon-feed him, hold a cup of water to his lips, trim his hair and beard, cut his fingernails, prop him up in his chair (in winter by the fire, in summer beside the open window, just far enough back so that he cannot be seen from the road), read to him, talk to him, put him back to bed again at night – an endless cycle, month in month out, year in year out. It is hard physical labour: Colonel Whalley even shrunken by old age, is still a heavy man. Little wonder Will is fit, with arm muscles more powerful even than in his youth, as if Ned has bequeathed him his strength.

He does not resent it. On the contrary. It is the Lord's work he is doing. 'Bear ye one another's burdens, and so fulfil the law of Christ' (Galatians, 6:2). Or again: 'Who sees his brother have need, and shutteth up his bowels of compassion from him, how dwelleth the love of God in him? Let us not love in word, neither in tongue, but in deed and in truth' (John, 3:17). With every task he performs – the humblest and most squalid especially – he feels himself drawing closer to God.

When Ned was first struck down, Reverend Russell consulted a doctor in Springfield. The symptoms described in his medical textbook – 'a malady, very sudden in its attack, which arrests more or less completely the powers of sense and motion, caused by an effusion of blood or serum in the brain, and preceded by giddiness, partial loss of muscular power, etc.' – plainly matched those of apoplexy. There was little hope of recovery.

To begin with, a nineteen-year-old young woman named Lydia Fisher, of a good Puritan family in Dedham, Massachusetts, came to stay and help. But Ned became agitated whenever she touched him, and Will found her proximity aroused feelings within him he had managed to suppress for the best part of a decade. She made it plain, by smiles and the occasional hand on his arm, that she felt the same about him. After a few months, he had had to send her away, not least because tending to Ned brings Frances into the room. He can see so much of her in her father, especially now his flesh has thinned, and his cheekbones have become more prominent, his expression innocent and trusting. It is another blessing of old age, he has discovered – it peels away the layers built up by years of suffering and experience; it lays bare the child inside the man. Sometimes he feels he is gazing down at her face. He wonders what, if anything, goes on in Ned's mind. The thought troubles him.

One day, not long after Lydia's departure, when he had brought up a broom from the kitchen and was cleaning Ned's room, he shifted his father-in-law's old army bag to sweep away the dust that had gathered behind it and noticed a thick sheaf of papers tucked inside. *Some Memories of the Life of His Highness, the Late Lord Protector.* He glanced across at Ned. As usual, he was asleep. Overcome with curiosity, he carried the manuscript into his own room and started to read.

I was born in the Year of Our Lord 1598 . . .

He read on until Ned needed feeding and cleaning, and then went back to it, lighting a lamp as the day faded. The early part was unobjectionable enough – fascinating, indeed. It kindled memories of his own – his early years as a pikeman in Colonel Pride's regiment of foot, marching fifteen miles a day with sixty pounds upon his back, fighting at Naseby, storming Bristol, where they had been the first to scale the city's walls, the meetings at Saffron Walden and Putney, where his sermons and visions had brought him to prominence, the purging of Parliament, in which he had played an eager part, his wooing of Frances after the King's execution.

It was only when Ned began to introduce Frances's name, and address her directly, that the tone changed and Will started to become uneasy. *You may wonder – many did; I did myself – at the action of an army that had gone to war in the name of Parliament now treating it more roughly than the King had ever dared . . .* What was this? And then there was the curious sympathy and respect for Charles Stuart – shocking, really – and his doubts about the King's trial, and then the most disturbing passage of all: *Dear Frances . . . one question troubles me. If the victories God gave us were proof we were doing His work, how are we to interpret what has happened since? Has he withdrawn his favour from our cause, or were we in error all along?* His portrait of Cromwell hinted at sins of personal ambition, pride, anger, duplicity, cynicism – a strange instrument for God to choose. The legibility of the manuscript declined badly towards the end, full of crossings-out and misspellings and repetitions, but the final page was clear enough:

I have read that my colleague Col. Hacker, a neighbour to me in Nottinghamshire, a good soldier and a pious man, declared to several of his friends a little before he suffered execution that the greatest trouble he had upon his spirits was 'that he had formerly borne too great a prejudice in his heart towards the good people of God that differed from him in judgement'.

If he chose that for his epitaph, it may also stand as mine.

Thanks be to God, and may He forgive his humble servant.

Edw. Whalley

Will had sat back, appalled. It was as if the ghost of Ned had risen from the husk of his body across the landing and started raving in utter madness. This could not be the man he knew. Some devil had seized his pen. Little surprise that God had struck him down. The thought that Frances might read his words was especially dreadful. She must be protected from the effect of her father's sickness. And Ned must be protected from himself.

He lit a fire in his grate and burned the memoir, page by page.

In the summer of 1671, four years after Ned's seizure, Russell had announced that Reverend Mather was now willing to risk forwarding a letter to Frances. Will had spent a long time in its composition. He did not disclose their whereabouts. He hinted at her father's state of health without going into details. He most certainly did not mention his writings. In case the letter fell into the hands of the government, he had addressed her as 'Mother' and signed himself her son. The following spring, he had received her reply.

My dearest Son, How your letter, so greatly longed for, has revived my spirits! Through mercy we are all in health and do experience much of the love & care of our good God in supporting & providing for us in such a day of trial as this. I rejoice to hear that America agrees with you & that you thrive so well, though I am sorry to hear your friend is sickly. I know not whether this will come to you safe, & therefore shall be the briefer to let you know how dear you are to me & your little brothers and sisters, all in good health, only Betty is weakly, & all longing greatly to see you. If the Lord says it is good for us, He will bring our reuniting to pass in His own time. We are compelled to be thrifty but if there is anything I can serve you in, pray command me, for I shall do it to the utmost of my power, if the Lord permit. I beg your prayers and promise mine, & with my dear Love to yourself, & duty & service to all friends, committing you & them to the safe protection of the Almighty, I take my leave & till death remain, Your dear & Loving Mother

A few more exchanges had followed. Then had come a long gap, caused by the Dutch war and the interruption of shipping across the Atlantic. On that August morning in 1674, the day of his visit to the Norwottucks, it was a year and a half since he had heard from her.

Once he had settled Ned in his chair and opened the window wide to admit some air into the stifling room, he packed up the beaver skins and took them downstairs to Russell.

'And how is our friend this morning?'

'The same as ever. Perhaps a little weaker.'

'God will take him when it pleases him. It cannot be long now.' They had had the same exchange for years. Sometimes Will wondered if Ned would outlive them both. Russell glanced at the sack.

'More business with the Indians? You weren't seen, I trust?'

'No, I'm always careful. Two dozen beaver, ready to go to Boston. Five shillings a pelt. Six pounds total. I have made a list of goods I require from Hartford.' It was a source of pride that he could pay his way. With the profits from his Indian trading, and the income from the investments Gookin had made on their behalf in 1661, plus gifts from home and a legacy of fifty pounds given to them by Richard Saltonstall of Ipswich, he and Ned were nearly wealthy, despite the rent he paid to Russell.

'A letter has come from England for you.'

He recognised Frances's handwriting. 'Thank you, John. God be thanked.'

His hand shook slightly with anticipation as he carried it upstairs.

'Here, Ned, is news from Frances at last.'

The old man murmured.

Will pulled up a chair to the bedside, broke the seal and started to read it aloud. 'It is dated the twenty-ninth of March. "My dear Son, much has happened since last I was able to write to you, and I must give you first the hardest tidings of all, that sweet Betty has been taken from us by the Lord in her eighteenth year." '

He looked up. Ned was staring at the ceiling, his expression blank. He wished he had read it to himself first, but he did not feel he could stop now.

'Her health was always sickly, & we were prepared, but she had survived the plague & the fire, & the blow has been most grievous. May our Maker & Redeemer provide to you the comfort in her loss that he has shown to us. Also, you should know that Frankie is newly married to a salter by trade, a gentleman, though not in very high condition, as business is poor. She is with child, & the time of her deliverance does now draw on. My dearest, I fear you must be angry with me, that this was done without your knowing or advice, & though I strive to be a goodly mother & pray for guidance, I cannot but be sensible that I lack your wisdom & guiding counsel . . .'

He crumpled up the letter and crept away into his own room. His image of Betty, rubbed away by time, had become a pale blur. Frankie was still to him a little girl with a doll. He had missed their lives. Now, one was dead and the other wed and pregnant. He cried for them both and he wept for himself. When he went back in to see Ned, his father-in-law had turned his face to the wall and would not look at him.

A few days later, after he had fed Ned his supper, Russell brought him another letter, inserted into a packet containing one from Reverend Hooke. The letter from Frances was brief, a single page, dated a few weeks after her last.

Dear heart, a line to tell you that Frankie was delivered of a boy two days ago, but the child, named William in your honour, lived only a few hours. She suffered grievously but the Lord appeared in her needful hour, & she now seems likely to recover, thanks be to Him who watches over us.

Once Ned was settled for the night, Will sat at the table in his father-in-law's room, moths fluttering round the candle. He had been putting off replying. Now he tried to find some words.

I shed my tears upon the hearse of her that is deceased, whose loss I lament. But my dearest, let me not renew your grief by speaking of my own sadness, for I know you will have grieved enough, if not too much already. Let us give thanks for her life, and also that you should have been made the joyful grandmother of a son, however shortly. They are at rest with God.

You say you fear I might be angry with you concerning the matter of Frankie's marriage. Oh, my dear heart, how could you fear such a thing from me? You know I never yet spoke an angry word to you, nor conceived an angry thought towards you, nor do I now, nor shall I ever, for you never gave me the least cause, and I believe you never will. Let us praise the Lord who has so united our hearts together in such a love that it is a thing scarce possible to be angry with one another.

It was a hot night. In the bed behind him, Ned muttered and tried to move. Will went over and turned down his blanket to let him cool. He looked at him for a while, waiting for his breath to become more regular in sleep, then went back to the table.

Your old friend, Mr R., is yet living, but is scarce capable of any rational discourse, his understanding, memory and speech do so much fail him, and seems not to take much notice of anything that is either done or said, but patiently bears all things and never complains of anything. I have sometimes wondered much at this dispensation of the Lord towards him. The Lord help us to profit by all, and to wait with patience upon Him, till we shall see what end He will make of us.

There was a fit of coughing from the bed, and more muttering. He went to look at Ned again. He seemed agitated by something. For the first time, Will sensed the end was near. Was his father-in-law dying in the hope and expectation of resurrection, or was his faith now lost to him, like his belief in the cause he had fought for? He knelt beside the bed and took his hand. 'Ned? Can you hear me? Our struggle was just. The Lord was with us. We have borne witness to the truth, you and I. Tell me you know it. Give me a sign that you are ready to meet God in the certainty of mercy and the life to come.' But the only sound was Ned's breathing, creakier perhaps than before, with a slight rattle, as if he was finding the effort difficult.

Your old friend, being asked just now whether he desired anything more to be added concerning himself, said I desire nothing but to acquaint myself with J; Chr: & that fullness that is in him for those that believe and have interest in him. This sentence he uttered with some stops, yet with more freedom and clearness than usual.

He sealed the letter and gave it to Russell to dispatch to Boston the following morning.

Two days later, when he went into Ned's room to wash him and give him breakfast, he found him, as so often, with his eyes open, staring at the door, waiting for him, but even before he touched his shoulder, he knew that he was dead.

He and Russell made the coffin together out of some of the seasoned oak planks stored in the barn, and at nightfall, hidden by the darkness, they carried it into the house and up the stairs. Will took off Ned's nightshirt and dressed him in his old cavalry coat and boots, then they lifted his body, Will at his head and Russell at his feet, laid him in the coffin and placed it on the bed.

Outside, at the back of the house, Russell's second son, Jonathan, now a hefty sixteen-year-old, and Abraham, the black slave, were waiting for them. They set about digging a grave in the moonlight, close to the cellar wall, beyond sight of the road and the nearest houses. The work to start with was easy, the topsoil sandy. But then they hit compacted stones and roots and had to take it in turns, wielding a pickaxe as well as shovels. The sound of metal striking rock carried on the still August air so clearly, Will was sure it could be heard from one end of Hadley to the other. Even so, nobody came to see what was going on. They went deep, the full six feet, and when it was dug, they brushed the dirt from their clothes and went up to Ned's room to fetch him. Just before they nailed down the lid, Will kissed him on the forehead. His wrinkles had gone. His skin was smooth and cold and white as marble, like the effigy of a knight in an English church. In his army coat, he looked as if was sleeping on the eve of a battle.

The four of them struggled to carry the coffin down the staircase. Only when they reached the parlour were they were able to lift it onto their shoulders and carry him to his final rest with dignity. Once they had lowered him into the grave, Reverend Russell recited the burial prayer – 'dust to dust, ashes to ashes' – then they covered the coffin with flagstones to protect it against marauding animals and shovelled in the earth.

By the time they had finished, it was getting light. The distant mountain was pink in the dawn. The others left. Will lingered, reluctant to go. He contemplated the rough patch of unmarked ground, so far from home. For once, no prayers came to him, no phrases from the Scriptures. He stood there for a long time, until he heard voices coming closer along the road. Then he remembered where he was, and hurried indoors so as not to be seen.

CHAPTER THIRTY-THREE

FTER THAT, HE fell into a deep despair, and lacked the energy to leave his room. Without Ned to care for, his days were empty. He lost all interest in trading, failed to order goods from Hartford or keep his appointment with the Norwottuck woman. He stripped Ned's bed, brought his belongings across the landing and put them with his own — his sword and pistols, a couple of shirts, a pair of stockings, his telescope. It made him weep to see how little there was.

Autumn came, and winter, and no letters from England. His fifty-seventh birthday passed at the end of April, unremarked. With Ned gone, he thought more about his family than he had since he came to America; not just Frances and the children, but his mother, who had died when he was eight, his father, the unflinching Reverend Goffe, from whom he had inherited his zeal for Christ and his gift for preaching, and his brothers, Stephen and John, both priests – John a moderate, Stephen, the eldest, a zealot on the other side, a Catholic convert, God save him and show him the error of his ways. Were they even still alive? All he knew for certain was that he would never see them again.

Spring brought a slight revival in his spirits. He forced himself to order a new selection of goods to barter, and towards the end of June, a few days after the summer solstice, he set out to walk to the forest. He left long before dawn, when the moon was full and the stars were bright, and when he was midway across Pine Plain, a most startling phenomenon occurred. The moon gradually began to shine blood red, then went through all its phases, from full to crescent, and vanished into darkness before starting to wax again – a disturbing and total eclipse that set all of Hadley's cattle bellowing in alarm. Will spread out his coat on the damp grass and lay down and watched it, and then the shooting stars that followed. Such a portent he had never seen before, although he had read of it in the Book of Revelation, when the sixth seal was broken: 'The sun became black as sackcloth of hair, and the moon became as blood.' The sky was alive with prognostications, more so even than in 1666. Something terrible was coming. He could feel it.

After an hour or more, he gathered his sack of household tools. He was in two minds whether it was wise to continue, but he had come so far it seemed foolish to go back. He resumed his journey.

It was one of those summer nights when it never becomes properly dark. He could make out the path through the trees quite clearly. He wondered what the Indians, with all their primitive heathen superstitions, would have made of the eclipse. Perhaps it would deepen their hostility to the foreigners. Once again he was glad of the comfort of the pistol in his pocket, although if they attacked him, he would soon be overwhelmed.

The moment he came down the track into the Norwottucks' camp, he sensed that something was wrong. Hunched against the silver of the lake, the dozens of wigwams were black and silent.

No fires had been left burning outside. He approached the nearest hut. The animal skin that usually covered the entrance was missing. Inside, it was deserted, everything gone – bedding, cooking utensils, food. There was no need for him to check the rest of the settlement. It had clearly been abandoned. He went to one of the firepits and ran his hand through the ash. It was still just warm. They must have left only in the last day or two.

He retrieved his sack and set off back through the forest to Hadley, half walking, half running, imagining evil spirits all around him, heedless of the branches that slapped his face and the vines that caught at his ankles.

That morning, he told John Russell of the Norwottucks' disappearance. 'Have they ever done such a thing before?'

'Never. And this is their fishing season, when they always stay close to the river.'

Russell went off to talk to Peter Tilton and the other leading men of the town.

A few days later, news from Boston gave the empty camp an ominous significance. It seemed that at the beginning of the month, three Indians had been convicted of murdering an Englishman, and had been hanged. Among them was the chief counsellor to the Indian *sachem*, Metacomet, leader of the Wampanoag people in south-east Massachusetts, who styled himself King Philip. In a fury at the insult, he had united the scattered tribes of New England into a war coalition to drive out the foreigners once and for all. The Norwottucks near Hadley must have abandoned their camp to join him.

'Our position here is most exposed,' said Russell. It was the first time Will had seen him seriously worried. 'We must wait upon events and pray.'

At first the fighting was all in the south of the state, around Providence. But one afternoon in the first week of August, Will heard shouts and the rumble of approaching ox carts. His side window looked east, towards Pine Plain, and from it came a sorry little convoy of three carts, a few dozen sheep and a couple of horses, with families trudging alongside, their faces and clothing blackened by smoke, their possessions piled in two of the carts and wounded sprawled in the other. They passed beneath his window, and a minute later he heard a loud hammering at the door.

It was the first time for years that he had been forced to hide.

He lit a candle and went into the passage, lifted the planks, climbed down the ladder a few rungs, replaced the boards above his head and descended the rest of the way to the cramped space. He could hear Russell's voice – commiserating, soothing, occasionally outraged – and that of another man, who must have been standing close to the fireplace. Pressing his ear to the brickwork, he was able to make out most of what he said. From what he could gather (the man was in a state of shock, and his story tumbled out in haphazard order), they had fled from Brookfield, a tiny place about twenty-five miles to the east of Hadley. Earlier in the week, a certain Captain Hutchinson and about twenty men of the Massachusetts militia had arrived to try to pacify the local Indians, had been lured into an ambush three miles out of Brookfield and lost half their force, had retreated to the house of a man named John Ayres, into which the entire community had crammed themselves, and had managed to hold off the besieging natives for two full days and nights, while the town around them was burned to the ground. Two settlers had been killed – one shot dead at a window and another when he ventured outside. On the evening of the third day, they had been relieved by the arrival of a Captain Parker with four dozen soldiers. The Indians had retreated, and the survivors had scattered to seek refuge where they could.

More people came inside, more voices added to the hubbub, and after that Will could understand little of what was said. An hour passed and gradually the volume diminished. The door closed. He heard footsteps on the stairs and then the boards were lifted. John Russell's face appeared.

'You can come out now. It's safe.'

'From what I overheard, I don't know that "safe" is the word I'd choose.'

'Indeed not. Those poor people.' Russell put out his hand to help him up. In Will's room, he sat on the bed and put his head in his hands. 'Because of you, I had to send them away to find shelter in other parts of the town.'

Will sat next to him. 'If that's the case, I'll leave today, John. I'll not deprive desperate women and children of a bed.'

'No, you can't leave, not now. As you say, it isn't safe, especially for a solitary traveller in the middle of a war.' Russell looked up. He shook his head and smiled sadly. 'And the old problem arises, my dear friend – where would you go? But the fact remains, this is a large house and I fear I've raised suspicions by not taking anyone in. No doubt there will be more coming – soldiers too. You may have to get used to spending more time in your hiding place.'

'I can't expose you to such a danger.'

'Danger lurks all around us. No more talk of leaving. Will you pray with me?'

They got down on their knees and prayed silently together, and for the thousandth time, Will wished Ned was still with him. He would have known what to do.

★

That night, while the rest of the household slept, Will went softly down the stairs in his stockinged feet. He sat on the steps and pulled on his boots, then ventured out into the night. *This* was what Ned would have done, he had decided: reconnoitre the terrain of the battle.

God will grant us victory if He wills it, but He expects us mortals also to make sound plans. It was a risk, but he calculated it was warranted.

He had never walked around the town before. He went south, past a dozen houses, all the way to the great broad expanse of the Connecticut, shining in the moonlight, then followed the riverbank west, past the ferryboat, to the point where it curved sharply and came back on itself, exactly like the bend of an elbow. Where the joint would have been was what they called the Great Meadow, or the Honey Pot – fertile common land. Then, as he moved east, the houses and their lots began again. It was the perfect natural spot for a settlement. He could understand why the Norwottuck would have regretted parting with it.

In the middle of the town was a green with the newly built meeting house. That is the obvious place, Ned whispered in his mind. A touch too obvious, maybe? He studied it for a while in the moonlight, then moved on. He estimated that the circumference of the town was perhaps three miles. With frequent stops, it took him two hours to complete his circuit.

When he was back in his room, he drew a sketch from memory, and in the morning, he showed it to Reverend Russell.

'You walked around the town?' Russell was shocked.

'No one saw me – and that, John, is a problem in itself. An entire tribe of natives could have moved around unnoticed.'

'There is supposed to be a nightly patrol.'

'If so, it isn't good enough. To cover such an area, you need three patrols. The town is not easily defensible, but we do have one advantage. Three sides are protected by the river, so if they come – unless they have canoes, which would be vulnerable to defensive fire – it must be from the east. Every man in Hadley is armed, I take it?'

'Of course.'

'With what? Muskets? Pistols? Matchlock or flintlock?'

'A mix of both.'

'They should carry them at all times, even working in the fields. Spare weapons and ammunition should be lodged in the meeting house – swords, pikes, daggers, anything that may be used. There is a signal agreed in case of attack?'

'The meeting house bell is to be rung. But let us pray it will not come to that. I have had word from Boston that a company of dragoons is now searching in the area. That should deter an assault.'

'Excellent,' said Will, though he could not help but wonder how farmers mounted on horseback, however heavily armed, might fare against the Indian warriors he had seen in the Norwottuck camp.

He spent the rest of the day preparing, shifting Ned's old bedding down the ladder into the cavity behind the fireplace, along with most of their possessions, their money – he still thought of it as theirs – a stock of candles, a pitcher of water, their swords, pistols, bullets and powder. Afterwards, he kept watch from his window with Ned's telescope. Towards the end of the afternoon, he noticed a column of smoke rising from the forest. It grew slowly over the next few hours, spreading like a thundercloud above the trees, immense and ominous. Some of the townspeople, armed with muskets and pikes, passed beneath his window and went out onto the meadow for a better look. There was cheering.

That evening, when Russell brought him his supper, his face was grim. 'Our soldiers have burned the Norwottucks' settlement – fifty wigwams torched.'

Will was aghast. 'Why?' He thought of the woman he dealt with, her unfailing offers of food.

'Revenge for Brookfield.'

'But we do not even know for sure they were the ones who attacked Brookfield.'

'I doubt they were. However, they are Indians. That is sufficient. Daniel Gookin has written to tell me that even the Christian Indians have been seized and put in irons. He is accused of being too sympathetic and will lose his seat on the governing council. Now it is a war to the death. There is something else you need to know – the soldiers will be here tomorrow, and every house in Hadley is ordered to provide a billet.'

'I am ready.'

'I presume they will be out often on patrol. I shall bring you food and water whenever I am able. But it will not be comfortable. In the meantime, I shall try to find you another place to stay.'

'Don't trouble yourself about my comfort, John. It will still be better than a cell in the Tower.'

Russell brought him a stock of food and more water, which he carried down into his shelter. The next day, he stationed himself at his window again, and around midday saw a line of dust rising on Pine Plain. He trained his telescope and a minute later was able to make out the figures of mounted soldiers, fifty or sixty at a guess, galloping towards Hadley. He picked up his Bible, took a last look around his empty room, and descended to his hiding place.

★

The gap behind the fireplace was eight feet long but only four across. The boards were roughly four feet above his head, so at least he could stand upright. To make room for his mattress, he had to take down the ladder and lay it lengthwise against the wall. Once that was done, he felt as if he was in a tomb, with only a single candle flame to pierce the darkness.

It was the last week of August, stiflingly hot. There was nothing he could do except lie on his mattress, damp with sweat, and listen to the soldiers. Their noises all around him were inescapable, like Job's tormentors, or hallucinations in a fever. They came and went from the stables through the parlour, clumped up the stairs, shifted furniture in the bedrooms, thumped along the passage above his head. Once, one of them complained that the boards were loose and tested them with the toe of his boot, but mercifully someone – an officer, by the tone of his command – called him away. The militiamen talked and laughed and swore and prayed and snored. Sometimes they shouted in terror in their sleep.

For a while he tried to differentiate between them – the Ipswich man, the Swansea man, the young one whose wife was with child – but there were so many he lost track of them, and eventually gave up. It was impossible to tell the time of day except when the house fell silent for several hours. Even then, he could not sleep. He stretched, did press-ups, paced the few yards in either direction. There was barely room to turn. Otherwise, he read the Bible endlessly by candlelight, lying on his side, until his eyes ached, returning again and again to the thirty-first psalm, which spoke to him directly as never before.

Have mercy upon me, O LORD, for I am in trouble: mine eye is consumed with grief, yea, my soul and my belly.

For my life is spent with grief, and my years with sighing: my strength faileth because of mine iniquity, and my bones are consumed.

I was a reproach among all mine enemies, but especially among my neighbours, and a fear to mine acquaintance: they that did see me without fled from me.

I am forgotten as a dead man out of mind: I am like a broken vessel . . .

He was sure he would go mad. He was sure he *was* mad. He tried to think if any other human soul had lived a life such as his, and could not conceive of one. For what terrible sins was he being punished? For what purpose was he being tested?

The days passed. The house was never empty. Russell never came.

O love the LORD, all ye his saints: for the LORD preserveth the faithful, and plentifully rewardeth the proud doer.

Be of good courage, and he shall strengthen your heart, all ye that hope in the LORD.

He tried to welcome the curses as blessings, to greet his trials as chances to move nearer to God, as he had with Ned's illness. But it grew harder, especially when not only his food and water were almost gone, but most frightening of all, his candles. The prospect of having no light at all was intolerable.

On the seventh day, he cried for hours, his hand over his mouth to deaden the sound, until at last, for the first time in a week, he fell into an abyss of sleep. When he awoke, there was absolute silence.

★

He couldn't tell how long he had been unconscious, or even whether it was day or night. Always there had been sounds of some sort, whatever the hour, if only creaks or coughs, but now there was nothing. He lay there listening.

Finally he got to his feet. The movement guttered his last stub of candle, sent his shadow dancing across the brick; then it went out. He felt around in the pitch black for his sword, tucked two of the pistols and their powder and bullets into his pockets, slipped the telescope inside his coat. He leaned the ladder back up, moving it around until he found the joist. He put one foot on the bottom rung. Slowly he began to climb. When he reached the top, he waited for a few more minutes, straining his ears again, then pushed up one of the boards. The light struck his face so painfully he had to turn his head and shut his eyes. It was a moment or two before he could open them fully. He came up into the passage and crouched there. Then he straightened, pulled out one of his pistols, and with his sword in his other hand edged along the wall to his bedroom.

It looked to have been abandoned in a hurry, possessions and dirty plates strewn across the floor.

He went over to the window. The plain appeared as deserted as the house. He felt a prickle of fear. Something must be terribly wrong. He took out his telescope and began to scan the open country – methodically, north to south, starting in the distance. The lens locked onto a smudge, like a smear of dust, a couple of miles away. Had the soldiers found something else to burn? He adjusted the focus a fraction. No. Not smoke – figures, moving. And they were more than a smudge now. Men on foot. A few on horseback. The image wavered lazily in the haze of morning heat. Were the soldiers returning? But again, no – these men were not in military formation. They were scattered in a wide line across the plain. And those on foot were running, raising dust like a lit fuse burning straight towards Hadley.

He closed the telescope, hurried out of the room and down the stairs. He was shouting, his voice strange in his ears after days of silence. 'John! John! Anyone?'

He threw open the front door and strode across the yard to the gate. Not a soul to be seen, as if the place had been abandoned.

He sprinted towards the centre of town – past the empty houses towards the green, the meeting house. He paused on the threshold. He could hear Russell's voice, preaching a sermon. He hesitated. But what did it matter now if he was seen? He threw open the door and marched up the aisle. Two hundred or more surprised faces turned to look at him. Russell was in the pulpit. Will climbed the steps and stood beside him at the lectern. For the first time in many years, he found himself facing a congregation. So many people. He waved his arms.

'An attack! They're coming! Arm yourselves! Ring the bell!'

For a moment, no one reacted. Then they started muttering to one another. And of course, he realised, why wouldn't they? What a sight he must have been to them – a stranger, old, griz-zled, wild-haired, wild-eyed, his face as white as ash after his years indoors and his days in his cell, brandishing a pistol, wearing his old Cromwellian coat. A madman.

Russell looked at him in shock. 'Are you certain?'

'I've seen them, coming across the plain. Where are the soldiers?'

'Gone to Deerfield – it's burning. There's fighting.'

'For God's sake, John, we must be quick! They mean to attack here as well!'

Russell's glance searched his eyes, trying to gauge if he was entirely sane, then turned to his followers. He shouted above the murmuring, 'He speaks the truth! Ring the bell! Lock the door!'

Suddenly, activity. The scrape of pews being pushed back. A clatter of muskets being produced from underneath them. Wails of alarm. Cries to God. The bell ringing.

Will jumped down from the pulpit and started pushing his way back towards the doors. As he walked, he surveyed the windows. Too many. Too large. And set in a building made entirely of wood. Fire was plainly the natives' chosen weapon. They would burn them out. For sure, that was what he would do – what he had done, countless times in the war.

'Open the door,' he said. It had just been locked. He hammered on it with the butt of his pistol. 'Open it!' he demanded.

Someone produced a key.

He stepped outside, half expecting to find the enemy, but the green was clear. Quite close, on the northern side of the grass, no more than fifty yards away, was a house.

'There!' He pointed. 'Every man with a musket, follow me.'

He set off a few paces, then stopped. Nobody had moved.

Russell was just behind him. 'He knows his business,' he said. 'Do as he says.'

'Fetch water,' Will shouted over his shoulder, 'to put out the fires. Then lock the doors and stay inside.'

He led a detachment of perhaps forty musketeers – some so old they could barely keep up, others scarcely more than boys – across the green and into the yard of the house. 'Find a position at a window, but don't open it. Stay quiet – not a sound – and stay out of sight. No one to fire till I give the order. Then pick a target, aim and shoot. Understood?'

A chorus of 'Aye!'

They were following him without question now – the only one among them who seemed to know what he was doing. By God, he would make soldiers of them yet.

They deployed into the house. Two storeys. He moved from window to window. Six faced south to the church. Four men at each, the rest of the force spread between the windows east and west. He went downstairs and stood at the door. God forgive him, he had not felt so alive in years. The women of the town were passing buckets of water from hand to hand in a line stretching back to the well. If they were not careful, they would be caught in the open. He cupped his hands to his mouth and shouted, 'Enough!' He gestured to them to retreat. The line broke up and they hurried into the meeting house. The door closed. And just in time, for barely a minute later, he saw the first of the attackers moving stealthily onto the green, holding a musket across his bare chest.

He stepped inside, closed the door and ran upstairs.

Pistols cocked, he stood behind the men crouched at the window and watched. Thirty attackers, maybe more, armed with muskets and bows, some on horseback. Young men, well muscled, half naked, they moved straight towards the meeting house. The riders peered down through the windows. Another two on foot tried the door. Suddenly they started yelling – no plan of attack, no strategy, no fear, just rage and excitement. A few shots rang out. The sound of smashing glass. Then a flaming arrow, beautifully aimed, swooped across the green and through a broken window. The others stood watching to see what would happen, yelling their encouragement. Another fiery arrow was unleashed. This one hit the timber frame just below the roof and stuck there, burning.

Will aimed one of his pistols, even though it was useless at this distance. 'Fire!'

The house seemed to explode with noise and smoke. The sting of sulphur briefly blinded him.

When he looked again, the green was carnage – the war party

scattered, men sprawled on the ground, riderless horses stamped-
ing in fear, one man with his foot caught being dragged across
the grass. Those who were still upright were looking around to
see where the shots had come from. One fired his musket at the
house.

'Reload!'

Half a minute to reload a flintlock – prime the pan, ram the
powder and the ball down the barrel – and take fresh aim. In the
meantime, the Indians had started running towards the house.

'Fire!'

He used Ned's pistol, saw his target drop, drew his sword.

'Charge!'

He was the first man down the stairs. They poured out of the
house. Bodies on the grass. Some of them still alive. The rest of
the attackers running. All very young. He gave chase to one who
was wounded in the leg, limping, hopping like an injured bird.
He caught him at the edge of the green and hacked at his neck.
He went down with a cry of pain. Behind him he could hear
gunshots and screams as the righteous men of Hadley finished
off the wounded.

*God made them as stubble to our swords . . . Give glory, all the glory,
to God.*

He stood astride the Indian, grasped the hilt of his sword in both
hands, raised it and plunged the tip of the blade with all his force
into his victim's sinewy back. He pulled it out and wiped off the
blood on the grass. Then he walked back to the Russells' house,
up the stairs to the passage, climbed down the ladder, replaced the
boards, and sat huddled on his mattress in the darkness – his hands
clasped around his legs, his knees drawn up, his head pressed hard
between them – shaking with cold despite the summer heat.

★

Hours later. Shouting. A rumble of people talking all at once – a crowd, by the sound of it, milling around in the parlour and the yard. He lifted his head to listen. He could hear Russell's deep voice – soothing, placatory, and finally commanding – then the door slammed. Heavy footsteps ascended the stairs and passed above his head. The boards lifted. A shaft of light. Russell's head appeared.

'Will?'

This was the situation, as Russell explained it. Twelve Indians were dead. Three Englishmen wounded. No wounded natives had been left alive. The survivors had fled. The fire on the roof of the meeting house had been put out. A mass grave was being dug on the edge of the Great Meadow.

'They were all very young. I wonder if the elders of the tribe even knew what they were planning. It seems the main fighting is all to the north, around Deerfield.'

'So, we slaughtered boys?'

'Murderous youths,' corrected Russell. 'They would have killed us if they could. You saved the town. People are calling you an angel sent from Heaven. They are looking for you. They want to know who you are.'

An angel!

'I had to show myself, John. There was no choice.'

'Yes, and God be thanked that you did. But you see how it is? I've ordered them away for the present, but they can talk of nothing else. It is a certainty they'll return.'

'Then I must leave.'

'Yes,' sighed Russell, 'I fear you must – and soon, before the garrison returns from Deerfield. I've arranged for you to stay in Hartford. There's a good Puritan there named Captain Bull, seventy or thereabouts, an old sailor, who lives alone with his wife and is willing to take you in.'

'Good. I'll go tonight.'

'No, no! The hurry's not so great as that! Stay and take another meal, at least. I'll find a man to guide you tomorrow.'

'I have no need of a guide. You say the fighting is all to the north. Well, Hartford is the opposite way, and I know easily enough how to find it – merely follow the river south.' Will smiled and clasped Russell's shoulder. 'You see how well I know the country after all this time? I can be halfway there by morning. I should like a horse, though.'

'Of course.'

'Which I shall pay for.'

'How can you suggest such a thing?' Russell looked offended.

'I should prefer to leave with all things straight between us. You have done so much these past eleven years.' He looked around the room. *Eleven years* . . . In truth, he would not be sorry to get away. 'To everything there is a season, John. And my season here is done.'

His belongings were already packed. It was merely a matter of fetching them up from his hiding space and loading them onto the horse in the barn. By half past seven, the sun had set, and he was ready. In the golden dusk he walked around to the back of the house. The grass had grown over Ned's grave. Nothing marked it. The birds sang their evening chorus. The breeze stirred the leaves of the apple trees, and the last of the summer bees hummed among the wild flowers. He knelt and put his palm to the ground. There ought to be a headstone, but he knew there never could be. *Here lie the bones of Colonel Edward Whalley – husband, father, man of God – who broke Prince Rupert's line at Marston*

Moor. He stayed like that for some time, then stood and walked back to the barn.

Nobody observed him leave the town. By midnight he was at Springfield. He rested a few hours in the woods a mile beyond it, and at first light moved on. He reckoned it was safe enough to travel in the daytime – the authorities would hardly be looking for him in the middle of a war. Still, when he met a column of troops marching north, he was careful to put his head down, and it was a relief when they passed without giving him a glance. In the middle of the afternoon he reached the ferry station at Windsor, crowded with people carrying their belongings, heading south to safer territory. He answered their questions curtly, to avoid being drawn into conversation. No, he had seen no Indians. Yes, he had heard that Brookfield and Deerfield had both been burned. No, he did not agree that the war must go on until every last Indian had been killed – he did not mind what the Scriptures said about the right of Christians to slaughter the heathens: it was contrary to Christ's teachings. After that, they left him alone.

At nightfall he entered Hartford, and had barely gone a hundred yards before he was stopped by a patrol carrying pikes and muskets. There was a curfew, was he not aware of that? Who was he? What kept him out so late? He gave his name as Walter Goldsmith and said he was looking for the road to the South Meadow, for Ward's lot. He had no idea who Ward was; he simply wanted to avoid mentioning Bull's name, and Russell had told him his lot was next to Ward's. They waved him on his way.

It was dark when he reached his destination. A lamp had been set in the window. A man came to the door – short, wiry, the antithesis of his name.

Will removed his hat. 'Captain Bull?' How many times had he done this – greeted a stranger in the dark? 'John Russell sent me.'

'Thomas Bull, sir.' A handshake. 'God be thanked for your safe arrival. My wife, Susannah . . . Let me show you to your room . . .'

The familiar routine. Up a winding staircase to an attic. A narrow bed. A table. A chair. An iron-hooped chest – a seaman's chest – with a basin and a large jug of water set upon it. It occurred to him that he had no means of letting Frances know where he was or what had happened to him. He felt so exhausted and lonely, a sob rose in his throat. He put his hand to his mouth and disguised it with a cough.

'This will do me very well. God bless you, Captain Bull, for taking me in.'

Once he was alone, he took his candle over to the tiny window. The world beyond it was completely dark. He could see nothing except the reflection of his face, watery in the rippled glass, pale as a drowned man's.

CHAPTER THIRTY-FOUR

FOUR YEARS LATER, in Paris, on a July afternoon in 1679, an Englishman left his house in rue Saint-Denis and set off on his habitual daily walk. Montorgueil was a rough neighbourhood, in the city's northern quarter, a district of narrow winding streets and wooden houses, gambling dens and fortune-tellers, thieves and whores. In his left hand he carried a stout stick, in his right-hand coat pocket a small pistol. Even at sixty, he gave the impression of a man who could handle himself in a fight. A familiar figure, L'Anglais – people generally stepped out of his way. He was bearded, and heavier around the waist than he had been in London, and beneath his periwig he was almost bald, but his shoulders were as broad as ever, and he still exuded a faint sense of menace, as if he knew something about you that you did not want known.

He walked, unmolested, down the centre of the street, avoiding the chamber pots occasionally emptied out of the upper windows, and a few minutes later emerged onto the right bank of the Seine. The weather was warm, the river stinking even more than usual. He strolled alongside the turbid brown water, stopping at some of the wicker boxes where the booksellers had laid out their wares, picking up the odd volume and leafing through it. Nothing took his fancy. Too much religion. The Pont Neuf was a likelier bet. Spread out along the parapets of the bridge were all manner of quacks and hustlers – purveyors of wooden teeth, glass eyes, and Spanish fly for drooping cocks; card sharps and ticket touts; jugglers and acrobats. He felt a pickpocket brush his coat and knocked the woman's hand away with his stick.

In the middle of the bridge was a *vendeur* who specialised in the latest English publications. This was more like it. Fifty *sols* secured him a two-week-old copy of the *London Intelligencer*, stamped by the censor as fit to read. He wandered on across the Pont Neuf to the Île de Notre-Dame, but by now the jostling crowds were boring him – he was often bored – and after a quick circuit of the Sainte-Chapelle, he turned for home.

In truth, Nayler had been bored most days ever since Hyde had died in exile, and that was four and a half years ago.

The Lord Chancellor had fallen, exactly as he had feared – felled like some great ancient oak by a combination of old age, rotting limbs, heavy storms, and the well-aimed blows of his enemies. The Great Fire had first exposed his weakness. Not long afterwards, the Dutch had burnt the English fleet at the mouth of the Thames, a national humiliation for which he was unjustly held responsible. Hostile graffiti had been scrawled on the walls of his enormous house, alleging that it had been paid for by corruption. His gout and age and corpulence rendered him not only immobile but repulsive to the court.

Even so, he might have survived, with royal protection, had it not been for his unconcealed disgust at the morals of the King, whose habitual greeting to any woman entering his presence had become to feel her breasts and thrust his hand between her legs. There had been a terrible final interview between the Lord Chancellor and His Majesty, with people gathered in the garden outside to eavesdrop, among them Lady Castlemaine. The certain fate of impeachment by Parliament, imprisonment in the Tower, followed by execution by beheading was bluntly laid out, with the King claiming he was powerless to save him. Exile was his only hope of survival. As he was carried out of the meeting, Nayler at his side, the King's chief mistress had laughed and pointed. 'He cannot rule. He cannot even walk!'

'O madam, is it you?' responded Hyde. 'Pray remember that if you live, you will also grow old.'

A coach had been arranged to take him along the Thames to Erith, where a ship was waiting. When Nayler came to see him off from Clarendon House, his master had looked so forlorn that on impulse at the last minute he had jumped into the seat opposite. Hyde had looked at him, nodded, and looked away, as if he had expected it.

'I am grateful, Mr Nayler, but be warned – I cannot pay you.'

They had sailed to France and settled in Montpellier, then Moulin, and finally in Rouen. The old man had been an embarrassment to the French, who didn't want him. On one occasion he had nearly been killed by a mob of English sailors demanding to be paid the arrears on their wages. After the initial shock of losing power, he had occupied himself, like many another ruined politician, by writing his memoirs – with Nayler acting as his secretary – a brilliant work of rolling prose and pointed insight; and when those were done, at sixty-four, he lost the desire to live. According to his doctor, he had eaten himself to death. The King, who had refused his pleas to be allowed home to die, graciously consented to permit his body to be returned for burial in

Westminster Abbey. Nayler had been due to accompany the massive corpse to London, but at the last minute he had succumbed once more to impulse. This time he had clambered *out* of the coach.

What was there left for him in England? Nothing. The place disgusted him.

Nokes, with whom he had maintained a regular correspondence, and who was now secretary to the clerk of the Privy Council, wrote to him about the funeral, which took place in January: *At six o'clock in the evening we gathered in the Old Palace Yard, at the little brick house going up to the House of Lords, & from there the coffin was borne to the door of the abbey, where, it being met by the Dean & Chapter, my Lord Clarendon was laid to rest in darkness with only the faces of a few old friends to see it.*

Once he had sorted out Hyde's papers and dispatched them to his heirs, Nayler had drifted from Rouen to Paris, rented the squalid timber-framed house in rue Saint-Denis that was all he could afford, acquired a mistress, gambled successfully at cards, drank too much cognac, acquired a taste for laudanum, and generally went to ruin, his life entirely lacking aim or purpose – until that July afternoon.

Catherine Louvois was the illegitimate child of the illegitimate descendant of some noble family in the Loire, reduced to dependence on a succession of men whose standing in society had declined over the years in direct proportion to her fading beauty. Now she found herself at forty living with Nayler in Montorgueil, and God alone knew what her next step down might be. She was out when he arrived home. She was out a lot these days. He was sure she was unfaithful. He didn't mind. He would have been unfaithful himself, if he could be bothered.

He poured himself a glass of cognac and sat down in an arm-chair with the *London Intelligencer*. There was little news of any interest. He rather regretted parting with his fifty *sols*. Indeed, he was on the point of throwing the newsletter aside when his eye was caught by a small headline: *The Angel of Hadley*.

Intelligence reaches us from His Majesty's Province of New England of a most singular incident in that late Struggle with the Indians known as the King Philip's War. The little remote town of Hadley, close by Connecticut River, at a time of public worship in September 1675, was Surpris'd by Natives called the Norwottuck, and thrown into the utmost confu-sion, and all seemed lost, when there appeared in their midst a grave elderly Person. In his mien and dress he differed from the rest of the People. He did not merely encourage them to defend themselves, but put himself at their head, rallied, instructed, and led them on to encounter the Enemy, who by this means were repulsed with heavy losses to the Heathens and none to the Christians. As suddenly as he had manifested himself, however, the Deliverer of Hadley disappeared, never to be seen again. The People were left in Consternation, utterly unable to account for this Exceptional Phenomenon, except that it be conjured by the Providence of God, and the Stranger himself an Angel, sent from Heaven to confound the Savages.

Nayler set his cognac down on the floor and read the passage a second time, then a third.

Since leaving England, he had managed to forget about the regicides. There was nothing he could do about them. Why tor-ment himself? Now they thrust their way back into his mind.

Whalley would be eighty; he could safely be regarded as dead. But Goffe? Goffe, if his memory served, was born in the same year as himself.

He read it a fourth time.

'By God,' he muttered, 'I do believe it's him.'

He tried to tell himself the notion was ridiculous. There must have been dozens of old soldiers living in obscurity in New England in 1675 who could have put on their uniforms at a moment of crisis and sallied forth to fight. And there might be any number of reasons why they had afterwards 'disappeared, never to be seen again'.

Also, it had happened nearly four years ago. This 'grave elderly Person' might well have since died. And even supposing he was still alive, and it was indeed Goffe, he would scarcely have lingered in Hadley – a place so tiny, Nayler had never even heard of it. If he had broken cover, he would have been obliged to move on at once. He could be anywhere by now.

He sat motionless and brooding in his chair as the day ended and the street lamp was lit beneath his window.

He heard the front door open, Catherine coming in, her voice calling out to him. '*Es-tu là, mon amour?*' Her tone was unusually soft and affectionate, which generally meant she had just made love to someone else.

Wearily he responded. '*Oui, ma chérie, je suis là.*'

Why did he even hesitate? There had been nothing to keep him in England when Hyde went into exile. There was nothing to keep him in France now.

The trail was warm. The hunt was on again.

He told her the next morning that pressing business demanded his return to London. He assured her he would be away no longer than a couple of months. He gave her all the money he could spare, and his permission, if she started to run short, to sell some of his possessions, beginning with his books. They both suspected he would not be returning, and their farewell was more affecting than either of them had expected, clinging to one another like a pair of survivors before they parted. By the middle of August, he was in London.

He took a room above a tavern in Milford Lane, still as rough as ever, but at least it was familiar. From his window he could see his old chambers in Essex House. He set up his miniature of Sarah on the nightstand, then lay on the bed and studied his thin file on Goffe, which had accompanied him on all his travels – the message he had sent his wife before his departure in 1660, the letter she had written to him that Nokes had intercepted in 1662, his likeness as a young man, the record of his attendance as a judge at the King's trial – he had attended every session – the report in the *London Intelligencer* and various notes Nayler had compiled over the years. When he had finished his planning, he took his file and went to see Nokes.

It was an odd sensation to walk his old route along the Strand to Whitehall, and even odder to be stopped at the door of the palace and to have to send up a message that he would like a word. When Nokes came down, he walked straight past him, and Nayler had to call him back. 'Mr Nokes, I am here.'

Nokes turned and peered at him. 'Mr Nayler, is it you?' He could not conceal his shock. 'I did not recognise you.'

'Oh come, is it really as bad as that? I am older, stouter and a great deal balder, but not alas any richer or wiser. May I trespass on your time a little?'

'Of course, sir. I shall always have time for you.'

He led him up the staircase and along the corridor to Nayler's old office. For a few minutes, they made polite conversation. Nayler asked after Nokes's wife and children, in whom he had no interest whatsoever, and related a few stories of Hyde in exile, then Nokes asked him how long he proposed to stay in London.

'That rather depends upon you.'

'Upon me, sir?' Nokes smiled uneasily. 'How so?'

'I rather believe I have located our old friend Colonel Goffe.'

At the mention of the name, Nokes's smile became somewhat fixed, and when Nayler laid the *London Intelligencer* on the table before him, open at the appropriate page, it shrivelled to nothing. 'What is this?'

'Digest it, Mr Nokes, and tell me if I am wrong to suspect our old quarry has revealed himself at last.'

He sat back and watched with satisfaction as Nokes bent his head over the paragraph. When he had finished reading, he looked up and vaguely shrugged his shoulders. 'It is a possibility, I suppose.'

'A possibility? I should say it is closer to a certainty. I am amazed no one in the government has acted upon it.'

Nokes grimaced slightly, as if he had a toothache. 'Frankly, Mr Nayler, we are no longer keeping much of a lookout for the regicides. Nearly all of them are reckoned to be dead.'

'This one is not.'

'Perhaps he is not. But even if he lives, I doubt the Council will sanction another hunt.'

'I am not proposing the involvement of the Council. I am willing to undertake the task myself.'

'I am not sure that is wise, sir.'

'It is not a matter of wisdom, but of honour. I made a vow some years ago, to one who was very dear to me, and I mean to keep it. I require two things only from you – private favours, if you will.'

'And what might they be?'

'First I would like to know the address of Mrs Frances Goffe.'

'We have not kept track of her for years.'

'But I presume you still have your network of informers amongst the Puritans?'

Nokes nodded. 'It is possible we can find her. And the other?'

'The services of your best forger.'

He spent long hours composing the letter, sitting at the table in his room in Milford Lane, Goffe's note to his wife beside him, the portrait of Sarah propped up against the candlestick. He tried to think what he would say to her if she was still alive, what infinite longing he would try to express, but each draft seemed more hopeless than the last. 'Dearest heart' seemed a safe enough beginning – that was how Goffe had addressed Frances in his note. Yet anything he wrote thereafter – *I yearn to hear your voice again, I dream of your sweet face, I have longed for your gentle caresses every hour we have been apart* – rang false when placed in the mouth of that stern fanatic. Love, he decided, was wasted on the Puritans.

The one thing he could be sure of was that Goffe would mention God, so he went next door, to the chapel of Exeter House, and spent an afternoon leafing through the Bible, looking for some appropriate quotation. He was acutely aware of sitting only a few feet away from where he had last seen Sarah, and that there in front of him was the spot where Whalley and Goffe, in all their arrogant power and bigotry, had directed a company of soldiers to prevent them celebrating Christmas – Christmas! As if it were a festival of the Devil! – and killed the best woman who ever lived. Hatred coiled within him, as sharp-toothed as on the day it had happened, twenty years ago.

He closed the Bible. It was hopeless. Come then, God, he thought, if you exist, show me what to write. He opened it again at random, and there it was.

The forger came to his room – a clerkish, scholarly man, with long white fingers stained with ink, who gave his name as Carby. He sat at the table, took off his coat and rolled up his sleeves, studied Goffe's note and asked for extra candles.

'An interesting hand,' he remarked. He made a few attempts at copying it. 'An intelligent man, but perhaps not well educated – a deficiency he attempts to conceal by over-elaboration. What is it you wish him to say? The shorter the better.'

'It is short.' Nayler gave him his composition. He had decided that brevity was the key to authenticity.

Mr Carby made no comment on the content. He worked quickly. Within a couple of hours, he had produced two versions, which he held side by side close to the candle and scrutinised carefully. 'This one, I think. The hand is freer.'

'As you wish.'

'To whom should it be addressed?'

'Mrs Frances Goffe.' Nayler spelt it out. 'Now, Mr Carby, how much do I owe you?'

'Nothing, sir. Mr Nokes has already paid.'

A couple of days later, while he was lying on his bed studying a newly purchased second-hand copy of the Bible, a liveried messenger arrived from the office of the Privy Council. He looked appalled to find himself in such mean lodgings. Nayler broke the seal on the note: *The person you seek resides at 2 Spital Yard, Bishopsgate.* That was all.

'Thank you,' he said. 'There is no reply.'

★

He set off at once, along the Thames to London Bridge, then north through the gate into the city. This was the spot where the Great Fire had started, in some wretched baker's shop. Wide areas of open ground, filled with weeds, shimmered in the afternoon heat. Still, he marvelled at how much had been rebuilt. He pressed on, past Finsbury Fields – where he had arrested Colonel Jones, walking as if he hadn't a fear in the world – past scaffolding and building sites, until he reached Bishopsgate. Spital Yard was a narrow cobbled alley of terraced houses close to the city wall. Children were playing in the street. Two men in Puritan black strolled towards him and gave him a suspicious glance. This was clearly the district where the vipers had their nest. He walked along the alley quickly. Number two was at the far end – cramped, cracked, the brickwork still scorched from the fire, apparently derelict. He turned the corner and whistled to attract the attention of one of the boys.

'Here's sixpence for you if you deliver this letter to the lady in that house. Into her hands only, mind. If she's not at home, bring it back to me, and if she asks who sent it, say a gentleman gave it you.' The boy grinned at his good fortune and took the letter. As he turned away, Nayler caught him by the arm. 'And no tricks, lad.' He tightened his grip until the boy winced. 'I'll be watching you.' He released him.

The boy ran across the road to the house and knocked on the door. For a while nothing happened, and Nayler feared the worst – the place looked uninhabited: perhaps Nokes's intelligence was out of date – but then the door opened a crack and a woman's face appeared. It was impossible at such a distance to tell if it was Frances Goffe – it was eighteen years since he had seen her. She was talking to the boy. She opened the door wider and peered up and down the street. Nayler drew back around the corner, and when he dared to look again, the door was closed. He settled down to wait.

It was a long time since Frances had heard from Will. Something seemed to have happened to make their friends in Boston reluctant to run the risk of handling his letters. Now her uncle was dead, and her only link to America had died with him, and she had been forced to move out of their old house without any means of passing on her new address. But she recognised her husband's hand well enough.

She took the letter into the tiny parlour and had to sit down to steady her nerves before she could bring herself to break the seal.

Dearest Heart, after many long years, the words so longed for may at last be spoken, as in Leviticus 25, 18–19, & if you have the strength & desire for the undertaking, which I pray you do, I implore you to carry this message to Mr Daniel Gookin in Cambridge, Massachusetts, who will render all assistance.

That was all. She had to read it several times before she grasped the meaning. He was inviting her to join him in America! She fetched her Bible and searched it for Leviticus.

Ye shall dwell in the land in safety. And the land shall yield her fruit, and ye shall eat your fill, and dwell therein in safety.

She wept. She laughed. She fell to her knees in prayer. She had given up all hope, but the Lord was good, the Lord was full of mercy. He had made her wait until the time was ripe – until Uncle William was dead, and Frankie married, and Dickie apprenticed and living with his master, and the girls with their widowed Aunt Jane in the country; he had brought her safe through plague and fire until there was nothing left to keep her from joining her husband. Hallelujah! Hallelujah! Thanks be to God! Thanks be to God in all His glory!

Nayler watched her leave the house and hurry away from him down the street, walking so quickly it was hard for him to keep up. He noticed that she didn't look back, or duck into alleyways. Her old instinct for taking precautions was forgotten in the excitement of the moment. He could scarcely believe his luck as he followed her all the way through the city to the river, to the Pool of London, where she walked along the crowded wharf, stopped to ask directions, moved on. Outside the offices of a shipping company, she finally thought to check over her shoulder, then went inside.

He lingered twenty yards from the entrance, pretending to watch the colliers from Newcastle as they were unloaded. If nothing else, her actions showed she believed that Goffe was still alive. After less than half an hour, she emerged and paused in the doorway. He watched her refasten her bonnet. She glanced in his direction, but didn't seem to see him: smiling so much in the sunshine she was apparently unaware of anything except her own happiness. And even if she had noticed him, he was sure she wouldn't have recognised him – not from a single meeting so long ago; not if his appearance had changed so much his own former secretary had walked straight past him.

She stepped onto the quayside and headed back the way she had come. He tried to imagine her slim figure beneath her dowdy gown as she wove through the crowds. It was strange how often he had thought of her.

He went to find the shipping clerk in his tiny cubicle. A bribe of ten shillings bought him a look at the passenger manifest, where she had registered herself as Frances Stephenson. A further five pounds secured him the last berth on the same ship – the *Blessing*, sailing from Gravesend to Boston three days hence, on Thursday 21 August.

CHAPTER THIRTY-FIVE

S HE BARELY HAD time to say her goodbyes, trailing on foot
from one child to another – to Frankie and her children
(two of them now, a boy and a girl) living in Clerkenwell;
to Dickie, apprenticed to be a grocer in Shoreditch, lodging with
his master; to Nan and Judith, looking after Aunt Jane, close to the
common in Clapham. She swore each of them to secrecy, showed
them the message from their father, and announced she would be
leaving before the end of the week. To their appalled objections,
she replied that there wasn't another boat to Boston for a month,
that if she didn't take the *Blessing*, she would risk sailing into the
start of the winter storms, and besides, that she had waited so long
to see Will again, she couldn't bear to prolong their separation by
another day.

It was Frankie, always the sensible, cautious one, who made the
most determined effort to dissuade her.

'This is madness, Mother – for a woman to travel alone to the
other side of the world at your age.'

'Forty-five I may be, but I'm as strong as any man – I've had to
be, to raise you all without a father.'

'But we shan't ever see you again!'

She clasped her daughter's hand. 'Dear Frankie, if there's no longer any danger as your father says, you shall join us – all of you. America is a better place for people of our faith than England. "The land shall yield her fruit, and ye shall eat your fill, and dwell therein in safety." ' She had the verses off by heart. The idea that after all these years of waiting she might refuse Will's summons was unthinkable. 'It is our Promised Land.'

They argued for an hour, until eventually Frankie surrendered. She knew her mother's stubbornness too well. 'Then go with our blessing. I can see that you've made up your mind, and nothing any of us can say will change it.'

Frances gathered her grandchildren in her arms and kissed them, tried hard not to cry – she wanted their last memory of her to be joyful – hugged her daughter, and hurried out of the house before she broke down completely.

God would reunite them, she was sure of it, either on earth or in Heaven.

She spent Wednesday morning packing – warm clothes for New England, a bowl and cup and cutlery, some biscuits and cheese, her Bible. It did not take long. She had not much in the way of worldly possessions. The children could have what remained. She told none of the members of her church of her plans. That afternoon, she walked down to the pier next to London Bridge and hired a boatman to row her to Gravesend, and by dusk she was aboard the *Blessing*, in the cramped communal cabin below decks, its timbers creaking on the rising tide.

Nayler passed the night before the *Blessing* sailed at an inn close to the quayside. He knew from experience what the voyage would be like. He wanted to spend as little time on board as possible. He had brought a pair of pistols, bullets and powder, wrapped up in a spare shirt. In his pocket he had a razor-sharp knife, protected by a leather sheath. At first light, he walked down to the harbour.

He was dressed in dark, drab clothes. He had dispensed with his wig and wore the flat-crowned hat favoured by the Puritans. In one hand he carried his leather bag and in the other his battered second-hand Bible. He showed his ticket to the purser – he was listed on the manifest under his usual pseudonym of Richard Foster – surrendered the larger of his two bags to be taken to the hold, and was directed to his hammock. This time he did not have a cabin to himself. Instead he was crammed into a space beneath the main deck with roughly a hundred others. The ceiling was only five feet high. He had to crouch like a hunchback and push his way through the press of bodies – old and young, men and women (some heavily pregnant), children of all ages, mothers and babies, pet dogs – until he found an empty hammock. From the hold below came the grunts and squawks of livestock – pigs, goats, chickens. He placed his Bible, his hat and his smaller bag onto the canvas to secure it, then peered around for Frances. If he could not see her – if, at the last minute, she had become suspicious or had been persuaded not to travel – then he promised himself he would disembark. Indeed, such was his dread of the ordeal ahead, he found himself almost hoping she had changed her mind.

He groped his way the length of the cabin – some eighty feet in all – bent double in the dim light, between the hammocks, up one side and down the other, stumbling over crawling infants and dogs and baggage, trying to spot her. It wasn't until he was almost back where he started that he saw her, face turned towards him, lying in her hammock, close enough to touch. She looked white and frightened. He glanced away at once. After all his searching, her berth was no more than ten feet from his own.

He squeezed his way to the foot of the ladder and climbed up onto the deck. There he stayed, leaning over the gunwale, listening to the cries of the seagulls, watching as the last of the passengers and cargo came aboard, the gangplanks were hoisted, the cables cast off fore and aft and the ship pushed away from the quayside, until he was certain she had not escaped.

The one luxury he had – if such a word could ever be used in connection with a voyage across the Atlantic – was time. Weeks of close confinement stretched ahead. There was no need to arouse suspicion by making a hasty move. He could stalk his prey with patience.

For the first three days he kept himself apart, spending most of his time in his hammock, ostentatiously reading his Bible by candlelight. On the fourth day, when they were out of sight of land, he joined the Puritans for their Sabbath prayer meeting, crowded onto the raised half-deck close to the stern. They made up perhaps half the passengers. A congregation from Essex was emigrating with its leader, a minister named Humility Fuller, who insisted on lecturing the entire assembly. He preached a two-hour sermon, his words about sin and temptation fighting against the wind. Nayler, stationed at the back next to the ladder down to the main deck, tried to maintain an expression of interest. The extensive prayers at least were easy enough – it was a relief to bow his head and close his eyes – but the unfamiliar chanting of the psalms he found impossible to follow. He mouthed the words as best he could. At the end of the meeting, he uttered a loud and heartfelt 'Amen', then stood back to allow the worshippers to leave ahead of him. As Frances brushed by, he murmured, 'God be with you.' She turned and gave him a surprised look. 'And God be with you, friend.'

For the midweek prayer meeting he tried a different approach. Once again he positioned himself at the back. This time, however, as soon as the session ended, he quickly descended the ladder and stood at the bottom to offer his assistance to the womenfolk coming down the final rungs. Some shrank at the prospect of a strange man's touch, but Frances briefly took his hand.

'Thank you.' He felt a jolt run through his fingers before she released them.

'God bless you, sister.' He touched his hat. 'Richard Foster.'

She nodded briefly and moved away without making a reply.

Plainly, the wooing of a good Puritan woman would be no easy task. Still he persevered – Perseverance Foster! – contriving to run into her occasionally over the following weeks when they were taking the air on deck, remarking on the weather or the condition of the sea, which heaved around them to infinity – sometimes grey, sometimes oily black and flecked by whitecaps, with never a glimpse of a passing sail to relieve the monotony.

' "And the Spirit of God",' he quoted, ' "moved upon the face of the waters." '

'It does indeed, Mr Foster. It is a most awesome sight.'

These carefully arranged but seemingly chance encounters were the chief purpose of his day. Everything else was boring, squalid, hideous.

The further they voyaged, the worse the food became. He warded off hunger by gnawing at the ship's biscuits they were issued with each morning, first picking out the red worms and spiders. Sometimes he took his ration of fatty, green-tinged meat to the firebox in its bed of sand and tried to cook it. He drank a lot of beer (as did the Puritans, for that matter, and their children too – the *Blessing*'s supply of fresh water was brown and, like the biscuits, full of tiny wriggling creatures). He pissed and shat in the communal buckets and scraped the lice off his skin when they started to appear. Otherwise he spent his time out on deck when the weather was clement, and when it rained, as it did most afternoons, he lay in his hammock and leafed through his Bible. The most frustrating aspect of posing as a Puritan was that it prevented him from joining in the constant games of cards the less religious passengers played to while away the time. With every page of the testaments, his dislike of God intensified. What a monster he was, smiting, punishing, testing, sending his son to be killed and ignoring his pleas for help.

Throughout, he kept an eye on Frances. He noticed how social she could be in her quiet way, laughing with the other women, helping to look after the children and nursing the babies – something else about her that reminded him of Sarah. It gave him an idea, and he went in search of the occasional offcuts of timber that lay around the ship and used his knife to carve figures, which he presented to her for the children to use as toys.

Gradually their exchanges lengthened until they began to border on something like conversation. One day, as they were leaning on the gunwale contemplating the ominous black thunderheads forming on the horizon, he decided to take a risk. 'May I enquire your destination?'

It was a mistake. For the first time, she looked at him suspiciously. 'My plans are not yet formed.' She returned her attention to the clouds, and he feared he had thrown away all his careful work. But then she said, as if making amends for her curtness, 'May I enquire yours?'

'A little town called Hadley, on the Connecticut. Doubtless you have never heard of it.'

He watched carefully for her reaction. She shook her head. 'No, I do not know New England at all.' Her tone was neutral. Unless she was a consummate liar, which he was certain she was not, she was telling the truth. But his question had clearly unsettled her. 'God be with you, Mr Foster,' she said, and moved on.

'And with you,' he called after her.

Still she did not give him her name. That evening, as the crew closed the hatches as a precaution against the looming bad weather, he saw her talking to an elderly man whose name he did not know. Something in the way the pair glanced at him, and quickly looked away when they saw him watching them, suggested he was the subject of their conversation.

Later that night, the threatened storm struck. The wind roared and moaned through the rigging. Each crack of thunder sounded like the splintering of the masts. Seawater crashed across the deck above their heads and poured in thin torrents, occasionally lit by the lightning, through the gaps between the planks. The ship pitched so violently, Nayler was almost tipped out of his hammock. The buckets of waste upended. The candles blew out. From the total darkness arose a cacophony of screams and shouts of panic, pleas to God, children crying, babies wailing, guttural sounds of retching. The cold, damp air was filled with the emetic stink of vomit. Nayler gripped the sides of his hammock, leaned over and heaved up what little there was in his stomach.

The storm went on all night and did not let up the following morning. A pale grey light filtered through the cracks in the deck, faintly illuminating the devastation – scattered belongings, bloodied heads, limbs dangling limply. The *Blessing* swung like a pendulum. Possessions hurtled from one side of the hull to the other. Unable to stand, too exhausted to shout or scream, the passengers clung to their hammocks and cots, silent mostly, apart from the occasional sob and moan, and the wail of a man crying out repeatedly that his wife was dead. Nayler lay shivering, drenched by salt water, knees drawn up to try to relieve the pain of the cramps in his belly. This was far more terrible than his last voyage. Any moment he expected the keel to crack and send them plunging to the bottom. His wretchedness was such he would almost have welcomed it.

He endured the day and another night, twisting and turning, his mind possessed by dreams, but when he woke at dawn on the second morning, the wind and rain had stopped, the keel was even. Passengers with hammocks closest to the hull started to open the shutters to let in fresh air.

He put his feet to the floor and tried to stand. The wood was wet and slippery with a mixture of seawater, vomit and human waste. The soles of his boots skidded. He almost fell, but managed to catch himself, grabbing the ropes of the hammock. He pulled himself upright. Cautiously he moved between the sleeping bodies to the ladder, climbed it to the hatch and tried to push it open. It was hard to shift it. When at last he succeeded, a cascade of seawater drenched him all over again. Protests rose from below. Ignoring them, he went up onto the deck.

It was a relief to be out of the stinking darkness. He breathed in the cold salt smell of the ocean. The sea was flat, the sky a smooth pearl grey. Thank providence the masts were still intact. Apart from a couple of sailors clearing up the debris, he had the deck to himself. He made his way aft and peered over the side. Her sails furled, the ship was drifting in the current. She must be miles off course. He heard footsteps behind him and turned to see the thin, elderly man to whom Frances had been talking before the storm.

'God be thanked,' said the man, coming to stand next to him. 'I thought we were lost for certain.'

Nayler turned back to the sea. He had no desire for conversation.

Nevertheless, he felt some comment was required. 'It was the worst weather I ever encountered.'

'So you have made the crossing before?' And when Nayler didn't answer, he added, 'But of course you must have, if you are a Hadley man.'

Nayler's hands tightened on the gunwale. He sensed trouble.

'You must know the magistrate there,' the man continued, 'John Russell. And Peter Tilton, the minister.'

'Naturally I do.'

The man gave an unpleasant croak of triumph. 'But naturally you do not, Mr Foster, or whatever your real name may be, for if you did, you would know that Mr Russell is the minister and Mr Tilton the magistrate.'

'I never said I lived in Hadley, sir. It is my brother who resides there. I'm on my way to join him.'

'Another lie! There's no one in Hadley named Foster. I know, *because it is my town!*'

Wearily Nayler turned again to examine him. What were the odds against this? A thousand to one, at least. And yet here was this skinny old fellow, poised to wreck his plans – a typical interfering, pinch-faced Puritan, eyes alight with self-righteousness, as if he had just sniffed out a witch. Rage, long suppressed, boiled within him.

The man continued, 'I believe you must have been sent among us as a spy. Either that—'

The rest of his words were stifled. Nayler clamped his left hand across the man's mouth, forcing him backwards against the gunwale, checked swiftly that he was unobserved, then drew his knife with his right and stabbed him with all his strength below the ribs, thrusting up and twisting the tip of the blade towards his heart. The man's eyes widened with shock. He managed a muffled grunt before Nayler scooped his arm under his knees and tipped him backwards. His body hit the sea with a splash so loud it made the sailors look round.

Nayler shouted and pointed. 'Man in the water!'

He was breathing hard, had a pain in his back. He leaned out to check if the old fellow was dead, but he couldn't tell. If they fished him out and he was still alive, or even if they simply discovered the knife wound, he would be finished.

The crewmen hurried down the ladder from the half-deck. By this time, more passengers were emerging from below. They ran and crowded along the side of the ship. The man was floating face down, drifting away from them.

'What happened?'

'Did anyone see him fall?'

Nayler clambered up onto the gunwale, collected himself for an instant, and jumped into the water. The shock knocked the breath out of him. He came up tossing his head, spluttering for air, looked around, then struck out towards the body. When he reached it, he rolled it over. The man was dead right enough, riding the swell, staring with wide-open eyes and mouth at the heavens, as if he had been granted some final wondrous vision. Nayler could hear shouts from the ship behind him. He put his hands on the man's shoulder and pushed the corpse under. For a few moments it hung, suspended, and then slowly it slipped from his grasp, the white face gradually dissolving as it sank, until it disappeared.

He turned and struggled back in the direction of the *Blessing*, already dangerously far away. The weight of his sodden clothes was dragging him down. A sailor shouted to him, threw a rope. It took the last of his strength to reach it and hold on, wrapping the end around his hand. He was towed towards the side. By the time he reached it, he was almost dead himself. He was dimly conscious of another sailor coming down a rope ladder, of a cable being tied around his chest, and then he was roughly hauled up the side of the ship, over the gunwale and onto the deck, where he lay on his back coughing salt water, gasping for breath, staring up at the faces of the passengers, Frances's among them – a murderer and yet, miraculously, a hero.

He passed out.

Frances took charge of him. He was trembling with cold. Crewmen carried him below. She showed them his hammock. They stripped him of his sodden coat, boots and trousers and laid him out to recover. He had a cord around his neck, she noticed, with a pouch. She hurried to the firebox, begged a cup of hot chicken broth from one of the wives and carried it back to his hammock. She cupped her hand behind his head – his hair was thick and sticky with salt water – and raised it so that she could hold the liquid to his lips. His eyes flickered open. He took a few mouthfuls, then sank back, shivering, unconscious. She fetched her own blanket – it was drier than his – and wrapped it around him.

She felt obscurely guilty about what had happened. He had been so friendly, always asking after her health and giving her dolls for the children, yet she had kept her distance. There was something about him (God forgive her) that she hadn't altogether trusted, and as the voyage had gone on and he had lost weight – thanks to the poor food and the constant diarrhoea they had all shrunk to skin and bones – she sometimes fancied she knew him from somewhere. Goodman Jones, her neighbour in the next berth, a widower returning to America after burying his wife in England, had observed her talking to him and asked who he was. She told him what little she knew. That had been just before the storm. And now Mr Jones was drowned, despite Mr Foster's gallant attempt to save him, and the fault was somehow hers, a punishment for her lack of Christian charity.

She carried his clothes up to the deck and laid them out to dry. When she returned, she saw a small leather bag beneath his hammock. Perhaps he had a spare shirt. She rummaged through it, lifted out his Bible and an object wrapped in oilcloth. It was hard to her touch, not a piece of clothing, but she was too curious not to look. It was a miniature of a young woman, very pretty, finely dressed, with a fashionable hairstyle.

The figure in the hammock stirred. She replaced the miniature quickly and stood. He opened his eyes and tried to sit up.

'Soft,' she said, laying her hand on his forehead. 'Rest.'

'You are very kind.' He lay down again. 'And I do not even know your name.'

'Frances,' she said. 'Frances Stephenson.'

By the end of the afternoon, he was back on his feet, dressed in his dried clothes, a little hesitant in his movements but otherwise seemingly none the worse for his ordeal. He acknowledged the praise of the other passengers with a shrug. 'I did no more than any other Christian would have done. I trusted my life to God in the knowledge that he would protect me. I am only sorry I could not save the poor fellow.' Asked by the captain how the unfortunate episode had come about, he repeated the same story: that he had seen Goodman Jones leaning dangerously far out over the gunwale, had bade him good morning, moved on, then heard a cry and a splash. The captain seemed satisfied. Such things happened on a long voyage. They had already lost two dead in the storm, a woman and a child. He would enter the incident in his log as a fatal accident.

But later, when Frances and the modest hero were walking around the main deck and came to the spot where the incident had occurred, he swore her to secrecy and quietly told a different tale: that he had seen Jones climb up onto the gunwale, and after a moment's hesitation, jump.

She looked at him in horror. 'You mean he took his own life?'

'I fear he must have done.'

'But that is a mortal sin.'

'True enough.'

'And yet he appeared so devout.'

'Who can say what is in a man's heart? Perhaps the storm had briefly robbed him of his reason, and he was in despair. Forgive me for sharing this burden with you. There is no one else I can tell. Will you join me in a silent prayer for his soul?'

Together they knelt.

After that, she was the one who sought out his company rather than the other way round. She was curious about him.

'Forgive me,' she said one afternoon about a week later, 'but I have a confession to make. I looked in your bag while you were asleep to see if there was a shirt you might put on, and I saw the portrait. Is she your wife?'

'She was.' A shadow of sadness fell across his face. 'She died of a miscarriage. Our baby, too. He would have been our first.'

'I'm most sorry to hear that. She looked a very fine lady.' After a minute, she said, 'You did not remarry?'

'I never found anyone I cared for as much. So you see, I have nothing to keep me in England. I went to America many years ago, and I've decided to go back. I shall join my brother in Hadley and live whatever years God grants me among people of faith.' He was quiet for a while. 'And you, Mrs Stephenson? You are married, I assume?'

'Yes indeed, for many years.'

She revealed as much as she dared while avoiding an outright lie. She said she knew no one in America, that her husband had gone out to make a new life for them, that he had now summoned her to join him but he had been moving around the country so much she was no longer sure where to find him.

She knew it made her sound like a fool, but it was a relief to have someone to confide in.

'Is there no one who can help you?'

'He has directed me to a man in Cambridge whom he says will have the latest news of his whereabouts.'

'Who is that – if you do not mind my asking?'

She saw no reason not to tell him.

'I know Daniel Gookin,' he said. 'Or rather, I know *of* him. I can certainly direct you to his house. It is barely a half-hour ride from Boston.'

She put her hand on his arm. 'You are very kind, Mr Foster. I am not sure what I should have done without you.'

The remainder of the voyage was calm. As they neared America, they spent hours standing together at the gunwale, watching the whales and dolphins playing around the ship. Soon afterwards, sea-gulls began to appear overhead, and on the morning of Thursday 30 October, after a voyage of sixty-nine days, the *Blessing* dropped anchor in Boston Harbour.

She had nowhere to stay, so when the time came to disembark and he said he knew of a place near the port, she readily fell in with his suggestion. He carried her bag away from the bustling harbour and down a narrow street to an inn. There were two rooms available, one single and one communal. He insisted she have the one to herself. It was a rough place, full of sailors and merchants with loud voices, smoking their pipes and talking business, and she was glad of his company when they dined together that afternoon. He suggested he hire two horses for the following morning. He would show her the way to the Gookins' house.

She protested. 'But you have done enough already.'

'Nonsense. You do ride, I hope?'

'Yes, although not for many years. My father was a great man for horses. I grew up with them all around me. But I should hate to put you to any trouble, Mr Foster.'

'It will be no trouble. I am in no hurry.'

'Very well.' She smiled. 'Thank you.'

She noticed how he never asked her questions about her husband, although he must surely have been curious. She was grateful for his tact.

The next day, they rode together side by side along the Charles River the short distance to Cambridge. It was All Hallows' Eve, a beautiful clear day, the last of the autumn leaves falling golden brown, a hint of winter in the air. Riding brought back memories of her father – the smell of the stables in the Mews, his voice telling her to sit up straight, his strong arms lifting her down from the saddle. *We shall have you in the cavalry yet . . .*

At the end of a bridge, Mr Foster halted. He pointed across the river.

'That is the Gookins' place, the first house on the right. I'll wait for you here. Take all the time you need.'

She walked her horse over the bridge. The grand building dominating the skyline was Harvard College, she knew that much. Cambridge seemed a fine place, hardly different to England, except bigger, cleaner and less populated. She felt a rush of optimism. Will had written the truth. It was safe.

She reached the Gookins' gate and dismounted, tied the horse to the fence, and went into the yard. She knocked on the door. It was opened by a woman in her fifties, wiping her hands on a cloth, wearing an apron dusted by flour. She ran her arm across her forehead and squinted at the visitor. She seemed half blind.

'Yes?'

Frances said, 'I am looking for Mr Daniel Gookin.'

'He's in the barn. I'll fetch him. May I ask who wants him?'

'My name is Frances Stephenson.' She swallowed. 'He might know me better as Frances Goffe. I believe he is acquainted with my husband – and my late father, Colonel Whalley.'

The woman was so surprised, it was a moment before she could speak. 'Wait here.'

She walked quickly across the yard to the barn, and emerged a minute later with a tall, strong-looking man with iron-grey hair and beard.

'Is this true?' he said.

She clasped her hands to her heart. 'As God is my witness.'

He glanced over her shoulder at the road. 'Are you alone?'

'Yes. A man from the ship showed me the way, that's all.'

'Does he know your real identity?'

'No.'

He went to the gate to check again. 'You had best come in.'

She sat at the kitchen table and produced the letter from Will. Gookin read it first, then passed it to his wife. 'This quotation from the Scriptures . . .'

' "Ye shall dwell in the land in safety. And the land shall yield her fruit, and ye shall eat your fill, and dwell therein in safety." ' She smiled. 'It is typical of Will to find the most apt passage.'

'That is true.' Daniel glanced at his wife and then back at Frances. 'And you are certain this is his hand?'

'There is no doubt. Look. These are all his other letters to me.'

She produced the precious bundle, tied with ribbon, and spread the contents over the table.

Gookin picked one up and compared it to the message. He repeated the process several times. 'I can see no difference.' He turned again to his wife. 'To have so many is testament in itself. I believe she speaks the truth.'

Mrs Gookin said, 'How many children do you have, Mrs Goffe?'

'Five – four now. One is dead.'

'And their names?'

'Frankie, Nan, Judith, Dickie and Betty – Betty is the one who died.'

'And the name of your uncle, who lived in New Haven, and his wife's name?'

'William and Jane Hooke. Uncle William is dead now too, alas.'

Gookin said, 'I am sorry to hear it, God rest his soul.'

'The years have been hard on us. But my children are now grown and settled. I saw no reason not to come at once. I have travelled thousands of miles.' Frances began to cry. 'Please, Mr Gookin, for the love of God, tell me where he is.'

Gookin blew out his cheeks and ran his hand through his grey hair. 'This is difficult for us, Mrs Goffe. I have not seen Will for many years, nor heard of him for two or three. He may be dead, or have moved again, for all I know. As to whether it's safe – that I am not at all sure of.' He exchanged a final look with his wife, who nodded. 'The last I heard, he was living under the protection of a Captain Bull in Hartford, Connecticut.'

'Thank you.' She bowed her head in relief, then started gathering up her letters. 'I need trouble you no further.'

The Gookins stood at the door to see her off. It was eighteen years and three months since the regicides had first arrived. Mary took Frances's hand. 'God speed you, Mrs Goffe. I hope you find

Will, and if you do, give him our love. Tell him we are sorry we could not do more.'

Nayler was waiting on the other side of the bridge, sitting on the grass with his back against a tree, watching the passing traffic. He had a craving for a pipe of tobacco but had to make do with sucking a long stem of grass. Despite his calm appearance, he was in a state of some anxiety. It had been hard enough to win Frances's trust. But this was the real test. Gookin was not some lonely woman, eager for companionship. From what he recalled of him, he was a real leader of the community – experienced, shrewd, and doubtless still on his guard against all questions concerning the regicides. He had faced down Colonel Nicolls when he had been questioned after the expedition to take New Amsterdam fourteen years ago. He might insist, before revealing Goffe's whereabouts, on first checking with him that he had indeed invited his wife to join him. Then everything would be lost.

He saw her coming down the slope towards the bridge. That had not taken long. A good sign, or bad? He scrambled to his feet. He couldn't make out her expression. Even when she had crossed the bridge and was waiting for him to mount, her mood was unreadable. They rode together in silence. She was full of her own thoughts. He longed to know what had happened, but he knew better than to ask.

It was not until they were back in Boston, had given up their horses and were walking towards the inn that she finally spoke.

'Thank you for all your trouble today, Mr Foster.'

'I only hope it was successful . . . ?' He let the sentence hang as a question.

She did not rise to it. 'What are your plans now?' she said.

'To find a guide to take me to Hadley.'

'Soon?'

'In the next day or two. It's a long journey, and tomorrow it will be November. The weather is already turning colder.'

She was quiet again, thinking something over.

'Where is Hadley in relation to Hartford?'

'Close, I think. Certainly in the same direction.' Now he could not resist it. 'Why Hartford? Is that where your husband is living?'

'I know it is a great deal to ask, and you have given me so much help already, but might it be possible for us to travel together?'

'It would be my pleasure.'

So there it was.

Hartford.

That night, he lay in his shared bed listening to the snores of the men beside him and contemplating what lay ahead. He had developed a strong liking for Frances Goffe. The prospect of a week travelling alone together was pleasant. They would sleep out under the stars or find shelter with friendly Indians. He would display his knowledge of New England. And at the end of it, he would kill her husband. He wondered if it might be possible for him to do so without her knowing he was responsible. In such a circumstance – alone and widowed in this vast and alien land – might she not turn for support to her loyal and only friend Richard Foster? It was conceivable. He would try to devise his plans accordingly.

CHAPTER THIRTY-SIX

THE MORNING OF Sunday 9 November 1679 found Will Goffe, as usual, in his attic refuge in the Bulls' house, staring at the rafters. The place was empty. The captain and his wife had gone to the meeting house for the Sabbath assembly. He was sixty-one years old and in despair. Three letters in the past year to Reverend Increase Mather, pleading with him to help him re-establish contact with Frances, had gone unanswered. The business in Hadley, the myth about an angel who had miraculously appeared in the form of an old soldier to save the town, had spread across New England and frightened away his helpers. They seemed to think that by showing himself he had betrayed their trust. But what else could he have done?

The Bulls were pleasant enough folk, yet he could tell that even they were weary of this guest who never left. His life was friendless and entirely without meaning. He longed for death, but his body stubbornly refused to part with its earthly existence. He could have endured any number of the torments described in the Scriptures – fire and scorpions, locusts and nails: these would have been of no account to him – but this endless loneliness was too much to bear.

All had come to nothing.

His Bible lay unopened, even on this Sabbath morning. The battered volume reproached him. He was on the point of nerving himself to open it, in the hope of receiving some fresh inspiration from God to lift him out of the dark valley through which he was passing, when he heard a faint sound downstairs.

He sat up.

Was it someone knocking? It was most unusual for the Bulls to receive visitors, and on the Sabbath, during the time set aside for prayer, unthinkable.

He rose from his bed and went over to the window. He couldn't see the front door, but when he unfastened the latch, he could hear the noise of frantic hammering and a woman's voice, faint but distinct, carrying up from the yard. 'Will? Will? It's Frances!'

He stumbled backwards into the centre of the room. This was madness. Torturing visions. The final torment.

The knocking went on for another minute, then stopped. She had gone.

He stood in the silence, trying to make sense of what he had heard. It could not be. Yet what if it *was* her? He launched himself out of the attic and down the stairs. He unlocked the door. The yard was empty. He ran out into the road.

A woman was walking away, carrying a bag.

'Frances?'

She stopped and turned. Looked at him. He was a stranger.

'Frances?' he repeated.

His voice, though, the sweet lilt. That was Will, no question.

She ran towards him, then halted shyly a few paces away and dropped the bag. They stared at one another, each trying to reconcile the unfamiliar figure that stood before them with the one in their memories. Then he closed the distance and took her in his arms.

'Is it you?' he said. 'Are you real?' He ran his hands across her back, felt her arms, her shoulders, her soft flesh, her sharp bones. He placed his palms gently on her thin cheeks and stared into her eyes. 'Are you real,' he kept saying, 'or a phantom sent to taunt me? Is it you?'

So long without his touch, his smell. It was both exactly as she had dreamed it and utterly unexpected. She took his hands away and kissed them. 'I am real,' she said. 'God be thanked.'

He put his arm around her waist. She existed, right enough – as fragile as a bird perhaps, but she was not a dream. He would not let go of her. He picked up her bag, led her back into the yard and into the house. 'How is it possible?'

She was laughing and crying. She put her arms around his neck and kissed his mouth. 'You wrote. I came. Did you think I would refuse?'

In the ecstasy of his happiness, the words seemed to come from a long way away. He didn't take in the meaning at first.

He continued to hold her, but broke away slightly. 'I wrote?' He was puzzled. Some mystery he couldn't quite grasp lurked within the miracle. 'Did I?' he said in wonder. 'Did I write?' Perhaps the truth was twofold: that she was real, but he was crazy. And then, a little uneasily, 'How did you find me?'

'Mr Gookin told me.'

Relief for a moment. That made sense. 'Ah yes,' he said. 'Dear Daniel . . .' He kissed her again. And then the shadow returned. He had always been so careful never to mention any names. 'But how do you know of Daniel?'

'Your message.'

'What message? I sent no message. I didn't know where you were living.' He stepped back from her, saw the flash of alarm in her eyes, felt his stomach hollow. 'Did you come alone?'

'No.' The sudden tension in his voice frightened her. 'Mr Foster—'

'Mr Foster? Who is Mr Foster?' Without waiting for a reply, he shut the door and locked it. 'Upstairs!' he said. 'Quickly!' He steered her ahead of him, up onto the landing and then up a second flight to the attic. 'Was it just the one man with you, or were there others?'

'Just one, and a guide.'

'When did you last see him?'

'A few minutes ago. Perhaps a quarter-hour, no more. He left me at the edge of the town. He said he was going to Hadley.' She pictured Foster turning his back on her. It had been a cool parting after such a long journey together, but she hadn't wanted him to see where she was going, and he had seemed keen to get on his way. She started shaking. 'Will . . .'

'It's no matter.' He opened his bag and took out two pistols. He kept them both loaded. 'Take this.' It was one of Ned's old weapons, cleaned and oiled. 'Stay here. Don't come out unless I call you.' He strapped on his sword. In the doorway, he turned. 'I'm eternally glad you came, my dearest love, whatever.'

He went downstairs, moving quickly from room to room, checking each window. The yard, the vegetable garden, the orchard with the chickens pecking between the trees – all looked deserted. He unlocked the door and opened it, only a crack at first, to which he put his eye, then wider. Nothing. He moved towards the gate, his pistol aimed and fully extended at shoulder height, turning in full circles, alert for any movement. He reached the gate and scanned the surrounding country – the street, the big south meadow opposite separated from the road by a ditch, the Connecticut beyond it.

Still nothing.

'Colonel Goffe.' A man's voice close behind him, terrible in its calmness. 'No, don't turn around. For the sake of your wife, whom I have no wish to harm, drop your pistol.'

He weighed his chances, reckoned them at nothing, and let the gun fall to the ground.

'Kneel down.'

He knelt. *Oh Frances, Frances . . .*

He heard the explosion and fell forwards.

What a moment of triumph this was for Nayler! What a consummation, after nearly twenty years of searching, to have his enemy kneeling helpless before him, like the King he had killed on that dreadful winter morning. He would have liked to have savoured the moment a little longer. That had been his intention – a taunt, a final word, something memorable to round it all off. He had imagined the scene for so long. But his gun must have fired prematurely. He experienced an instant of bewilderment, followed by an intense pain in the back of his neck. His mouth was full of liquid. He couldn't breathe. He staggered, half turned.

Frances was on the doorstep. The pistol in her hand was aimed directly at him. Hatred and love twisted in him. His legs buckled. He tried to say something, but all that emerged was blood. For a fraction of a second, he saw Goodman Jones's white face slipping away beneath the waves, and then the black depths rose and swallowed him as well.

Frances dropped her father's pistol and ran past the body to Will. She feared she had somehow managed to hit him too. 'Will? Will, my dear heart?' He started to rise. She helped him to his feet. 'Thank God!' She flung her arms around him. She could feel his heart. For a long time, they stood entwined, swaying to its beat, until he whispered that they would have to move.

They dragged the corpse across the road and heaved it into the ditch. Will clambered down and covered it as best he could with leaves and a few branches. It would suffice for a day or two, with luck. He had to hurry. They didn't have long before the church meeting ended.

He left all the money he could afford on the kitchen table, then went up to the attic and gathered his belongings, carrying them down to the stable, where there was a little two-wheeled buggy the Bulls used for visiting their neighbours. He hitched it to the horse and led it into the yard. He threw in Frances's bag as well as his own, helped her up onto the seat and opened the gate.

A minute later, they were on the road heading into open country. She had her hands around his waist. Whatever happened, she would never be parted from him now.

He had no idea where they would go, or what they would do, or what dangers lay ahead. But with their love, and their Bible, with their absolute certainty in the power of the Lord and the protection of their guns, and with the plentiful vastness of America spread out before them like God's table – see Corinthians, 10:21 – he had faith that they would make a future.

ACKNOWLEDGEMENTS

Edward Whalley suffered a stroke and lingered in a twilight state for a number of years, nursed by his son-in-law, before dying in the Russells' house, probably some time towards the end of 1674. The eventual fate of William Goffe is unknown. Following the attack on Hadley in 1675, and his removal to Hartford, he was still desperately trying to make contact with his wife in April 1679, and a letter was written to him by Peter Tilton from Hadley in July of that year. Thereafter, all trace of him vanishes. He may have died soon afterwards. He may have decided to take the chance of returning to England. Or perhaps Frances really did come out to join him and they disappeared together. Like so much else in this novel, I can't say it happened as I describe it. The best I can say is it might have happened.

There are two excellent general histories of the hunt for the regicides, *Killers of the King* by Charles Spencer and *The King's Revenge* by Don Jordan and Michael Walsh. There are also two specific recent studies of the regicides in New England, *Charles I's Killers in America* by Matthew Jenkinson and *The Great Escape of Edward Whalley and William Goffe* by Christopher Pagliuco. Long before these, there was *A History of Three of the Judges of King Charles I* by Ezra Stiles, published in 1794 but still very useful.

I was fortunate in being able to track down an unpublished MPhil dissertation submitted to Southampton University in 1973 by Geoffrey Jaggar, 'The fortunes of the Whalley family of

Screveton, Nottinghamshire'. His widow, Mrs Margaret Jaggar, was kind enough to lend me the only extant copy. My thanks to her for her generosity, and to her late husband for his scholarship.

In the course of my research, I read scores of books and articles on the Civil War and its aftermath, some very old, others published while I was writing. This is by no means an exhaustive list, but those I found most useful include:

W. C. Abbott, *The Writings and Speeches of Oliver Cromwell* (four volumes)

G. E. Aylmer, *The King's Servants; The State's Servants; The Crown's Servants*

Harral Ayres, *The Great Trail of New England*

Michael Braddick, *God's Fury, England's Fire*

Francis J. Bremer, *Building a New Jerusalem: John Davenport, a Puritan in Three Worlds*

Lisa Brooks, *Our Beloved Kin, A New History of King Philip's War*

Edward Clarendon, *The Life of Edward, Earl of Clarendon*

C. H. Firth, *Memoirs of Colonel Hutchinson* (editor); *Ludlow's Memoirs* (editor); *Cromwell's Army; The Last Years of the Protectorate*

Antonia Fraser, *Cromwell, Our Chief of Men*

S. R. Gardiner, *History of the Great Civil War* (four volumes)

Malcolm Gaskill, *The Ruin of Witches*

Peter Gaunt, *The English Civil War, A Military History*

Ian Gentles, *The New Model Army*

Richard L. Greaves, *Deliver us from Evil: The Radical Underground in Britain, 1660–1663*

Ronald Hutton, *The Making of Oliver Cromwell*

Sylvester Judd, *History of Hadley*

Anna Keay, *The Restless Republic*

Paul Lay, *Providence Lost, The Rise and Fall of Cromwell's Protectorate*

Margarette Lincoln, *London and the 17th Century*

Alan Marshall, *Intelligence and Espionage in the Reign of Charles II*

David Masson, *Life of John Milton* (six volumes)

J. G. Muddiman (editor), *Trial of Charles I*

Richard Ollard, *Clarendon and his Friends*

Rebecca Rideal, *1666: Plague, War and Hellfire*

Geoffrey Robertson, *The Tyrannicide Brief*

Ruth Spalding (editor), *The Diary of Bulstrode Whitelocke, 1605–75*

Simon Thurley, *Palaces of Revolution*

John Thurloe, *State Papers* (seven volumes)

C. V. Wedgwood, *The King's Peace; The King's War; The Trial of Charles I*

Blair Worden, *God's Instruments; A Voyce From the Watch Tower* (editor)

I would like to thank those who read and commented on the manuscript and helped make this novel possible: my wife, Gill Hornby, to whom it is dedicated with love; Venetia Butterfield, Helen Conford and Gail Rebuck of Penguin Random House in London; Deirdre Molina of Penguin Random House Canada; Noah Eaker of Harper in New York; Jocasta Hamilton, who read this one as a friend rather than an editor; my American agent, Suzanne Gluck; my foreign rights agent, Nicki Kennedy; and my film agents, Anthony Jones and Bob Bookman.

ROBERT HARRIS is the author of fourteen bestselling novels: the Cicero Trilogy—*Imperium*, *Lustrum* and *Dictator*—*Fatherland*, *Enigma*, *Archangel*, *Pompeii*, *The Ghost*, *The Fear Index*, *An Officer and a Spy*, which won four prizes including the Walter Scott Prize for Historical Fiction, *Conclave*, *Munich*, *The Second Sleep* and *V2*. Several of his books have been adapted into films, including *The Ghost*. His work has been translated into forty languages and he is a Fellow of the Royal Society of Literature. He lives in West Berkshire with his wife, Gill Hornby.

www.robert-harris.com
Twitter @Robert_Harris
Facebook @RobertHarrisAuthor